PRAISE FOR *STARS UNCHARTED*

"An absorbing space opera, in the tradition of *The Expanse* and *The Long Way to a Small, Angry Planet*."

—Charles Stross, award-winning author of *The Delirium Brief*

"[A] brilliant female-driven tale. . . . Readers of Asimov, Lois Mc-Master Bujold's Vorkosigan saga, or Anne McCaffrey's Pern series will enjoy this story." —*Booklist* (starred review)

"A fresh concept, cutting-edge technology, and characters that pop! A must-read."

—William C. Dietz, *New York Times* bestselling author of *Battle Hymn*

"The prose is fluid, easy to take in, but never simple, and keeps readers entranced by the action, making *Stars Uncharted* a superb sci-fi novel." —Seattle Book Review

"*Stars Uncharted* is a precarious space odyssey of epic proportion. The crew battles political machination, corruption, and betrayal all while trying to stay alive. Complex world building, characters with true depth and intense action." —Tome Tender

"An engaging plot and high-octane escapades. . . . A fun, exciting ride." —Fantasy Literature

"Compelling. . . . Dunstall might be my favorite new science fiction author." —Richmond News

STARS BEYOND

S. K. DUNSTALL

ACE
NEW YORK

ACE
Published by Berkley
An imprint of Penguin Random House LLC
penguinrandomhouse.com

Library of Congress Cataloging-in-Publication Data

Names: Dunstall, S. K., author.
Title: Stars beyond / S.K. Dunstall.
Description: First Edition. | New York : Ace, 2020. | Series: Stars uncharted
Identifiers: LCCN 2019024901 (print) | LCCN 2019024902 (ebook) |
ISBN 9780399587641 (paperback) | ISBN 9780399587658 (ebook)
Subjects: GSAFD: Science fiction.
Classification: LCC PR9619.4.D866 S72 2020 (print) | LCC PR9619.4.D866
(ebook) | DDC 823/.92—dc23
LC record available at https://lccn.loc.gov/2019024901
LC ebook record available at https://lccn.loc.gov/2019024902

First Edition: January 2020

Printed in the United States of America
1 3 5 7 9 10 8 6 4 2

Cover art by Fred Gambino
Cover design by Judith Lagerman
Book design by Kelly Lipovich

CAST OF CHARACTERS

THE CREW OF *ANOTHER ROAD*

Hammond Roystan—captain
Josune Arriola—engineer
Carlos Almeida—engineer
Jacques Saloman—chef (and cargo master)
Nika Rik Terri—modder
Bertram Snowshoe—modder (Nika's apprentice)

JUSTICE DEPARTMENT

Alistair Laughton—agent
Cam Le-Nguyen—agent (works with Alistair)
Paola Teke—coordinator (Alistair's boss)

1

LEONARD WICKMORE

It might have been coincidence—the chairman of Eaglehawk Company standing in the foyer of the Grande Hotel, watching the news vid on the three-floor-high screen—but Leonard Wickmore didn't believe in coincidences. Not when Chairman Keenan was as unlikely to frequent midlevel hotels like this as he was. Nor when they'd both just come from a board meeting where Keenan had told Wickmore, in the cold, nasal way that irritated Wickmore so much, "Ten of your own staff dead. Sloppy, Wickmore. Downright sloppy."

And every head around the boardroom table had nodded.

"Drawing attention to our company at a time when the Justice Department is cleaning itself up is bad form," Keenan had continued. "They already suspect Woden worked with us. Woden was your assassin. You lost control."

Tamati Woden had become a liability. Wickmore was glad he was gone. "The Justice Department is easy to take care of."

Keenan had fixed Wickmore with his cold, flat gaze. "Not as easy as it used to be, Wickmore. If you don't realize that, then maybe you're no longer fit to—" He'd broken off before he'd finished, because he wasn't stupid enough to cross Leonard Wickmore without the board a hundred percent behind him. Not even with ten of his elite staff gone.

But Wickmore had seen the nods. He knew who backed whom.

Wickmore made his way across the foyer of the Grande. "Were you looking for me?"

Keenan glared at the man on the screen. "Honesty League. Two months ago they were nobody." He sipped the coffee in his hand, curled his mouth as if the coffee was curdled, and scowled at the screen again. "Now the whole galaxy is on their side."

"The Honesty League has been around for ten years." Not that Wickmore disagreed with Keenan. They had been unknown. Just another fringe group trying, unsuccessfully, to bring so-called law and order to an unlawful universe. Until Santiago—one of the Big Twenty-Seven companies—had been stupid enough to convince the Justice Department to blatantly look the other way while they murdered the brother of the man who owned most of the free media inside the legal zone and outside it. The Honesty League had used this to call the Justice Department to account. Santiago had given them a martyr, and a voice, and they were taking full advantage of it.

"One month and we have to watch everything we do," Keenan said.

It was closer to three months now, but you didn't correct the chairman of the board for minor inconsistencies like that.

"We can't even dispose of anyone now without the Honesty League, and hence the Justice Department, jumping all over it."

"How many people have you disposed of lately?" Wickmore's department looked after jobs like that.

"Metaphorically speaking. That's not the only thing the Justice Department turns a blind eye to." Keenan looked at the coffee again, looked at the recycler. "I hate this stuff. They coat the container with some sort of wax."

The coffee hub that made up the center of the foyer was doing roaring business, with customers waiting five-deep for their order. Keenan's bodyguards were nowhere in sight. They'd come looking for him soon.

"Fact is, the Justice Department's becoming unreliable," Keenan said. "We can no longer count on them. We need other ways to get things done." He turned away from the screen.

There would be a point to this. Keenan would get to it eventually.

"Nika Rik Terri was my modder, you know."

Wickmore had known. It wasn't something he'd thought about, except to wonder if he could slip something into Nika's studio to eavesdrop on conversations. He'd discarded that because she was obsessive about cleanliness, likely to find hidden bugs, which might just tip her over the edge. Instead Tamati Woden had done the tipping. He would have killed Woden personally for that alone, if Nika hadn't done it for him.

"I had an appointment three days after she disappeared." Keenan looked at his coffee again, looked at the recycler. Wickmore bit back the urge to tell him to throw it in if he hated it that much.

"I ran into Tamati Woden," Keenan said. "I admired his mod. We got talking."

And no doubt Woden had identified himself.

"A device that can temporarily exchange bodies," Keenan said. "I can see uses for it."

Woden had no right to discuss that with Keenan. The exchanger was Wickmore's, as soon as he caught up with Nika again. There would be no mistakes this time.

Keenan's gaze came up to meet Wickmore's properly for the first time. "Your department budget has been curtailed for the moment."

Thanks to the man in front of him. Wickmore forced his expression to politeness.

"The company has discretionary funds. We would find an exchanger useful. Very useful. Deliver it, and there might even be a promotion in it for you."

Might? Wickmore doubted it. He was already a part of the Eagle-hawk executive. There was only one possible promotion he could get. A seat on the board.

And he could get that by using the exchanger himself.

More concerning was the fact that Keenan had known to come here, to the Grande, where Wickmore was following a trail that might lead him to Nika Rik Terri, the modder who had built the original exchanger and had since disappeared, taking all knowledge of how to build another with her. How closely was the other man watching him?

"I might take you up on your offer of those funds," Wickmore said slowly. "If I have the need."

Keenan nodded. "Mention our mutual deceased friend if you do." He glanced across the foyer. "Ah, here are my bodyguards. Must go." He tossed the coffee into the recycler and disappeared into the crowd around the coffee counter.

Wickmore skirted the crowd the other way and made his way over to the lifts, to the restaurant on the two hundredth floor, where they served coffee in elaborate gold-patterned glasses.

"Pol Bager has a reservation," he told the maître d'. He could see her now, looking around the restaurant as if wondering if Wickmore had stood her up.

He slid into the seat opposite. "Apologies for my tardiness." No point in getting her offside immediately. Not before he'd learned what she knew. If he chose to work with the chairman, he didn't need Pol and her schemes, but he hadn't decided what to do about Keenan yet.

He ordered, then turned to her. "So, Pol. You say you were on Hammond Roystan's ship, *The Road to the Goberlings*."

"Yes. I was there when we found the *Hassim*."

"And after?" He probably knew more about her movements than she did. She'd led a mutiny on Roystan's ship, stolen the memory of the *Hassim*, and escaped with it. Wickmore's employee, Benedict—now dead—had made a deal with Pol. He'd help her find the treasure in return for the memory. Unfortunately, the memory couldn't be opened. Pol claimed that Roystan had opened the memory, so Benedict had taken the crew of *The Road* prisoner. Pol had gone with the crew when they'd escaped. It was the crew who held Wickmore's interest now.

They talked through details already familiar to Wickmore. How *The Road*'s crew had escaped, how they'd taken a ship down to Lesser Sirius to rescue Nika Rik Terri. Pol glossed over why she'd been left behind. Wickmore knew. He'd seen the records from Benedict's ship. Pol hadn't been working with the crew, as she'd implied, although she wasn't lying when she claimed she had helped them escape.

Wickmore's staff had kept track of Pol, but he hadn't expected to ever want to talk to her. Not until an unrelated casual conversation with the captain of a cattle ship had mentioned a name he recognized.

"So when you got to Lesser Sirius," Wickmore said, "who was left? Yourself, Captain Roystan. Who else?"

"Jacques and Carlos." Jacques Saloman had been cargo master, Carlos Almeida the engineer. "And Josune, of course." The hatred in her voice ran deep when she mentioned the name. Good.

"Was that all?" She hadn't mentioned the name he needed to hear. "Did anyone else escape with you?"

"What? No. There was just us." She stopped to think. "And the body modder, of course."

Finally. "What was his name?"

"Snow, I think. I mean, it wasn't his real name. I don't know what his name was. He was just there when Benedict captured them. Us," she corrected herself.

She didn't even know Wickmore had been on the ship with them for a time.

"What about Nika Rik Terri?" Nika was already on her way to Lesser Sirius. Just in time to blow up her own studio, and Wickmore with it. He realized he was grinding his teeth, forced himself to stop.

She frowned. "Not her. She was already gone. They had some plan to rescue her."

Wickmore brought up an image of Bertram Snowshoe. "The man who was with you?"

She considered the image. "Maybe," then, "Yes, but he's younger in that picture."

Good. Wickmore smiled. "Well, Pol. I think you and I might have a deal."

Leonard Wickmore watched as Captain Oliver Norris strode toward him. Norris wasn't a big man, but he walked as if he owned the world. Wickmore walked the same way. Image mattered. Act as if the world was yours; prove it by everything you say and do, and people believe you. Especially if you could back that up with a harsh hand and absolute control. Unfortunately for Norris, young Bertram Snowshoe had provided a recent setback.

The captain had brought guards. Eight witnesses. All the better.

"Executive." Norris scanned the empty street, flicked a glance toward Pol, beside Wickmore. "You're alone?"

Wickmore also glanced at Pol. "Not quite."

"Not what I meant, as you're aware." Norris dismissed the woman, but a smile tilted one corner of his mouth. "So the rumors are true. Your team has been decimated. I hadn't believed it possible."

Wickmore ignored the almost-question and smiled himself. He was satisfied to see Norris's amusement change to wariness. He would have made Norris sweat longer, but he needed him onside.

"This meeting is for a side excursion of mine. I plan to present it to the board fait accompli. I don't need spies."

Norris nodded slowly. "I'm intrigued."

Of course he was.

"But allow me to introduce you to my companion. Pol, meet Captain Norris, of the mercenary ship the *Boost*. Norris, Pol Bager, a former crew member from the cargo ship *Another Road to the Goberlings*."

Norris inclined his head in a greeting. "*Another Road*. It sounds familiar."

"Of course it's familiar," Pol said. "We found the *Hassim*."

Wickmore noted the flash of interest that sparked in Norris's eyes and kept his own expression bland. Nothing excited men quite so much as treasure. But Norris was a careful man, not a stupid one apt to chase dreams. It wasn't treasure that swayed Norris, although it would sway his crew. It didn't matter—that was just the bait. Wickmore had done his research.

First, however, the small talk.

"Allow me to draw your attention to Pol's bracelet. It came from one of the worlds Feyodor and the *Hassim* crew discovered." The bracelet had been among Benedict's effects. Wickmore had returned it to Pol earlier that day.

"May I?" Norris asked.

Pol hesitated, her hand over the bracelet.

"Go ahead," Wickmore said. "Captain Norris is not a thief." He was a soldier who'd kill you if you crossed him, which Pol was sure to do. Norris would probably even return the bracelet once he'd killed her. Wickmore didn't care whether he did or not. The bracelet was simply to prove Pol had seen the *Hassim*.

Pol handed it over. Her wrist showed red where the bracelet had stained it.

"One of my men had it analyzed," Wickmore said. "The red veins are a mineral composite, nothing we've seen before."

"Interesting." Norris handed it back. "How long does the stain remain?"

"Forever." Pol rubbed her wrist.

"I can send you our findings if you're interested."

Norris shook his head. "Not really."

He was lying, but Wickmore didn't call him on it. "As you wish."

"I'm not sure where you're going with this." Norris glanced up and down the empty street again. "The *Hassim* was sold to Brown, the backup memory supposedly destroyed, and the crew of the *Hassim* are dead."

"Not all of them," Pol said.

Norris frowned and glanced at Wickmore.

"One of the crew survived." Norris would be wondering why he let Pol take part in the conversation. Yes, Pol was annoying. She never knew when to keep quiet, but for the moment, he didn't want her quiet. It made it easier for Norris to believe. "The engineer, Josune Arriola. She has her own records of their trip."

He had no idea if Arriola did or didn't; all that mattered was to make Norris believe that they believed it.

"Benedict, one of my men, was convinced of it. Therefore, I am sure there is substance to the tale. When I bring this to the Eaglehawk board, though, I want irrefutable evidence." It sounded credible. Wickmore's team had followed up some crazy ideas in the past that had made money for Eaglehawk. "Hence it's a side project at this time."

"I don't chase dreams, Executive. No matter how lucrative you make them. Finding some woman who may or may not have access to records from the *Hassim* is hardly my style. We're a fighting ship. We fight other people's wars for them."

Wickmore didn't even have to consider his answer.

"We're in a period of stability right now, with companies working together instead of going to war. Not to mention the Honesty League keeping the Justice Department honest, relatively speaking. Your mercenaries are becoming . . . redundant. You're spending money feeding a lot of deadweight."

Norris's eyes narrowed.

Wickmore didn't push. He had the reaction he wanted.

"I am sure you are looking for something new. We can come to an agreement on terms. Or we can split the profit."

Norris started to shake his head.

"Before you refuse, Captain Norris, hear me out. I have one more item of interest that might change your mind." Wickmore glanced at the eight bodyguards. "Indentured?"

Only half of them would be. No matter how well protected Norris was, he would have loyal bodyguards alongside the not so loyal, to keep them in line.

"The term is contracted. Once they have paid off their contract, they are free to leave."

They never worked off their debt, but Wickmore didn't mention that. He wanted these people listening. And they were. Avidly. Norris might not give credence to the *Hassim*'s treasure, but his crew certainly would. Not that the crew's interest would influence their captain, but if they knew about it, they'd work that much harder to find Roystan's crew.

"Don't they try to escape?"

"Nobody, but nobody, escapes the *Boost*."

As predictable as ever. Wickmore damped his spark of triumph.

"Not even Snowshoe Bertram?"

Norris could kill him with a single lunge. He wouldn't. The loss of control would cause him to lose face in front of eight soldiers—two of whom were looking at each other with small, knowing sniggers; silent sniggers to be sure, but it was enough.

Norris, after a few seconds, regained his speech and made a pretense of looking puzzled. "Who? Oh, Bertram Snowshoe. He didn't escape, Executive. I let him go temporarily. He dreamed of becoming a body modder. Who am I to stand in the way of a boy who wants to become qualified? Especially when he's prepared to pay for the tuition himself."

"But you intended to collect him again afterward, Captain."

"I intend to," Norris corrected him.

"Snowshoe graduated months ago, Captain. He should be back on board by now."

A tic started to pulse in Norris's right cheek.

"But he's not, is he. He disappeared not long after graduating." Wickmore leaned close. "How many deserters have you had since?" For no one deserted the *Boost* and lived to boast about it. Captain Norris tracked them down and killed them or forced them to sign a worse contract than before.

Snowshoe's disappearance would have given the crew hope. If one man could do it, so could others.

Norris bared his teeth. The tic had grown into a full-grown twitch. "There had better be a point to this."

"I can get you Bertram Snowshoe. Or Snowshoe Bertram, as he calls himself now."

"Where?"

"Let's talk about what I want in return."

"You didn't tell him which ship," Pol said.

"Of course not." He wasn't a fool. "You can give him the name once you are on your way. But not before." Pol Bager was no match for Captain Oliver Norris. Wickmore was sure she would discover that the hard way. It wasn't his concern. "Call me as soon as Norris disables *Another Road*."

Captain Roystan and his crew—including the long-missing Nika Rik Terri—had evaded capture before, and until Keenan's unexpected offer of funds, Leonard Wickmore hadn't had enough manpower to be sure of finding them, let alone be certain to capture them when he did. But even Roystan and his crew would find it impossible to evade a warship filled with four hundred trained, armed mercenaries.

"Arriola is mine," Pol said.

"Of course." Norris didn't care about Arriola, except maybe as a bonus. Wickmore didn't care about her either, no matter what Pol thought, no matter what he'd told Norris. Even if information from the *Hassim* database would be useful in cementing his place in the Eaglehawk hierarchy.

No, he wanted Nika Rik Terri. He hoped Norris hadn't realized that.

Norris would do his job if he wanted to get Snowshoe. Pol had better do hers as well.

"I got you onto the *Boost*," Wickmore told Pol now. "Just do your job when you get there."

2

NIKA RIK TERRI

The Netanyu 3501 was a serviceable machine, good for its time, but up against a Songyan, it didn't rate. "Only six inlet tubes," Nika said. "How are we supposed to fine-tune a body with six inlets?"

The human body was a complex factory that responded to minute chemical changes, and she was used to being able to control them right down to the DNA. The Netanyu worked for basic repairs, but it only worked down to the cellular level. She missed the fine-tuning she could do with the fourteen inlets and tenfold increase in accuracy in the feeds that came with the superior machine.

She had an apprentice now too. How could she train Snow properly if she couldn't teach him how to modify any lower than cellular level?

Snow, who had taken the Netanyu apart to clean to Nika's exacting standards and was now putting it together again, snapped the last coupling together. "We could always get a Songyan."

She wanted one as much as Snow did, maybe more so because she knew what they could do. A Songyan had fourteen inlets, and those extra inputs made a difference when you wanted a perfect mix. She had a new name, Nika James, and a new look. She'd removed all her hair and added diamanté in a line of faceted jewels that trailed over her forehead and down the side of her face and neck. It wouldn't make any difference, for as soon as she put the order in, Leonard Wickmore would find her. One day they'd have to get a Songyan, but not yet. Not until she could work out a way to order it without Wickmore using it to find her.

The chatter of the crew through the internal links was comforting. At first it had been strange to see and hear what was happening in the crew room, down in engineering, or on the bridge, while she worked in her studio. She was used to working in quiet areas with nothing but ambient music to soothe her clients. Here on the ship the only thing that soothed was the chatter of daily life, the knowing that everyone was safe. The only private conversations were the ones you had in your cabin or when most people were off ship.

"Ready?" Josune asked. Nika could see her at the shuttle bay, waiting with Roystan while Carlos and Jacques made their way down. "The merchant closes shop at 20:00."

They had plenty of time, but today Nika was as impatient for them to go as Josune was.

Josune and Carlos left first—they had to get to the other side of the station where Josune had a part on order.

"Come on," Nika said under her breath as Jacques hesitated for some quiet words with Roystan. Snow looked at her.

"Set up for an examination," Nika said.

"I can't keep setting up the machine and pulling it apart again. I eventually need someone to practice on."

It was a problem, and one she'd have to address, but they had a bigger problem right now. "I'll give you someone to practice on soon."

He set it up, one eye on her. "I don't know how we lucked onto a ship where no one wants to be modded. What are the odds?"

Four months ago she'd have asked the same question. "High."

At long last Jacques left.

"About time." Nika made her way up to the crew room, which was where Roystan would go.

She got there before he did.

Roystan stopped in the doorway. He knew.

"When were you going to tell us?"

"I . . . it's probably nothing. Something I ate, maybe."

"Roystan. You know the symptoms. You've had this problem before."

He moved over to make himself some coffee. He made her a mug too. "I was hoping it was temporary. I've got used to feeling so well lately. I wanted it to be—"

There was nothing but silence through the speakers, not even the sound of Snow setting up the Netanyu.

"Come on down," Nika said. "We need to see the damage."

"I have to watch the ship while the others are out."

"It'll take ten minutes. Don't you trust us to hold the doors for that long?" Nika ushered him out. "I've got an apprentice. We'll be talking things over. If we wait until the others get back, everyone will hear the discussion." She paused. "Unless you want us to turn off the feed to the studio."

That would bring everyone down, sure something was wrong.

Roystan brought his coffee with him. "It might be a virus."

She didn't honor that with an answer. If he'd thought it was something others might catch, he'd have been down at the first symptom.

"Are you ready?" she asked Snow.

He nodded.

"Are you sure it will only be ten minutes?" Roystan asked.

"Your coffee will still be hot." She looked from the mug to his face. "Lukewarm, anyway."

"There's no point arguing with her," Snow said. "She always wins."

Nika should find that in the ship record and play it back the next time Snow disagreed with her.

Roystan didn't argue anymore. The other crew members would be back on board in less than an hour. He knew as well as she did what would happen then. They would have him in the machine as soon as they knew there was a problem. He ran the ship mostly on consensus, which meant he wouldn't pull rank to ignore her, probably didn't even want to. He just didn't want to face the truth.

His body was deteriorating.

Hammond Roystan—formerly Roy Goberling—had spent the last eighty years just surviving while his body rejected the modifications Gino Giwari had made, at Goberling's request, to take away his memory. He wouldn't want to know he was going back to that.

But if he didn't tell them he had a problem, they couldn't fix it, could they.

"Good," Nika said. "Into the machine."

"Clothes on or off?"

It was always better with clothes off, but the machine could take a reading either way, and Nika was good at gauging moods. "On," she said.

"That's okay, then." Roystan put his mug down, crawled into the machine.

"They should make these things easier to get into."

Snow looked pointedly at Nika. "If we had a Songyan, all you'd have to do is lie down on a bench."

Yes, if they had a Songyan, they could do lots of things. But Songyans had to be custom built. She didn't remind Snow about Wickmore. Snow would only tell her again that she was paranoid. She was paranoid, but Snow didn't know Leonard Wickmore the way she did. He didn't like to lose, especially not when he could see benefit in it.

Like being able to swap bodies and use the swapped body to commit a murder.

She wished she'd never invented the exchanger.

"Run the diagnostics." She watched Snow's sure fingers on the controls. He was better with a Netanyu than she was, despite his oft-repeated claim that fixing genemod machines was for technicians, not body modders.

She turned to the results that had started scrolling up.

"What can you see?" she asked Snow.

He frowned down at the screen. "It looks normal."

Nika knew this body down to the DNA. She zoomed in on the cells around Roystan's kidneys. It wasn't just the kidneys, anywhere would do, but it gave her something to target. "Compare it to the read we took thirty days ago."

Snow studied the two reads carefully. "Some of those cells should have died off. But it's nowhere near Giwari's changes."

Gino Giwari had modded Roystan's body nearly eighty years earlier, wrapping the end of each gene tightly in what Nika hoped was a code to how to restore Roystan's memories. The issue might have been related to that. It might have been related to the changes Nika was making to restore his memory. Or it might be something else altogether.

"The human body is complex." It would take days to work out what the underlying cause was, but they could do something to alleviate the problem while they worked on it.

"Maybe it's the start of a tumor."

She didn't think he believed that any more than she did.

"All over his body?" That much was a fact. She could see it in the stats scrolling up.

"It isn't bad at the moment. Sometimes you see problems where there aren't any, Nika."

And sometimes she saw problems while they were small. Before they became large ones. She fixed her gaze on Snow.

He sighed heavily. "How do we fix it?"

Nika turned back to the scrolling data. Body mods had a flow-on effect. One tiny change, like fixing a chemical imbalance in one part of the body, could end up affecting other parts. The challenge was keeping the body balanced long enough to make the changes permanent—before it started its own repairs. Like Roystan's was doing now.

Extra growth in cells like this was normally easy to fix. Put the person in a genemod machine, and let the machine set the body back to its norms. Except Nika's ongoing adjustments had forced Roystan's body to accept Giwari's changes as if they belonged. His body was healthier, the cells stronger, but it wasn't normal, by any measure.

All they had to work with was a Netanyu. It was like trying to use a freighter to maneuver into a shuttle bay when you needed a little one-man shuttle. Still, it could be worse. It could be a Dietel. Or a Dekker.

The Netanyu pinged to show it was finished. Nika helped Roystan out of the machine. "That wasn't too bad, was it?"

She watched his face, trying to gauge what he really thought—Roystan was an intensely private man, although in Josune's presence he was relaxing that shield—while he took a sip of his no-longer-hot coffee and grimaced.

"What's the damage?"

How could she describe it without getting technical?

"Cells in your body die every day. When they do, they break down into smaller components so your body can get rid of them. Unfortunately, your body isn't doing the breakdown properly, and it's not doing it fast enough."

"My body is finally starting to fall apart?"

She wasn't sure. Roystan had lived eighty years with Giwari's mod without his cells starting to multiply this way. He'd had other problems—like his body starving itself because it couldn't get enough food—but the cells behaving this way wasn't one of them. "It's just as likely to be what I'm doing to try to restore your memory."

"It's still close to acceptable bounds," Snow said.

Not for Roystan, it wasn't.

"Look at Nika's face. She doesn't agree with you." There was a glint in Roystan's eyes that hadn't been there before, the hint of a smile at the corners of his mouth that showed no matter what he said, he was relieved they were looking at the problem.

"Nika doesn't agree with anyone who doesn't agree with her. You should account for all the factors that make up the body. Including environmental factors, emotions of the person, even the food they ate the night before."

Roystan tipped the rest of his coffee down the studio sink. "That sounds familiar. Almost like a lecture I heard Nika giving the other day." His eyes lightened as he smiled.

Yes. He was happier.

"Give me time to look at the read," Nika said. "We'll do something." It wouldn't be the fine work she could do with her old machine, and Roystan's body wasn't exactly standard anymore. Sometimes the more basic genemod machines could tip the balance trying to restore things to human normal. She could do something temporary and fine-tune it later, but to really fix it, she needed more control, and that meant a Songyan.

She might save Roystan's life, only to have Wickmore turn up and kill them all. Everyone but her, because he'd want her to turn the Songyan into an exchanger.

She could put it to the crew to vote on what they wanted to do. She knew what they'd say. Get the Songyan. All except Roystan, who would pull rare captain's rank to prevent them going. But they'd go anyway, and it would be more dangerous and more divisive because they were doing it behind Roystan's back.

She'd never before had friends who'd put their own lives above someone else's.

Nika sighed. There was no choice, really. "Snow, it's time I showed you how to order a custom-built Songyan."

Nika left Snow to wipe down the Netanyu and joined Roystan in the crew room to work through the gene read.

Their ship, *Another Road*, was twice as large as *The Road to the Goberlings*—which it had replaced—and fifty years more modern. It had five levels, and when they'd bought it, four of them had been given over to cargo. Three of those levels were still closed off with no life support. The fourth was now divided into three roughly equal parts. One-third for cargo, one-third for engineering, and one-third a modding studio.

When they'd bought it—two months ago now—the top level had contained more cargo space, a cramped set of cabins off to one side for crew quarters, and a small bridge. In the intervening weeks, Roystan, Carlos, and Josune had stripped it down, separating the area into more spacious living quarters, adding emergency bulkhead doors around and across the ship, and building an entirely new, larger crew common room, with a full commercial kitchen opening off it. Jacques refused to let them call it a galley—he was a chef, after all.

Josune was adding weapons. The ship now bristled with them. The weapons themselves were on the outside of the ship with an access corridor all around. The corridor served as another protective layer that could be sectioned off and sealed in case the ship got hit. She wanted to add panels that could control the weapons from their shared common room, but that, she said, was a long-term project.

So far no one had fired at them.

Nika wanted to believe no one would.

The whole ship was a work in progress. Even now, there were half-assembled weapons on the smaller counters at the back of the crew room.

Nika looked away from the read, frowned at the weapons. It was unlike either Josune or Carlos to leave them out, but they'd been there for three days now.

Roystan looked to where she was looking. "They're planning something." He smiled for the crew who weren't there.

"Do you know what it is?"

He shook his head. "We'll find out soon."

It was a funny way to run a ship, but it worked for Roystan.

Nika tapped the schematic in front of her. "I've ordered a Songyan, but that will take weeks." She watched his expression fall. "I can prevent some of the symptoms in the meantime." His face brightened. "But I can't fine-tune it. Your body will take time to adjust when you come out of the machine." She'd taken her Songyans for granted. Now she knew just how good they were. "There'll be things you can't do for two days." He'd be fine after thirty hours, but it was better to play safe, especially with Roystan's fragile body. "You can't exercise strenuously. Can't get too excited." She paused again. "No sex."

"Okay. No sex. No exercise. No excitement."

"Two days of absolute calm."

If his body started producing adrenaline, it would trigger a cell reaction that wouldn't stop.

"Got it."

"Have you? Really?" She held his gaze with hers. "This is important, Roystan. You think you're bad now, but do the wrong thing and it'll get worse."

It wouldn't just be worse. It would be dire.

"It's getting worse now, isn't it?"

She couldn't argue with that.

"Does it matter either way?"

"If you don't follow my instructions exactly—" Nika paused. "You could die." She nearly said "will die," but until it happened, she was not going to say it.

"And if I'm sensible, I'll feel better." Roystan's smile was crooked. "There's no question, really."

There wasn't.

"We'll do it after dinner." After the crew got back, she meant, because although Roystan might go into a genemod machine for ten minutes without the rest of the crew here, he wouldn't do it for longer. No one felt truly safe, but this part of space was quiet. They were in the legal zone. Wickmore would take days to track them, if he even tried and didn't just wait at the Songyan factory.

"Thank you, Nika."

Josune and Carlos arrived back from their shopping in high spirits, dragging an antigrav trolley behind them. The engine on it was twice as big as the one they'd installed two weeks ago. At least Nika thought it was an engine. It was like none she'd seen before.

They shooed Snow—who was researching body modder Giwari at one of the three secondary screens near the disassembled weapons—over to the main table.

Giwari was eighty years dead, but Nika had told Snow that she expected him to know everything about the man and his work. He had, after all, been the genius who had modded Roystan.

So far as Nika could tell, Roystan's body hadn't aged since his late thirties, and that was more than eighty years ago.

Jacques arrived back not long later, with another antigrav trolley. His was laden with fresh food.

"The hydro farms on this station are amazing," Jacques said. "Look. Melons, grapes, greens." He rubbed his palms together. "Everyone out of the kitchen. I'm cooking dinner."

Nika's mouth watered at the thought. "How long to dinner, Jacques?"

Roystan would enjoy his dinner better after being modded.

"An hour."

They had time. "Then I'd like to fine-tune some of Roystan's chemical pathways." The crew were used to her working on Roystan, with her trying to help him regain his memory.

"Let me move away from the station first," Roystan said. "Overstay fees are heavy here."

Six months earlier Nika wouldn't have known that if a shuttle stayed longer than its booked time, it incurred overstay fees, let alone known how high those overstay fees were. "Sure," and she waited until they'd moved before she took him down to the genemod machine.

"We're going to force the destruction of some of those excess cells," she told Snow. "Make our own initiator caspases to trigger the destruction of the cells."

Snow chewed his bottom lip. "How are you going to target the cells?"

"Turn it off and turn it on." It was like throwing red paint at a wall and hosing it off immediately after. Do it often enough, and you ended up with a slightly pink wall, which was all they wanted.

Stopping the reaction was the bigger problem. "We need to slow the cell destruction immediately after." She tapped the screen. "These ions will speed up that process. Get me the rate of blood circulation. I want you to calculate how much we need to give him to stop the cell breakdown within thirty hours of us starting the repair."

"Sometimes I think I'd have been smarter to stay home and be beaten up by Banjo," Snow muttered.

"You can always go back, Snow. Banjo loves you now. And he did say he'd look after your studio until you got back."

Snow didn't even hear her; he was already immersed in his calculation. "And I tell you what I'm not doing," he said. "I'm not going to cannibalize his body to get the proteins."

The mod took half an hour. "Now remember," she warned as she helped Roystan out of the Netanyu, "nothing strenuous. For how long?"

"Two days. Thank you, Nika."

Back in the crew room, the smell of their forthcoming dinner wafted. Nika breathed in. This was her home now.

Snow went back to studying Giwari.

"You know," he said as he followed another link of data. "Gino Giwari thought a lot of himself." He reached over for a piece of the flatbread that was keeping them all out of Jacques's way. He chewed reflectively. "Rather like other body modders I know."

"There's no point hiding what you are," Nika said. "When you're good, you know you're good."

"Some people think they're better than they are," Snow said.

Josune and Carlos were packing up. They'd cleaned up whatever they'd been installing, and Josune reassembled the disassembled blasters. They didn't take long to put together. She locked them into a weapons drawer. Every public room on ship had weapons drawers, coded to the crew. Josune had made it her mission to fill those drawers with weapons.

"Are we talking about the great Nika Rik Terri, Snow?"

Snow didn't answer.

Instead he scrolled through the data he was looking at. "Did you know that Giwari was the first modder to purchase a Songyan gene-mod machine? When it was still a start-up company." He tapped the screen. "There's a picture of him here with Conrad Songyan himself."

Nika came over to look. The flaxen-haired man standing in front of the big black box looked to be around Snow's age. He radiated confidence.

"He's young."

Had she looked as confident at that age? Probably. Although she'd never admit it to Snow, she'd been rather full of herself for a while.

"He's a body modder," Snow said. "He was probably sixty."

"Songyan machines have been around a hundred and fifty years." Nika did quick calculations in her head. "Giwari was eighty when he modded Roystan's memory. Ninety when he died. That makes him in his early twenties when he bought the Songyan."

Songyan himself didn't look much older. But then, Nika knew Songyan's story. How the young engineering genius's mother had died being modded. How he'd been driven to build his own machine to prevent that happening again.

"So Giwari got it cheap," Snow said. "New engineer, brand new machine he's trying to convince people to buy. It's untested. Conrad would sell it at cost to anyone who'd buy it."

The machine of choice for professional modders back then had been the Maestro. Even the Netanyu was unheard of. And as for the Dietel, that would take another seventy years to come onto the market.

After which it would spread like the parasite it was, because it was cheap and easy to use. They even had one in the studio here on the ship.

"You'd have taken it too," Snow said.

He was right. Even now she checked out all the new modding machines. Just in case. But then, people used to send them to her. "I wonder if Giwari used anything except a Songyan."

Snow rubbed his hands together. "And soon we get our own." He beamed at the others. "You're not the only ones who went shopping today, you know."

Carlos slapped his palm against Josune's. "You owe me fifty credits."

"I thought she'd take longer." Josune glanced over at Roystan, opened her mouth to speak, closed it before she did.

Nika would have to tell them soon that Wickmore would be after them again.

"Five minutes to food," Jacques said from the kitchen. "If you people are doing something, do it now."

Josune and Carlos scrambled in a last-minute flurry of activity.

"Right," Josune said. "Switch her over."

The big wall-screen came on.

"You're on." Josune and Carlos slapped palms again. "Come on over, Roystan."

Josune wiped down the smaller table, which had earlier held disassembled weapons, dusted the seat behind it, and pointed. "Try it out."

"The seat?" Roystan asked.

"Sit down."

Roystan sat. The webbing around the seat—which had looked like simple emergency webbing—snapped into place around him. A full flight seat.

Roystan's eyes widened.

Carlos cackled gleefully.

The table came up, tilted to look like one of the boards on the bridge.

"Oh." Roystan put his hands on the board. "You built a pilot's console." Familiar screens came up. "We can fly the ship from here, Nika," for the table next to Roystan's had come up as well, and there, on-screen, were the calibrator controls. And no doubt that innocuous-looking seat behind it would turn out to be a full flight-deck seat as well.

Not that they needed Nika to calibrate any longer. They had a fully functioning ship calibrator that Carlos and Josune kept spot on. Even so, Nika liked to keep her hand in. It improved hand-eye coordination and gave the modders something to practice with. As Snow had pointed out, there weren't many people to mod on this ship.

She'd have to do something about that eventually, if she were to train her apprentice properly.

"Ahem," Jacques said. "Play later. Dinner is served."

Roystan ran his hands across the console, then reluctantly stood. "Later," he agreed.

Carlos's grin was wide.

"Bet you didn't see that coming." Carlos made way for Roystan to sit down.

"No." Roystan's smile was almost as wide. "We can run the whole ship from here."

Only Roystan would think that doing everything from the one room was a good thing. But whoever had thought of it—it had to be Josune—was a genius. Roystan lived in the crew room.

"You didn't build that in a day," Snow said. "You couldn't."

They hadn't. Nika looked at the weapons drawer, containing the blasters Josune had put together in under a minute. The blasters had littered the table for three days.

"We would have finished days ago," Josune said. "But we needed—" She broke off as a communications link sounded.

Roystan opened the link.

A woman's face appeared on-screen. Her face was modded in a style Nika had made famous five years earlier. She wore a burgundy suit and dark eye-covers. "*Another Road*. This is the Justice Department. Prepare to be boarded."

3

JOSUNE ARRIOLA

Josune's hand automatically went to her stomach, to her sparker tucked under her shirt. Back when Roystan had claimed salvage on the explorer ship the *Hassim*, the Justice Department had sent out a fake arrest claim for him. The crew of *Another Road* now believed the claim had been instigated by Eaglehawk Company, headed by Executive Leonard Wickmore and his elite team of assassins. After Benedict, Alejandro, and Tamati Woden had died, the crew had checked to see if Roystan was still a wanted man. Josune had paid an investigative service to make doubly sure. According to the investigative search, and their own lesser searches, Roystan had never been wanted by the Justice Department at all. None of them had been. She'd checked them all.

So what did they want now, and how had they snuck up on them without any warning alarms?

Roystan was already answering, his voice relaxed as he said, "Please identify your ship." He muted the link and brought up coordinates for a space jump. "We might get to test out our new boards sooner than we planned." He moved over to the pilot's seat. "Nika, I need you on the calibrator. The part of space I plan to nullspace to has anomalies that interfere with communications links."

Nika moved over to the calibrator board. "Remember to stay calm." Low. A murmur. Josune only caught it because she'd moved to a nearby screen to check the weapons. She glanced at Nika, then to Roystan.

Roystan avoided meeting her gaze. He unmuted the link as the Justice Department details came through and the ship matched their speed and came alongside. "Thank you. We have received the Justice Department seal. Please hold while we confirm the details." He sounded almost apologetic as he added, "After all, we need to prove you aren't pirates who've stolen a Justice Department seal."

The woman on the link snorted. "Pirates. We're in the legal zone, mister."

"It's captain, not mister, and as you point out, we are in the legal zone. Confirmation of identity is a standard requirement for an official wishing to board a ship."

Another standard requirement was that the agents would ID themselves as they came on board. Josune was looking forward to that. She and Nika had built the scanner together, to the same design as the scanner Nika had built in her studio. It recorded more personal details than anyone might reasonably expect it to. As Nika had said, sometimes it came in useful.

"Ooh. A man who knows his rights. Very well, Captain. I am Agent Brand. Agent Bouwmeester and I wish to board your ship to investigate the report of the illegal use of a genemod machine."

A genemod machine. The Justice Department had boarded the *Hassim* three times. The usual excuse was a stolen engine. Once it had been a stolen calibrator. It had never been a genemod machine.

These people knew who they were.

Josune pulled up the schema for the other ship onto the big screen built into the table. "A standard ten-man carrier." They'd be armed. If they tried to run, the Justice Department had every right to shoot them.

"We have to let them board," Roystan said.

An impatient sigh came through the speakers. For a moment

Josune thought Roystan had accidentally unmuted. Brand said, "Of course, you're going to deny you have a genemod machine. I'll bet you're packing it away right now."

"Is she for real?" Nika demanded. "Let me." She opened the link without waiting for Roystan to agree. "Do you know how long it would take to hide a genemod machine that is set up? We're not packing anything away, and if you break anything, we'll sue you from here to the other side of the galaxy."

They were lucky the crew had only had *Another Road* two months. Josune was sure that within twelve months there'd be a whole room of genemod machines waiting to be inspected, instead of just the Netanyu and the Dietel that they had now.

"It's a trap," Josune said.

"Unfortunately, we have to spring the trap before we can do anything." Roystan unmuted again to say, "As captain, I welcome you both to *Another Road*. We have nothing to hide. I will meet you at the docking station." He hesitated. "Also, for the record, we are recording this."

"And you're sending it on to headquarters?" Brand grinned. "Good luck with that."

"Of course not. You're most likely jamming our long-range signal. I thought I'd mention it because once we prove we are legitimate, we expect you to leave the ship quietly."

Jamming long-range signals was standard procedure with the Justice Department out at the fringe. Mostly so the ship the agents were boarding couldn't call for support. Josune's old captain, Feyodor, had refused to allow anyone on her ship while signals were being jammed. She'd said that if you used a jammer, you were a pirate.

The Justice Department generally turned a blind eye to the way their agents handled things out here on the edge of the legal zone, but a spate of public vids showing their agents getting away with bad behavior had swept across the pirate media over the last months. It was just a pity no one had copies of what the Justice Department had done to the crew of *Another Road*, back when they'd last been hassling Roystan and his crew.

Not that Josune would have known where to send the vids.

When you didn't trust the law, there was no law. The Justice Department claimed to be cleaning the department up. Josune would believe that when it happened. You didn't get rid of two hundred years of corruption overnight.

"Ooh. Now you're threatening to expose me. I'm scared." Brand rubbed her hands together. "Your modder had better have his proof of registration ready."

His registration? Were they looking for Snow? Or was that a guess? Nika must have thought they were, because she crossed her arms and moved over to him. A mother protecting her cub. Josune and Roystan exchanged smiles.

Off-screen, a voice demanded, "What's the delay? One might almost think you're obstructing justice. Prepare to be boarded now, or we'll fire on you."

"There is no problem. I have already agreed to allow you to board. I repeat, I will meet you at the docking station." Roystan switched off the link.

"Warm up the plasma cannon," Josune suggested. "The small one. Snow?"

Snow was their gunnery expert—not counting Josune.

"Not yet," Roystan said. "If he's waiting by the cannon, they'll know we have one."

"Blasters?" Josune asked.

"Stunners," Roystan said. "I wouldn't want to be up for murdering a real agent of the Justice Department."

If anyone was going to do murder right now, it would be Jacques, glaring down at the unfinished meal congealing on the table.

Maybe that would be a good thing. An agent attacked by an enraged chef with a meat cleaver wouldn't be suspicious; it would be justice.

Josune touched her shirt where her sparker rested underneath, against her stomach. Not that she planned to use the weapon while on *Another Road*, not when it meant she could burn out their wiring, but it was easy to hide, and most people didn't realize it was a weapon till she used it. She nodded to Roystan. "Let's go meet Agents Brand and Bouwmeester."

Four Justice Department agents boarded. All were heavily armed, with blasters and stunners. Definitely not friendly.

"You said there were two of you, not four," Roystan said.

Brand hoisted her blaster in a deliberate show of menace and dragged her eye-covers to rest on the tip of her nose. "Someone with your legal expertise, Captain, would know that it is no longer safe to travel in pairs."

"We are a peaceful ship. We don't want trouble."

"Neither do we, Captain. Neither do we." Brand tried to push past him.

Roystan put up a hand, indicated the ID scanner near the airlock.

"This is a waste of time."

"As you pointed out, Agent, a man with my legal expertise knows the rules. That's the rule. One of your own department's rules. Let's make sure we complete all the right checks, shall we."

The woman with Brand pushed forward. "It doesn't matter," she told Brand. "We have every right to be here. Get this over with."

The scanner identified her as Agent Calista Bouwmeester, certified Justice Department agent. The other two agents stepped forward as well. Agents Korel and Pelin. And finally, Brand.

"Now the preliminaries are over," Brand said. "Let's see this modder of yours. You understand if you have a genemod machine but don't have a registered modder, you are breaking the law."

Technically, they could have one; they just couldn't use it.

"We understand," Roystan said.

"And your proof of purchase must be in order."

"Understood," Roystan said again. "Do you want to see the genemod machine first?" He stood aside and indicated the passage.

"I want to see your modder. And you go in front of us. I don't trust you."

Josune's gaze crossed Roystan's. She nodded.

"Crew room it is," Roystan said.

Hopefully the others had thought to arm themselves—discreetly—with weapons. Roystan was giving them enough time to do so.

Josune's back itched all the way.

"Quite a big ship," Brand said as they went. "For how many of you?"

She knew exactly how many; Josune was sure of it. They'd sent just enough agents to overcome a crew of six. She smiled grimly to herself. Six regularly armed crew, that was. These people didn't know what they were in for if they made any trouble.

"The report you had of our genemod machine," Roystan said. "What made you think it was illegal?"

Josune couldn't tell if he was having a dig, fishing for information, or changing the subject.

"Our sources are our business," Brand said.

Sometimes, in the screens as they came up to them, Josune could see the images of the agents behind. All four were muscular and trod with an aggressive firmness that implied intimidation. They wore their blasters low and kept their hands close to their weapons. Trigger happy, maybe? Best not to give them cause to draw, then.

Brand stopped in the doorway to the crew room. Her gaze swept the set-up table. "Pardon us for disturbing your dinner." She failed to hide a snigger.

Jacques, standing in the doorway to the kitchen, crossed his arms and changed his posture. He was holding a frying pan. The meat cleaver, his usual go-to weapon, was attached to his belt. Brand glanced at him and dismissed him in the same look. It wasn't exactly subtle, but the agents didn't seem to see either as weapons.

Carlos had a small, cigar-shaped stunner tucked into his shirt pocket. It was the smallest in their armory but packed a nasty punch. Nika was wearing the dart gun that looked like a heavy, gold, jeweled cross. It was loaded with fast-acting tranquilizer darts and coded so that if any of the crew curled their fingers around the crossbar and applied pressure, it would fire one of those darts. Snow had a spray bottle hanging from his belt. Josune hoped it wasn't the lethal naolic-and-mutrient mix Nika had used on their original ship. Not only did it eat away skin—the mixture was corrosive enough to dissolve metal.

"Quite the party. Now, which of you is the modder?" Agent Brand's gaze stopped at Snow. She pulled out her scanner. "Let's ID you and check your registration."

Did they want Snow, specifically, or did they just recognize him as the modder? Josune put up an unobtrusive hand. Snow nodded, once, and stayed back.

Young Snow was a quick learner.

Nika stepped forward. "I'm the modder."

"You?" For a moment Brand looked nonplussed. "I don't believe you."

"Why don't you ID me and find out?"

Brand waved her blaster in Snow's direction. "Our reports say a male modder. I want to know who he is first. He looks familiar."

Yes. They specifically wanted Snow, but why?

"They're body modders," Josune said. "Any one of us could have been male yesterday." She glanced at Roystan. He gave a slight shake of his head. Not yet.

Brand hesitated. "Later. I'll deal with you later." She gestured at Snow. "Come on, ID yourself."

"I thought you wanted to ID the modder?" Snow said.

"I want to ID you. Do you have a problem with that?"

"Get on with it." Bouwmeester picked up one of the plates and breathed in the aroma. A look of pleasure flashed briefly across her face. Josune wasn't surprised. Even half-cold, the food still smelled divine.

"Can't let this go to waste, can we?" The agent forked up a mouthful, and her eyes widened. "Hey. This is not bad. Would you believe, it tastes better than it smells. It would be better hot, though." She walked over to Jacques. "Heat it up for me, will you?"

That move positioned the agents evenly around the room. Was it deliberate? Probably.

Jacques uncrossed his arms, and Bouwmeester dodged sideways to avoid the frying pan. "No."

"It is a little impolite to come on board and eat our food without asking," Roystan said.

"So sue me." Bouwmeester thrust the plate at Jacques again. He stepped back.

"Hey," someone said sharply through the link. "Do your job."

Bouwmeester shrugged and forked up another mouthful. "You are missing some great food, Ewan."

Snow looked at Josune, and she gave a slight nod this time. He stepped forward to ID himself.

No one spoke.

Agent Brand studied the result. "Well, well. Snowshoe Bertram. Who would have guessed." She sniggered. "You've changed your name."

Snow huffed out a breath. "It's Bertram Snowshoe. I did not change my name. That's a computer error."

Josune's hand rested on her hidden sparker as she watched Agent Bouwmeester murmur into her jaw-link. Roystan leaned against the newly converted pilot's console.

Brand looked at Roystan. "Your modder here is a wanted man. That means we'll have to take him with us. Your other modder, if legitimate"—and she glanced at Nika—"is likely on our wanted list too. How unfortunate for you, as it means we'll have to take both, and the machine as well."

"Not likely," Nika said over Roystan. "A wanted man?"

"I told you. You never know who you may have taken on as crew, unknowingly."

"I know who comes onto *Another Road* as crew," Roystan said. "I'm more concerned about the people who come onto the ship pretending to be officials."

"Pretending?" Brand said. "You've had your proof."

"But not proof that Snow is a wanted man. As far as we know, this could be a personal vendetta of yours. You will need to back up your claim."

"He was an indentured doctor. He left his post."

"Irrelevant," Nika said loudly, talking over Snow's muttered denial. "Snow is an apprentice. He signed a contract with me. It's legal. His registration as an apprentice is recorded in the modders' database and takes precedence over all other claims if not disputed within the first month. Unless I agree to release him." She put her hand up to curl around the cross containing the tranquilizer darts. "And I don't agree to release him. Not to you, not to anyone."

Apprenticeships were binding. The master became responsible for feeding the apprentice, for housing them, and for any legal issues.

"You?"

"Yes. Snow is apprenticed to me, and I do not agree to release him. And for your information, I also own the genemod machine. You can't take either."

Josune hid her smile. It wouldn't stop the coming fight, but the Justice Department, corrupt as they were, couldn't deny legal rights, and all this was being recorded.

Snow blinked at Nika. He looked distracted. "Are you saying that if I was an escaped merc, which I'm not, and I signed on as an apprentice, then no one can take me back?"

"Temporarily," Nika cautioned. "While you are an apprentice, I have first rights. Once you've finished, though, I must hand you over to the other party. It's part of the apprenticeship agreement. Didn't you read it?"

Snow ignored that. "So why don't more people do apprenticeships to escape?"

"It's a no-brainer, Snow. What do you think would happen to me if I let you go, or you did a runner on me? When you signed, you became my responsibility. If you disappear, who do I have to offer up, with the skills I've just trained you in? I wouldn't take your place willingly, nor would another apprentice."

"So why—"

"Snow, have you signed any contract, other than the one you signed to become my apprentice?"

"No, but—"

"Therefore I am under no obligation to anyone, except to make sure you get a proper apprenticeship. I get to keep you. I get to keep my machine. And no matter what these thugs want, I also know that you are not on any wanted list, Snow." Nika looked at the Justice Department agents. "Don't you think I would have checked that?"

"All this is interesting but it's not getting the job done." Agent Brand turned to Nika. "The Justice Department overrules your claim. Now. Your turn, lady. Let's ID you as well."

"Go ahead. Check my ID. If you recall, I offered to be identified first." Nika stepped forward and allowed the scanner to record her details.

Brand dragged her eye-covers to the end of her nose again and stared at Nika while they waited for the results. Nika stared back. The silence stretched. Josune's money was on Brand to look away first.

Whoop, whoop. The klaxon warning broke the standoff, and *Another Road* bucked from the proximity of the new ship. Josune automatically adjusted her balance to compensate but froze for a few seconds as she swallowed bile and memories. The last time they'd had a proximity alert, it had been her old ship, the *Hassim*, out of control and overrun with company men. Her friends and shipmates had been dead.

Roystan swung around to the nearest screen; Carlos ran to another one. Korel, Brand, Jacques, and Nika lost their footing.

"They've stabilized." Roystan brought the image of the other ship up on-screen. Josune took a deep breath and moved to Roystan's side.

Bouwmeester's face creased into a smile. "Look at that. Company."

Brand was white. "Damn that man. He doesn't have the sense of a turd."

Snow, one hand on the table for balance, stared at the screen. "The *Boost*."

Roystan brought the ship details up on the screen. Sure enough, it was the *Boost*. Captained by one Oliver Norris.

Roystan glanced at Nika, glanced at the calibrator board, which they hadn't tried out yet.

Nika rolled to her feet smoothly and moved close to the board. She casually set the calibrator. At least Josune assumed that was what she'd done. It looked as though she'd wiped a speck of dust off the board.

"What's so important about the *Boost*, Snow?" Nika asked.

Snow's gaze went blank, and he looked incredulously at her.

Josune kept her gaze unwaveringly on the four agents. She managed to keep her face neutral. They'd all heard the horror stories he'd told.

"This is your plan?" Roystan asked. "The *Boost*?"

"You might call it a little side business," Brand said. "About time, Norris," as the communications link chimed and the captain's image filled the screen.

Nika's eyes turned speculative, as they always did when she was assessing a mod. Josune guessed that Oliver Norris had been modded by a master. Even she could see that the mod wasn't standard. And she was going to have to stop thinking about modding. Nika's passion was becoming a bad influence.

Josune moved to block the screen as the nullspace timer started a silent countdown in front of Nika.

"Excuse me," Nika said to Norris. "But is your modder Samson Sa?"

"Is she for real?" Brand asked.

The stars on-screen collapsed into the center of the screen, then disappeared altogether.

They had nullspaced.

When they came out the other side, the *Boost* was gone.

Josune's sparker was aimed at Agent Brand's head. "Don't move," she told the Justice Department agents.

"Outmaneuvered." Carlos pushed his stunner into Korel's ribs.

Bouwmeester yawned as if it were of no consequence. "They're stunners. They won't kill us."

A chime sounded on the console. The Justice Department ship trying to contact them. Roystan opened the link. A man in a suit scowled out at them. Ewan, presumably. "What in the hell do you think you are doing?"

"Nullspacing," Roystan said mildly. "Couldn't you tell?"

"With us linked to your ship?"

"Well, naturally. After all, I couldn't warn you about what I was doing, could I?"

The Justice Department man scowled again, looked around as far as the camera would let him. "And what were you thinking, Brand? You know to never let them onto the bridge."

"This isn't the bridge," Brand snarled.

"Kill them and get back here."

"Killing them wasn't part of the deal. Besides, we don't quite have the upper hand here, Ewan. And one of them has a sparker." Agent Brand picked her eye-covers up off the floor where they'd fallen and pushed them back into place, ignoring Josune's sparker.

"How badly can you botch a simple job?"

"If you think you can do better, come and do it."

"Believe me, I will. And let them fire the sparker. It won't kill you, but there's a good chance it will destroy the wiring on their ship and leave it dead in space, just waiting for the *Boost* to catch up."

Roystan closed the link and pulled two stunners out of the weapons drawer Josune had locked earlier. He handed one to Snow. "We can count on at least fifteen minutes before the *Boost* gets here. Their own jamming tools will work against them. The *Boost* will have a difficult time pinpointing the ships. It won't be able to come too close. Enough time to finish this."

He gestured to the passage and said to Brand, "Let's walk you back to your ship."

"Hands above your head while you walk." Josune kept her sparker aimed at Brand. She had out her stunner by now, too, and it was aimed at Pelin. "All of you. Keep them high, or one of us will shoot."

Brand gave her a filthy look but raised her arms.

Jacques collected the agents' weapons.

"Move," Roystan said. "Jacques, you and Carlos wait here and watch. Nika, you and Snow come with us. Stay alert. Josune?"

"I'll come with you. Be your eyes."

They were halfway to the airlock docking station when a *wumph* of hot air almost knocked them off their feet, sent Josune staggering back. The smell of burning plastic and heated metal hit them like an almost-physical force.

Roystan brought up the screens even as Carlos called from the crew room. "Five more from the Justice ship have boarded. They've destroyed the docking door."

Roystan tapped a code into his handheld. "Close breach door two." On-screen they watched the big breach doors snap close.

"One made it through," Josune said. "She's coming this way. Fast. Carrying a—" She squinted at the screen. What was it they had? A long cylinder with a ball on the end. "It's a riot gun. Stay low and cover your eyes and nose. It won't knock you out, but it gets in your eyes and throat. Like a pepper spray."

She wasn't fast enough. Two riot bombs hit the floor in front of them with a soft *wumph*. Acrid smoke billowed.

Josune dropped to get below most of the smoke, forced her suddenly burning eyes to stay open so she'd be ready to shoot at the first sign of movement. Through the haze, she glimpsed the edge of a sleeve. She rolled, continued rolling, and fired a long burst of her stunner in a wide arc. She tried to take shallow breaths even though her mind screamed for more air. She heard two thumps, couldn't see whom she'd hit.

Roystan had rolled in the opposite direction. He fired at Bouwmeester and Korel. Both went down.

Agent Brand grabbed Snow and pulled him into an embrace. She twisted a wire around his neck while she held a blaster to his temple.

"Drop your weapons. All of you, or I'll shoot."

Snow twisted in Brand's grip, choked, and put his hands to his throat as he tried to tug away the thin wire.

"Patience, boy. Your turn will come. Struggling will make you bleed more."

He took his hands away and pressed back, leaving a smear and a thin, glistening red necklace of blood.

Nika, shirt pulled up to cover her nose and mouth, one hand clutching her cross and eyes half-closed, crowded as close as she could to Brand. "You're not taking Snow."

"Back up, lady. Or I will shoot. He's a wanted man. Dead or alive. It doesn't matter either way. You shoot me, you'll be garroting him."

Nika held her hands in the air. "My hands are empty. You shoot me and it's murder. Shoot any of us and it's murder."

Roystan touched Josune's arm lightly and indicated the four unconscious agents. Josune nodded.

"Good idea." Brand had seen the movement. "Put my sorry shipmates onto an antigrav unit and bring them along. We're heading back to our ship."

"There's a trolley in that room." Josune indicated a door farther down the corridor. The genemod studio. "We have to go past you to get it."

"Not likely." Brand backed down the corridor, dragging Snow with her. She kept a firm hand on the wire and the blaster. Snow scratched at his neck, trying to loosen the wire.

"Be careful with my property," Nika snapped. "If he's damaged and can't do his work, I'll sue you." Nika's hand had gone back to her cross.

"His problem if he refuses to move."

"No, your problem. We can simply stun you both as you stand. You'd both collapse together."

"But you can't take that chance, can you? Back up, all of you."

"We need to get that antigrav trolley," Josune said. "The nearest one is in the room to your left."

In the background, Roystan was talking to Carlos over the link. "Get down to breach door two and wait by the lock. Don't go in. Make sure you are armed."

"There's four of them waiting behind the door there."

"I know."

Brand risked a quick glance sideways, to the studio door. Josune was too far away to use the opportunity. The agent backed into the room, dragging Snow with her. Nika followed close behind.

"One at a time, and go right as you come in." Brand's back was against the far-left wall. She wasn't taking chances. A pity the trolley wasn't to the left.

"All of you. Or Snow here dies."

Nika stood just inside the door, her eyes still fixed on Brand. Josune edged past her, went over to the trolley, and picked up the controller. She flicked a button, and the trolley lifted off the ground. She headed back out. Roystan stood in the doorway.

He was breathing heavily, his face the color of Jacques's uncooked flatbread.

"Roystan?" Something was badly wrong. She hoped it was simply the effects of the gas he'd inhaled.

"Let's get this lot loaded so we can get rid of them."

"One of you only." Brand's voice was sharp.

"I can't lift four of them onto the trolley," Josune said. "Not without help."

Brand's finger twitched, and Josune held her breath. Nika took a quick step sideways, into the line of fire. Her eyes never left Brand's face. "As Josune said, it needs two. You are not a stupid woman. And you are in a hurry. Let's get it done."

Brand's finger visibly tightened.

"So far you've shot no one. You have a hostage. You don't want all-out war, and with three of us against one of you plus your hostage, you know who is going to win."

"Get on with it, then," Brand snarled. "When this is over, you are going right to the top of the wanted list, you know that. With a bounty so high it won't keep the bounty hunters away. You will spend the rest of your short life running. You will wish you were dead. All of you."

"Tell us something new."

Josune went out quickly. She didn't want to leave Nika alone, but they needed these people off the ship. Fifteen minutes, Roystan had said. Now ten.

Roystan went with her, and they quickly lifted one of the bodies onto the trolley. He made hard work of it.

"Are you okay, Roystan?"

"I will be when these lot go. Although," he admitted softly, "between you and me, I need another stint in that machine soon."

If Roystan thought he needed work, then it was bad. Josune had been gentle with the first body. Now, speed was more important. The bodies loaded, she headed back. The scene had changed subtly. Brand was leaning against the open Netanyu with Snow still in her embrace, the necklace of blood starting to drip. Nika was against the left wall, clutching the cross.

Brand gestured toward Nika as Josune and Roystan came to the doorway. "Leave the trolley and the controller. Both of you up against that wall and turn your backs."

Josune grimaced. She didn't like to turn her back on her enemy like that.

"You forget we have the firepower."

"And I have the hostage."

"I'm not sure why we should worry," Josune said. "You take

Snow, or you kill him. Or we do. Either way, he's gone. So why do we care? We should just shoot you and be done with it."

Brand opened her mouth, closed it again. She turned her glare full on Josune, then flinched. "What the . . . something just bit me."

Not suspicious yet. Good. Even a super-fast-acting tranquilizer like the one in Nika's dart gun took time to take effect.

Please let her not tighten her hand as she falls.

Brand's movements slowed even as her hand rose to check. The other hand, the one holding the wire, loosened, and the garrote slipped. Josune charged across the room and flipped Brand into the modding machine.

The lid began to close on its own, and Josune tried to stop it. "What?"

Nika tossed a cloth to Snow. "We'll fix your neck as soon as we're safe." She turned to Josune. "It's automatic. It's taking a read. We'll have to wait." She rounded on Roystan. "What part of forty-eight hours didn't you understand?"

"I didn't have much choice."

Nika shook her head, checked Snow's throat. "You'll live." She called through to Jacques. "Start heating up that garfungi stew."

Josune looked from Nika to Roystan. "That bad?"

"Worse," Nika said.

How bad was worse?

Nika glanced at the time and held out a hand. "Can I borrow a stunner?"

Josune handed her stunner over, wondering for an insane moment if Nika would shoot Roystan with it. Josune's hand moved to her sparker.

Nika followed the movement, could have been reading her mind. "It's tempting, but that won't fix stupidity." She raised the stunner and waited. The Netanyu lid opened. Nika fired at Brand. The agent didn't move.

Nika tucked the stunner into her waistband. "It was only a read, but it pays to be safe."

"Let's get her onto the trolley with the rest," Josune said.

"Not you," Nika said when Roystan came over to grab a leg. "You've done enough."

"Nika, I will keep going for as long as I need to. Don't write me off yet."

Josune moved him aside gently. "We've got it, Roystan." She didn't know what the problem was, but if Nika didn't want Roystan doing any lifting, he wouldn't be doing any lifting.

Carlos waited for them at the breach door. "There are four of them in there, getting in each other's way. I think everyone except their captain is on our ship now." He indicated the screen in front of him showing the room. All four were trying to force the door open. "They're amateurs. Can't get past the first defense even. Even you airy-fairy modders could do better."

"I don't think their captain likes failure." Josune turned to Roystan. "How do you want to do this?"

"Fast," Roystan said. "When I open the door, Carlos, you aim left and sweep to the right in continuous blast. Nika, you do the same, but right to left. Snow, you aim straight in front and sweep right. I'll do the same but go to the left. Josune, watch for anyone we miss. We should get them all in one pass, with no mistakes."

"Aye, Captain," Josune added to the soft chorus.

"Ready. Okay, on three. Three, two, one, open breach door two."

It was over in seconds. Josune looked at the four inert bodies in satisfaction. "That was easier than I thought."

"Don't tempt fate," Carlos said.

"I'm going to prep for nullspace." Roystan turned away. "And talk to the captain. Josune, can I leave you to get this lot off our ship? There should only be the captain, and maybe one other remaining."

"It will be my pleasure. If anyone comes out shooting, they'll hit their own people first."

"Thank you. Snow, if you and Carlos could help Josune, it would be great. Once we've unlinked, we can check for trackers they may have left behind."

He turned to Nika. "Come with me. The calibrator awaits you."

"You don't need me on the calibrator. It's not like we haven't got a good one in place now."

"I know, but you are better than any automatic calibrator. I like to have you watching that needle. Besides, you enjoy doing it."

Nika snorted but didn't argue. She handed Josune back her stunner and followed Roystan. "Think you won't be able to pilot this thing accurately, is that it?"

Josune hoped Nika didn't mean that. She heard her call Jacques.

"Garfungi takes time. It will be ready in five," Jacques said.

This time it was Roystan who snorted. Josune chewed her lip and watched Roystan until he turned the corner. He had better be all right. She turned to Snow. "Are you up to this, Snow?"

"Of course I am." He wiped his neck. "As Nika said, my injury isn't life threatening."

"Good. I'll have Carlos watch the door, if you don't mind coming in with me. As soon as Roystan has the captain on the line and they come to an agreement, we go in."

Roystan's voice came through the link even as she spoke.

"Captain Ewan. We are returning your agents. Unfortunately, they are not conscious. Permission to bring them on board your ship. Our crew will leave as soon as they are in your space. I advise you and your ship to unlink as soon as they exit."

"Captain Roystan, this is not the last you will hear of this. Norris is close by."

"Even if you have managed to get a message out—which I doubt—he's far enough away that it won't matter. Do we have your permission to board with your people?"

Josune sent the antigrav trolley in front of her as she listened to Roystan continue to talk. She checked the pile of human bodies. They were all still unconscious.

She brought out her sparker again. The familiarity settled her.

"Permission granted." Ewan snarled the permission. "No one steps past the docking bay. Unfortunately, there is no one to greet your people."

"I don't think they'll mind that, do you?"

That was easy. Too easy. He didn't complain. He didn't object. He didn't ask questions. He simply agreed to Roystan's request after a token growl and opened the docking-bay door.

What had she missed? Josune didn't trust Ewan. She didn't trust the Justice Department. Ewan could try to pull his ship away early, but he'd kill his crew. He wouldn't do that.

"I don't like this." She turned to Snow and Carlos. "You two wait here."

"No way." Snow was adamant. "You think it's a trap. You need someone to cover you, to watch your back."

"And to watch for any sneaky attacks coming through secret doors," Carlos added.

They were right. "All right, Carlos. You watch from the entrance. Snow, you wait with him and watch the other side."

"No. I'm coming with you."

Josune didn't have the time. The longer they argued, the more chance there was of Ewan staging an attack of some sort.

"Then let's do this." She pushed the trolley forward. The distance was only ten meters. Snow followed, stunner sweeping the cargo hold as he did so.

There was no one in the hold, but the cold, prickling sensation at the back of her neck told her Ewan was watching, biding his time.

Snow shoved his stunner into his waistband and grabbed Brand's arm to pull her off the trolley.

"Leave the trolley, Snow." Josune backed away, her sparker out. "We've more. They can have this one as a gift." Ten seconds and they'd be gone.

"Josune!" Carlos's cry was a warning.

She spun around, just in time to watch the *Justice VII*'s airlock door—the door linking them to their own ship—clang shut.

"Get back behind the breach door, Carlos." Back to where, if the two ships did pull apart while *Another Road*'s airlock was open, he'd have oxygen.

Roystan's snarl on her link was more menacing than any she'd heard so far, and the Justice Department agents had snarled a lot. You never could trust the Justice Department. She hadn't expected anything less.

"Captain Ewan, explain your action."

"Of course, Captain. Unfortunately, we now have another standoff. I have your people trapped in my landing bay. I have the one person I need. You may unlink and go your way and we will not bother you further."

Ewan thought he had Snow, did he? He could think again. One, maybe two people against her and Snow. Did he think they'd survived this long on pure luck?

"Roystan. Give him one warning. If he wants his ship, tell him to let us out now."

She glanced at the floor while Roystan repeated Josune's warning. Good. Insulated. At least there was no skimping on flooring. They wouldn't electrocute themselves.

"Wait near the exit to *Another Road*, Snow. Stay on this black flooring. Stay in shadow if you can." Ewan wouldn't show himself, not without provocation. He was outnumbered. But he had smarts. Well, she wasn't going to give him time to come up with a plan.

"Ready? And focus. You have one job. Hit the manual close on our lock as soon as we get out."

Snow moved to the door. "But how—"

Josune looked directly into the camera Ewan would be watching, waved her sparker. She turned to Snow. "This disables ships. Once I use it, their ship will be dead in space. Ewan has had his warning."

She had to believe Ewan thought she was desperate enough to kill both herself and Snow to get to him.

The back of her neck prickled; she spun around as an inner door opened. Captain Ewan stood in the doorway, blaster in hand, pointed at her.

Josune dived to avoid Ewan's blaster, didn't need to. Snow fired his stunner.

The captain slumped. Unconscious.

"Good shot, Snow."

"Now we have to go to the bridge to open this door so we can get back to our own ship." Snow looked at the body. "Sorry."

"No, we don't. Help me pile him onto the trolley." She was tempted to kill him, knew better. Justice Department agents might slink away from a fight they'd been bested on, but murdering some of them would bring the whole Justice Department out for revenge.

Snow helped her lift the captain onto the trolley, on top of the others.

"We just leave them and go? It seems unfair."

It was unfair, but there were ways to make it fairer. "He had his warning." And she had her sparker.

Josune pushed the trolley experimentally. It was almost at limit, for it hovered only millimeters above the floor. Snow helped her push it into the nearest room with a door with a manual override on the lock; she locked the door manually. They didn't want it coming open when the systems failed. Just in case everyone got sucked out before the breach doors closed.

Back in the shuttle bay Josune looked around for the nearest power board. Ship circuits were all linked. She knew her smile was feral as she aimed her sparker at the nearest electrical panel. "Be ready to close that door."

The panel sparked and smoked. She didn't stop firing until it exploded in a cacophony of lightning flashes and bangs. Josune ran for *Another Road* as the flashes and bangs continued in a chain reaction throughout the Justice Department ship.

Snow shut the outer airlock as soon as she slid past.

Josune channeled her best Brand. "Oops. I think the ship will need a few repairs before it is serviceable again."

"So sad," Snow agreed, without a trace of regret. "A pity it wasn't the *Boost*."

"There are four hundred people on the *Boost*. I'm glad it wasn't. Besides, Norris would be more used to action than this lot. These people rely on their name to intimidate. They don't expect people to fight back."

Carlos hit close on the breach door of *Another Road* as soon as they were through. "Good to see you still have that thing, but please don't use it on our ship."

"Not likely." Josune laughed. "Roystan?"

"Are you all on board?"

"Yes, but—"

"I saw. Well done. I'm tempted to blow them to bits. Instead I'll set an emergency beacon for them. A signal will get out eventually. It will bring every space scavenger in range to their door, but that's their problem. Come on up so I can see you are all safe. Then we can get out of here." He sounded breathless.

In the background, Josune heard Nika yell, "Jacques, where's that damn garfungi?" She ran. *Another Road* unlinked and broke away. She reached the crew room just as they nullspaced.

Roystan smiled over at her. "Nice job."

Jacques trotted out of the kitchen, a steaming bowl in his hands.

"Thanks." Roystan's hands shook as he took it. He dropped the bowl. Josune caught him as he slumped unconscious.

4

ALISTAIR LAUGHTON

The parcel from Zell—half a galaxy away—had taken one month and five ships to arrive.

Alistair looked down at the note Melda had scrawled. Handmade paper, handmade ink.

Prison life isn't so bad. We get to trade with the warders.

It wasn't a prison, not officially, but Alistair knew as well as Melda did that if the colonists tried to leave, or to send out an unsupervised message via the link, they'd be stopped. Maybe even meet with a little accident.

Fresh food. Medical attention. Mayeso cut her hand the other day. She was in a genemod machine, and out again in another hour.

Before the Santiagans had arrived with their machine and their doctor, a cut like that would have taken weeks to heal.

Don't stress on our behalf. While you're busy hunting modders, we're living the good life.

How long would that continue if Alistair didn't deliver?

He handed the note to Cam, who was kneeling in front of the low table on which the contents of the parcel were strewn.

Cam shook his head. "I read it already."

The setting sun struck the gifts, bathing them in a red-gold light, bathing Cam's face, so that for one unsettling moment Alistair thought he was sitting across from a bronzed statue. He glanced away, out the window that made up the two corner walls. Anything truly bronze nowadays had blue tones for him.

Unless it had been warmed by the sun.

His changed eyesight hadn't been this disconcerting on Zell, where he'd had nothing to compare it with, but he'd lived his entire adult life in Dartigan Capitol. Coming back to the same scene, but seeing it so differently, was hard to take. Alistair closed his eyes and forced his thoughts away from the strangeness and onto his immediate problem.

One month, and still no sign of Nika Rik Terri. "How can someone just disappear?"

"She's a modder, Alistair. But we'll find her. We'll keep looking until we do."

They would find her, but would it be too late to save the colony?

He moved over to the window. Below, in the city of Dartigan Capitol, it was raining. Here above the clouds the sky was clear. That same sun colored the heavy rain clouds below a darker gold, creating outside the window a fluffy carpet that seemed to extend forever.

"Santiago knows we're looking. They'll wait." Cam held up a pair of felted boots. "I swear, Yakusha's designs get worse every time."

"I like them," Alistair said. To him, they were green and deep crimson, with a smattering of yellow. Then, because it was Cam and he could ask: "What color do you see them as?"

"Bright green and pink." Cam tossed them over with a shudder.

"They are loud." He picked up a carved wristband. "Who do you think they meant this for?"

Some things, like the boots, were obvious. Cam had never worn felted boots in his life—and Yakusha would have had to make them four sizes smaller—while Alistair would never consider the painting of the lake his. He didn't collect paintings.

"Do I look like I'd wear a bracelet?"

"You wear those boots."

Alistair pulled his new boots on. "They're comfortable."

The entry link buzzed.

Alistair brought up the image of his guest. His former boss, Paola Teke. It was the first time anyone from his former life—before Zell—had come visiting. What did she want with him?

He opened the link. "Paola. This is a surprise."

Paola was immaculate in a modern-cut purple silk suit. Purple to him, anyway. She must have come straight from work. She pushed against the lobby door. Paola didn't like heights. Being out on the roof of a building 214 floors high was bound to worry her.

"Let me in." Paola pushed at the door again. "The wind up here is about to blow me away."

The lift lobby was on the roof. The car had let her off in a section screened from the wind, but it could be disconcerting for the first-timer. Especially if your aircar didn't have good stabilizers.

"And I swear I can feel the building sway."

That was because she knew the building was built to allow a sway of three meters, not because she could feel it. There were stabilizers built into each floor—and on the roof where Paola currently stood—that prevented you feeling the sway. Paola didn't care. She'd gone through the specs and warned Alistair against buying the unit.

That had been three years ago, when it was still just an image on an architect's computer.

Alistair wished she'd spent less time worrying about the physical structure and more about the solvency of the company he'd bought his unit from. The company had gone broke two days after Alistair had moved in. Which was why his ex-wife had left it to him in the divorce settlement.

Three years later the lawyers were still arguing over who was responsible for the bankruptcy, which was why, when Alistair had returned from Zell after a two-year absence, he discovered he remained the sole resident.

Not that he minded the quiet. There were advantages to living in an empty building.

"Just look at the services," Paola had said at the time. "There's a hundred pool cars for two hundred and fourteen floors, with four units on each. When you need an aircar, you'll have to wait hours. Or call an aircab."

Right now Alistair enjoyed being the only client in the building. When he called a car, it came immediately. Not to mention, with the divorce, his time on Zell, and now the hunt for Rik Terri, he didn't have enough money to move anyway.

He buzzed to let Paola in.

"Thank God. I don't know why you live here, Alistair."

"My old boss," he told Cam.

"From the Justice Department?"

"Yes."

Paola stopped in the passage and stared at the long wall hangings that ran along it.

Alistair sighed. "I'd best go and rescue her." He stood up and padded down to the front door.

"You like my wall hangings?"

He could see Paola struggle with a lie. "They're—"

Alistair hid his smile but decided not to leave her floundering for a compliment she didn't mean. "Some people find them loud."

Mostly pinks and browns, if you believed Cam. A discordant cacophony of color that hurt one's eyes.

She nodded, vehemently.

"I find them restful." In his eyes, at least, they were a riot of verdant greens, blues, and crimsons that offset the sterile cream of the walls. "Come on down."

Paola started after him. Stopped. He turned. She was staring at him.

"What?"

"Those boots. My God, Alistair, you've really let yourself go. You used to be such a—" She shook her head.

"Handsome man," Cam suggested from the door of the study.

"He was never—" Paola bit that off too.

"Whatever you say next you're going to put your foot in it," Cam said.

Paola stared at Cam. That, Alistair had found, was most people's initial reaction to Cam. And their second. And their third.

"Who are you?"

Cam smiled and held out a hand. "Cam Le-Nguyen."

Paola smiled back.

That was the usual reaction you got with Cam too. When Cam smiled, people smiled back.

"I'm a friend of Alistair's."

"Delighted to meet you, Cam." She glanced sideways down at Alistair's boots. "Maybe you could give him tips on how to dress. Take him to your tailor."

"I couldn't afford his tailor," Alistair said. "Do you know how much his clothes cost?"

He was sure Cam had money. Why he'd even been on Zell was a mystery.

"Probably better than you do, Alistair."

Cam looked at Paola with interest. "You're a friend of Alistair's."

Alistair's pre-Zell past was over with. "I used to work for her," he said. "What do you want, Paola?"

"I just want to chat."

Paola never made idle chat.

Cam, who knew what was in Alistair's liquor cabinet better than Alistair did, held up a bottle inquiringly.

"Yes, please," Paola said. "I've had a harrowing day." She sank into one of the lounge chairs. "The Honesty League." She shuddered. "They weren't key players when you left, were they, Alistair?"

When he'd left. That was a polite way of putting it, even for Paola. "No." But they'd received vids, even on Zell. "The Chester case?"

Jack Chester was a miner who'd made a living buying up the rights to abandoned asteroids. Except, one asteroid supposedly mined out wasn't, and he hit a lode of gold and platinum—along with a small amount of transurides. The company who'd staked the original claim had muscled in and taken over, murdering Jack Chester in the process.

Except Jack suspected he might be murdered and had set up cameras, and he'd transmitted the whole thing to his brother, who just happened to own the largest non-company media network in the galaxy.

Despite the fact that the murderers were caught on tape, that their faces were displayed around the galaxy, and that one of the them was easily identifiable as a midlevel executive from Santiago, the executive had never been arrested.

"The public's been on our back ever since, and they're watching us closely. Justice Department's had to clean up its act."

"About time," Alistair said. "Although, it's only been, what, two months? It might die down soon."

"No sign of that happening. You wouldn't believe the extra work it's given us. The Honesty League's onto anything and everything." Paola stared broodingly into the glass Cam brought over to her.

"Like this latest case." She drank a mouthful, sighed with pleasure. "It's even aged."

That's because it had been sitting in Alistair's liquor cabinet for the two years he'd been on Zell.

"This latest case?" Alistair prompted. Paola didn't visit for no reason.

"Landed in my lap today, and the Honesty League knew about it before I did, can you believe. They were onto me before I even got into my office. Is it true? A Justice Department ship? Taking bribes?"

"That's hardly unusual."

"Were they taking bribes?" Cam asked.

"I wish. No, they ran a profitable sideline using their powers as Justice Department authority to board other ships and hold them there until whoever'd paid them to do the holding came to collect. Cattle ships mostly. Inside the legal zone too." She took another appreciative mouthful. "They got unlucky. Someone fought back and left them all unconscious on their own ship. We had to decode the backup memory to see what had happened."

Criminals cleaned their primary ship memory, but most of them forgot about backup memory. Alistair had pioneered using evidence from backup memory in Justice Department cases.

"We had to arrest them all," Paola said. "We'll take them to court and charge them. Keep this blasted Honesty League happy for now. But that's not what I came here to talk about."

Paola opened a link on Alistair's big wall-screen. She hesitated, looked at Cam. "This is confidential."

"I don't work for the Justice Department any longer," Alistair said. "And we're in my apartment."

"It's okay," Cam said. "I'll get dinner." He went down to the kitchen.

Paola watched him go, waited for the sound of the door, which didn't come. "Where did he go?"

"Kitchen."

"You mean he's preparing it himself?"

He wasn't. He'd brought it with him from a high-class restaurant near Cam's apartment. The food was in the warmer, waiting till they'd finished with the parcel from Zell.

"My God, Alistair. What sort of place is Zell?"

"It wasn't as if you could go out and order food in, Paola. There were fifty of us colonists."

"I know, but—" Paola rested her head in her hands. "You should have stayed, Alistair. You weren't sacked; you were asked to take leave."

It was close enough to being sacked. Besides, he hadn't wanted to work for the Justice Department after the farce of Lisbet's trial.

He heard, rather than saw, when Cam came out of the kitchen and padded back up the passage. He paused where Alistair could see him, but not Paola.

Cam had his back.

"Show me what you were going to show me, Paola."

Paola brought up the image again. "Executive Shanna Brown, from Brown Combine. She's dead. Been dead for six months. She was murdered at a party." The image changed. Security camera footage from inside a house. Judging by the way the view changed from camera to camera, the security was strong. The image stopped on another woman, who paused in the doorway.

Alistair's trained brain automatically took in the statistics. Medium height, black eyes—no one had black eyes for real, she had to be modded—pearlescent skin that appeared to glow slightly. Where had he seen a look like that before? Her hair was spiked, black underneath with white tips.

It was a striking look. She was beautiful, in a unique and compelling way.

"The man with her is Samson Sa, Brown's body modder. He was invited to the party. This woman wasn't."

"Who is she?"

"I'll get to that. Watch."

Alistair watched as the woman circled the partygoers. Always with her gaze on Brown. Given that Shanna Brown was dead, and that Paola was here showing him this video, he guessed what would happen.

"Why did she want Brown dead?"

"Your guess is as good as mine." Paola waved him silent. "Here it comes."

The woman moved in, and Shanna Brown smiled. She'd been watching for her, waiting to speak to her. Alistair saw Samson Sa scowling in the background.

The sound, which had been muted for the rest of the video, became louder, the two women's voices picked out of the background noise by a clever engineer.

"I've been admiring your mod all night," Brown said. "Did Samson do it for you?"

The woman leered.

Alistair stepped back, startled. Such a leer should—would—never have come from a face like that. Moreover, he recognized it.

"Tamati Woden. That's impossible." Ice crept up his back, his fingers, his toes. "He's too tall to be modded like that."

On-screen, the two women moved close; then Shanna Brown gasped, clutched her stomach. The other woman pushed closer, turned her arm.

"Hasn't got the strength he was expecting to have," Alistair said. Tamati Woden committed his murders with one thrust, not a thrust, a turn, and another thrust. He—or she—had thought it would take one thrust. Not familiar with that body, then.

Another leer, and the stranger turned away.

Shanna Brown stood for a moment longer, face bloodless with shock, clutching at her stomach, then crumpled to a heap on the floor.

The beautiful stranger made her way casually out of the room as screams started. She stopped at the front door for a final leer at the camera.

Paola turned the video off. "The knife wound alone wouldn't have killed her."

"Poison?" Alistair knew how Woden worked. He'd spent three years chasing the man.

"Fast acting. Her heart had stopped before the blood had finished pumping out of the wound. She was dead before the paramedics arrived."

Alistair shivered. "No wonder we have never been able to catch him. If he can mod like that." The Tamati Woden that Alistair had been chasing was at least ten to fifteen centimeters taller. "I thought you couldn't mod height." Not without major trauma, anyway.

"She left the knife," Paola said. "With fingerprints all over it."

"Deliberately careless? A copycat? Or maybe she's just sloppy and doesn't know how to hide her tracks."

"Tell me you'd take out a contract on someone and then leave your fingerprints all over it. Or look at the camera like that. It was a deliberate taunt."

"So maybe it wasn't a contract. Maybe they were friends once. Or enemies."

"With Tamati's trademark leer? I've asked the experts. It matches perfectly."

"Only if you had a scar. You can't leer like he does without that scar." Tamati Woden would never have given up his trademark scar.

"If you had once had a scar and had it removed, and you tried to leer like he does, that's exactly what you'd get. It's in your case files, Alistair. You ran that scenario with every expert you could."

"Is it my advice you want, Paola? Or do you want my opinion on whether or not it really is Tamati Woden?"

"I know it was Woden, Alistair. I also know it wasn't his body. He was just controlling it."

"That's not possible."

"But what if it was, Alistair?"

"I think you'll find it's more likely he found a modder who could change his height, as well as his looks." That was worrying enough in itself. A good modder could already change the voice and an iris pattern enough that biometric recognition didn't work. Hell, bad modders could do it by accident.

Which was why the Justice Department used height as one of their primary search tools. Until now, you could disguise it—you could stoop or wear heels—but you couldn't change it. If Woden could change his height, he could become anyone. Then they'd never catch him, because Woden didn't leave evidence behind. Not normally, anyway, and especially not DNA. So why had he allowed the cameras to record the murder this time? What was different?

Not his problem anymore, Alistair reminded himself. He had more pressing ones of his own, like finding a body modder who had seemingly disappeared without a trace. He'd find that trace.

He just hoped he didn't find her too late to save the colonists on Zell.

"Woden became more brazen after you left," Paola said. "I think you kept him reined in."

Woden had been getting that way anyway. Nothing annoyed an assassin more than not being recognized for his work. It was why he kept his trademark leer.

"Why are you looking for Nika Rik Terri, Alistair?" The subject change was so abrupt Alistair knew Paola had planned it.

"That's my business."

Cam stirred from his post, came into the room. "Because she's my modder, and she's disappeared."

Both statements were true. She was Cam's modder. She had disappeared. They were everything and nothing to do with the reason Alistair was looking for her.

Paola looked from Alistair to Cam, back to Alistair. "Are you two—?"

"No." Alistair wasn't in Cam's class, wasn't sure he wanted to be. "You've heard of these things called friends, Paola. Some people have them."

Their reasons for hunting Rik Terri were their own. It wasn't the Justice Department's business, and time was short. Alistair frowned at the now-blank screen, steered the conversation back to safer questions. "Are you asking my opinion on if this murder is a copycat, or my opinion as to how likely your scenario of Woden taking over someone else's mind is? Because I can tell you, it's unlikely."

"I want you to come back to the Justice Department and solve the case for me."

He laughed. He couldn't help it. "I was kicked out, Paola."

"You were placed on suspended leave."

"I was escorted out of the building."

"Your wife was up on a fraud charge."

His ex-wife, even if they had still been going through the divorce. He still ground his teeth sometimes over how demanding she'd been about getting her half of their assets—including his savings, for she'd claimed she had none of her own—when she was sitting on a fortune of ill-gotten assets in anonymous bank accounts.

"Why did you walk out, Alistair? We all knew you wouldn't be part of it. If you'd waited another month, you'd have been back in your old job. Hell, you could even have gotten Lisbet off. You're a good talker, and she was a minor cog."

She'd still been a cog, and Alistair should have known. He'd worked in the Justice Department for twenty years, been married to Lisbet for ten. He knew the signs of someone on the make, and Lisbet had exhibited every classic symptom.

"I'm not coming back to the Justice Department. I have a new life. Other responsibilities." He wasn't the dedicated agent he'd been two years earlier. He had people to protect. Different priorities. His old life was a long way past.

"Yes, you are," Paola said. "I'll expect you in at work tomorrow."

"Not happening."

Paola stood up. "In the office tomorrow, Alistair."

He didn't bother to say no again.

She paused at the door. "I told you the woman left prints on the knife."

"You did." Alistair waited. Paola's pauses always preceded a dramatic announcement.

"When you're looking for someone, Alistair, you should at least know what they look like."

She couldn't possibly mean what she was implying.

"The woman was Nika Rik Terri."

When Alistair and Cam had started their search for Nika Rik Terri, they'd thought it would be easy. But Rik Terri had disappeared, leaving a bombed-out studio and seven dead bodies behind.

"It doesn't have to be her," Alistair had told Cam. "Any modder who works with transurides will do."

"I don't know." Cam sounded doubtful. "It's not common. Plus, it's expensive. I paid a fortune for mine, and she told me it was because of the transurides."

Modders always charged big money.

They discovered Cam was right. Most modders couldn't work with transurides.

"Wouldn't waste my time," one of the lecturers at Landers, the best-known training college for modders, told them. "Fraught with danger. I mean, sure, we use trace transurides when we can, when we have to; it helps to stabilize a mod. But adding it for cosmetic purposes?" He shook his head. "I can't imagine it would add any value."

"Not to mention hugely expensive. The only modders who could afford to experiment with it would be the top-tier modders. Nika Rik Terri, Samson Sa, Jolie Sand, Esau Ye. And only on their wealthy clients."

"How easy would it be to do, if it could be done?" Alistair asked.

The lecturer glanced pointedly at the time. "I have another lecture to present. Can't afford to miss these classes, you know. We are training the new generation of skilled modders." He paused, as if struck by a sudden idea. Alistair knew a fake pause when he saw one. "Why don't I give you the name of one of our retired lecturers. He might be able to help you more. He loves to talk."

Igor Chatsworth could certainly talk.

"Let me have a look at you," he said to Cam, and dragged him over to a window to study him. "Modded, not natural?"

Cam nodded.

"Beautiful, beautiful. Done by a master." He turned Cam around, studied him from every angle. "Amazing."

"Let me know if you need rescuing," Alistair said to Cam.

"It's rather weird."

Chatsworth didn't hear. "Who did your mod?"

"Nika Rik Terri," Alistair said. "Mr. Chatsworth, we'd like to talk to you about transurides and modding."

"Of course she did. She was such a brilliant student. One of my own, you know. She was my special protégée."

If Rik Terri was on the run, as seemed likely, would she go to her old mentor? Maybe this trip would be more fruitful than he thought it would.

"She's turning out such beautiful work nowadays. Such a pity about that accident in her studio, and her body still not found."

"Mr. Chatsworth—"

"Please call me Chatty. It's what the students used to call me behind my back." He sighed wistfully. "I miss teaching, you know."

"I can imagine." Alistair steered Chatsworth to a seat. Since he'd mentioned Rik Terri, maybe they should start with that. "We're actually looking for Rik Terri. We don't believe she was in the explosion. We're trying to find her."

"Such a terrible business. Such a terrible, terrible waste of talent. Some modders are followers, you know. They won't experiment. Others experiment but they don't know what they are doing. They're the ones who kill people by accident. Nika, she was one of those rare people who understood the body. The kind of person who could change modding." He sighed, looked defeated, and said again, "Such a terrible, terrible waste."

Rik Terri had gone to a lot of trouble to make people think she was dead. Why?

"We heard that before the accident she was working with transurides."

"Transurides are difficult. But Nika—maybe. She apprenticed to Hannah Tan after she graduated. Hannah learned from Gino Giwari. And Giwari—well, no one uses his techniques anymore. Too dangerous. He started mucking into DNA—a disaster. He was discredited. I tried to talk her out of it. The apprenticeship, I mean. I had ten modders lined up for her, but she insisted on choosing her own. And she chose Hannah Tan."

It took two hours to extract themselves.

"All we learned from that," Alistair said, "other than that your mod is remarkable"—which they already knew—"is that everyone works with transurides, but no one does either." Which didn't make sense. "Can we just send in a normal modder or not?"

"I don't think another modder could do it," Cam said. "I think we have to find her."

Unfortunately, Alistair found he agreed with him.

Except they'd been looking a month now and they hadn't found anything.

Maybe, with the resources of the Justice Department behind them, they would.

Alistair called Paola long after Cam had gone home. Long after he should have gone to bed. It was two in the morning, but she answered immediately. "You'll take the job."

"If you'll do something for me."

She'd say no, and then he'd have to beg for the job anyway, but finding Nika Rik Terri was only part of saving the colonists on Zell. They also had to get the colonists safely off-world afterward.

"You're not exactly in a position to bargain, Alistair."

"You're the one who wants me to take the job. Come on, Paola."

Maybe she heard the edge of begging in his voice. Maybe she really was worried about Tamati Woden. Maybe she was tired and just wanted to be rid of him.

"Spit it out."

"If I take this job, then you organize a ship and have it ready to pick up a hundred people from an isolated world when I ask for it."

The Justice Department had a ship that could do it. Two ships, in fact.

There'd been silence at the other end of the link.

"I'll do—" He bit off a promise he couldn't keep.

If he could arrange transport, and if he could somehow get rid of the warship orbiting Zell, maybe he could buy the people on Zell extra time.

"A hundred people," Paola said at last. "How many people contracted to that isolated place you went to, Alistair?"

"Fifty-one."

Her silence spoke volumes; he just wasn't talking the language.

"I'll see you in the morning. My office, 8:00 A.M."

5

NIKA RIK TERRI

Nika checked the settings on the Netanyu. "Eight minutes," she told Jacques before he could ask. "You know that because nine minutes ago I told you it was seventeen."

"That wasn't me, that was Carlos."

"On this ship, when one person hears, everyone does."

The only one who hadn't bothered her was Josune, who was sitting in the crew room drinking her third cup of coffee, watching the screens for signs of pursuit, listening to the public links for reports of a chase.

That's what Roystan would have been doing if he'd been conscious.

Roystan's body was producing too much of the protease enzymes that triggered natural cell death in the body, especially for someone who'd spent the last hour in a genemod machine. Nika circled the machine. "Switch inlet five over to the iron solution again," she told Snow. The Netanyu was a solid machine, but it only had six inlets. How had the early modders ever managed to get results? Adding trace elements must have been a nightmare. If anyone added them.

"Will he be all right?"

"What do you think, Jacques?"

She'd paused too long.

"Jacques," Josune said. "None of us have eaten in hours." She'd thrown the congealing remains of the earlier dinner into the recycler. No one had wanted to eat that. "And Roystan is coming out of the tank in eight minutes."

"Please," Nika said, "don't call it a tank, Josune."

"Eight minutes." Jacques looked around the genemod studio, as if realizing where he was. Or wasn't.

Seven minutes now, but Nika didn't tell him that. "And Jacques. Don't give him coffee."

Nika circled the Netanyu again. When Jacques was worried, he made for the kitchen. This time he hadn't. She forced herself to breathe naturally.

Snow snapped the new module in. Switched inlet four over to mutrient half a minute later, without Nika needing to tell him to do it.

"You're learning."

"We've got one client," Snow said. "I won't know what to do for normal people soon."

Even Snow was behaving strangely today. But then, that was to be expected.

"You escaped from the *Boost*," Nika said.

Carlos entered with a clatter. Nika held up five fingers.

He nodded and stood away. "You can fix him, Nika. You have before."

They'd better get this Songyan soon so she could at least feed multiple trace elements into Roystan's body at the same time. Another problem with the Netanyu was that it didn't allow complex add-ons. Otherwise she'd have built one that combined the trace elements for her.

In the kitchen Jacques started throwing pots around with unnecessary vigor. "We should have made her stop when she fixed him the first time." Ostensibly talking to Josune, but talking to the modders as well. "We shouldn't have let her play. We shouldn't have tried to get his memory back."

Josune said, "Roystan's a grown man."

Eighty years older than any of them.

This problem hadn't come about as a result of Nika trying to restore Roystan's memory. It was a direct result of what Giwari had done all those years ago interacting with the mods Nika had done back when Roystan had almost died while they'd been imprisoned on Benedict's ship, interacting with the changes Nika had made earlier to fix those, and all of that interacting with the sudden spike of adrenaline Roystan's body had produced.

"Let me tell you," Nika said to Snow as they switched the feeds, all four of them this time. Two each, in quick succession. "Giwari could never have modded Roystan the way he did without the Songyan."

Snow nodded, intent on what he was doing.

Timing was important here.

"He's doing it for you, Josune. You tell him to stop. Tell him—"

Nika hardly noticed Josune interrupt Jacques. "Carlos. I need you here. A ship just appeared."

Carlos left at a run.

"I don't think even a Songyan could cope with this," Snow said as they switched the feeds again.

"But you can build add-ons for the Songyan. Feed more through a single inlet."

"You can build add-ons for a Dietel too."

Another quick switch. Roystan's body was now killing off cells too fast. She'd almost preferred it the way it had been. He'd been fine when he'd come out of the Netanyu two hours earlier.

"Ore carrier," Carlos said. "A million kilometers away."

One of the big, armored company ships, bringing in a load of ore from outside the legal zone, with enough firepower to blast them out of space.

"Let's hope he's checking us out as carefully as we are checking him," Josune said. "The ship should move in an hour, when it's stabilized."

Meantime, it would be watching them. Nika had learned a lot about ship jumps in her time as a member of Roystan's crew. The bigger the ship, the harder it was to calibrate, so the jumps were generally smaller, leaving less margin for error. Even automatic calibrators could give problems. When a ship came out of a jump, it was never a hundred percent stable; it always moved a little from opposing forces. A larger ship took longer to stabilize than a smaller one.

"Do you need Snow on the cannon, Josune?"

"Not yet."

Good, because that was a bad idea.

The Netanyu chimed. Nika looked at the container she held in her hand, at the one Snow had in his. She didn't like it when the machine and she didn't agree on the definition of *done*.

She'd be glad when they collected the Songyan.

She put the new feed down and helped Roystan out of the machine. "They're watching some ore freighter."

"Thanks." Roystan made for the door, raising his voice as he went. "What's the status, Josune?"

"Ore freighter, a million kilometers. Identifies as a Santiago ship. So far it looks legitimate. How do you feel?"

"I'm fine."

He had no idea how he was, and Nika didn't either. She hoped it was legitimate. She wanted to watch Roystan for a few days, to see the effects of today's two mods without them having to run from something.

She cleaned out the Netanyu while Snow put the inlet containers into the sterilizer. "So the *Boost*? Why does he want you so badly?"

She thought Snow wasn't going to answer. Eventually, he did.

"I told you about Gramps?"

The modder who'd taken him in. "Yes."

"He signed onto the *Boost*. To save me."

Snow had told her that before. How Gramps had taken the contract because they were both starving. But that was all he ever said about it. Nika still wasn't sure how that had come about. Few experienced modders were paupers, and if Gramps had taught Snow the trade, he was no newcomer.

"The *Boost*—" Snow ran his hands through his hair. "How much do you know about mercenaries?"

"Cattle ships?" A lot more than she had six months ago. She'd heard a lot of horror stories.

"Nika." Snow pulled at his hair. "This is not . . . a mercenary is not a cattle ship. A merc is a fighting ship. It's full of armed people who go to war."

She knew there were wars. When two or more companies claimed the same world, or when one company tried to take over a world belonging to another company, they hired ships full of mercenaries to fight that war for them. It was the cattle ships she hadn't heard about until she'd met Roystan's crew. She'd thought they were different names for the same thing. Snow hated them equally.

"Cattle ships go around in space finding people who are vulnerable." Snow looked a lot older suddenly. "In space, if you don't have money to buy air, or fuel for your ship, or food, you don't survive. They pick on small ships—like *Another Road*—and attack them, take them over."

"But we can afford food and air."

"It doesn't matter, if you're caught by a cattle ship. They work outside the legal zone, so there's no law but salvage law. They take your ship and sell it for salvage. And you either pay them to go free or they sell you to a merc ship."

"Sell you?"

"Technically, it's not selling. You sign a contract to work for the merc ship. The cattle ship takes a down payment up front, then a percentage of your wage until you've paid your way out of the contract." Snow looked at his hands. "I've never heard of anyone paying off their contracts. The money's poor. The interest increases."

"Interest?" They'd just been sold.

"They charge for food and board. Add that to the end of the contract, and start charging interest from day one."

She'd bet the interest compounded too. "So don't sign the contract. Don't join the mercs."

"You're on a cattle ship," Snow said. "There's only two ways off. Sunward, or by signing a contract."

Nika suspected sunward wasn't anything good. "So the cattle ships supply soldiers for the companies. By kidnapping people and selling them to ships that do the fighting." She had been so sheltered on Lesser Sirius.

"They don't always go to the merc ships. Sometimes they are sent to work on asteroids. They do the dangerous jobs humans have to do or that no one else will work on."

It got worse. "So Gramps signed on to a merc ship, and you went with him. You didn't sign on, did you?"

"I ate food. Used water and air. I have a debt. Captain Norris can't afford to let anyone get away. Otherwise other people will try to escape too."

"I see." If Nika ever came across Captain Norris and the *Boost* again, she might make a little reckoning of her own.

Big thoughts, for according to Snow, the *Boost* had four hundred armed soldiers on it.

"I hope Gramps is all right," Snow said. "It was dangerous what he did. Helping me get away. But Gramps said Captain Norris was too stingy to take on a doctor when he had him for cheap. Said he wouldn't do anything. Once I'd made enough money, I planned to go back and buy out Gramps's contract."

Gramps might have been right. Or he might have been saying that so Snow would go. Nika silently packed away the last cleaning rag. "Come on, let's go up and see what's happening."

The ore ship nullspaced out half an hour later.

"One less thing we have to worry about," Roystan said. "I presume we do have to worry about the *Boost* in the future, Snow."

Snow nodded.

They also had Wickmore to worry about, and Nika hadn't told them that yet.

"So where do we go next?" Roystan reached out as if to grab something, closed his hands on air. "I admit I'm not used to not having something to do."

They couldn't randomly wander through space either, hoping to find Goberling's lode. Plus, Nika had an apprentice; she had a responsibility to train him. He needed clients to work with. Unless Snow wanted to work on longevity, in which case he was in exactly the right place. But first they had to collect the Songyan she'd ordered.

Roystan said, "Josune, where did Feyodor think Goberling was most likely to be? Maybe if we go there, I might remember something."

Josune wrinkled her nose. "For the last two years Feyodor was convinced you'd spent time near the Vortex."

Roystan shuddered. "Never. I'm sure I'd remember if I'd been there."

"What's the Vortex?" Nika asked.

Everyone turned to look at her.

Snow pulled at his hair. "She doesn't know anything outside of modding." It was almost apologetic.

Nika didn't laugh, although she wanted to.

"The Vortex is a massive electromagnetic area in space." Roystan tapped the tabletop as he thought. "It's twenty light-years across, closer than most of us ever want to go toward the galactic center. You have to travel slowly, and carefully, because a careless—or plain unlucky—ship can get caught by the force of the field. There's only one way to get to the Vortex. That's an area called the Funnel, which is like a hole through one edge of the Vortex. Don't ask me how it works."

Even Carlos was rubbing his arms, as if he was cold, and nodding vigorously.

Roystan shuddered. "The Funnel's almost worse than the Vortex itself. A kilometer wide, like a pipeline through the middle, and you have to go right down the middle. Any deviation gets you caught up against the sides, and the forces pull the ship apart. Then, once you're out of the Funnel, there's less than a million kilometers between you and the Vortex itself. No. Goberling would never have been stupid enough to go there. Never."

Nika looked from his face, to Josune's, to Carlos's. If it were that dangerous, "Why would anyone go there?"

"Transurides."

Of course.

"It was a popular theory when I was young," Roystan said. "Scientists believe transurides take massive energy to create, to push the atoms out past an unstable configuration into a stable one, and the Vortex certainly has that energy. And there's a planetary system, just where you come out of the Funnel, with a barely human-habitable world, but every twenty years or so someone tries to set up mining there, because it has a higher-than-average level of transurides in the water."

"No one has made money from it yet," Josune said. "We stopped at Zell on our first trip in. It's a bleak place, abandoned. And past the Zell system—" She shuddered. "It's terrifying, so most people turn right around and go back up the Funnel."

"Those that don't get sucked in by the Vortex," Roystan said.

Josune shivered. "The funny thing is, not far past that dangerous part, you can nullspace out. It's just nobody ever goes far enough to find out. Except Feyodor."

Feyodor had been obsessed.

"Out past the Zell system there are patches of wider, safer space with star systems. We found one with an Earth-type planet. We called it Sassia." She looked at Roystan. "Back when I had to prove to you who I was, I showed you specs of a bracelet made of a mineral that came from there."

"I remember that bracelet." Roystan's mouth curved in a smile. "The one Pol took."

"Let's not go there," Carlos said.

Nika wasn't sure if he meant don't talk about Pol or not go to Zell. "Before we go anywhere, we collect the Songyan."

"Yes, the Songyan." Josune looked at Roystan. "Which you already ordered."

"I didn't order it."

"Nika did, which means she thinks there's something wrong."

Roystan looked around as if looking for an escape, thought better of it, and sat back.

"And there is, or she wouldn't have ordered a Songyan, as well as put you into a genemod machine as soon as we left that last space station."

"There was something wrong with him after he came out of the box," Carlos said.

"Machine, please. It's not a tank. It's not a box. It's a machine." Training them to use correct terminology was a slow job.

"Can't trust these modders. Not even the great Nika Rik Terri."

"There was something wrong with him before that." Josune fixed her gaze on Roystan. "She told you to stay calm."

If Roystan had hoped to keep quiet about his problem, this wasn't the way to do it. But it was better out in the open so everyone knew. "Initially his cells weren't dying off fast enough." Nika had learned to tailor her explanations to this crew. "Which led to cells multiplying when they shouldn't." The rampant, unchecked cell growth would eventually have killed him. "So I sped up the die-off." The transurides in Roystan's body meant you couldn't just put him into a machine and have it repair him. You needed a machine—like a Songyan—that would allow you to tweak the mod as it went. "Over the next two days his body would have settled. Unfortunately, excess adrenaline sped up the die-off and now we have the opposite effect, and while it's great that Roystan's body is full of dellarine, it is binding with the proteins that speed the process up, making it difficult to stop."

In the body, dellarine was the most powerful of the transuride elements. Nika didn't know of any modder besides herself who used that element exclusively. Other modders used a cocktail of any of the transurides they could get, and as few as they absolutely had to use.

Most modders couldn't afford to use them at all.

"So you botched it," Carlos said. "And you can't fix it."

"She's doing better than you," Snow said. "You didn't even notice anything was wrong."

"She did fine, Carlos," Roystan said. "I'd been feeling unwell for days. She tested me, said she could do something, and warned me I wasn't to excite myself for two days. None of us planned on being attacked by the Justice Department."

"She shouldn't have done something so dangerous, then."

Roystan held up his hands. "No more, Carlos. Let's not argue about this. You either," to Snow, who'd opened his mouth to say something. "Let's talk about more-pressing problems, like what we do after we get the Songyan. Where do we go?"

"Where is the Songyan?" Josune asked.

"Kitimat."

Josune thought for a moment. "Sagittarius arm. Old and established."

"Justice Department headquarters," Carlos said, voice laden with doom.

That hadn't been a problem when Nika had ordered the Songyan. "I can ask for it to be sent somewhere else."

"No," Roystan said. "Kitimat is the last place the Justice Department will think to look for us. It's the perfect place to go." He rubbed his hands together. "Let's set a course for Kitimat."

6

ALISTAIR LAUGHTON

The Justice Department hadn't changed. Same offices, same soaring interior, designed to impress the tourists. Same full-body scan.

The door remained closed.

Paola had better have cleared this.

Alistair went over to the desk, where a young man and a young woman—who might almost have been twins, with their short purple hair and green suits—looked up with the same inquiring expressions. Purple and green to him, at least.

"Can we help you?"

He gestured vaguely toward the door. "I'm supposed to have clearance." He didn't bother explaining who he was. He didn't know them—hopefully they didn't know him.

Both looked at the screen in front of them.

"You only passed two of the three points of reference for ID," the woman said.

His eyes. Which were never going to pass a scan. Alistair wasn't even sure they were organic anymore.

"Terribly sorry, Agent Laughton. But you should have completed the Intention to Mod Form before you were modded. We'll require a certificate from your modder and proof of identity from three independent sources before we can let you through."

He hoped Paola was in her office today. "Then can you call

Agent . . . Wait." Three points of reference. There were four options. Iris, fingerprint, image, and voice. "Let me try again."

He went back to the entry, waited out the body scan, then said, "My name is Alistair Laughton. I am an agent of the Justice Department."

The door opened to let him through.

Cam waited for him inside the security doors.

"I'm not going to ask," for Cam didn't talk about his past, and the Justice Department didn't let anyone in who wasn't supposed to be there.

Cam followed, looking around with interest. "I came here when I was a kid," he said. "Back when—" He cut off what he was going to say. "We got the grand tour. Twenty of us."

Families of company executives or members of the board got the grand tour. Nobody else.

There were twenty-eight people on the Justice Department board. Twenty-seven company representatives, and the combined-worlds rep, who represented the combined, non-company worlds.

They made their way up to Paola's office. Cam didn't set off any alarms.

"What's he doing here?" Paola asked.

Cam smiled the smile that made everyone smile back. "I'm working with Alistair."

Paola did smile, but afterward she scowled. "You can't afford to bend the rules right now, Alistair. You need to be squeaky clean for the next few months. People will be watching, waiting for you to do something wrong. You already had a lot of enemies."

"Not my doing," Alistair said. "Cam, you sort out your security so that Paola is satisfied. Meantime, I want to see the file. Is there somewhere we can work?"

"Your old office."

His old office smelled musty and unused. There was no dust, of course, because the bots cleaned the office daily, but the biscuits he'd kept in the drawer were still there, along with his special brand of coffee. Both two years stale.

The room looked different to how he remembered it. Not only because of two years' diminished memory, but because of his changed eyesight.

The battens in the wall were crisscrossed, the design he'd come to recognize as being supplied by one of the subsidiaries of Santiago. The fabricated walls might hold up well on a building on Kitimat, but in the harsh world of Zell, they'd fallen apart quickly.

A lot of things had fallen apart on Zell.

The wall was full of cabling and pipes. Most of them seemingly active. The wires were warm, the pipes cool—except for one, which looked to run hot water. It was flimsy, for he could see the faint shape of someone in the next office.

He settled down to look at the files.

Cam came back half an hour later. He looked tireder than usual, and his ready smile was gone.

"Are you all right?"

"I'm fine. I just want out of here. I didn't go to Zell for two years just to come back and sit in an office and play politics."

"Don't play with Paola. She'll always win." Alistair sat back. "Why did you go to Zell, Cam?" He waved a hand. "No. You don't have to answer that."

You didn't go to a world like Zell because you wanted to see it. You went because you wanted to escape. It wasn't his business to pry into Cam's secrets. He sent Cam the list of names he had ready and stood up. "Let's go and talk to Samson Sa."

SaStudio was on Lesser Sirius. One of the few worlds to have an independent government rather than a company, which meant they used their own police force rather than call in the Justice Department. Consequently, Alistair didn't know much about the world. It was, he found out from Cam on the trip there, the place to go if you wanted a top-of-the-range mod. Half the elite modders in the galaxy lived there.

Nika Rik Terri's studio had been on Lesser Sirius, on the same street as SaStudio.

Sa's assistant told Alistair to make an appointment. The waiting list was three months.

"We're from the Justice Department." Alistair had called ahead, so the assistant was just being difficult. "We're not trying to make an appointment for a body mod."

The assistant's gaze flickered over Alistair's body. It was clear he thought Alistair should be here for that. Alistair gritted his teeth. He hadn't been to a modder since Zell and was unlikely to ever go to one again. They wouldn't understand about his eyes.

"I'm sorry, but you still need to make an appointment."

"We'll wait."

"He's with a client."

"That's fine," Cam said. "We'll wait till he's done."

Cam got his usual approving smile in return. Did he ever get tired of it?

"I love your mod," the assistant said. "Is it Samson's?"

"Nika Rik Terri."

The assistant's eyes widened, but he didn't comment further. Alistair noted that not long afterward he touched the jaw-link and murmured something. He hoped it was a message to the modder.

Five minutes later a man came out from behind the closed double doors on the left. Alistair recognized him from the recording of Shanna Brown's murder. Sa's classically handsome body was a perfect advertisement for SaStudio. His gaze centered on Cam.

"You're taking lead on all our body-modding queries from now on," Alistair said under his breath.

The man smiled, held out his hand. "Samson Sa." He looked Cam over.

Cam shook hands. "Cam Le-Nguyen. And this is Alistair Laughton. From the Justice Department."

Sa turned his gaze on Alistair, looked him over too. He smiled again, only this one was the professional smile of the salesman. Alistair blinked at the brightness of the teeth.

Sa turned back to Cam. "My apologies, for I do have a client at present, but I am happy to talk to you once the session is over. I will be another hour. My apprentice can make you comfortable while you wait."

He waved a hand in the apprentice's direction.

"Thank you," Cam said, and Sa disappeared back through the inner doors.

The assistant, now demoted to a lowly apprentice, offered them a choice of alcoholic beverages. "Just coffee, if you have it," Alistair said. Real coffee was nonexistent on Zell. It was still a luxury to be able to get it whenever he wanted. He was offered his choice of five blends, and seven ways of having it served, while another apprentice hurried over to offer a tray of delicacies for them to pick from.

Alistair could get used to this.

There were three apprentices, all differing ages, if Alistair had to guess, with the oldest more senior than the other two and ready to give orders. After they'd offered refreshments, they gathered around the desk, staring at Cam, whispering occasionally among themselves.

"If it gets too bad," Alistair told Cam, "you can always go for a walk."

"I'm fine." Cam leaned back and closed his eyes. "Maybe it is a little unnerving."

Alistair considered going over to scare the apprentices into looking away. Even as he considered following up on the thought, one of them smiled. Which reminded him. "Did Sa's teeth glow for you too?"

Cam opened his eyes. Blinked. Burst out laughing. "Really?"

It seemed to have broken up the awestruck audience, for when Alistair glanced across, two of the apprentices were talking over something on a screen while the third was polishing glassware. "Shining white. Like beacons in his mouth."

"It must be strange to be you, to see what you see. Do you ever regret it? I mean, if you lived your life over, would you wish it had never happened?"

Would he? Alistair remembered the terror of that first night.

The dark. The pain. The disbelief.

And overriding everything was the realization that he was blind. On a world with fifty people, no doctor, and no way off.

It had been all he could think about. Not even his final memory of . . . beings . . . as tall as he was, only half as wide. It had been instinctive to raise his blaster, because on Zell everything was out to kill humans. He'd realized, as he fired, that the other creature had its own weapon, raised it at the same time. He'd turned his aim, saw the other turn its aim as well, but the edge of the blue light had struck his face. It had happened so fast he hadn't even felt the pain until it was over.

That, and the secondary realization that he'd been hired as security, and now he couldn't do his job.

Alistair shuddered.

"I don't remember how I used to see," he told Cam now. "Zell. It's normal. All this"—he waved a hand around Sa's genemod studio—"this is alien, unusual." Not that he'd ever been in a studio like this before. Prior to Zell he'd used a modder close to the office who did a basic job of keeping his body in shape and healthy. Their shop front hadn't looked like a ten-star hotel.

He could normally block the memory of the time that had followed the blinding. Not today. It all came crashing back.

Three-fingered hands touching his face. Cooler than human hands. Trying to get away. Him, a former twenty-year veteran of the Justice Department, panicking like a rookie. They'd tied him down. He realized later that the restraining was a kindness, to prevent him damaging himself while he healed or running off into the wilderness before they were done.

He'd just started to think rationally about what he was doing when they'd placed the hypodermic against his arm. At least he assumed it was a hypodermic. Everyone else had described it as a circle of metal, slightly cold.

As cold as the fingers, Alistair would have said, but no one else had felt the fingers.

Two hours later he had a raging fever. He didn't know how long the fever had lasted. It had felt like forever.

He'd come around to silence. Or not silence, exactly. There was a murmur of sound at the back of his hearing. A whisper that might have been words, waves on a distant shore that came and went. "Uncles . . . accepted the graft . . . wait and see."

He was untied. He'd pulled up the bandage, dreading what he would see. If he could see. He could make out shapes. The heat-shape of a weapon that had recently been fired. Circular windows. A circular door. He'd grabbed the weapon and made his way out.

Something knocked his ankle. He twisted, raised the weapon, realized he didn't have it in his hands, and instead threw his weight at what he'd felt. Couch, Alistair, and another body went down.

Cam. Who'd kicked his ankle.

They were at SaStudio.

"I am glad I didn't tap you on the shoulder, like I was going to. You weigh a ton, Alistair."

Alistair climbed to his feet and hauled Cam up. "You okay?"

"Somewhat flatter than I was a moment ago." Cam helped him right the couch. "This young man offered us more coffee."

That young man was backed against the wall, coffee pot tilted so far it was starting to pour out.

"Coffee," Alistair said, because if he tried to rescue the pot the apprentice would jerk back and scald himself.

Cam swooped forward and righted the pot. "Alistair's a big scary bear, I know. Do you need to sit down? Here, I'll pour us some coffee." He did so. "I'll take the pot over to the counter here"—suiting action to words—"and you come over here too."

The apprentice sidled around, keeping to the wall.

"Sorry," Alistair said. "I forgot where I was."

Cam gave the apprentice a friendly pat on the shoulder. "You'll be fine." He came over to sit across from Alistair again.

"Big scary bear?" Did he scare Cam?

"You must have been in a bad place."

Alistair rubbed his face. "There are times in my life I'm ashamed of how I behaved."

"Me too, Alistair. Me too."

Alistair sat back, sipped coffee, and watched the apprentices sidle as far around him as they could on their trips into and out of the room. "Does every modder have apprentices?" No one had mentioned Rik Terri's apprentice. "Including Rik Terri?"

"That's an unfounded rumor."

He'd been so focused on watching the apprentices, he hadn't heard Samson Sa open the double doors. "Nika Rik Terri doesn't take apprentices."

There was no sign of the client, so they must have gone out another door. Or maybe they were being modded.

"What do you mean? Rumor?" Alistair asked.

"She didn't have one two years ago," Cam said.

"And she still doesn't have one," Sa said. "Despite what the records say. The apprenticeship was registered after the explosion in her studio. She's dead." He ushered Cam to his feet, stared at him for a long, silent minute. "Your skin is so clear. It glows."

It did glow. At least to Alistair it did. A soft, golden color. All Cam needed was the white teeth to go with it, and Alistair would have to wear eye-covers when he looked at him.

"And the eyes." Sa might almost have been talking to himself. "It's amazing the way she didn't make you classically handsome. You look—"

"Striking?" Alistair suggested.

"Put you beside me." Sa drew Cam over to a full-length mirror. "People will notice you before they notice me. I'd give anything to know how she did it. But come, let's talk in my office."

Alistair followed them in.

"Nika certainly knows how to mod to make someone stand out." He leaned close, said confidentially, "I'd never have admitted it while she was alive, of course, but some of her designs were outstanding. Yours especially." He hesitated. "It's a pity she's gone, of course, but if you need a touch-up, my studio would be honored to oblige."

Cam's own smile flashed out. "I'm rather hoping Nika's still alive."

"What makes you think she's dead?" Alistair asked.

Sa turned his attention to him. "Well, there's the explosion, of course. At her studio."

Did he know Rik Terri's body hadn't been found there?

It was the best introduction they were likely to get. Alistair said, "I believe you were seen with Nika Rik Terri only a few weeks before the accident."

"I haven't seen Nika since Festival. There's a big gala dinner. Anyone who's anyone goes. It's the only event Nika is sure to attend. Not like she used to. Not like she did before she hooked up with Alejandro Duarte."

Duarte's body had been one of those in Rik Terri's studio.

Sa sighed reminiscently. "We've had some great discussions over the years." He laughed this time. "Quite energetic ones at that."

"What about Shanna Brown's event?"

"Oh, my—" Sa put a fist to his mouth in what Alistair thought was an instinctive, rather than feigned, reaction. He shuddered. "Terrible business, and my client too."

"But the woman you came in with—"

"Was not Nika Rik Terri. I've already told your agents that. She was no more Rik Terri than I am."

"Yet you came in with her."

"It was an outstanding mod. I mean, look at the images." Sa waved a hand. "You can only get skin like that from a Songyan, and Nika only ever uses a Songyan. I only wish I knew what she was using to create that glow." He looked hopefully at Cam, who shrugged. Sa sighed and turned back to the image. "Of course, I sought the woman out as soon as I saw her. When your rivals are producing work like that, you need to know about it."

"But you don't believe it was Rik Terri?"

"I did at first, until I spoke to her. It had all the characteristics of a Rik Terri design." He looked at Cam. "The woman's skin had that same, clear look yours does." Nodded. "Beautiful eyes. Which explains why you're so mixed up about the woman's identity, but the modder is not the body they produce, Agent."

"But it could have been Rik Terri herself." Alistair had checked Rik Terri's stats. She was the same height, same build, as the assassin.

"Agent, Nika and I are professional rivals. We know each other's work; we know each other's bodies. We're modders. We know how the other walks, how they talk, how they smile. If they do smile, that is," and Sa smiled his own teeth-blinding smile again. "I can't answer for the smile, but that woman did not walk like Rik Terri. She did not talk like Rik Terri. She did not converse like Rik Terri."

"What do modders talk about when they get together?"

"Small talk initially. Pointed barbs aimed at each other's modding work. Then they get down to business. There is only one topic of conversation when two top-class modders get together, and that is modding."

"And what did you and the woman—the murderer—discuss?"

"The weather. Of course, I tried to find out about her mod, but all she spoke about was how cold the night was." Sa rubbed his chin. "You know, on reflection, that was unusual. Someone who's just been modded generally wants to talk about how wonderful the mod is."

"So you didn't know her at all before you got to Brown's that night?"

"No."

"There's a rumor that before the woman was modded she was taller."

"Couldn't happen," Sa said. "It's not worth the effort. Too much modding. Too fiddly. Too dangerous. Although, if anyone could, it would be Nika Rik Terri. She had a mind that went right down to the molecular level. Rather too much detail, if you ask me."

"What about the theory that someone else was controlling the body?"

Sa laughed. "Now you're getting into fiction. They only do that in the vids, Agent. No one can physically swap bodies."

"Not even Nika Rik Terri?"

"No. Not even Nika."

They escaped an hour later, knowing more about body modding than Alistair had ever wanted to know.

"Samson Sa can certainly talk," Alistair said as they made their way back to the hotel they were staying at. "Was Rik Terri like that too?"

Cam laughed. "Nika? She made you talk. She hardly said a word. She just listened, and before you knew it, you were pouring out your soul."

Alistair wasn't sure which would be worse.

"Where to now?" Cam asked.

"Eaglehawk Prime," which was the headquarters for Eaglehawk Company. "We have an appointment with Leonard Wickmore, the sole survivor of the attack at Rik Terri's studio."

At the Eaglehawk head office, Alistair and Cam passed through five outer offices and spoke to seven personal assistants before they finally got to speak to Leonard Wickmore.

"I'm so glad you made an appointment," Cam said as they waited for the seventh assistant to clear the way. "Imagine if you arrived unannounced."

There was security, and there was excess. This was excess.

The seventh assistant ushered them into Wickmore's office.

Alistair shook hands with the Eaglehawk executive. "That's some gamut to run out there."

Wickmore laughed, deep throated and musical. "One can never be too complacent." He indicated the two seats in front of his desk. "Please."

Alistair pulled off the eye-covers he'd worn on the way to cut the infrared and ultraviolet and clipped them onto the edge of his pocket. There were occasions when it paid to see colors approximately as others saw them. It saved a lot of misunderstanding, and the occasional near miss.

Without the blocking lenses, Wickmore's body took on the

more familiar, warmer red and yellow overtones. Through the walls Alistair could see the heat from the power conduits. And the cameras. Wickmore had five cameras hidden in the walls around his office. Along with two weapons. One of which was pointed directly at the chair Alistair was about to sit on. The other at Cam's chair.

What sort of man hid weapons in his wall?

Sometimes the extra sight was a blessing. Sometimes he'd rather not know.

Alistair moved over to the window instead of sitting. He wanted to warn Cam not to sit down either, but Wickmore would know he knew. "An amazing view." The weapon followed, remained targeted on him.

He tried not to sweat. This was a regular visit. Nothing to worry about. But it was amazing the junk people had hidden in their offices that most people didn't know about.

The view from Wickmore's office was purported to be amazing. Alistair supposed it was, but the rushing aurora in the sky outside reminded him of the Vortex. He hid a shiver, went back to the chair Wickmore had proffered, and tried to ignore the weapon focused on him.

He noticed that Wickmore walked around them both to get to his own desk.

"You've fallen on your feet," Wickmore said. "Not so long ago you were up on a fraud charge. I see you got off that. Your wife didn't. It was generous of her to take all the blame."

An immediate declaration of war? Or just another powerful man trying to gain the upper hand? Alistair ignored the jibe. "Executive Wickmore, we'd like—"

"Yet here you are, large as life, still working for the Justice Department. Back in your old job, even."

When Wickmore smiled, his teeth were almost as blinding as Samson Sa's. Maybe it was fashionable.

"We'd like to talk to you about the explosion at Nika Rik Terri's studio on Lesser Sirius."

"And this is what my attack has been reduced to. A cold case being investigated by a discredited agent on trial for fraud."

Wickmore might have guessed they were there to talk about the explosion, but his pat answer sounded rehearsed, as if he'd already thought of what to say and now had to deliver it. He'd known why they were here before Alistair had told him. But then, he was a company executive. He'd have called up the Justice Department Eaglehawk board representative as soon as Alistair had made the appointment. A few discreet questions later and he probably knew more about the case than Alistair did.

"Your attack?"

"It was directed at me."

That was an interesting view of an attack at Nika Rik Terri's studio.

"Why do you feel the attack was directed at you and not Rik Terri?"

"Why would anyone target a body modder?"

Alistair could think of a lot of reasons, but he left it. He was looking for Nika, not investigating an attack on the executive. "You should be encouraged," Alistair said. "At least someone is looking at it."

"Somehow I might be more encouraged if I knew it was an agent who didn't have a hidden agenda. Last time we met, I recall, you attempted to intimidate me."

He had? The last time he'd seen Leonard Wickmore had been three months before he'd left for Zell. He'd linked Tamati Woden to three possible companies—Eaglehawk was one of them—and he'd gone around to see executives at each of the three. Alistair would have said the meeting was quite civil. It was interesting that Wickmore remembered it as otherwise.

Or maybe he was out-and-out lying.

Cam laughed. "I didn't think anyone could intimidate you, Executive."

Wickmore's gaze swiveled to Cam for the first time, although Alistair was sure he'd been observing him. "I did say attempted, Agent Le-Nguyen."

Alistair hadn't given Cam's name to any of the assistants. "You were at Rik Terri's studio on the day of the explosion. Can you tell us what you were doing there?"

Wickmore hid a sigh. "Agent Laughton, I have told the Justice Department what happened. Three times, if I recall."

He recalled correctly.

"Maybe you should read the reports."

"I'll do that. Meantime, can you tell us what you were doing there?"

"You really should read the reports. It would save you a lot of time."

They didn't have time to play word games. Alistair couldn't stop his gaze drifting to the wall. He forced his attention back to the executive. Why not try the crazy approach? Get the weird ideas out of the way, and Wickmore might relax enough to give him some real information.

"So, body swapping, Executive. What do you know about that?"

The red tones of Wickmore's body intensified. Increased heart rate, for sure. A massive adrenaline surge. Certainly not the reaction Alistair had expected. Did Cam see a change in color too?

Alistair pulled his eye-covers on momentarily. Wickmore looked more relaxed, if anything.

"I have no idea what you are talking about, Agent Laughton."

"Haven't you heard?" Alistair said. "Executive Shanna Brown, murdered by Tamati Woden, who borrowed Nika Rik Terri's body to do it."

Wickmore laughed, but there was something off about the sound. "Agent Laughton, I fear your time in exile has turned your mind. That's not possible."

"Isn't it?" and Alistair's gaze locked onto his.

Wickmore refused to look away. "I have never heard anything so unlikely in my life and I have heard many unlikely things. If only something like that were possible. Think of the opportunities. The possibilities."

Like using someone's body to commit murder.

"You were at Nika Rik Terri's studio a month after the alleged incident, Executive. Right at the time her studio was blown up. Maybe you planned for it to blow up after you left."

"Agent Laughton." Still matching stares. "I hope you aren't insinuating anything. Words like that could get you a visit from company lawyers."

Alistair held up his hands in mock surrender. "No," he said. "I am sure that if you planned to bomb a place, you wouldn't do it yourself. You'd pay other people to do it."

Wickmore's eyes narrowed.

"What were you doing at Nika Rik Terri's studio, Executive Wickmore?"

"If you cared to read your reports, you will find I was there with one of my staff. Alejandro Duarte. Alejandro and Nika were partners. She was also his modder. I admired his mod, was thinking of using her next time. He offered to introduce me."

All of that was in the report.

"What did she say when you met her?"

"Say, Agent Laughton? She wasn't there. I did not get to meet her."

"But you waited inside her studio?"

"Alejandro had access to her rooms. She lived upstairs."

That, too, was in the report. "And Alejandro Duarte? Where did he live?"

"I'm not sure why that's even a question, but if you read the report, I'm sure the address will be there. He is dead, you know. He was at the studio with me."

"But Rik Terri wasn't."

"You think she might have taken refuge at his apartment?" Wickmore's smile chilled. "I'll have our personnel department send any known addresses through."

Alistair stood. "Thank you, Executive. You have been most helpful." More helpful than he knew, with his adrenaline-fueled reaction at talk of body swapping. Maybe Paola had a reason to worry.

Wickmore escorted him and Cam to the door. The weapons swiveled to follow them. Alistair's back prickled all the way.

7

ALISTAIR LAUGHTON

Paola came down to Alistair's office when he got back. "Most people's underlings have to go up and see them, you know. Not the other way around."

"You could have called me."

"Then waited while you did whatever you thought was more important before you came up. You never did have any respect for authority, Alistair."

"I'm hardly in a position to ignore you." She'd given him the only lead he'd had in a fruitless month of searching.

"No, and you won't be after I give you this." Paola looked around the office. "Where's your striking assistant?"

"Gone down to the desk to collect dinner." Living on takeout wasn't much different to what he'd done in the old days, but he had to admit, Cam took takeout to a whole different level.

"Alistair, don't get involved in the companies. They suck you in and spit you out."

Had she waited till Cam was out of the room to say that? "I'm not sure I—"

"Even when it's legal. They still dump you when you're done, and Santiago is almost as bad as Eaglehawk or MGK."

Only almost?

She must have read their report on Zell. The one they'd made to divisional headquarters on New Capy on their way to Lesser Sirius, back when they'd both thought it was a simple matter of going to Rik Terri's studio and asking for help. Back before they'd seen her burned-out studio and realized how hard the task would be.

"I can't not be involved."

"I can't help you if you won't help yourself, Alistair." She held up a hand to forestall him. "The other thing you asked. The condition."

She was going to say she couldn't do it.

"A ship has been organized." Paola pushed a code through. "This is the authorization. Use it wisely."

"Thank you." Alistair leaned back in his chair, suddenly drained. "Thank you, Paola."

"I don't know what mess you've got yourself into, Alistair." She stood up as Cam came in, nodded at him, and made for the door. "Just don't drag me into it."

"What was that about?" Cam asked.

"Paola can get us a ship if we need it. To get everyone off Zell." If they could get around the not-so-minor issue of the warship orbiting it.

"Including the Ort?"

"A hundred people."

Cam served out exotic beans and a bright-red vegetable Alistair had never seen before. "Paola's going to have cats when she finds out about the Ort."

It was Mayeso who finally gave them the clue to finding the Ort.

Alistair had been woken by a distress call. It had come through at 03:34 standard time, four minutes to midnight local time. Even though there was nothing he could do, Alistair pulled on the pants and fleece-lined jacket of his company uniform—and the totally non-company felted boots—and padded outside.

Zell, the world he was on, was four light-minutes away from the Vortex. He linked in to check the ship. It was an old prospecting ship with four people on board. They'd been there two weeks, risking the Vortex to mine some of the asteroids caught in the Vortex's gravitational field.

Dicing with death for two weeks now.

They all thought they could do it, but the Vortex got everyone in the end.

When Alistair had arrived on Zell, the Vortex had been a writhing gray hole that took up most of the northern sky. Nowadays he saw it as a full-colored, writhing spiral in that same space. At night it was bright enough to light up the whole area. At least it did for Alistair.

They'd already be dead, those four miners who'd risked their lives to make money. Pulled apart by the stresses of the Vortex as their ship accelerated in an attempt to break free from forces they had no hope of escaping from.

That was how he imagined it, anyway, for no one lived to tell what the Vortex did to you, and Alistair certainly wasn't going close enough to find out. He shuddered. Did the forces literally pull you apart, as some scientist theorized? It certainly pulled the ships apart.

Alistair gave a last nod of acknowledgment to the now-dead miners and turned to go inside. They'd all been putting in long hours lately. They were so close to making bonus, and they only had two weeks to do it in.

Two more weeks. It was hard to believe their time in this hell was almost over. And yet—he had friends here.

He'd signed on because he'd been running. Running from a broken marriage, running from a destroyed career. And so was everyone else on Zell. From poverty, from failure, from despair. A group of broken people who'd forged a community together.

The whisper of noise that had been in his head ever since those first months cleared momentarily, turned into words he imagined he could hear. "Mutated again," heavy with disappointment, and a resigned, "Start over."

It did that occasionally.

A light went on in the residency building.

There were two buildings on Zell. A massive machinery shed—five hundred meters long and two hundred meters wide—and the one where they lived: offices, common rooms, and food hall on the ground floor, living areas on the second and third. This light was on the third floor.

Another light went on. Then another.

Trouble.

He took the steps three at a time, could hear Yakusha's voice before he reached the third floor.

"What's the problem?"

"Mayeso didn't come back from her run," Yakusha said.

Mayeso jogged after work, before dinner. She should have been back hours ago.

"And no one noticed until now?"

"She had a call from her daughter earlier today. It upset her."

There'd been a few of those calls lately. This close to the end of the project, people were making plans for going home—and finding their families had moved on without them. People who chose to spend two years on an isolated world away from their families were unlikely to have families who missed them. Alistair supposed he should be grateful he didn't have the illusion of family to go back to. His ex-wife was in jail; none of his former colleagues would want to see him.

"We assumed she ate dinner in her room," Yakusha said. Which was understandable when you wanted to brood about a family who didn't have time for you. "But I thought around now she'd be wanting to talk, so I went to see her."

No one locked their doors here on Zell.

"Her clothes are all strewn on the floor, you know like she does when she gets back from the mine."

There was no privacy, either, and after two years everyone knew everyone else's habits and rituals. Mayeso came in from work and changed into her running clothes. She left her dirty mining clothes on the floor of her bathroom. When she got back from her run, she tossed all the dirty clothes—mining and running—into the washer, showered, and changed into one of the many weird outfits she'd made herself out of local materials. If the clothes weren't in the washer, it meant she hadn't come back from her run.

"We checked inside the first bounds." The first of two electric force fences that protected the settlement. "We couldn't see her."

Alistair nodded. "Let me look, anyway."

Everyone was there. They parted, making a narrow path for him to walk through.

"The Ort have taken her." Cadel Jones had initially scoffed at tales of the Ort, but after he'd been taken, he started blaming them for everything. Even things they couldn't possibly have done, like the big generator going down. As mine supervisor, he should have known better, but the pressure was getting to them all.

Melda pushed her way through. "We all know it's the Ort, Alistair. I'm not wasting staff to go look for her."

"She could be hurt." Worse case the salynxes had caught her unaware, not that they came this side of the cutter bushes anymore. If they had, all he'd find would be bones. He didn't mention that.

"We're two weeks off finishing up, and we've a bonus to make. Mayeso will call in a couple of hours. We can't afford to waste the time."

Melda fiercely protected every one of her crew. This was out of character for the camp boss.

"Melda," Alistair said. "I'm going to look for Mayeso. Come with me." If he didn't get her away from this muttering crowd, she'd likely be lynched. "You're right. We all need to work tomorrow." He looked at the others. "I know where she runs." Inside the second bounds. That force fence went all the way down to the lakeshore and for a kilometer either side of the camp. It was the one safe place she could run.

He wouldn't find her there, not if the Ort had taken her. "She'll be in shock, no matter what's happened. Can someone prepare a warm drink and something for her to eat?"

"I'll do it," Yakusha said. "Look after her, okay?" And they all pointedly didn't look at Melda.

Alistair took Melda's arm. There were advantages to being tall and bulky and your boss being short and skinny. You could drag her along, even lift her at times, and it wasn't noticeable.

Except for the sound of her dragging feet.

"Get your hands off me." Melda sounded as if she'd clenched her teeth. At least she'd said it quietly.

He made his reply soft as well. "Not until you revert to being sensible. Honestly, Melda. You'd think you'd had bad news from home the way you're acting."

He felt her arm stiffen.

Alistair sighed. Melda's had been the only stable family group in the whole fifty of them. He should have realized that stability was only in Melda's mind. He gave her arm an encouraging shake. "Hey, they'll get over it." Whatever it was. The only knowledge he had of both her partners was from Melda herself. Bob sounded like a company sycophant, Angel little better.

He didn't say anything further until they were out in the aircar. "You want to watch the left or the right?"

"Left."

He set the autopilot as slow as it would go—little more than walking pace—and close to ground. He kept the lights on full—for Melda's sake—beaming out around the car the whole 360 degrees.

There was nothing inside the force fence. Alistair called Cam. "No sign of Mayeso inside the bounds. I'm going to try outside."

"I'll tell the others."

He lifted the aircar high enough to hop over the fence, then came down again and resumed his path.

The Vortex colored the sky in front of them. Alistair shivered and pulled his jacket closer. The soft clop of the propellers and the fan recycling air around the cabin were the only noises in the silence. If you didn't know better, you'd think it was the sound of the Vortex, because you could see it swirl. Back when his eyesight had first changed, he'd watched the center till it made him giddy.

Nowadays he only looked at it when he had to.

Small creatures scurried away from their lights. Off to the right an enormous bovine turned one head to look at them; the other head continued feeding.

"You want to talk about it?" he asked eventually.

"This bonus is our future, Alistair. If we can get it, everyone will be set for life. I know Mayeso is gone, but we all know where she is, and we know she'll be all right. And if she isn't, then there is nothing we can do."

Melda truly was thinking of the future for them. She looked on these fifty contractors as her own personal family, wanted them to succeed. But she was in charge. She was paid to make the hard decisions.

"Every time someone disappears, we lose two days' work from them. And from whomever you set to watch them. When you find Mayeso, you'll set Yakusha to mind her. Yakusha's our best miner."

The two women were friends. Yakusha was the logical person to sit with Mayeso, and she wouldn't get much work done if she was sitting on a float in the middle of the lake, wondering how Mayeso was doing.

"I meant did you want to talk about your family."

"If you weren't so big, Alistair, I'd hit you."

No. She didn't.

The aircar crept on through the night.

Melda's link beeped. She brought the call up on the aircar screen. Angel, one of her partners.

"Melda." Angel had been modded. She looked nothing like the image of the three of them that Melda kept on her bedroom wall.

How must it be to have a partner you wouldn't recognize when you went home?

Her voice was the same, though. A hard voice, Alistair had always thought, with no warmth. But then, that was a prejudice, because he didn't like the woman.

"Angel." Melda's voice was guarded.

Angel smiled. The smile didn't reach her eyes. "You clicked off earlier."

Definite accusation in the tone. Or was Alistair reading that into it because he wanted to?

"We've a problem here. One of our miners disappeared on a run. We're searching for her."

Melda didn't normally tell her family about the problems they had on Zell. Only about the positives—like the fact that they were about to make bonus. She pointed, blindly, to nothing on the side of their path. "Over there."

"Yes," Alistair agreed, stopping the aircar. He even opened the door and stepped out.

"Got to go, Angel," Melda said. "We've found our missing person. I'll call you back." She clicked off and sat shivering while Alistair returned to his seat and started the aircar back on its course.

"If you need someone to talk to," Alistair said softly, "you know where I'll be."

They finished the east ridge in silence. Melda didn't complain when Alistair turned the aircar down the southeast route, prickly with plants that would scratch the vehicle. Normally she'd complain about that. She wanted to return the vehicle in as good a condition as she could. They'd be docked for repairs. It was part of the contract.

"You tell her about—" Alistair inclined his head toward the undergrowth.

"I'm not stupid."

Alistair still didn't know if that was a wise decision or not. He hadn't agreed with Melda's decision to play down his own early encounter, didn't agree with her holding off now.

This was his first job with Santiago Company—Melda was a lifer—but surely a company would be reasonable about first contact with another sapient species and make some allowances.

Or maybe they wouldn't. Companies cared about profit first, and Melda knew more about how Santiago worked than he did.

"I'll tell them after the bonuses come in. We have worked for them. We have earned them."

Even Alistair admitted the bonuses were exceedingly generous. It was clear to him that Santiago had never expected to pay them. Alistair hadn't expected to earn them. But the team was a good one. They'd worked well, and innovatively, together. So here they were, two weeks and a hundred grams short of ten kilograms of transurides that would make them all rich.

Melda's link beeped again. She ignored it.

"Maybe Angel just wants to see you."

Melda laughed. "Angel wouldn't go out of her way to see you if you were in the same city. They call her the Hatchet, you know."

"Because she ignores people?"

"It's her job. Closing unprofitable departments. She loves it. Cutting off the deadwood of the business, she calls it."

He had no idea what Melda saw in Angel, but then, he couldn't talk. Lisbet wasn't any better. "What about Bob?"

"Depends whether his boss is watching or not."

At least she was realistic about her family.

He saw a warm red body to their left and set the aircar down gently.

Mayeso had fallen among a copse of bushes known as cutter bushes—because get in among them and that's exactly what they did. Cut you to pieces.

She was hotter than normal. Still in the throes of the first bout of fever.

Alistair killed the lights.

"What—"

"Shhh." He bounded out of the aircar. Nothing. Not even the usual night sounds. Alistair turned a full circle. There. Heading east. A long straight streak of heat, rapidly cooling, like the heat trail the engine of an aircar might leave. Alistair took a careful reading. "Got you."

Of course, they may have just lifted off that way, but it was a clue. The first they'd had in all the long months.

He waited a full five minutes after, to be sure they were alone, before he turned on the lights again.

"I swear," Melda said as he turned the light onto the huddled figure, "even the Ort can't have changed your eyesight that much, Alistair."

"It's my magic trick." Alistair looked down at his felted boots, which were fine in the confines of the camp but totally useless out here among the bushes. No one went into a copse of cutter bushes willingly.

This was going to hurt.

He scanned the area. He had a stunner and the fire-breather. Bovines—who had two heads and absolutely zero brains between them—loved the taste of the bushes, but the sharp leaves cut the inside of their mouths and their stomachs and sent them crazy. A bovine in pain was a rampaging monster. If it came your way, the only thing you could do was kill it. The fire-breather was for emergency use only. Setting the cutter bushes alight accidently was not the way to help Mayeso.

There were no bovines close.

He'd have liked an ax, but there was nothing in the car. Where were his brains today? In bed, where he wanted to be. A heavy iron bar was the only tool. He grabbed the bar and stepped out.

"Be ready to grab her when I hand her out."

He used the bar to push the leaves aside, but they still cut into his hands, and—as he pushed in farther—into his fleecy coat as well. He swore under his breath. It was the only good coat he had left.

Mayeso was as far into the bushes as she could get. Alistair was bleeding and scratched all over by the time he backed out with the inert body in his arms. At least he wasn't hurt badly, not like Mayeso was, for she was in running shorts and a sleeveless top.

"My God," Melda muttered. "How long will she be off work?"

"Melda."

"I know. I'm sorry, but we've only two weeks and our bonuses depend on us delivering. We were so close until this started happening."

Right now Alistair was tired of hearing about the bonus, although that was all any of them could think about this close to the end. The bonus, the end of the job, and going home.

He checked Mayeso over. She didn't seem harmed, but who was he to say? They didn't have a doctor to fix things. Their doctor had wiped himself out two months into the first year, rock climbing.

What had possessed him to go rock climbing on a world where the closest help was five nullspace jumps away was beyond Alistair's comprehension. But then, Lennie had been an adrenaline freak.

Which was fine, providing you weren't the team doctor.

So now they had a machine coded to a dead man, which none of them could use, and no way to heal anyone. Not that Alistair himself had ever used the machine while on Zell, but there'd been times when it would have been useful.

Like now.

As he laid Mayeso carefully in the back seat of the aircar, a thunderous roar had him reaching for his fire-breather. He looked up.

The entry burn of a shuttle lit up the sky. It came closer and closer, a massive ball of heat.

They watched it come.

"It's headed our way." Alistair set the aircar on auto. "Let's get home."

He called Cam as soon as they were airborne.

"Got it," Cam said before Alistair could say anything. "We're on it."

Cam was the settlement lawyer—although why Santiago had bothered to send a lawyer on a mining expedition Alistair didn't know. Or maybe he did, for Cam was the worst lawyer Alistair had ever met. But in a crisis, Alistair wanted Cam behind him. His levelheadedness calmed them all. You could rely on him to do what you asked of him. And people talked to him.

He was everyone's favorite. Cam played on it rather well, but he had a charm and diffidence that offset his obvious enjoyment of his own looks. Most of the camp babied him, even though he was—according to Alistair's records—thirty years old and three of the miners were younger.

Mayeso came around as Alistair carried her into the warmth of the shared lounge. She was dazed and disoriented and clutched at Alistair as if he were a lifeline.

Alistair helped her stand. "Do you think you can walk?" He guided her to one of the couches. The lounge was full of strangers in suits. Strangers who all turned to watch as they entered.

Cam was off to one side, talking to a woman whose suit looked as expensive as those that Alistair's old boss, Paola, used to wear. For a moment he thought it was Paola. Then sanity returned. He'd seen the woman's image less than an hour ago.

"Angel," Melda said. "What are you doing here?"

Why hadn't Melda's partner told her she was coming? Or had Melda cut her off before she got around to it?

Cam gave a quiet thumbs-up from where he was and kept talking to Angel. Melda went over to join them.

Mayeso stared around the room as if she'd never seen it before.

Cadel came over with a warm blanket, Yakusha with hot soup. The rug was a brightly patterned, felted weave. Yakusha had spent the whole of last cold season making it. Alistair gently unclenched Mayeso's fingers from his arm—he would be bruised tomorrow—and curled them around the rug instead. "Look, Yakusha's rug."

She clutched at the rug convulsively.

"And some hot soup." He kept his voice low, tried to sound reassuring.

"Seaweed nut soup," Yakusha said. "Strong, healthy."

Alistair would have picked something out of the freezer, something that didn't taste like the sludge out of the recycler, but it seemed to work, for Mayeso lifted her head to take a sip.

He turned to Cadel. "Can you get me a first-aid kit?" To Timoty, the miner next to Cadel, "And some warm water and a clean cloth."

Yakusha's rug was already spotted with blood. He hoped it came clean.

He moved to prevent a spot of his own blood dropping onto it.

The first-aid kit was in the cupboard. Cadel didn't have to go far. "What did you do? Fight off the—?" He looked at the suited people staring at them, cut off the rest of what he'd been going to say.

"Ended up in a cutter copse," Alistair said.

Had the Ort put Mayeso there? If so, why hadn't they returned her back to where they'd found her, to where it was safe? Maybe because they thought the cutter copse was safer.

Mayeso shuddered and clutched at Alistair's arm again. Another bruise for tomorrow. "They're big. Bigger than us. Like a pole on four legs."

Bigger than Mayeso, but they hadn't been taller than Alistair.

A stick insect, others had described them. Long, skinny legs set around the body to balance. Four smaller forearms and an oval head with four bulbous eyes.

"Claws like needles."

They hadn't been claws. More like leathery fingers, but Mayeso was telling the truth as she believed it. He could see it in the way her color stayed constant.

"It took my necklace."

"What was the necklace made of?" He thought he remembered it. A clunky gold flower. "Gold?"

"Yes. It was. A gift from my daughter. I wore it because—"

She started to cry.

They liked gold, these aliens. Ravi had lost a gold signet ring. Teena had lost a pair of gold earrings. He had lost his wedding ring. That wasn't a loss. He shouldn't even have been wearing it, for the divorce papers had come through a week after he'd arrived on Zell.

Alistair took the bowl of warm water from Timoty, started wiping Mayeso's arms. He made it as gentle as his voice. "Tell me how it happened. What were you doing when you first saw the Ort? What did it do?"

"I didn't see it. I felt this . . . sting. I thought it was an insect. I put my hand up to swat it."

One of the suited men moved across. "What's the problem here?" He wore a blaster. Security, Alistair guessed.

Right now he didn't want to go through the whole story. He wanted bed. They all did, and Melda hadn't yet mentioned the Ort to Santiago. "Didn't Angel tell you? One of our people went missing." He nodded at Mayeso. "We found her."

"She came up against wild creatures?"

He wasn't sure he'd call the Ort wild, but, "There are plenty of dangerous creatures on Zell. I'll give you a rundown later." After he'd convinced Melda it was time to talk about other sapient species. "But not tonight. For the moment, please don't go out of our camp without one of us." He looked around the room, counted the visitors. Ten. "Is this all of you? Bedding will be tight."

"We don't plan on sleeping," the Santiago man said. "We're here to pack everything up. We'll do it in shifts. We've ten here now, and we've ten more upstairs."

"Upstairs?"

"On ship." The man smiled, as if at some private joke Alistair wasn't privy to. "But this shift is ready to make a start."

"We're still using most of the equipment. There won't be much packing up done for two weeks."

"We have our orders."

"I don't care what your orders are. We have another two weeks. You'll need to talk to Melda and Cadel." Was this how the company got out of paying the bonus? He quashed the uncharitable thought. They probably thought they were doing them a favor by arriving early and starting the packing. "Regardless, you can't start tonight. Everyone is exhausted." Cadel would have to make the decisions about what equipment could go early. And Yakusha, who oversaw stores. "It's been a long night."

"We'll see." The Santiago security man moved over to talk to Angel and Melda.

Alistair turned back to Mayeso. "Tell me the rest."

Mayeso would have spilt her soup if she'd had any left. "When I come around, I'm strapped on a table, with this . . . with this . . ." She gestured, to indicate height. "Four legs."

They were slowly building up an image.

"Green. Like a big stick insect. Four smaller forelimbs that it used like arms." Mayeso stared into her empty bowl. "A cold circle on my arm. Then it left the room, and the table went down, and I heard a click, and I wasn't restrained anymore."

They all told a similar story.

"I was so tired. I couldn't get off the bed. I went back to sleep. I couldn't help myself. Then you found me."

"Why did you go into the cutter bushes?"

"I . . . I don't remember."

Whatever the Ort injected them with knocked them out for a few hours. Alistair himself remembered blacking out several times before Cam had found him. At the time he'd thought he was lucky to survive while he'd been unconscious, but given what they knew now about how deadly salynxes could be, he hadn't been lucky—he'd been helped.

They'd put Mayeso under the bushes. What kind of—presumably—sapient creature put a fragile-skinned body under leaves so sharp they could cut?

One that thought it was the safest place for them.

Melda's voice rose above the noise in the room.

"Leave her with me." Yakusha handed Alistair a filled beaker. "Drink this first, then you can go over and sort that out."

He drank in one long swallow. It burned on its way down. His eyes watered, and he choked. "Thanks for nothing." But he needed it. He was tired, he was cranky, and he did not want to face strangers.

Time to be civil. He went over to where Melda, Cam, Angel, and the security person who hadn't introduced himself yet were standing.

"You are not packing up anything until we finish here," Melda said. "We've people still working."

"Let's sort this out tomorrow." Alistair stifled a yawn. "No one is doing anything tonight. We need sleep. All of us."

"We don't work to planetary times," the security person said.

"I'm sorry, whoever you are, but that's too bad. You are on planet. Here, I'm your security. It's not safe to wander around. If you don't plan on sleeping, don't leave the fenced-off area. I've already said I will give you the full rundown later. Until then your people can bunk down here on the floor. We need sleep, even if you don't."

"You are not—"

"Maybe we will tonight, Barry," and Angel looked at Alistair, as if committing his face to memory.

Remembering the past didn't help with the future. And if Nika Rik Terri wasn't alive, what then? Would the Ort take matters into their own hands? Would Santiago slaughter the colonists at the settlement and take the prize of alien technology for themselves? Once, Alistair wouldn't have believed they would. But that was before Zell.

"Where to now?" Cam asked as they finished another delicious meal Alistair probably couldn't afford.

"Songyan Engineering." One of the people killed in the explosion had been a Songyan engineer. According to Wickmore—at least, according to what Wickmore had told earlier agents—he thought the engineer was there to service the genemod machine.

Cam sighed. "This is the life of a Justice Department agent.

Plodding from one interview to another. Spending our life in ships en route to other planets."

"Songyan Engineering's on Kitimat."

"Or aircars."

Alistair called one from his own building. He knew that would come immediately.

"We don't even get to travel executive class."

Alistair could have gone up a class because Paola had reinstated him at the same seniority level, but not Cam, who was a junior agent.

"I've been meaning to ask. How did you get this job?" There was always competition for the few jobs going.

"I used my contacts." Cam glanced at him. "I didn't sell out."

He hadn't wanted to think that, but he had wondered. "I'm glad we cleared that up."

Cam punched his shoulder lightly. "Don't feel guilty. It's in your nature to wonder."

What sort of nature was that?

"I went to Manu Pascale and asked him to get me in." Pascale was the Santiago board representative at the Justice Department. "I'm pretty sure he doesn't know about the other business."

By "other business" Alistair presumed he meant Zell and the Ort.

"I think they've told no one they don't need to. Because Manu—" Cam broke off, took a breath.

There were some parts of Cam's life that were out-of-bounds. Alistair recognized the limits. They'd just hit one.

"Do you think we will find Nika?"

"There's no evidence that she's dead." Time to change the subject. "What was she like?"

Maybe as a change of subject it was a bad choice, for Cam took a long time to answer.

"She was . . . a goddess."

Strong words. Unusual words.

The aircar arrived. Cam didn't notice. Alistair had to push him into it.

"You're so confident, Alistair. You don't know how important body image is to some people. Before Nika got hold of me, I was just another fifth-generation rich kid."

Cam rarely spoke about his past. Once or twice he'd said things that made Alistair suspect he belonged to an executive family in one of the Big Twenty-Seven companies, but he'd never asked. And given what he'd just said about going to the Santiago representative for a position at the Justice Department, Alistair was certain he knew which family he'd come from. He just hoped Cam wasn't there to spy on him.

"I wasn't ugly. I'd been modded before. Latest fashion, you know. But I was bored, and I had an income I could never spend. I became a lawyer because that was what my family expected, but I never worked as one. Not before Zell." He shrugged. "I'm a lousy lawyer."

"You get a new body and suddenly you're a different person?"

"It's hard to explain." Cam leaned back in his seat. "Nika is . . . was . . . demanding, abrasive. Honest. She's a lot like you, in fact."

Was that how Cam thought of him?

"It's a compliment."

It was?

"You go in and you think you'll come out soon with a new body. Same inside but new package. Nothing really changes. Because that's what always happens. But you don't. You sit down and talk. And talk. And talk. You start off talking about the body you want, then suddenly you're talking about how bad a lawyer you are, or how you hate law, anyway. How you don't like your family. How you hate your work, your life, yourself."

Cam rubbed his eyes. "I hope she's alive." He rubbed his eyes again. "She didn't just give people new bodies; she gave them what they needed. I mean, look at me." He gestured down at himself. "I wanted to be handsome."

Cam's look was striking rather than handsome, and he had that smile that made everyone swoon. And the first thing he'd done was taken himself and his new body off to a nowhere world with fifty other people.

"This is not handsome." Cam pointed a thumb at his chest. "This is me. This is what I always wanted to be but didn't know it until I got it."

Alistair was still trying to think of something to say when the aircar arrived at the Songyan factory.

"Nikolas Comantra was servicing the genemod machines," Dagar Songyan told them.

She was lying. Alistair could see it in the color generated by the extra heat that flowed around her body. There were advantages to being able to see beyond the visible spectrum. An increase in adrenaline increased the heat emitted from the body. To Alistair, Dagar may as well have blushed bright red instead of the spots of color high on each cheek. He put his eye-covers on momentarily to check what Cam would have seen.

"Let's start again," Alistair said gently. "With the truth this time."

The color intensified. "Are you calling me a liar?"

"Nika wouldn't have let anyone look at her machines without her being there," Cam said.

He said it with conviction. Alistair wasn't sure if he was guessing or he knew that for certain.

"The body modder wasn't there. Leonard Wickmore said one of

his own staff—who happened to be the woman's partner—let them in."

Dagar scowled. "This is business confidential. I can't tell you what it's about."

"We are the Justice Department. People were murdered."

"Which is why I refuse to talk about it. A prize like this. People will kill for it."

This time she was telling the truth.

Alistair had interviewed a lot of people like Dagar Songyan. The longer she dug in, the less likely she was to talk. He tried the shock approach. It had gotten a reaction from Leonard Wickmore.

Which he'd forgotten to mention to Paola.

"Are we talking about body swapping?" He was embarrassed to say it. He still didn't believe it was possible.

"Exchanging, please. Swapping bodies sounds so crude."

"Is there a difference?" How did Paola hit the target every time? Body swapping should have been impossible.

"A swap implies a physical transfer of bodies and minds. This is only temporary. And one of you has to be unconscious."

"So it's more like taking over someone else's mind." He wanted to rub his eyes, the way Cam was doing. Instead he called on all his twenty years of experience at the Justice Department to keep his expression neutral.

"Of course not."

"So how does it work?"

Dagar Songyan hesitated. "I've only heard about it, never seen it."

"And it takes a body modder to do?"

"It takes a genemod machine. A Songyan."

"And you build these things."

"You sound appalled, Agent. Don't be. This is the most important invention since the genemod machine itself. Human progress," she said dreamily. "The things we can do. The Justice Department should love it. You can use it in undercover work." She must have seen something in his expression. "Seriously. You will. All you need to do is switch bodies with someone you know will be at the scene of a crime. Catch them in the middle of doing it."

"I don't quite see—"

"Suppose you hear someone plans to rob a warehouse. You know one of the people who's working with the ringleader, but you can't get close to him, because if you do, the mastermind will know."

The best heists nowadays were all done by computer. By the time the empty warehouse was discovered, the missing goods had long disappeared.

"You could grab the worker one night off the street, switch bodies, and you go in and do the heist. You catch them red-handed."

"What about the body you've snatched?" Cam asked. "Even a lawyer as bad as I am can see a winning lawsuit coming."

Dagar waved that away. "I'm sure you could cover it."

Alistair tried not to look as appalled as he felt. It was time to stop talking horror stories and get some real information. His current urgent need was not to get sidetracked by trails Paola could follow up herself, and she certainly needed to follow this one.

"Did Comantra break in to Rik Terri's studio?" Because Wickmore knew about body swapping, it was a fair assumption that Comantra had gone with Wickmore, but Alistair wanted to know if Dagar would admit to it.

"What a terrible accusation. He accompanied Executive Wickmore and Alejandro Duarte." She sighed. "Such a loss. A lovely man, and so charming."

"But Nika wasn't there."

"Well, no. But Alejandro had access. He was her partner."

"What were Wickmore and Comantra doing at Rik Terri's studio?"

"Waiting to see Nika, of course."

According to the reports, Nika hadn't been seen for two weeks prior to the explosion, probably longer. "Are you sure?"

"Why don't you ask Executive Wickmore?"

He kept his gaze steady, fixed on her.

She waved a hand impatiently. "Nikolas was there to look over the Songyan."

"In someone else's studio?" Cam said.

"Nika had disappeared."

"You just said Wickmore and Comantra were waiting for her."

Dagar looked flustered. "They must have been expecting her back."

"I don't think so. You know Rik Terri has disappeared and you don't ask why? You don't report her missing. You don't ask how these people know she is missing. Instead your engineer and his friends just walk in, and . . . look?"

Dagar pressed her lips together and didn't say anything.

"Why?" Alistair asked. "Why her Songyan?"

"Duh." Dagar Songyan turned away. "We've just been talking about why."

"The exchanger was built into Nika Rik Terri's genemod machine?" It made a crazy kind of sense. "Nika Rik Terri has a body-swap machine?"

What kind of person was Rik Terri if she made technology that allowed people to swap bodies?

"Exchanger."

"And because you don't have an exchanger, you sent your engineer off to steal the technology."

"Of course not," Dagar said. "Executive Wickmore asked about the machine, asked whether we could make one. Nika had disappeared, so I sent Nikolas along to see if he could figure out how it was done."

"Now he's dead and you don't know where Nika Rik Terri is." This was a waste of time.

Dagar straightened her shoulders. "Rik Terri is dead, Agent Laughton."

"You know this for certain?"

"I . . . no."

Samson Sa had said that Nika only used a Songyan. It had been months. If she wasn't dead, she'd have ordered a machine, surely. And modding machines could only be sold to registered doctors and modders. Maybe she had ordered one. Alistair said, "I'd like to see any Songyan orders that have come through in the last six months."

"All of them?" Dagar's mouth became a thin line.

"All of them."

"We are breaching client confidentiality there."

"Or I can arrest you for obstructing a murder investigation."

Dagar pushed the list of orders through to Alistair's link. "You won't find anything there."

"Thank you." Alistair forwarded it to Cam, and they both took a moment to read it. There were only three orders. Three names, one of which was familiar.

"The apprentice," Cam breathed.

Alistair nodded. Bertram Snowshoe, who, according to Samson Sa, was not an apprentice. He looked up to Dagar, who was staring at the list as if something had finally clicked. "I want that machine." He tapped orders into his link. "Someone from the Justice Department will be around to collect it."

"But you can't—"

"I can, and I just have. It's a potential weapon."

Something about her expression made him add, "Make sure it's the right machine. You have all the part numbers here. Be sure we'll be checking them." Thank God the Songyan was custom built, with custom-made, numbered components. It was all on the order. "Thank you for your time." He hesitated. "Tell Snowshoe he can collect his genemod machine from the Justice Department. Tell him to ask for me. And please call me when he arrives."

8

ALISTAIR LAUGHTON

"Do you think this will work?" Cam asked as they supervised the loading of the just-completed Songyan onto an antigrav trolley.

Alistair used his thumb to sign for it. "It's the closest we've come. I don't know about you, Cam, but I'm getting desperate. Just because we have an agreement with the Ort doesn't mean Santiago won't decide they can do better by getting rid of the colonists. They won't wait forever."

It wasn't even a formal agreement, just an understanding that the Ort worked with the colonists rather than the Santiagans. A bluff, perpetuated by Melda and Alistair, to try to save their people.

Angel was gone, and Barry—nominally in charge for the moment—had encountered the Ort and was therefore more cautious, but how long would that last? First contact would be a boost to anyone's career, and someone was bound to be ambitious.

"But we're the only ones who can understand them."

"So far." The Ort might have sided with the settlers for the moment, but they had bigger problems, and if Alistair and Cam couldn't deliver what they'd promised, the Ort would turn to someone who promised they could.

After the Santiagan visitors had settled for the night, Alistair had gone to his office, where he added Mayeso's kidnapping to the map of instances.

He sat back and studied the result.

The captures were starting to make a loose circle, each capture closer than the last. Now they were coming inside the bounds, inside the force fence around the perimeter.

The fence had been set up to stop salynxes—small, furred creatures, a pack of which could strip the flesh off a human in under five minutes—but it was strong enough to discourage a three-ton bovine as well. There were gates. The shuttle landing field was outside the bounds, as were some of the settling ponds. Alistair had no doubt the Ort were intelligent enough to figure out how to operate the gates.

What did they want? Why didn't they come straight out and visit?

If the Ort were close, they'd have heard the shuttle arrive. That's if they could hear. They'd certainly see the heat trails if they'd made Alistair's vision match their own.

Maybe the settlers should bunker down for the next two weeks.

Tomorrow he'd see if Barry was amenable to loaning out people for security. For tonight? There wasn't much he could do except know if any of the Ort tried to enter the building. Alistair padded downstairs and set the old motion detectors they'd used early on, before they'd built the bounds, and made sure the physical locks—which they hadn't used in months—were also set.

If the Ort tried to come in, they'd have warning.

He sent a link to everyone in the building, telling them he'd set the perimeter motion-detector alarm. The last thing he wanted to do was wake everyone up by someone stepping outside early.

After which he dropped into bed, exhausted.

The klaxon blare of the perimeter alarm woke him.

He fell out of the bed in his hurry to get up.

They were here.

He flicked on the screens to see. Small, catlike creatures

swarmed at the east corner. Not Ort. Salynxes. How had they gotten past the force fences?

Alistair dressed quickly and put on the oiled jacket Yakusha had improvised. It helped with the teeth. He grabbed his firebreather, which he slipped into the holster on his back, and a knife. Cutting a salynx off a human without a knife was impossible.

Cam met him at the door.

"Salynxes," Alistair said. "Stay inside. You'll never see them." The first light was chasing away the night. He flicked on the infrared security lights. To him, everything in the compound would be visible.

The Ort had given him two advantages when they'd restored his sight. Salynxes were visible in both ultraviolet and infrared. Alistair could see them long before anyone else could.

The second advantage he had was the weapon he'd stolen when he'd escaped. Cam had christened it a fire-breather. Its closest human relative was a sparker—if a sparker shot out a flat, horizontal voltage. It looked like a sheet of lightning. It was ideal for getting rid of a pack of salynxes fast.

He had no idea how to power it, but it hadn't failed yet. Alistair was glad of that. He'd used it a lot, for their last three blasters had run out of charge months ago. And no matter how many times they requested new ones, no new blasters, or charges, had arrived with any of the six-monthly ship deliveries.

Someone screamed, kept screaming. Molten beams of blaster fire punched through the early-morning light.

The Santiagans. What were they doing outside this early in the morning? Packing? "Keep everyone inside." Alistair ran.

Someone had turned on a light. It didn't help, for most people couldn't see salynxes well at any time. The only thing they had going for them was that salynxes were pack animals and stayed in the pack.

Someone else screamed.

As soon as Alistair was close enough, he sprayed the fire-breather. White light sheeted out. Half the salynxes dropped.

The Santiagans were firing in all the wrong places.

"Hold your fire," Alistair roared as one of the blasters burned past him. "Do you want to kill us all?"

He sprayed another sweep. Then a smaller burst at one of the Santiagans' feet. When he was sure the salynxes were all dead except those on the two screaming guards, he switched to the knife. Came in sideways and slashed at the first animal, slicing it so that it bled out. For all their toughness, they had thin skins.

When it was over, he inspected the area around them. Not a salynx moved.

Behind him he heard Barry order, "Get these two back to the main building."

Alistair turned. There were six of them. They could manage.

He joined Barry as they started back to the main building. "Was there a reason you turned off the force fence? You put us all in danger?" He managed to keep his voice mild but had to grit his teeth and force his lips into a smile to do so. They'd shipped fifty-one people in two years ago. Fifty of those people were still alive. It would be stupid to lose them two weeks before the end due to some ignorant visitor.

"It wasn't deliberate," Barry said.

"It wasn't? A force fence doesn't turn itself off."

"We weren't trying to turn off the fence. We turned off the motion detectors. The one you so kindly sent us the message telling us you'd set."

That was worse. Alistair waited until the pounding anger subsided before he asked, "Why?"

"If you didn't want us wandering, we wanted to know why."

He was serious.

"Couldn't you have just asked?" Alistair nodded his thanks to Cam, waiting inside the door, and moved over to the fence controller. They hadn't turned it off; they'd set up a bypass. The bypass had created a feedback loop that had finally surged and reset everything. "You're lucky the reset turned the alarms back on. Otherwise the first we'd know of your early-morning walk would be coming out to find you stripped to bone this morning."

"Some of us would have heard the screams," Cam said helpfully.

Barry looked at him, scowled.

"We'd have woken Alistair. He is, after all, responsible for our security."

"It's quite a patch job," Barry said, gesturing at the panel.

"Our engineers did well, considering the amount of equipment they asked for from Santiago and didn't get." Still, as Melda had said, every piece of equipment they'd ordered and hadn't received was one less piece they had to pay for.

Alistair turned his attention to the two injured Santiagans. One of their companions sprayed nerveseal.

"Nerveseal," Yakusha said faintly from the other side of Cam. "Do you think they'd notice if I sneaked a pack or two."

"They'll charge your whole bonus for it," Cam said.

Barry flashed them an unfathomable look. "How bad is it, Gai?" he asked the woman who'd sprayed the nerveseal.

"He needs a doctor."

Alistair turned away. "We don't have a doctor." That was another thing they had requested and never received—a replacement for the medic who'd wiped himself out rock climbing.

"We have one on ship."

A doctor. Nerveseal. Luxuries they'd forgotten about. Santiago charged for everything.

"Take the injured up there. Get them into a machine." Should he ask them to take Mayeso too? No. They'd probably charge the whole bonus for any repair. Besides, the rest of them had survived.

"You're hurt too. We'll take you up."

Alistair looked down at himself, covered in salynx blood. Human blood, too, for salynx blood shone blue to his eyes.

If they put him into a genemod machine, what would it do to his eyes?

Cam laughed, clapped him on the shoulder hard enough so that even Alistair rocked. "The bugs around here are too scared to bite our Alistair." He gave Alistair a push. "Go and wash up, to show there's nothing wrong. We'll handle everything here, including getting these people onto the shuttle."

The shuttle had gone by the time Alistair came downstairs, clean, shaven, stinking of the astringent ointment he'd put over his own bites.

"You okay?" Cam asked as Alistair grabbed breakfast from the servery.

"Ask me when I've had a full night's sleep, but I'm fine." He cocked his head, listening. Down the other end of the large lounge, voices were raised. "What's up with them now?"

"Who knows?"

Alistair moved over to the sink, where he poured instant into two cups of boiling water. He handed one to Cam.

"Thanks." Cam took a sip, made a face. "I don't know how we drink this stuff."

It was all they had left. With two weeks to go they were running short of the necessities, let alone the luxuries.

"Do you know the first thing I'm doing when I get home?"

"Drinking real coffee."

"Yes."

Yakusha wanted to eat lavaberries. Melda wanted to soak in a hot bath. Personally, Alistair wanted a decent whiskey. Lack of alcohol wasn't an issue—humans could make alcohol from anything, and the cutter bushes made a potent drink that had spoiled most of them for other alcohols. Alistair thought it was more the memory of the whiskey than the actual taste of it, but he wouldn't know until he had that first drink.

"Angel Penn." Cam glanced at the group at the other end of the room, turned back to Alistair, and kept his voice low. "They call her the Hatchet. Her job is to close unprofitable departments." He put the mug of instant down onto the bench, leaned forward. "She shouldn't be here. We're on a shoestring budget. They can't lose money on us."

They could if they had to pay out excess bonuses they weren't expecting to.

"I'm worried they'll try and pack everything up under us," Alistair admitted. "They came prepared to work."

"And us with two weeks to make bonus."

Cam was quick. Alistair had no idea why he was such a bad lawyer. "Maybe we're imagining issues where there are none," Alistair said. "Angel is Melda's partner."

"That relationship was over before yours was. No one comes out to an isolated world like Zell if they have people to leave behind." Melda talked a lot to Cam. If anyone knew how strong her partnership was, he would. "We can't let them take away the bonus, Alistair. Everyone has worked hard for it."

"Delay them," Alistair said. Which was easier said than done. "I think Melda can delay them for today, at least."

They stopped as Angel's voice cracked out. "Then find her so we can all get back to work."

Alistair walked over to the group. "Is there a problem?"

Barry ignored the frown from Angel. "We've lost contact with one of our team," he said.

"Lost contact?"

"Her link dropped out."

"Inside the settlement?"

How had they gotten in? To the Zellites, a dead link meant only one thing. Ort. Alistair couldn't stop his sigh. Two in two days.

"Outside."

"How long ago?"

"I was talking to her. She cut out."

Alistair thumped his empty mug down onto the table. "I told you to stay, told you that I would give you a security talk this morning. For someone in security yourself, you are stupidly careless." Newcomers. They always thought they knew everything. "I'll get weapons." He stalked off without waiting for Barry to speak.

This time he grabbed the ax and the six-meter-long pole they kept for outside trips. It was hard, and strong, and he could use that as a secondary weapon, or for things like pushing cutter leaves aside.

He hoped they wouldn't need it.

"Where was the last signal from your missing person?" he asked as he, Barry, and Cam left in the aircar. He didn't ask what the missing person was doing wandering around, on their own, in the cold, early morning. Especially not after the salynxes. That would come later.

Barry pushed the location through.

It was close to where one of the miners had disappeared two weeks earlier.

Alistair tapped the screen. "They're watching us. They've been there before."

Cam leaned over to look. "If you say so. It looks like dots to me."

"Who are they?" Barry asked.

"The Ort." He didn't expand further.

Barry looked at the dots. "You're telling me there's another company here and you haven't reported it?"

"We tried to." Back when his eyes had first been damaged. "We were informed that no one besides us had a right to this world. It was intimated that we should remove any opposition." He hadn't been specific about the details when he made the initial report. After all, no one wanted to be thought crazy.

"Another company trying to muscle in on our territory is not something we take lightly."

"Nobody said they were another company," Cam said.

"Who are they, then?"

Alistair said, "Locals, most likely. Objecting to Santiago muscling in on their territory."

"There are no locals. You should remember that we have the rights to this world for another two weeks. If another company is here, we have a right to sue them. You could have been gathering evidence." Barry glared at Cam. "You're the lawyer. Surely you know that much."

Two more weeks of this. Alistair was tired of the Santiagans already.

The aircar beeped. They were coming up to where the signal had dropped out. "It's a long way out for someone on foot."

"She had a personal rider."

"You came prepared." A personal rider was a small platform with a motor on an antigrav unit. The rider used balance and skill to stay upright. They could have used a few of them to get around over the last two years. But the company hadn't offered that.

Alistair brought the aircar down. "Let's see what we can find." He took the pole as well as the fire-breather.

They found the rider easily. However they did it, the Ort had stopped the signal dead. Alistair turned a full circle. There was no one with the rider.

He was sure someone was watching him. Something.

"What are we looking for?" Barry asked. "Other than Talli, that is."

He wished he knew. "The Ort. Anything that looks odd, out of place."

"Big, long, green sticks on legs," Cam said.

A whisper of sound. White noise in his ear. Like waves coming into a shore . . . only . . . The white noise slowly turned into words.

"Ancestors . . . revered ancestors . . . Uncle's uncle's uncle . . . self is as our . . ."

Alistair turned.

A white cylinder propped up on four supports. As tall as he was. Two appendages jutted out from either side. A human, a woman— draped loosely in one of the appendages, hanging down, her head almost touching the ground. Something blinked at the top of the cylinder. Eyes.

They stood frozen, staring at each other.

Barry cried out as he reached for his blaster.

"No shooting," Alistair snapped.

But Barry had already fired.

Alistair felt the sting of something against his neck. He swung around.

Another white, cylindrical creature stood in the shelter of the cutter bushes, arms raised.

Barry dropped to the ground. Then Cam.

Alistair raised his hands. It was an effort. "We mean you no haarrrrmmm." The word stretched out.

He felt himself falling.

Alistair came around strapped to a table. An Ort leaned over him. White. It was white. Everyone said they were green. Even Alistair remembered them as green. Yet now they were white.

Something hissed against his arm.

He would not panic. He would not. Breathe.

"Why are you doing this?"

The Ort reared back, then leaned over him again. Before he could do or say anything, a wash of white noise swamped Alistair. It was followed by high-pitched cries. An emotion of excitement swept through him. Alistair's Ort didn't turn, just used the back two legs—now the front—to move, while the two now-back legs supported the movement. Alistair would bet it had eyes around the other side of its body too.

His Ort joined the three around a second table. Chatters and chirps filled the room.

Another wash of excitement. Was it some kind of emotional backlash? Was it genuinely excitement? Or was that just how his brain interpreted it?

"I don't understand any of this," came Cam's voice, weakly, from in the middle of the excited group.

The chattering grew louder.

"What did you do with Alistair?"

"I'm over here. Strapped to a table." He could slide out of the straps if he wanted to. They weren't tight.

All attention swiveled to Alistair momentarily, then back to Cam.

The chattering grew to a bursting crescendo. Suddenly all of them took off.

It was unnerving seeing them change direction without having to turn.

"I think it was something you said."

Alistair slid his body under the top straps, then sat up to pull his legs out. "They certainly got excited about something."

He crossed over to Cam's table, helped Cam to slide out. Barry and Talli were laid out neatly on the floor.

"Aren't we supposed to be woozy?" Cam rolled off the table. Staggered as he stood up. "I feel fine."

"Are you sure?" Although, he'd regained his feet faster than Mayeso had the night before.

Cam held his hand in front of his face, peered at it. "Yes."

"What did that achieve?"

"I can't see any whorls. Apparently, that's what you're supposed to see when you first stand up."

No one had told Alistair that.

"We were all sitting at dinner one night, trying to describe something, and Cadel said it was like the whorls he first saw when he woke up on the Ort's slab."

Slab made it sound like a mortuary.

"Anneke and Timoty agreed. But they said that mostly all you remembered was the wooziness, which comes after the cold circle on your arm." Which Alistair had just had. "Maybe it takes time." It was Alistair's second cold circle. "They might not have got to you yet."

"How do you feel?"

"Surprisingly well," given he'd just been dosed. Alistair turned to Barry, who was stirring, and hauled him to his feet.

Barry couldn't stay upright without support.

Cam took Barry's other side. "I've got him."

Alistair turned to Talli. She, too, couldn't stand on her own. "Let's go."

He stopped on the way to snatch up two of the fire-breathers lined up against the wall. Placing them against the wall seemed to be the traditional way to store them. There'd been four Ort, four weapons. Did that mean there were only four altogether? Or did they belong to the four in the room? And what had made them run off?

"I need to get fitter," Cam said as they staggered out like drunks.

"And I am really glad they have doors we humans can work," as Alistair stopped and lifted the bar to let them exit. "Imagine how silly we'd feel if we couldn't get out."

How long did they have? Would the Ort chase them? How far had they come?

"Do you think we'll all turn into Ort one day?"

If they did, Alistair was going to turn long before anyone else. "You'll have plenty of warning, anyway."

They'd panicked when the aliens had first started injecting them, and Mayeso and Timoty had spent weeks talking about divine retribution for what humans had done on the worlds they'd claimed. But you could get used to anything, especially when there was no alternative. The injections didn't harm them, or not outwardly. Besides, the Ort had saved Alistair's sight.

They kept to the cutter bushes, which the Ort loved so much. It was risky, but it protected them a little, for it was only the bovines that went near the cutter bushes, and bovines had territories. If they could avoid this area's bovine, they'd be fine.

When they'd run as far as they could, Alistair pulled them into the shelter of the next set of bushes. "Let's rest."

Cam helped Barry down, then flopped himself. "Can you see anything behind us?"

Alistair's ability to see Zell creatures had been one of the things that had kept this little community alive and whole—except for the doctor who'd been stupid enough to indulge in dangerous sports. The mortality rate on a trip like this ran close to fifty percent, according to the contract Alistair had signed when he'd taken the job. Even with a doctor and a machine. Security was an especially risky task.

"Not that I can see." The area was blessedly free of salynxes. The Ort's doing, or coincidence? Alistair checked his link. It was dead. "What about yours?"

"Dead too."

Would Angel's people look for their own? Would Melda raise the alarm now their links had dropped out?

"How long do you think we were out?"

"No idea," Cam said. "It didn't feel long."

Alistair thought not long either. "Midmorning," he decided. The heat trail he'd seen when he'd found Mayeso led east. Assuming the Ort hadn't taken them too far away from their own settlement, if they walked with the sun to their backs, they'd eventually come to the lake and their settlement. "We'll head for the lake."

He saw something in his peripheral vision. Grabbed one of the fire-breathers, swung around. It was one of the small, harmless rodents. He left it.

"Let's go. I'll take Barry this time." Barry was larger than Talli.

Barry struggled as Alistair pulled him up. "Aliens." He shuddered. "Big, green." He convulsed and fell against Alistair.

"Aliens," Talli agreed.

"Technically, we don't call them aliens," Cam said. "We're the aliens."

Aliens or Ort, maybe there were only the four of them, as beleaguered as Alistair's own little settlement was. That would explain why they didn't follow. It would also explain why they only attacked singly.

Although, they had taken four of them this time.

Maybe Alistair was just hoping.

9

NIKA RIK TERRI

They'd ordered the Songyan in Snow's name, just in case.

Nika chose a simple mod for herself for their trip down to the Songyan factory. Nothing too obviously designed by a master, but good enough to accompany someone who'd ordered a Songyan. Or as good as it could be given that it was done on the Netanyu.

Snow went for something more flamboyant. His red-gold hair turned into golden curls that hung down his back, with a golden beard to match.

"I really like that hair add-on you made," he told Nika.

Hair would certainly be one of the ways other modders would identify Snow's work in future.

"Wait till we get the Songyan," Nika said. "You'll have so much control. Netanyu add-ons are limited."

"I hope you're not going to use the new machine for that," Jacques said. "We're not risking our lives coming here just so you can play with hair. You have people to fix first."

They'd all come to see them off.

"You are aware that seeing us off the ship like this looks ominous," Nika said.

"It's so we recognize you when you come back on board," Carlos said. "That's providing you don't stop to mod yourself before you do come back."

"Don't tempt me, Carlos."

"We should put Nika and Snow's images up on-screen near the shuttle bay so we know who they are," he told Roystan.

"Might not be a bad idea," Roystan agreed. "But Josune will be with them. She's taking the shuttle down."

They'd chosen Josune, as her name was less likely to trip alerts than Roystan's was.

"She might not recognize them. Won't let them back on board the shuttle."

"Don't worry, Carlos," Nika said. "We'll use the secret code word."

"What's that?"

"Airy-fairy modder types, of course."

Carlos scowled. "You think you're so funny."

They were all on edge. Kitimat was too far into the middle of the legal zone to make any of them comfortable.

"We'll be as fast as we can," Nika promised. "A quick in and out, Carlos. Get the machine and go."

Songyan had messaged Snow days ago to say his machine was ready.

"We'll be fine," Josune said. "And we need to go now, to get down on-world during business hours. Otherwise we will have to stay overnight."

No one wanted to stay overnight.

"Don't forget the food I ordered," Jacques said. If there was landfall, Jacques wanted fresh fruit and vegetables. Nika had bought up big too. To date they'd only been able to buy basic modding supplies. Here on Kitimat they could get rare salts and metals, along with some of the rarer plasmas. Even transurides, for a price, and she'd bought all she could.

"Take care," Roystan said.

"We will. You can be sure of that."

"If you get into trouble, I'll come find you." It was a promise.

"What have you got as weapons?" Josune asked as the shuttle headed toward Kitimat.

Nika touched her heavy gold cross and showed her the mini-blaster she'd secreted under her shirt.

"You'll have to get up really close with that. You'll be lucky to hit anyone. What about you, Snow?"

He had a similar mini-blaster and a projectile weapon.

"I feel like you're going in undressed. They'll stop you leaving the spaceport with those blasters." Josune unlocked the weapons cupboard—even the shuttle had its own cache of weapons—and studied the contents with a frown. "Here, Snow." Handed him a sparker.

He stepped back. "I'm not going to use that."

"You shouldn't need to. It's just a precaution. To make me feel better. What are the chances you'll have to fire it?"

"What if it goes off accidentally?"

"Then you didn't put the safety lock on, and you deserve everything you get."

Josune waited with the shuttle for the supplies while Nika and Snow took an aircar to the Songyan factory.

Snow rubbed the palms of his hands together. "Our first Songyan." It was Nika's third, but she didn't correct him. She'd been just as excited when she'd ordered her first one. "I hope they're as good as everyone says they are."

They were better.

Nika had never been to the Songyan factory. Her machines had all been delivered, with an engineer to install it for her. She looked around the foyer with interest.

It was opulent, reminiscent of a company headquarters, only nowhere near the scale. Tastefully done, but then it needed to be. Their clients were high-end modders. To the left, elegant pearl-white couches made a U-shape around a gold-flecked marble table. In the center of the room, enclosed in a flexiglass display case, was a Songyan. An early model, by the look of it. The wall to the right was covered with images. She recognized them all. Famous mods, probably all done in Songyans. One of her designs was there. The first one she'd done on a Songyan, in fact. Maybe she should send them another image. One that more expressed her current capabilities.

They'd put her design right next to one of Samson Sa's.

She gritted her teeth.

Snow practically bounced up to the counter. "We're here to collect a genemod machine."

The receptionist looked at him warily. It would be unusual for any client to pick up an order, so Nika wasn't surprised at the wariness.

"A Songyan," Snow added helpfully.

"A Songyan." The receptionist reached up to scratch her beautifully coiffed head, stopped just short of doing it. An old habit. She hadn't had that hairdo long. "What name shall I say?"

She probably didn't even know whom to call for a pickup. Nika had a private bet with herself. They'd get one of the salesmen first.

"Bertram Snowshoe."

The receptionist's eyes widened.

"I'll let them know. Please take a seat. They won't be long."

She'd recognized the name. Nika hoped that was only for the infamy of collecting his own genemod machine. She looked around carefully. They were the only ones in the reception area. She unclenched her fist from around the cross. Grabbing the cross was getting to be an automatic reaction. She'd have to work to eliminate that habit. After they were safe.

She moved over to look at the Songyan. Snow paced around the reception. Stopped at the images on the wall. Tilted his head. "Nika?"

She came over to join him. "Not my best."

"They should get a more modern image."

"Yes."

"The black-and-white was good."

"Thank you."

Snow resumed his pacing.

Nika turned back to the Songyan. They hadn't changed much. They'd always been a glossy black box. The corners were more rounded nowadays, but otherwise this machine didn't look much different from the two she'd had in her studio.

Snow stopped to read the placard at the other end of the Songyan.

An exquisitely modded woman came out of the lifts. Nika watched her come. Dagar Songyan, whom Nika had modded four months before Tamati Woden had walked into her life.

She made toward them.

"Nika." Snow's voice was so high she looked around quickly to be sure nothing was wrong. "Do you know whose genemod machine this was?"

"It's the first Songyan my grandfather built." Dagar Songyan answered before Nika did. She held out a hand. "Snowshoe Bertram."

Snow sighed. "It's Bertram Snowshoe, actually. That's an administration error."

Dagar's eyes were on Nika. "And you are?"

Nika hoped her disguise would hold. "Nika James."

Dagar looked at her, assessed, then dismissed her as she turned back to Snow. "You're the apprentice?"

They'd never said he was an apprentice. Nika hadn't expected Dagar to be up-to-date on who was apprenticed to whom. Dagar didn't normally lower herself to know modders until they became known. She moved around to read the plaque. "Gino Giwari's." This was the box that had modded Roystan. "Does it still work?"

"Of course. It's a Songyan. We service it once a year."

How different was it under the box? If they could look at it, would they discover how Giwari had modded Roystan?

"Would you let us examine it for an hour?"

Dagar swung back to Nika. "Why would you want to do that?"

That had been a mistake. "Your mod is impressive," Snow said smoothly into the sudden tension. "Who did it?"

She preened. "Nika Rik Terri, of course." She glanced at Nika and back to Snow. "But come, my office."

"Of course." Snow sneaked a glance back at Nika, who shrugged. If Dagar had been farther away, Nika might have chanced a quiet "Standing appointment, once a year, on her birthday," but she was too close.

"But your own mod isn't too bad either," Dagar said. "Who did it?"

Nika was as affronted as he was.

"I am a modder. I do my own mods."

"My apologies, Mr. Bertram. I thought—" She didn't finish her sentence, so they didn't find out what she thought. Why would she think a modder didn't do his own mod? Because she knew he was an apprentice?

Nika had done her own mods while she'd been an apprentice.

Snow made a half-placating movement. "It's okay." He looked at Dagar. "We came for the Songyan."

"As to that," Dagar said. "It's been confiscated."

"Confiscated?"

"The Justice Department took it."

They'd walked into a trap. And spent time making small talk

while the trap closed around them. Nika opened a link, discreetly messaged Josune.

"The Justice Department," Snow said.

"Look, I don't know what you did, but it's not my fault they want to talk to you."

"We paid you for a machine," Nika said. "You said it was here, ready to collect. When did the Justice Department confiscate it?"

"Two days ago."

"And you didn't think to call us and let us know?"

"I rather expected you to call before you turned up." Dagar held out her hands placatingly. "The machine is built. You simply need to collect it elsewhere."

They couldn't leave without the Songyan. Roystan would die without it, but Nika needed answers. "Why did the Justice Department take it?"

"I have no idea." Dagar sounded as if she wanted the interview finished.

Nika wanted it finished too. The sooner they were out of here, the safer she'd feel.

"Agent Laughton said he wants to talk to you. He left his details." She pushed them through to Snow.

"Thank you." They said it—equally frostily—in unison.

Snow turned and marched out.

Nika hesitated. "Do you know where the Justice Department took the machine?" she asked Dagar.

"Back to his office, he said."

Nika nodded and followed Snow.

He was waiting at the lift.

"I bet you didn't get that reception when you used to visit."

"I never came here. They always came to me."

"I don't think you should mod her in future."

"I won't."

"Hold the lift," someone called, and jogged up to join them.

Sinead Agutter. Nika's own engineer. Not to mention another of her clients.

"Thanks." Sinead punched ground.

The fact that Sinead didn't recognize Nika was more disconcerting than Dagar not recognizing her. It made her feel like the nobody Dagar thought she was. She straightened her back. Leonard Wickmore and Alejandro had tried to ruin her life. They hadn't succeeded. She'd fight back.

"Nice hair," Snow said of Sinead's knee-length platinum locks.

"Thanks." Sinead appraised him. "Yours isn't so bad yourself."

The lift opened into the lobby. It was crowded, filling with people in gray-and-black camouflage kit.

Snow stopped. "The *Boost*."

Where had they come from? Although, the *Boost* had used the Justice Department before. Dagar Songyan had probably called them before she'd come out to greet them.

Nika punched the top floor, pulled Sinead back into the lift. "You don't want to go out there."

Sinead pulled herself free and gave her a cold look. "Excuse me," and stepped out.

The lift door closed.

"Was that Sinead Agutter? Your engineer?" Snow leaned back against the wall of the lift. He looked exhausted.

Nika nodded.

"What are we going to do?"

"Call an aircar," Nika said, and did exactly that. She sent another message to Josune as well. They had an aircar on standby, but the *Boost* crew might have found that. "Captain Norris doesn't take no well, does he?"

"It's bad for his reputation."

The lift door opened. There were four more black-and-gray camouflage suits on the roof landing pad. All four looked their way, and two started toward them. If they went back down in the lift, the mercenaries would suspect something.

"Do you have that sparker?"

"They've got blasters, Nika. They're trained too."

"And we've got an aircar coming in"—she checked—"three minutes. We don't want them following us." The sparker would take out all the aircars on the roof. And the lift. They just had to worry about the blasters. "I don't think they recognize us." She hoped. "They're probably stopping everyone." Josune had shorted out the Justice Department ship with the sparker. It would be nice if it would short out everything here.

She didn't want to think of what would happen if it didn't, but there was no time to make other plans.

She forced her breathing to normal. She should have linked to Josune, but it would be obvious if she did so now. *Don't think, act.* She stepped out, gripping the short cross of her necklace as she did so.

Now to get close enough to shoot them with it. All four of them.

"You are crazy, you know." Snow pulled out the sparker—discreetly—one-handedly while he waited, head slightly bowed.

He'd told her that before, and this plan relied on them being crazy enough for no one to consider them a threat.

"Please identify yourself," one of the mercenaries said while the other closed a hand around his blaster.

Nika looked him up and down with all the arrogance she could muster. She was, after all, on the roof of the Songyan building. "Shouldn't I be asking this of you? Who are you, and what are you doing on our landing pad? Where is your pass?" She looked around. "Where is your engineer?"

The mercenary looked momentarily nonplussed. The second

one laughed. "These people are all the same. Let's put it this way, lady. If you don't identify yourself, I'll shoot you."

Nika stiffened her back further and looked down her nose at him. "Dagar Songyan will hear about this. Don't think it won't go further. But for the sake of expediency, I'll identify myself." She indicated the approaching aircar with one hand, the other tightening around the tranq weapon. "I have an appointment, and my car is approaching. I don't have time to waste, so get on with it. Do you want the full ID, or will giving you our names suffice?"

Three of the guards turned to the watch the aircar. The one who'd threatened to shoot her reached for his identifier. "Full identification, if you don't mind."

As soon as he looked down to his equipment, Nika pressed the release on the tranq dart. "Now," she hissed at Snow.

Even a massive overdose like this took seconds to kick in, but it slowed the guard's reflexes enough for him to react slowly as Snow raised the sparker. He crashed to the ground. The other three guards turned, drawing blasters.

The electricity from the sparker jolted them into a macabre dance as Snow sprayed them all.

The lift behind them sparked blue before its lights went out.

Nika dived for the nearest prone figure, grabbed his blaster, and fired. Turned to the second and third and did the same. Four down. Too lucky. Would their luck last? She shut down the hysteria before it took control.

Snow raised the sparker again, aimed for the closest aircar. The resulting crackle of power was fierce. There were three cars on the roof, and the power arced from aircar to aircar, then arced farther to connect with a pole.

An explosion threw her forward, onto her knees.

Lights went out in buildings around them.

Snow was still standing. He looked down at the sparker. "I don't know why Josune likes these so much." His voice shook. His hands shook.

Nika did. "Josune's all about best weapon for least effort." And the one that passed most security scanners. After all, who'd expect anyone to carry a sparker?

Especially given the aftereffects. Her head hurt. Her eyes ached. Even her teeth ached. She scooped up a second blaster, tossed it to Snow. "Someone will be here soon."

She tried to link in. The link was down. Realized the aching jaw was because the sparker had burned out the connection. Snow's too, for a spot on his chin was blistering. They'd both need time in the Netanyu.

Maybe she didn't know why Josune liked sparkers so much, after all.

An aircar descended to settle on the roof.

Their cab. They ran for it.

Only to be stopped at the door.

"Please identify yourself," the aircab said. "This car is hired."

What? "I hired you."

"This car is hired," the aircab repeated again.

"Our links are burned out," Snow said. "It doesn't recognize you."

Surely they weren't trapped on this rooftop. "Iris scan," Nika told the aircar, and prayed it was smart enough to check the scan against her ID. Some cars required the same ID you'd used to place the order.

The car took what felt like forever identifying her. She imagined the mercenaries from the foyer pounding up the staircases. They must know that whoever was on the roof had been taken out. Or maybe they didn't, for after all, no doubt they had problems of their own.

The aircar door opened.

Nika fell into the seat, Snow close behind.

"Spaceport," Nika said. Don't think about how she'd just killed three people.

The aircab drew smoothly away.

"Too easy," Snow said. "That was way too easy."

Except the last bit, which had been nerve-wracking, but they had gotten away. "I'll take easy every time, if it works." Nika watched the dark roof until it was out of sight. She shivered. Snow was right, though. It shouldn't have been that simple. She half expected to hear someone knocking on the roof of the aircar, then blasting their way in.

But they didn't.

"Sometimes the luck falls our way," she said. It wasn't over. They hadn't got the Songyan yet.

The aircab made it to the spaceport without incident. Nika let out a breath of relief as they exited and saw *Another Road*'s shuttle on the tarmac in front of them.

The jets were firing. The shuttle was ready to take off.

Thank goodness.

"Now we're safe," Snow said.

Even as he spoke, the shuttle lifted from the tarmac in front of them.

10

JOSUNE ARRIOLA

A cargo of fresh food was waiting when their shuttle landed. Josune had just finished loading that when two pallets of engineering goods arrived, followed by three crates of modding goods.

Josune smiled. Nika was stocking up. Judging by the insurance on one of the loads, there were some transurides in there. Good. Surely all this would help Roystan.

She stopped smiling.

This had to work.

There was no point worrying about the things she couldn't control. Worry about what she could.

Nika linked in to let her know they'd arrived at Songyan Engineering. An hour to get there, another to get back.

Josune called Roystan. "I'm going to grab something to eat."

"I'll tell Jacques he should have packed a picnic box. Take care."

"Believe me, I will."

It would be nice to hope that one day they'd be on a ship where you didn't have to watch your back all the time. What must it have been like to be Roystan, with eighty years of hiding, eighty years looking over your shoulder. Never able to say who you really were. Always worried someone would find you.

She chose a place to eat where she could see out onto the tarmac and where she could face the direction of *Another Road*'s shuttle. She had the screens, but machines could be hacked.

The food place sold everything from sandwiches to a full meal, from water to alcohol. Josune took a seat at the shared table at the window and ordered coffee and a sandwich. Her own shuttle was at the back—they weren't paying premium rates—but she could see it. She could see it even better on the small handheld she put discreetly beside her plate. Not that she needed the handheld, or the view. The shuttle was wired to warn her if anyone went near it. She could start the launch sequence from the handheld if she needed to. Not that she planned to, but if anything went wrong, it was always nice to have a ship ready to take off the moment you entered it. Or, for that matter, a shuttle that could take itself off if, say, Nika and Snow were on board and couldn't pilot it. It could lift off and take itself back to *Another Road*, where it would autopilot itself into the hold.

The table was crowded. There was something about spacers. They liked to see the ships. Half the people eating wore business suits, the other half coveralls.

A flower seller came into the bar. "Scented flowers. The Kitimat rose. Native to this world." She thrust the basket forward. "Here. Smell the roses. Take life back to your ship."

The scent rose, hot and pungent.

It reminded Josune of a flower the crew of her original ship, the *Hassim*, had found on Sassia. She blinked, shook her head. Sometimes she didn't think of the *Hassim* crew for days, but the occasional memory still welled up, overwhelming her.

She loved being on Roystan's ship, but she missed the crew of the *Hassim* too.

The woman next to Josune—her face permanently burned, as if she spent more time looking sunward than most humans—bought one. She touched a petal reverently. "We don't appreciate them enough. It's the one thing I miss in space."

"You don't grow your own?" Josune asked. *Another Road* grew herbs Jacques claimed he couldn't do without. Jacques hated tending them, though, so it was a task Roystan allocated out on rotation. Jacques had been throwing out hints that since modders liked growing things, they might like to grow vegetables as well.

Nika had replied, "Sure. We could do that, Jacques. Although, we'll probably mod them. What do you think, Snow?"

After which Jacques and Carlos had taken over Nika and Snow's gardening tasks for the next week, just in case they got ideas.

The woman beside Josune shook her head. "On our ship aeroponics is for protein. Edible only."

"That's sad." Even the *Hassim* had grown flowers.

A shuttle landed. The Justice Department logo was emblazoned across the side, half the height of the shuttle.

Josune hid a shiver. It wasn't after them. She was stupid to worry.

A woman in an immaculate cream suit with the distinctive collar of the Justice Department came out to stand at the entry, almost before the ground was cool enough. The soles of her feet must have been burning.

Figures dressed in suits branded with a symbol Josune didn't recognize moved up to stand on either side of her.

Interest around the table sharpened. Josune heard a few murmured "Paola Tekes" and "Honesty Leagues." Even those who hadn't been looking outside before looked up.

"Who's Paola Teke?" Josune asked her companion.

"A Justice Department higher-up. She reports directly to the board." The woman leaned forward, as interested as anyone else. "This must be those agents they caught." She looked back at Josune. "Justice Department agents. They were on the make."

That sounded like every Justice Department agent Josune knew.

"The Honesty League got hold of it."

"The Honesty League?" She'd never heard of them. Or maybe she had. They'd been on the news vids recently.

"The Justice Department is taking the agents to trial. If they don't, they'll prove the Honesty League is right, and the Justice Department is corrupt through and through."

"And so they are," a spacer from midway down the table said. "They do terrible things."

"There are some bad apples," the woman next to Josune conceded. "And it's getting worse, but they're cleaning them up."

Josune would bet she had never worked on the rim, or far away from the main populated worlds.

"It has to be bad if the Justice Department are hauling them in," the spacer from down the table said. "Lucky we've got the Honesty League is all I can say."

Josune was going to find out more about the Honesty League. Maybe she could send them vids of their own recent clashes with the Justice Department. If they were any good, maybe even the vids from the *Hassim*.

Paola Teke entered the shuttle. Not long after that an aircar dropped down, hovered at the entry. The Honesty League followed.

Everyone groaned.

"I wanted to see those lying scum," the woman next to Josune said.

"Not going to show their own," the spacer from down the table said. "They've probably bought a couple of contractors from a cattle ship, and they're pretending to be Justice Department people. Wouldn't surprise me to find they haven't arrested anyone at all."

He might even be right.

"Wouldn't be too bad," the woman beside Josune said. "They'd be in jail, then, eating at the Justice Department's expense."

"Lady, do you know what the jails do with their prisoners? They hire them out to merc ships."

"Not going to be an option much longer," another spacer said. A company man, but he'd nodded emphatically at everything the other man had said, so Josune thought he had a better idea of how the Justice Department really worked than the woman beside her did. "The war at Merkle is finished. So is the one at Newest Hebrides. Hard pickings if you're a merc ship nowadays. Or so I've heard."

"They won't care. They'll just make up another war."

Josune wouldn't put it past the companies to manufacture a war just to get rid of people they didn't want. Although, why would they bother? They could murder them and the Justice Department would turn a blind eye. Might even help with the killing, for a fee.

Her jaw-link buzzed. Nika, to say the Songyan wasn't there and that they'd probably walked into a trap.

She lost track of the conversation around the table. Nika and Snow were an hour away. What could she do to help? Find out where their enemies were.

She ran a quick check of the media for Leonard Wickmore. The media always reported on executive whereabouts.

He'd arrived on Kitimat three days ago.

Surprise.

Josune called Nika.

There was no answer.

She called Snow.

No answer there either.

Josune found a quiet spot to call *Another Road*. "I can't contact Nika or Snow. Neither are answering my calls, and they're an hour away by aircar."

"Stay put for the moment," Roystan said. "If they're on their way, you might need to escape quickly."

Would they have the Songyan with them?

"Wickmore's on Kitimat. I haven't checked the whereabouts of the *Boost*."

"I'll do that."

"Thanks."

Josune's security alert buzzed. She opened a screen. Figures moved around the base of the shuttle. She pushed it up to Roystan. "I need to check this out."

"We'll watch from here."

Josune left the link open as she made her way rapidly across the tarmac. She paused in the shadow of the recently landed Justice Department ship, but two armed Justice Department agents moved her on.

"Nothing to see here, go back inside."

"I'm heading for my shuttle," Josune said.

"Well head on, then."

They watched her go.

All the while Roystan kept up a monologue in her ear. "Three people in combat gear walking around the shuttle. One of them has just tried the entry. He's moved away. Don't go too close."

Carlos's voice came in over Roystan's. "We checked the *Boost*, Josune. They're at Kitimat."

Surprise on that one too. She'd bet money the people walking around the shuttle were from the *Boost*.

Josune risked a glance over her shoulder. The two Justice Department agents still watched.

Nearly there. She veered sideways, to a smaller shuttle than hers, and was finally out of sight of the agents. She slowed, edged around the shuttle.

"Still only the three people," Roystan murmured in her ear.

"I can't get any closer." Maybe she should walk up to them and ask what they were doing?

"I know what you're thinking, Josune. Don't. They'll be armed."

She was armed too. She had her sparker. Except if she used that, she'd destroy the electricals in the shuttle—and in those around it—which would achieve nothing. Maybe she could sic the Justice Department agents on them. Which would do exactly nothing except draw attention to them. Even if she fought and won, she still had to wait for Nika and Snow to arrive. Longer if they didn't.

"I'm going back inside. Let me know if the *Boost* takes off. If it does, we know they'll have Nika and Snow. If Wickmore leaves, we know they are with him. There is no point in me heading out yet." There was nothing she could do for the moment except keep watch on the situation.

"Good."

She went back to the same eatery she'd left from. A new batch of spacers occupied the long table. Josune put the handheld down and watched the three intruders at the shuttle while she checked up on the aircar Nika had hired. That was a dead end.

She frowned down at the screen in front of her. One of the intruders leaned against the shuttle lock. The other two stayed around the back. Presumably so that the rightful owners of the shuttle wouldn't see them until they were at the door.

She linked in to *Another Road* every five minutes to let them know she was still safe.

The sun set with a suddenness that reminded her Dartigan Capitol was on the equator.

"Should we turn on the external lights?" she asked Roystan during the next call.

"I think we'll have to," Roystan said. "If we want to see what they're doing."

"Next time I'm putting infrared lights and cameras on the outside." You couldn't be prepared for everything, but while on the *Hassim*, she'd learned that once you found a vulnerability, you needed to fix it.

Roystan sighed. "I'd give anything for us not to have to run."

So would Josune. Just to go exploring without forever looking over your shoulder would be bliss.

She spent the time setting up a request for takeoff, saved the request, and left it ready to send. She then programmed the shuttle so it was ready to take off automatically. They would have to leave in a hurry, and possibly fight their way into the shuttle. Time spent starting the engines would be time one person didn't have to fight.

Maybe next time they'd buy one of those newer engines that stayed warm all the time.

Forty-five minutes after Josune had lost Nika's signal, a shuttle landed between the Justice Department and *Another Road*'s shuttle. Ten people in combat uniform piled out.

This time Roystan called her. "Are you seeing this?"

"I wish I wasn't."

"Time to abandon the shuttle, do you think?"

All Nika's supplies, including the heavily insured pack that was probably transurides, were on board. She'd need that for Roystan. "Jacques ordered lavaberries. He says they're a local delicacy and you must eat them fresh. It'd be a shame to dump them just because some mercs got in the way."

"You can't take on ten—thirteen—armed mercenaries, Josune."

"If we wait long enough, the spaceport authorities will question why the mercs are there." It had to be worrying them.

"You think you can wait it out?"

"Maybe. But it shouldn't stop us delivering the goods." Josune pushed through the request for takeoff. "I'll send this one up on auto, hire a separate shuttle for us."

"I'm not sure—"

"Already done, Roystan."

Clearance took fifteen minutes. She'd have to remember that, factor it into any future escapes.

In that time the mercs spread out, covered the area. There was one positive to this. The gathering implied Snow was still free, given he was the *Boost*'s target.

Two of the mercs joined the guard at the door. One of them started to pick the lock. This might turn out badly.

Josune linked in to Roystan again. "I am sending the shuttle up before they get in. Even if we don't have clearance."

But blessedly, then, clearance came through.

She pressed for auto-takeoff.

"Watch them scramble," Carlos said gleefully, through Roystan's link, as the mercs moved back.

Right now Josune would prefer the blast to take them out. That would make fewer people to worry about later.

The mercs scrambled for their own shuttle. She smiled. They weren't going to catch it. They might violate the clearance, but by the time their shuttle had warmed up, it would be too late.

As they did so, two people stopped in the shadow of the shuttle Josune had loitered around earlier. Nika and Snow.

"Call you back," she told Roystan, and ran out of the eatery.

She slowed when she got outside—she wanted to run—forced herself to walk naturally, albeit briskly, toward the shuttle the two now sheltered near. Just like any spacer heading for their own shuttle.

"But we're not on it," Snow said as she got close enough.

"There'll be a reason."

Nika understood. She always did.

But Josune wished they'd both move back. Out of sight of the camouflaged mercenaries entering the shuttle not far from them. They'd both been so busy watching *Another Road*'s shuttle they hadn't seen what was going on around them.

She pitched her voice to reach them. "Keep moving."

They didn't hear her. Or didn't realize she was talking to them.

"Nika. Snow."

She had to call them three times before they heard her.

"Veer left."

They veered left, but it was too late. Someone in the shuttle would have been watching. "Do they know what you look like?"

"Unfortunately."

Josune kept pace with them but didn't join them. She called up an aircar. Naturally, it refused to come anywhere near the shuttles. "We have to go back to the cab pickup. That's to your left."

"We just came from there," Snow said.

A pity Josune hadn't known that. She could have met them there. "What happened to your links?"

"Fried."

That would make communication difficult. Josune glanced behind. Nothing. "Maybe quicken your pace."

They did.

A mercenary ran out in front of them.

Josune raised her blaster. Fired.

The merc went down.

They started to run.

Two more mercenaries ran in, one either side. Snow turned to one of them and pulled out a blaster. They veered away.

"I think they heard about the sparker," Nika said.

Josune fired two quick sparks from her own sparker. "They haven't heard about mine."

"I hope our aircar still works," Snow said. "You've probably shorted everything out for miles."

"Come, Snow. I'm not that bad."

They reached the aircab pickup.

"I am."

"Behind you," Josune said as another merc came close. She fired her blaster this time.

The aircar dropped.

They flung themselves into it. The door took forever to close. At least three seconds. Josune ID'd herself and told the aircar to take them straight up.

Hot blaster fire made the door glow.

The aircar, thank goodness, wasn't damaged enough to not take off.

Josune switched on every screen she could. A thin rod was in the hand of one of the mercenaries behind. "They have a sparker too." They wouldn't even have thought of using it if Snow hadn't used one first.

"Increase speed to maximum," she ordered the car. "Continue up to level three." The highest level they could take the aircar. It was risky, because if the sparker got them, they'd hit the ground hard enough to die.

Please let them be out of range.

"Level three incurs a surcharge of seventy-five percent," the air-car told her. "Please confirm."

Blue fire sparked. Kept sparking.

"Confirmed," Josune said, and held her breath as the merc she'd pointed out raised a thin rod. They should be out of range now.

Blue fire sparked out beneath them, kept sparking.

Their aircab kept rising.

Even if the *Boost* had paid someone to ignore them here at the spaceport, the authorities couldn't ignore that. It might even curtail some of the *Boost*'s activities. Those sparks would cut power to a considerable part of the spaceport, and it was all on the security vids. At least until everything had gone black, that was. The smartest thing the mercs could do would be to lift in their shuttle and go back to the *Boost*.

If they could even do that after the spaceport fiasco.

She turned to Nika and Snow. Both had red, blistering burns on their left chin.

"Sparker did that?"

Nika nodded. "And it hurts like anything."

"You must have given them a full dose." It was lucky they hadn't been in an aircar. At least she thought they hadn't, for they were still alive.

"It shorted out our original cab. Not that we planned on taking it."

Snow handed his sparker to Josune. "This thing is dangerous. I don't know how you use it."

She'd given him Reba's, which was twice as powerful as her own. "It must have caused some damage."

"It did."

"Where to now?"

"We still have to collect the Songyan," Nika said.

Josune had expected that. "So tonight we raid Songyan." Where people would be waiting for them to turn up.

"It's worse than that. We're going to the Justice Department."

They hired a room where they could talk in private.

"And eat," Snow said. "I am starved."

Josune called Roystan, let him know they were safe for the moment and they'd look at hiring a shuttle as soon as they thought safe enough. It felt dishonest, but she didn't tell him about the Songyan.

Nika might have noticed the omission, but she didn't comment. "What about the Boost? Will it go after Roystan?"

"I'm hoping the Boost will have enough to worry about. Kitimat will want compensation for what happened earlier."

You didn't hide ships around a world as busy as Kitimat. Each ship was assigned an orbit and monitored. The Boost would have to break its own orbit to attack *Another Road*. Captain Norris would be stupid to try. Not only was the Justice Department headquarters on the planet, but every company had offices there as well. Large offices. Any attack on any ship would force the Justice Department to act.

Or maybe not. Put credits in the right hands and you could get away with anything, as they knew well.

Agent Alistair Laughton's contact details that Dagar had sent through to Snow were lost until he got himself a handheld, and in this world of up-to-date technology and cutting-edge mods, they were hard to come by. You got handhelds out near the edge of the legal zone, where technology was limited, and you always needed backups.

"They know we're here," Nika said. "They knew we were going to Songyan. Which means they'll most likely know we have to go to the Justice Department. They are one step ahead of us all the way. We're walking into a trap."

How did you avoid a trap like that? "Let's not forget Wickmore's here too. Somewhere."

Nika shuddered. Josune was sorry she'd mentioned it, but it needed to be said. "I'll see if I can find where Laughton's office is." She opened a screen.

Old news about Alistair Laughton wasn't hard to find. Two years ago, he'd been suspended. The media had been full of it. Did he even work for the Justice Department anymore?

"I've got a bad feeling about this." Sometimes the direct way was the best way. Josune called the Justice Department.

It was a machine at the other end, not a human. "Please state which department you wish to speak to."

"General inquiry," Josune said.

After five more questions, she got through to a real person. "I have a sample I promised to send to Agent Laughton." Josune should have thought up a better excuse before she called. "I don't know where to send it."

"The address is on the site," the person at the other end said.

She was glad she'd looked up that much, at least. "Yes, but there are five addresses there. I don't know which one to send it to."

"Agent Laughton works out of the head office," and they closed the link before Josune could ask any more questions.

"Friendly." Nika prodded at the burned-out link in her jaw. Moved over to the mirror in the bathroom to look at it more closely. "We'll have to get these fixed, anyway. If we walk into the Justice Department and can't ID ourselves, they'll stop us at the first security barrier. Oh!"

Josune and Snow both leaned over to look into the bathroom. Nika was staring at her image.

"Are you alive in there?" Snow asked.

Nika turned. "I know how we can get into the Justice Department. We'll mod ourselves. And I know just who we're going to look like."

11

LEONARD WICKMORE

Leonard Wickmore was in the gym when Dagar Songyan called. "Snowshoe Bertram came by. Unannounced."

If Wickmore had been Snowshoe, he wouldn't have announced himself either. "When?"

"He just left."

"You sent him to the Justice Department?"

"Yes. I gave him Agent Laughton's details."

"Was Nika Rik Terri there?"

"No. He had a woman with him, but it wasn't Nika. I would have recognized her, and she would have recognized me. She's my modder, you know."

If Nika's boyfriend, Alejandro, couldn't recognize her at first glance, then Dagar wouldn't either.

"She was quite—" Her connection dropped out.

Wickmore didn't bother to call back. She'd given him what he needed. People like Dagar Songyan were generally a waste of space, but Dagar's greed for the exchanger kept her useful. Without her he wouldn't have known about Snowshoe's order or that Laughton had confiscated the machine.

It would take half an hour to get from the Songyan factory to the Justice Department, longer if they stopped to plan, which they were likely to. But they were coming, and they'd be here tonight.

Finally.

"Right into my trap, Nika. Right into my trap."

Provided Alistair Laughton didn't get in the way. Laughton had a habit of popping up in places he wasn't meant to. He should have been out of the picture by now. Wickmore hadn't wanted to close the net on Lisbet Cross-Laughton. She'd been useful, but in the end, it had been more convenient to expose her in an effort to frame her husband. If only that blasted boss of his had done the right thing and sacked him, as any sensible person would have done, instead of trying to save his career. And now he was back, as large as life, and as annoying as ever.

Wickmore didn't want Laughton in the way of tonight's capture. He called Manny, who'd been watching the agent.

"Where's Laughton?"

"At home. He's ordered takeout. Looks like he's settled in for the night."

Good, although he was likely to get a call very soon that would interrupt his dinner plans. "We're ready to collect. Have everyone assemble to meet me in fifteen minutes."

"Consider it done."

Laughton would go back to Dagar once he realized the Songyan was gone. She'd mention she'd called Wickmore. Hell, he'd probably get it from her link records. They didn't need interfering agents who couldn't be bribed getting in their way. It was time to get rid of Laughton. Permanently.

"And Manny, start Operation Pest Control."

12

ALISTAIR LAUGHTON

Alistair hadn't eaten a home-cooked dinner since he'd arrived back on Kitimat. Cam provided takeout every night.

"You realize I can't get used to this," Alistair said. "I can't afford it."

"Ask Paola for a pay raise."

Alistair knew how that request would go.

"Surely you didn't buy takeout every night before you came to Zell?"

"We had a kitchen staff. Or we ate at restaurants. I only discovered takeout when I left home."

Alistair could see by the way Cam twitched that they were creeping into forbidden territory again. What could be so taboo that talking about him being from a wealthy family was off-limits?

"I'm grateful for the food, anyway." Alistair served dinner.

They ate in silence for a while. Off to the north, a solitary drone showed black as it made its way across the sky. The drone was higher than it should be. Someone was about to cop a heavy fine. Aircars and drones had strict, segregated flight paths, and the maximum drone height was five hundred meters.

Cam followed his gaze. "What are you watching?"

"The drone." A red spot, cooling down into purples as the night deepened. "I can probably see it more clearly than you can."

"I can't see a drone at all."

Rather like walking into Leonard Wickmore's office with regular eyesight and not realizing he had weapons hidden in the walls. He'd been to Wickmore's office several times over the years. All it would have taken was one command. Alistair shuddered. He rubbed his eyes. "Do me a favor, Cam. Don't ever go into Wickmore's office on your own."

Cam blinked. "Let me backtrack." He ticked off topics on his fingers. "Eyesight. The view outside. Takeout for dinner." He paused. "How did we get there from here?"

"Eyesight. You don't want to see what's inside Wickmore's walls."

Cam helped himself to more food. "I thought for a minute you were going to say what's in his mind."

Alistair wasn't sure he wanted to know what was in Wickmore's mind. "For a long time I was convinced he controlled Woden."

"But you aren't now?"

"There's a fine line, Cam, where you have to step back and let others do the work because you're too biased. I couldn't let go of Wickmore as the bad guy, so I gave the case to one of my staff."

"You had staff? What happened to them?"

Good question, and not something he'd thought about. "I don't know." His had been a close-knit team, but no one had dropped by his office.

"Wickmore has a reputation, even among the companies." Cam pointed his fork at Alistair. "You don't cross him without consequences."

"He had that in the Justice Department too."

"Wickmore acted like he knew nothing about body swapping, but Dagar knew. Do you think it's real?"

Alistair honestly didn't know. "Someone's spreading rumors if it's not, for Wickmore reacted too, even if you couldn't see it. Maybe he's been listening to Paola and he's telling us what she wants to hear."

Or she'd been listening to him.

But to what purpose? Talking about body swapping wasn't something you'd draw attention to. Not if you were doing it. Even less if you weren't. Which meant he likely believed it.

Rik Terri had gotten herself involved in something crazy. Willingly, like Dagar Songyan had seemed to? Or unwillingly?

"I hope we find Snowshoe soon." They couldn't move far until they found him, for they had to remain close to the Justice Department in case he came for his genemod machine. "We need—" He stopped as the entry buzzed.

Paola, this time immaculate in a cream silk suit, clinging to the foyer door. "Hurry up, Alistair, and let me in. It's windy out here, and the building is swaying."

The sway was still her imagination, but it was windy tonight. Alistair sent the lift for her and buzzed her in. "If you called before you came, I'd have the lift waiting for you."

"If I call beforehand, people would know where I was going."

She entered the apartment indecently fast.

As she entered the living area of the apartment, the dot of red that was the drone came closer. It must be bigger than he'd thought if he could see the heat of it so clearly through the wall. Or it was closer than was safe.

A reporting drone? And Paola hadn't wanted people to know she was here. "Paola, I think you're being spied on."

Through the wall, the spot of red that was the drone blossomed and darkened. No, not the drone. Something had separated from it. Something hot. Coming toward the building. It took him a second to recognize the hot spot for what it was. A wasted second.

He pushed Paola back the way she'd come.

"Run, Cam," he yelled. "Run."

He hoped Cam was behind him.

An explosion rocked the apartment. Plastiglass disintegrated behind him. The inward force threw Cam forward and knocked Alistair and Paola off their feet.

The heat of the explosion made a mushroom cloud of red and yellow. The coolest part was on the floor.

The back of Cam's shirt was on fire. Alistair rolled him over, the smell of burning flesh making Alistair gag.

A fireball whooshed over them. Paola moaned. At least he thought it was a moan. His ears were ringing, other sounds deadened.

"Stay down. There's an emergency stairwell near the lift. Crawl toward it." He couldn't hear his own words.

His wall hangings were burning.

"What was that?" He thought that was what Cam asked.

Another explosion rocked the apartment. The lights went out. The building shuddered with aftershocks.

Paola would be feeling that sway now.

"Drone missile. Get to the stairwell."

Paola started to stand up. He pulled her down.

"Crawl. You okay, Cam?"

"What?"

Alistair pushed him toward the door.

This high up, the wind was fierce and the air thin. They didn't have a lot of time.

They made it out onto the tiny landing that was the emergency exit. Alistair slammed the door shut. The building specs indicated the landing was fire rated for two hours. He shook his head to clear his ears. Sound was beginning to come back.

"You've got to be kidding me," Cam said. There were no stairs, just a ladder. One side going up, one going down.

"Emergency exits are emergency exits," Alistair said.

Paola made for the down ladder. "Two hundred floors! We'll never get out."

Two hundred and fourteen floors. And no, they wouldn't.

"Go up." Alistair prayed to whatever gods might be listening that the company hadn't skimped on the building and that it was as structurally sound as the builders had claimed it to be.

Paola kept moving toward the down ladder. "The only way I'm going is down. We have to get out of here."

Alistair pushed her toward Cam. "A few extra floors won't make your landing any softer. You'll hit just as hard." The trouble with modules was that they were modular. Any holes, like emergency exits, were designed to stack over each other. If this top module had moved, they wouldn't get down to the next level.

The building swayed, tilted again. The three of them fell back against the door they'd just exited. If Paola had been on the ladder, she would have fallen.

They couldn't stay here. "Up," Alistair ordered. "Go."

Cam grabbed Paola's arm, guided her toward the up ladder, set her on the way, and started after her. "If anyone can get us out of here, Alistair can. He has—" Cam slid down the ladder he'd started up. Alistair caught him.

"Thanks . . . a plan. I'm sure." He started up the ladder behind Paola again. "Hurry."

Alistair linked in and called a pool car as he stepped onto the first rung. Let this not be the one time the car didn't arrive as soon as he called it.

Another tilt and the whole building shrieked. So did Paola. Alistair braced himself and stopped his two companions sliding farther.

A lot of the blast had been absorbed by stabilizers in the floor, which were designed to neutralize any external forces. It had wrecked the stabilizers but had saved Cam's life. Otherwise the force of the explosion would have killed him. Probably killed them all.

Unfortunately, the stabilizers were connected electromagnetically to other floors. With that connection broken, the top floors weren't connected to those below. It was only a matter of time before the building built up enough momentum for the floors to slide off. The floor was settling. Whether it would settle flat or tilt, Alistair didn't know. They were in trouble if it tilted. They were in trouble if it settled flat.

"Your foot, my face, Paola." Cam was more breathless than he should have been climbing a ladder. He was hurt and hiding it. "This is a Nika Rik Terri design, you know. If you scar me, you're paying the bill. I'll charge you what she charges me to fix it."

Something bounced off Alistair's head. Probably one of the shoes she'd scarred Cam with.

They couldn't afford to stop.

"Hang on tight and keep going. The faster you reach the top, the faster you're out of danger."

Then they were at the top, the three of them standing in the tiny space.

The exit door was jammed. At least it opened out onto the roof, not inward.

"Stand back." Not that there was anywhere to stand.

Alistair raised his foot, slammed it against the door. There was no room to get any power to the kick. He forced the door open the rest of the way with his shoulder.

They burst out onto the roof.

This wasn't the protected lobby where the aircars landed. It was the flat of the roof itself. The wind was almost strong enough to blow them away.

"Oh, God." Paola dropped to her knees, tried to bury her hands into the surface.

"Don't stand up," Alistair ordered. "Head toward the lift lobby." He crawled behind Cam, who was struggling.

The aircar approached the lobby.

Just in time. Just as ordered.

But the lobby was on the other side of the roof, which meant the aircar was too.

Could it land?

The roof tilted, stabilized. The aircar hovered trying to find a level surface. Alistair grabbed Paola and Cam to stop them sliding. Nearly slid himself.

"You called a car," Cam said.

"It seemed a good idea." He kept his grip on them both. They'd have bruises tomorrow.

If they made it to the next day.

The roof tilted the other way.

"Hold on." He used the tilt to slide across the roof, dragging them with him.

It took no more than five seconds, but those five seconds were the longest in Alistair's life. Finally they reached the lobby. They were out of the wind.

Alistair let Paola go and reached up to open the door of the aircar as it hovered a meter above the surface. Paola grabbed his legs, almost knocking him off balance. He steadied, then helped Cam through the open door. Paola staggered to her feet. Alistair scooped her up and threw her into the car behind Cam. A flailing foot forced him backward just as the building tilted again. He lost his footing, and his hold on the door. He grabbed in vain as he slid past the aircar toward the broken roof edge.

The roof teetered on an angle. Alistair didn't stop at the edge. He went over.

Paola's scream echoed behind him.

He hit an exposed beam. Grabbed hold of it.

Then the aircar was there, door wide open. A meter too far.

"I can't get any closer." Cam's voice was strained. "You'll have to swing over."

The beam he had a death grip on collapsed. The floor tilted the other way. He rolled.

The aircar swooped behind him. "Come on, Alistair. Hurry, hurry."

Another explosion rocked the building. Alistair was on his feet and running before the reverberations had stopped. He dived as the floor collapsed around him.

He caught the bottom edge of the open aircar doorway. The aircar tilted under the impact. His hands slipped. Cam grabbed him and held on. The aircar steadied. Alistair pulled himself up and inside. Cam's grip hindered rather than helped, but he was glad Cam didn't let go. He collapsed onto the floor, sucking in deep breaths. Paola slammed the door shut behind them as he lay gasping.

"State your destination." The monotone of the aircar.

"Justice Department," Paola said, and Alistair was glad he didn't have to answer.

"Only you, Alistair, would think to call an aircar." Cam put a hand to his stomach. "Remind me to throw up when I get back on solid ground."

"Take us to the nearest hospital," Alistair ordered the aircar. "Priority override."

"Alistair!"

"Hospital first. You can take the car on to the office once you've dropped us off."

Paolo looked at Cam and didn't argue.

The hospital took Cam straight in and wanted to take Alistair in at the same time.

"I'll wait till Cam's out."

He was glad he'd refused when the doctor drained the genemod machine two minutes after Cam had gone in.

"What's going on?"

"The man's a walking dellarine mine," the doctor said.

What did that have to do with it? "Don't touch the transurides." He didn't have his blaster, wished he did.

"You knew he had them?" The doctor rolled Cam into another machine.

"Yes."

"You're lucky I'm an honest man, or I'd be in heaven right now."

"What are you doing?"

"Preparing hu-skin. I'll fix his back by putting hu-skin on it, but I'm not touching his mod. Who knows what damage I could do."

"You're telling me he has to go back to Nika Rik Terri to be repaired?"

The doctor grunted. "Rik Terri. I might have known." He flicked switches. "I'm telling you to take him to a modder. Someone who's had more experience with transurides in quantity than I have. If he can afford mods like that, he can afford a decent modder."

"But you will fix his back."

"I just told you I would."

"Thank you."

The doctor shook his head. "You are lucky it was me. If you can imagine the temptation in that man's body."

"Thank you," Alistair said again.

The doctor moved on.

"Excuse me," an orderly said. "Visitors wait in the waiting room until patients come out of the machine."

After what the doctor had just said. No way. Alistair pushed through his Justice Department ID and stayed in the room with Cam. He leaned against the wall and called the Justice Department to report. The agent in charge—Dirk Cartwright—knew him. "You're not going to get involved in this, are you, Alistair? You know you can't work on a case that involves you."

"I've enough of my own work to do." It was the first friendly work voice Alistair had heard, not counting Paola's. He had fallen a long way.

"Where are you?"

"At the hospital. Agent Le-Nguyen was hurt."

Dirk grunted, glanced down at the screen in front of him. "Rookie," he said. "Sucks to be them, although I can't imagine Paola placing you with a junior. I'll get to you after we've investigated the scene."

"Thanks."

The doctor came by half an hour later. "There's a lounge outside where you can wait."

"I know."

"He'll be another hour."

"I'll wait."

Alistair leaned back against the wall, closed his eyes, and listened as the noises of the busy hospital flowed around him. He should go back to the office and report in. Or find a place to stay.

Cam had stayed by him in those horrible first months on Zell, when his eyes were healing and he'd worried he'd be nothing but a burden to the settlement. The least he could do was wait for him to come out of the machine.

The only time Alistair had been in a genemod machine recently was on the Santiago ship orbiting Zell immediately after their second capture by the Ort. For diagnostic purposes only, thank God. That was when he'd first begun to suspect that Santiago was trouble. That they wouldn't abide by the contract.

Angel had sent Barry and Talli up to the ship to be checked over by the ship's doctor.

"I want the other two as well," the doctor from the Santiagan ship insisted.

"I'm not going." Alistair had survived one treatment from the Ort. He could survive another, and he needed to understand what was happening here on Zell.

"He's hiding something," the doctor told Angel.

His eyes. He didn't want them touched. "I have work to do, and I don't want you charging for medical expenses I haven't asked for."

"It's also a security issue," Angel said.

Of course it was a security issue. "You've finally noticed."

"We are ready to work; you were stopping us. Barry sent Talli out to see what you were hiding."

Seriously?

"Thank you for the trust, Angel," Melda said. "Fifteen years of marriage and it comes to this. You don't even have the decency to ask your own partner what is going on." She turned away. "Enough discussion. Take your people up to their doctor. Leave my people alone."

She didn't see the contempt flash in Angel's eyes. Alistair did, and from the troubled way Cam's gaze met his, Cam had seen it too.

"You seem to forget." Angel's voice was ice. "I oversee the cleaning up here. If you get in my way—"

Alistair made his own voice mild. "I hope that's not a threat. Because I would like to remind you that under the terms of the contract, the head of the settlement is responsible for the settlement until completion of that contract."

"You work for a company. You answer to your superiors."

"Actually," Cam said, "most of them don't work for the company. They're contractors. The conditions of their contract are that they spend two years here, doing the work they are contracted to do."

And a lot more they weren't contracted to do, given the company left so many supplies off the semiannual supply shipments.

"They answer to the company-supplied person in charge. That's Melda." Cam looked apologetically at Melda. "While you may have to do what Angel says—if she's your superior—Alistair doesn't. He only does what you ask him to."

He shrugged at Alistair. "Contracts 101. Even a bad lawyer knows that. Sorry."

Alistair understood what the apology was for. Cam had left Melda in an awkward position. If Angel was her boss, Melda had to order Alistair to go with Angel. But Melda wouldn't do that.

"I'll go up with Angel and Barry," Alistair said. "The doctor can check me over. I know I got an injection." Though it hadn't impacted him. "We're not sure if Cam did."

Melda didn't thank him, didn't have to. They'd worked together for two years. She looked at Angel. "I want it under contract that we won't be charged for the doctor, or for you taking Alistair up to the ship and back. That you won't treat him, and you won't charge us."

Because they all knew how companies worked. Those medical expenses could cost the group their bonus.

"Fine," Angel agreed.

"And I want that recorded and signed before Alistair goes. No charges for any of this."

"Fine, I said."

"And I want to see it when you're done," Cam said. "I am the settlement lawyer, after all."

It was a pointed reminder that they still had a legal representative, and Angel would do well to not try to dupe them.

The doctor took Barry first.

Angel called the hospital fifteen minutes after Barry went into the machine.

"He's been injected with a virus," the doctor told her. "Gets into the blood. From there it goes to the heart and everywhere else. He's lucky we caught it in time. I'm clearing it from his system. He's also hallucinating. Hopefully he'll come out talking sense."

Alistair listened, trying not to worry about his own upcoming scan. What would the doctor do about his eyes? Alistair was used to the way he saw now, couldn't imagine what he'd do if they took the expanded sight away. Could they even fix it, or would his vision revert to what it had been like before the Ort had changed it? Destroyed.

He leaned back against the wall and tried to think of other things. Like, why had the Ort injected them all with a virus? It hadn't seemed to harm any of them. At least not yet.

"Is it contagious?" he asked the doctor.

"It doesn't appear to be, thank you very much, or this whole ship would be in lockdown."

After Talli, it was Alistair's turn.

"You've got the virus," the doctor told him when he came out. "It's all through your blood."

Alistair looked at the walls—his best indicator that he could see what others couldn't—and saw electrical circuits as warm lines. He looked around, trying to reassure himself everything was still functioning.

It was.

He tuned in to what the doctor was saying, didn't know what he'd missed.

"You've a knee that will give you real problems in around three years. You've a scar like an incision across the top of your head, it looks like an old surgical job. Barbaric. Your eyes—I suspect the virus got into them. You'll probably go blind. But I didn't fix a single thing. I can't. Your hastily cobbled together contract states no medical repairs, investigative scan only."

"Is he done?" Alistair hadn't noticed Barry, waiting on the same bench Alistair had waited on earlier.

"As done as I'll ever make him."

"We'll get something to eat on the way to my office." Barry led the way along a narrow passage. Alistair paused to let a crew member exit from a nearby cabin. He glanced inside. The cabin was small. He saw four bunks, two on two, so close they touched, with a single step between the bunk and the door.

The galley wasn't much larger than the room the crewman had come from. Barry dialed up two food packs. He handed one to Alistair—it was warm—and led them down another passage to an office that was no bigger than either room.

"They don't give you much space." They'd be extra cramped on this trip. There were fifty colonists to accommodate.

"Tell me about it." Barry sat down, tore the covering off his meal. "The ship's ninety percent cargo hold. It holds a regular crew of ten. With the twenty guards we brought along for this trip, plus Angel and me, we're bursting at the seams."

Alistair pulled the cover off his own meal. Where did they plan to house the colonists on the return journey? In one of the cargo holds?

"So," Barry said. "These creatures. Tell me about them."

The Ort. Melda had come up with the name, back when they'd finally accepted that their kidnappers weren't human.

"We can't call them aliens," Yakusha had said. "We're the aliens. They're local."

"We can't call them locals either. We're here as well, and we don't know where they are."

"The Hidden, then? Mantis?"

"You can't call them after a bug."

"Enough," Melda had said. "They are ort—'of this place.'" It was a word her grandfather had used.

"The Ort," they agreed, and they'd called them that ever since.

"There's not a lot to tell," Alistair said now. "Melda sent a report when we first became aware there may have been someone else on the planet." True, the report had been couched vaguely, but at the time they weren't sure of what was really going on. "I believe the reply was along the lines of 'deal with it.'" Alistair shrugged. "Then the incidents became more frequent. They kidnap someone, inject them with this virus, and we find them a few hours later." He shrugged again. "So far it doesn't seem to have harmed anyone." Not even him, and he'd been the first, nearly two years ago.

"And they're local."

"We think so. Tell me"—he should have asked Barry earlier—"what did you see?"

Barry shuddered. "Legs on a pole. A bright, leaching green that sucked the color out of everything."

Which was pretty much what everyone else had seen, right down to the color. Something in the ultraviolet or infrared must change that green to white.

"What do they want?" Barry asked.

"We don't know."

"Are they intelligent?"

They had transport with engines. Hospital rooms with padded benches. They'd damaged and repaired Alistair's eyes—without, so far as he could tell, a genemod machine. They'd deliberately injected humans with a virus. "What do you think?"

"They might have bitten us. Or maybe we just caught a virus. We don't know Zell all that well."

"That kind of denial will get you killed one day."

He hadn't wanted to believe either. Not the first time. When he'd finally faced up to it, he'd told Melda and Cam. Melda had initially flatly refused to believe it. Cam had shrugged and said, "At least they saved your eyes."

"What do they want?" Barry asked again.

Alistair shrugged. "It's going to take time to find out." Time they didn't have. Maybe this was how they got their two weeks. "Santiago has to decide their priorities. Is cleaning up here still the most important thing?"

He didn't mention the bonus. Barry might not know about that. Then again, he might.

Barry stared at the screen in front of him. Alistair couldn't see what was on it. "Let's keep this to ourselves until we decide what we're doing."

"I don't understand." It was better to know exactly what was being asked. "How do you mean, keep it to ourselves?"

The whole settlement knew about it, Barry's team, and the doctor. Whom else was there to tell?

"Don't tell anyone on this ship."

"I'm not the only one who's seen others. Nor are you. There's Talli as well."

"She's taken care of."

Alistair hoped he meant that differently to the way it came out. Barry moved over to the door—one step. "Let's go."

Alistair took his lunch with him.

As they walked to the shuttle, Alistair saw more crew quarters. It was a cramped ship. The warnings showed that this floor and the shuttle floor were the only ones with oxygen and heating. The shuttle bay, when they arrived, was surrounded by locked bulkheads. Each bulkhead had closed doors and huge, red warning signs. NON-LIVING CONDITIONS—NO OXYGEN, NO AIR.

"Those things were gross," Talli said, joining them at the shuttle bay. "What were they?"

Barry frowned at her.

Talli pantomimed zipping her lips. "Not a word."

"Talk about it on the ground," Barry said.

Alistair took a seat on the shuttle, looked around. It held eight people. "Is this the only shuttle you have?"

"We've two. The other one is back down on-world." Sixteen Santiagans on-world now. Alistair hoped they'd brought their own food. "They're small, but they get the job done."

"And they're armed," Talli said. "If we need to defend ourselves, we can."

Barry scowled at her.

Talli shrugged and sat in silence while Alistair finished the food Barry had given him earlier.

A thought niggled. This ship didn't have room to accommodate another fifty people.

Thinking about the past wasn't helping the present. Alistair looked at Cam's genemod machine again.

They'd reported Santiago, of course. As soon as he and Cam had reached the closest Justice Department branch office. They had both recorded the interview, although neither realized the other had until afterward. "Just in case," Cam had said. "Santiago legal team is worse than a pack of salynxes, and they'll rip you apart in the same amount of time."

How was the case going? Alistair opened his link. Once, he wouldn't have dreamed of checking up on a case that was none of his business, especially not one that he was personally involved in as a victim, but there was before Zell and after Zell, and each had different priorities. After-Zell Alistair had no compunction looking up the case.

Except he couldn't find it.

He went through the whole caseload for the branch office in the week before and the month after their report. Then he went through the caseloads of the two agents who'd listened so attentively and assured them they would deal with it. Nothing.

Their report, if it had ever existed, had gone.

Alistair stared at the screen. Santiago would take over the Ort as soon as they could, leaving fifty people who knew too much. How many other lonely worlds had this same scenario played out on, with the Justice Department blatantly ignoring the injustice?

He closed the link. The screen went back to what it had been playing before. News around the clock, updating and replaying the day's events. Just what your average patient wanted to see when he came out of a genemod machine.

The news feed changed to the spaceport. From the light, Alistair guessed it to be around midday, so not current. Paola waited with some sober-suited Honesty League people for a Justice Department shuttle to land.

Was that why the Honesty League had become so powerful? Because they were the only ones who could demand justice and get it at the moment? What would they say about how Santiago had treated the Zellites? About how the Justice Department had conveniently lost the report he'd made?

Maybe it was time to find out.

Alistair opened the recording he'd made of their meeting with the agents. Should he? Yes, if it helped him to save fifty people.

He forwarded the recording.

13

NIKA RIK TERRI

"We have ID," Nika said. "It's in the records on *Another Road*." And in her own personal database, as soon as she could access it. "Our old enemies, Agents Brand and Bouwmeester. We have Brand's full profile, right down to the fingerprints. I'll build a disposable lens that will fool the security for iris checks for both of us—it might obscure our vision a little, but we can take them out once we're in." She'd build extra sets in case they needed another iris ID to retrieve the Songyan. "We can build skin gloves over the top of ours so the fingerprints can work. Something temporary so it sloughs off in less than a day."

"You think you can do that?" Snow said skeptically. "If iris checks were so easy to do, everyone would be doing them."

"I changed Tamati's iris print."

"I bet that was permanent."

Nika grinned at him. "Snow, in olden times, before genemod machines, they put artificial lenses in the eye to correct sight."

"We're fighting for our lives, and Nika stops to give a history lesson."

"Some of those lessons have been useful," Josune said. "Giwari, for example."

"I thought when I apprenticed to Nika Rik Terri I'd learn cutting-edge modding. Not"—he flung a hand out, hit the wall—

"not continual repair and . . . and learning how to break into places by pretending to be someone else. I already know how to be a doctor. And I didn't really want to learn how to be a criminal."

Every word was a barb. And every word was true. Nika wasn't doing the job she was supposed to—teaching her apprentice.

"Do you want me to release you from the apprenticeship?"

Snow stared at her. "What? No. I earned this. You can't kick me out."

"I just thought—" What had she thought? She'd been feeling guilty all along because she wasn't training him properly.

Josune put a hand on Snow's arm. "Don't worry, Snow. She won't kick you out." She said to them both: "Our nerves are stretched. We've been on the run a long time. We're exhausted. Let's get this Songyan and get out of here."

Snow looked away, down at the floor. "Sorry, Nika." It was a mumble.

"I'm sorry too. I promise I will train you better."

"You are training me. Even if it is only how to clean genemod machines. Which I already knew."

"How do we get a machine to do these mods you want to do?" Josune asked.

Nika wasn't sure if Josune was asking because she was impatient to have it done, or if it was because she simply wanted to stop her and Snow.

"I don't know."

Neither did Josune.

"If I was to admit to being the criminal you are training me to be," Snow said, "maybe I could share some of the learnings from my short-lived commercial enterprise."

They both looked at him.

"You'll do anything for money on the docks," Snow said. "It's how you survive."

Except Snow, who'd refused to play by the dock rules. And that wasn't survival. When Nika had met him, he'd been about to be beaten up.

Josune was already scanning the link. "There's a whole street of modders here."

"Let's take weapons, then," Nika said. "We know how dangerous things can get down there." And their own supplies.

"Hey." Snow pointed to himself. "I'm the only apprentice. Okay? Even if you pick someone else up."

She thought he might be genuinely worried. "Believe me, Snow. You're a handful on your own."

"Good."

They stopped by a merchant and bought mutrient, Arrat crystals, naolic acid, and small amounts of minerals and other compounds that Nika insisted they needed. The next stop was an electronics shop. Nika bought two new links.

Then they went hunting for modding shops.

They weren't studios, not here. They were little more than body shops, and they reminded Nika of the shops she'd walked out of before she'd walked into Snow's studio. Back then she'd been arrogant enough to think of it as little more than a shop too.

How the mighty had fallen.

There were six modders in the street along the spaceport. By the time they came out of the sixth, even Snow looked dispirited. "Which one?"

Nika pointed to the one at the end of the street, the first one they'd looked at.

"But that's the strangest," Snow said.

"He has a Kedder in there," Nika said. "And it's in reasonable working order." She led the way back.

"This place gives me the creeps," Josune murmured to Snow. "I hope you know what you're doing."

"She usually does," Snow said. "Even if she is crazy."

The modder greeted them enthusiastically, rubbing his scaled hands together. The sound was like two pieces of wood rubbing against each other. "Back again. I knew you'd come back. I'm the best there is." He flexed his muscles for them, the way he had when they'd first walked in, and winked at Snow. "I can give you muscles you wouldn't believe." He leered at Josune. "A girl likes muscles."

Nika looked at the vest. She thought he might have cut the sleeves when he'd flexed his muscles once too often and the shirt had torn. He didn't understand his muscles, so hadn't had the mod long. There were other signs, too, that the mod was recent.

She tapped his chest. "Some people might like muscles, but what's your answer for the scales? You look like dried-out leather." She felt the rippled skin and frowned. "You used a low-grade coagulant. It won't last. The shine will be gone in a week."

"So you think you know about modding, do you. Let me tell you, little lady. This is my design, and I know how long it will last."

Nika turned away. "Did you use orange crystals for the blue? You've had this design for, what, three days? The color is already losing its luminosity."

"You're making that up."

"Check your hairline. Compare your scales." She took one of his hands and placed it against his scaled arm. "Color variation already. See."

"It's meant to be like that." The modder moved to a screen and examined his hairline. "I can't see any difference."

"Then you should get your eyes fixed. Snow, you note the variation. Using sodium salts gives a discoloration that fades. It's an effect that works beautifully for a short-term boost, but it doesn't last. Including orange crystals gives a longer intensity, up to a month."

"How do you know I didn't use orange crystals?" The modder was still examining his hairline.

Snow answered, "Because the scales would have an orange luminescence to them, not gray."

"Do you know how much orange crystals cost?"

"Of course we do," Nika said. "What's your name?"

The modder abandoned his hairline and opted for preening. "You can call me Drake."

Nika sighed and moved over the faded certificate on the wall. "Gregory Eames." She'd never heard of him. But not calling him by the name he wanted wasn't going to get them the use of the Kedder. "Well, Drake. We want to use your machine. We'll pay you for time."

He backed away. "I want nothing to do with illegal modding."

Out on the rim they'd probably have started talking price by now. Nika slapped down her ID. "Nika James. Body modder. Registered."

He looked from the ID to her, and back to the ID again.

"How much?" she asked.

"A thousand credits, and you don't use my supplies."

"Done."

"Nika," Snow said. "You're supposed to bargain. He would have taken it for seven hundred."

"Credit me with some brains," the modder said. "I would have insisted on at least eight. You really wanted to use a machine." He looked at the burn on her jaw. "And I don't do wiring either."

"We do." Nika said to Snow, "You're about to learn how. But first—"

"I know." He gave an exaggerated sigh. "We clean the machine."

"What do you know about Kedders?" she asked him as they pulled the inlet valves off. One of them was almost rotted through. She turned to Drake. "Have you another inlet?"

"If I had, don't you think it would be on the machine?"

Probably not. "Another hundred credits if you have one better than this."

She could see he wanted the money, wanted to lie.

"Okay. We're not using inlet three." She looked at Josune, who always carried some tools. "Unless you can pull something together."

"I'll see what I can do. It's liable to be expensive, given what he charges." Josune started to wander around the studio, stopped, looked at Drake. "I'd think a thousand credits would get us a private showing. Can I lock the door?"

"That'd be worth another two hundred credits," he said.

"Ten."

"Ten. What do you think I am?"

"Ten or nothing."

"Twenty."

"Twenty," Josune agreed, and pushed the credit through. After which she spent time working on the lock before she went back to searching the studio.

Nika was glad Josune was along. But then, if she wasn't, she and Snow would probably be dead. Or she would be dead, and Snow would be back on the *Boost*.

She scowled at the genemod machine. One thing they hadn't bought was disinfectant. "I suppose it's too much to hope you have some disinfectant in your cupboards."

"It'll be a hundred credits for you."

"Ahem," Josune said.

He looked at her sideways. "I'm dealing with her, not you."

"We're a team," Josune said. "Twenty credits, and there'd better be at least a liter."

"Half a liter."

"Half a liter and you get ten credits."

He came out with less than that. Nika paid for it but didn't quibble.

"Right," she told Snow when the machine was clean and washed out yet again. "Do you know how to put a jaw comms in?"

"You go to a tech shop."

And then came to a modder to have the scarring fixed.

"Here's what they do." She showed him how the wires connected to the nerves. The other modder watched over Snow's shoulder. "Now. Put me in and we'll see how good it is."

"Shouldn't I go first? I'm your apprentice."

"Snow. If you're not prepared to try something on yourself, don't try it on anyone else." She stripped quickly and climbed into the genemod machine.

Drake said to Snow, "That means if a client came in wanting wings, she'd give herself wings first."

Snow sniffed. "She wouldn't do wings. They were fashionable five years ago. Besides, only rookies do them."

The lid closed over her.

While Snow's jaw was being fixed, Nika used her new implant to call up the specs for Brand and Bouwmeester.

"Minor changes for you," she told Snow when he came out. "Just the hair and removing the beard." She indicated the lenses she'd designed from Bouwmeester's specifications. "They're yours. If anyone asks, say you've been modded recently." She didn't mention the finger pads she'd made. Drake was likely to make something of it. The less he knew, the better.

"By whom?"

Drake sniggered. "SaStudio, of course."

Nika glared at him, opened her mouth to argue, thought better of what she'd been about to say.

Josune spoke before Nika did. "Wouldn't pass. Not the right teeth or jaw." She touched Nika's arm gently. "Let's not kill him yet. Maybe later."

Nika blinked at her, then laughed. "You're right. Later would be better. Sorry."

"You're strange, you know that." Drake turned away to answer a call. "Drake's modding."

Josune leaned over to show her, privately, what she'd found while Nika was under. Alistair Laughton's office was at Justice Department headquarters, the massive building that took up five hundred meters of prime street across from the huge cultivated park that made up Dartigan Capitol's central district. The park was famous for its eating houses, all expensive, all in exquisite garden settings, showcasing cuisine from around the galaxy. Jacques would have fitted right in here. Agent Laughton could eat from a different world every day.

Josune pushed through the coordinates to three areas. She tapped the screen. "Office, seventeenth floor."

How likely was the Songyan to be in his office? Genemod machines weren't small, and unless Laughton's office was large, it would take up all the spare room. But then, the fact that Laughton had an office didn't bode well anyway. Senior people, in Nika's experience, could get away with more audacious crimes.

"It probably won't be in the office," Josune said, as if Nika had spoken aloud. She checked to be sure Drake was still on his call and not paying attention to them. "There are two storerooms. Both secure. Both on the ground floor. From what I can gather, all evidence is stored there. Not only that, Laughton has a distinct preference for storing his evidence in this one." She tapped it.

"I didn't know it was so easy to get information about places like that." Nika looked at Josune's expression. Maybe not that easy.

Drake finished his call. He rubbed his hands together, another dry, woody rasp. "I hope you're finished with my machine by morning. I've a client coming in at 9:00 A.M."

Plenty of time, given it was early evening. Still, Nika set the machine to do the fastest mod she could. "Cosmetic only for you," she said to Snow. "Hair and face. Not even the Adam's apple."

It hurt her soul to leave a body so badly underdone, but it only had to work for one night.

Snow fingered his curls wistfully. "I was getting to like this color."

Josune laughed. "Snow. Look at her face. You totally have your priorities wrong. And you, her apprentice."

"An extra dose of testosterone never hurt anyone," Drake said.

"I'm getting a headache," Nika said. "You first, Snow."

He crawled back into the genemod machine. "I hope you've got this hair color in your database, Nika. I might use it again."

She missed his original red-gold hair. She had that in the database. "I hope you have it in yours by now," and closed the lid.

14

NIKA RIK TERRI

There was a building site around the corner from the Justice Department, with a landing area for the heavy deliveries. It was big, it was private, and at this time of night, it was also deserted. Some cities had night building curfews. Dartigan Capitol looked to be one of them. Nika would have liked that on Lesser Sirius.

Josune opened the aircar door for them. "Don't take too long."

Now to see if their disguises worked. Nika checked her weapons, added new darts to the tranquilizer cross. They both carried the blasters they'd stolen from the *Boost*—surely agents would wear weapons, even at headquarters. She set her blaster to stun and made sure Snow did too. Killing Justice Department agents, even in retaliation, would ensure they were hunted down.

Nika adopted Brand's stance and swaggered down the street. Snow took on Bouwmeester's heavier stride. Good. A good modder should be able to imitate other bodies.

They hadn't even gotten to the security door, just inside the foyer, when two older agents stopped on their way out.

"Well, look who we have. The hicks from the sticks," one of them said.

Nika swaggered up close, the way she thought Brand would. "Ooh. Rhyming now, are we? Think we're so clever."

The agent who'd spoken stepped back a pace. Good, he was a

little nervous of Brand. Nika stepped forward again. This time he stood his ground. Maybe not so nervous, after all.

"We haven't got time for this." Snow's voice was almost too high. The deeper "gah" that followed was closer to Bouwmeester's growl.

The agent stepped around Nika, said to his companion, "They work on the edge of the legal zone, fancy themselves as hotshots because there's so much scum out there that their arrest record is high. They haven't worked out yet that only the dregs are sent out there, because they're expendable." He moved on, laughing at his own wit.

"Maybe you should have punched him out," Snow said.

Brand relied on her mouth. "That's more something Bouwmeester would do." They moved on to the security doors, stopped. There were six ID stations. Nika took a deep breath. "Here we go."

"This is not going to work," but Snow put his eyes to the scanner, his hand to the finger pad, and moved his mouth in time to the recorded words, "My name is Agent Calista Bouwmeester."

The entry opened in front of him. Nika did likewise.

They were in. Now for the next hurdle.

"Straight through to the end." Those were the instructions Josune had given them earlier.

The passage was long and straight, stretching the whole five hundred meters, and security could watch them all the way. Some of the staff traversing it even used personal riders.

"This building takes up a lot of real estate." Nika swallowed her nerves. Trust your work. They'd gotten in with no problems, hadn't they? "We should have brought one of Jacques's picnic packs."

They were still laughing when two agents stepped out of a cross corridor in front of them. Both pointed weapons—stunners, not blasters. Nika was learning to recognize the difference.

"Agent Brand. Agent Bouwmeester. You are under arrest. Please come quietly."

Was it their mod, or were they really after the two agents?

Brand would be the spokesperson. She had been on *Another Road*. "What's going on? We're Justice Department agents."

"And you're under arrest. Come quietly."

Snow reached for his stunner.

One of the agents fired at Snow's hand. "Away from the weapons."

"Gah." Snow shook his arm.

More guards approached from behind, running.

Nika lifted the cross with both hands, using one hand to hide the fact that she was curling her fingers around the cross. "What's the problem?"

"The problem, Agent, is that you are under arrest." The agent kept his eyes on her blaster, didn't notice what she was doing with her hands. At least something was going their way.

Nika turned to face the agents running toward them. Two of them. She fired darts quickly and turned back to the original guards. No one would expect darts.

"On whose orders?"

So much for a quiet break-in. They were attracting guards from everywhere.

"Where are you taking us?" Weren't they ever going to drop?

"Back to the nice, cozy jail cell you just escaped from. You're surrounded, so don't fight it." His finger on the stunner twitched.

Behind her an agent crashed.

Nika dropped to the floor, an imitation of what she imagined the agent behind her had done. Under the cover of her fall, she shot two quick tranquilizers, one at him, the other at the woman holding her stunner at Snow.

The woman put her hand to her chest. "What—?"

Snow took advantage of the distraction to kick the stunner out of her hand.

The second agent behind crashed to the floor.

Nika watched from under her eyelashes as the first agent turned to Snow, not sure what was happening, not sure whom he should be aiming at. Snow had his own blaster out now, in his left hand, and it was aimed at the first agent. His right hand flopped at his side.

The now-stunnerless female agent opened a link. "Assistance required. We are—" She dropped to the floor.

"You can't escape." The first agent tried to keep his stunner aimed, but his arm drooped, too heavy to hold his weapon. He fired. His aim was off. He raised the stunner again, with effort.

Snow shot it out of his hand. Got part of the hip instead. "Sorry." To both Nika and the agent: "I can't shoot as well left-handed."

Nika snatched the stunner as it fell from the agent's hand. "Move," she told Snow.

They took off running.

"Hold," someone called from the same direction the third and fourth agent had come. They heard more running feet. "Stop, or I'll fire."

They ducked left into the nearest cross passage. Turned right into the next one parallel to the way they had been going.

"This building can't be that big," Snow said. "We have to be near the stores. Let's hope they don't have breach doors, like they do on a ship."

It was easy to lose track of where you were headed. "Back into the main passage," Nika gasped.

They turned right. Then left, straight into two agents.

Nika kept running, braced herself for the impact.

Snow must have done the same, for both agents went flying.

Nika nearly went down on top of them. She righted herself and jumped the prone body instead.

One of the agents raised his blaster. The other lunged for his arm. "Alive, you idiot."

The blaster shot went wide.

"Hear that, Nika?"

"Yes." It meant they didn't have to worry about being killed, except by accident.

They still had to worry about getting caught. The next mod Nika designed for herself was going to be able to run fast. Sprinting relied on anaerobic energy, muscle strength, elasticity.

Although, maybe she'd have to work for longer-distance running, given this passage seemed like it would never end.

Snow stumbled, slightly off balance. Nika glanced at Snow's useless arm. His arms were always getting injured. She'd have to sound him out about reinforced limbs.

The agents were back on their feet, following. Two more ran out of another side passage. Who had designed this building?

They reached the end of their corridor. Finally.

For a moment Nika couldn't remember which way to go next.

"Right," Snow gasped.

They turned right, shouting agents closing in. None were shooting.

"Room 313." Snow was as out of breath as she was. Maybe give him anaerobic energy as well.

309, 311, 313.

The door was locked.

Iris on the scanner, thumb on the lock. *Hurry, hurry.* If the Justice Department had locked down their access, this was where they would run out of luck.

The door opened. They fell inside.

"Thank you, thank you," Nika said fervently. "Lock the door."

Snow shook his head. "How?"

She called Josune. "We need to lock a door." She sent the image through. "Like, right now."

"Eye scan," Josune said promptly. "Bring up the number pad. Type these numbers when I say. Seven, seven, three." Pause. "Six, five, two." Pause.

Outside a voice said, "On my count. Ready."

"Seven, seven, three." Josune's "three" came at the same time as the three-count finished outside.

"Go," from outside.

The lock clicked into place.

Nika sagged against the wall. "We've run into a slight hiccup," she told Josune. "Be ready when we come out. We'll be running." She closed the link. "Where's the Songyan?"

How hard could it be to find? Genemod machines weren't exactly small. And given that, how did they get it out when they had agents outside the door?

Worry about that when they had it.

"Songyan ships their machines in a crate." Surely they'd have crated it for the trip. It was a Songyan, after all. "The crate is green, with the black Songyan logo etched on each side." At least both machines delivered to her studio had. "It's about so high." She raised her hand to her chest. "Two and a half meters long, and roughly one and a half wide."

The noise outside the door was growing. It sounded as if they'd brought more people in. Nika heard the word *engineer* mentioned at least twice.

They found the Songyan at the back of the store. It was still on the antigrav trolley it had been delivered on. Right next to the loading bay exit.

"There is a god," Snow said.

There was a noise from the shadows, and Nika spun around, raising her blaster.

"Well, well. Here we are." Wickmore stepped out into the light, a needler aimed steadily at them. "As predictable as ever. And with all the drama on your heels. Hello, Nika. I must say, your mods are getting worse if that is the best you can do."

15

ALISTAIR LAUGHTON

Paola arrived in Cam's hospital room as the genemod machine lights went green.

"There you are. I've been looking everywhere for you."

"There's a waiting room, you know. Any sane person would use that." She'd called him a lot of things in their working life, but sane had never been one of them. "You've changed, Alistair, since you've been away."

Everyone changed. Alistair was a lot more cynical, less trusting, than he had been, and no wonder. "Maybe it's your memory of me, versus the reality."

"It's not that. It's . . . you used to care, Alistair. Now you're . . . I don't know, you've lost your passion."

Two years scraping to survive, then having the company who'd put you there try to kill you might do that. Besides, he'd never been more passionate about doing his job than he was about finding Nika Rik Terri.

The doctor came up as the genemod machine pinged completion. He checked the readings, then helped Cam out. "All done," he said. "You'll have a nice bill at the end of it. Hu-skin is expensive."

"Thank you." Alistair handed Cam a pair of coveralls he'd purchased from a vending machine. "Your clothes were wrecked."

Cam looked at the coveralls as if he'd never seen vending-machine clothes before—he probably hadn't, even on Zell he'd dressed well—then opened the pack. "What do you think?" he asked Paola. "Too large? Or too small?"

"Doesn't he know your size?"

"Paola. You have the wrong idea."

Her link buzzed. She held up her hand. "Got to take this one. It's a priority three."

Alistair had taken a number of priority calls in his time. Priority-one calls were major incidents involving a lot of people, such as an explosion that killed everyone at a function, or a large passenger ship being attacked by pirates in legal space. Priority two was for smaller incidents that had a big impact. Shanna Brown's assassination was one of them. Most of Tamati Woden's kills were priority twos. Priority three was important, but the impact was limited.

Cam was right. The coveralls were too big, and once they were out of the pack, they fluoresced with an orange luminescence—to Alistair—that increased as they took on the heat from Cam's body.

"They have?" Paola started to walk, beckoned impatiently to Alistair and Cam when they didn't immediately follow. "Restrain them. Don't make a big thing of it, unless they try to escape. And for God's sake, don't kill them. I'll have the Honesty League and the media all over it."

"Shoes?" Cam asked.

Alistair shook his head.

Cam sighed. "You probably would have got the wrong size anyway."

"Come on, you two. I need to get back to the office."

They jogged to catch up to her.

"Did you have something you wanted to say to us?" Alistair asked. "I mean, you came to see me."

"Or was it to warn us someone was trying to kill us?" Cam asked.

"Of course I want to talk to you." Paola was almost running herself.

"What's the hurry?"

"My prisoners have escaped." She stabbed impatiently at the lift button, stabbed it again.

"Prisoners?"

Paola didn't normally take prisoners. She prosecuted them, signed the warrants for them, but she didn't do the hard labor. Not usually.

"You know, wrongdoers who get caught. They're put behind bars."

"Why do you have prisoners?"

"Because the Honesty League is on my back." The lift arrived, took them to the roof, where an aircar swooped down. Paola was inside before the door was fully open.

Alistair grabbed the aircar door, held it while Cam got in, then jumped in himself. In the mood Paola was in, she was just as likely to forget they were there. She'd left him behind once, talking to no one as the aircar lifted. It had been ten minutes before she'd realized.

This time he made it in. Just.

"I spent the afternoon talking to them."

"Slow down, Paola. Tell us who the prisoners are."

"Rogue agents. I told you about them. In your apartment, when I offered you back your job. Remember? They were found unconscious on their ship."

He had forgotten. That must have been what she had been doing at the spaceport earlier, on the news. Arresting the agents.

Paola called the jail and got Walter Lanzo, who was always on night shift. Alistair had been bringing prisoners to him since he'd started at the Justice Department.

"How did my prisoners escape?"

"Hello to you, too, Paola. Which ones are yours? I've a hundred and seventeen in the cells."

"You've only got a hundred and fifteen now."

"Tell me who they are, and I'll find out for you."

Alistair had never heard Walter raise his voice, not even to prisoners.

"These two." Paola pushed images through.

Walter pursed his lips, looked at the screen in front of him. "Says they're still in the cells." He pushed the feed through to her; it came up on the aircar main screen. Two women in business suits. One paced the cell; the other sat back on a bunk, scowling. "Shall I go check?"

"Finally. Thank you."

Walter left the view on-screen.

Paola switched channels, called her own office. No one answered. "Where the hell are they?"

Hopefully out arresting escaped prisoners. A silent alarm sounded on Alistair's own link. He glanced at it. An incident at the Justice Department building.

"Oh, come on," Paola said.

"I'm getting an alarm," Cam said. "I have no idea what it means."

"Something's happened in our building. It's a warning to stay away if you're not at work, to be careful if you are."

Paola finally got through to her office. "What the hell is going on?"

"The prisoners resisted arrest, ma'am. We've cornered them in one of the stores."

"Gas them, then."

"We can't, ma'am. If we gas them, we gas the whole building."

Walter called Alistair. "I thought I saw you with Paola and I can't contact her. Is she still there?"

Alistair nodded.

"Tell her she was fussing about nothing." He stood outside a barred cell. A woman stood close to Walter, clutching at the bars. She looked like one of the women Alistair had seen in the earlier image. The other woman remained on the bunk.

The woman clutching the bar yelled at the screen. "You can't keep us in here like this. We're from the Justice Department. We've been framed."

Walter looked at Alistair. "Is it true?" Walter had a soft heart, but he'd never, so far as Alistair knew, let a prisoner go, no matter how much he sympathized.

"I don't know."

Alistair tapped Paola on the shoulder.

"Can't you see I'm—"

He pushed the link to the main aircar screen, pointed to Walter, standing outside the cell, zoomed in so Paola could see who was behind him.

Her eyes widened. She cut off her other call. "Who are they?"

"Walter thinks your prisoners."

The aircar pinged for descent to the head office.

"Then who are the people we're chasing?" Paola demanded.

"Someone trying to get into the Justice Department," Alistair suggested. It made more sense than someone escaping from jail and heading straight to the headquarters of their arrestors.

He didn't believe in coincidences. How likely was it that two people she'd arrested turned up at the Justice Department headquarters just afterward? "ID them," Alistair ordered Walter. "Let us know if their ID matches. We'll investigate the intruders at head office."

Alistair exited the aircar. "Do they know anyone at headquarters, Paola?"

"They're agents. They did their training here. Of course they'll know people."

"They're agents, yet you arrested them?" They hadn't arrested Alistair. They'd put him on suspended leave.

"I had to. I had the Honesty League on my back. Otherwise we could have sacked them quietly. Instead it's a media circus and we need to give them a trial."

Cam followed them out. Hopped. "This tarmac's rough."

He'd forgotten Cam had no shoes.

Cam waved him away when he would have helped. "Let me mince," and he did, across the roof. Alistair matched his pace.

Paola looked out across the roofs, looked back quickly. "Can't he go any faster?"

"I'm doing my best," Cam said.

Paola always had set a fast pace to the lift. How much courage did it take her just to arrive at and leave work every day? Alistair gave her a gentle push toward the lifts. "Go press the button for us."

"That's some phobia," Cam said once she was out of hearing.

"Yes."

They reached the lift, where Paola waited with one palm against the wall. "Ground floor's locked down. They have to authorize us, can you believe."

They were trying to catch intruders down there.

"We'll go down to second," Alistair said, because it had to be better for Paola than standing out here in the open, waiting for access.

"Thank God," Paola muttered, and punched the floor number.

They stepped out onto the second floor.

"They were brought in this afternoon. Which is what I came to see you about earlier tonight. Before I interviewed them, I reviewed the case file. They'd contracted to deliver some young man to a merc ship. But they underestimated the crew young Bertram Snowshoe was with. Finally," as she must have gotten clearance for the ground floor, for she punched the lift button.

"Bertram Snowshoe?"

"Get in the lift, Alistair. Stop gawking." The other two were already inside. He followed. "Yes. Snowshoe. I looked him up and found two people had inquired about Snowshoe recently. Leonard Wickmore and yourself."

This case was getting more tangled every second. "Why does Wickmore want Bertram?"

"That's something you can answer tomorrow, when you interview him. I hear he's on Kitimat."

"The other day when we interviewed him, he was at his office on Eaglehawk Prime," Cam said. "Not liking the coincidence."

"Executives travel all the time. They do most of their work on their way to and from places." They stepped out of the lift and Paola stopped to talk to the agent in charge. "What's happening?"

They were outside the storeroom. The room number was familiar.

"We cornered them in the storeroom," the agent in charge said. "They've locked themselves in. The engineer is about to open the door." He hesitated. "They know we won't harm them. They're using that to their advantage."

It was clear what he was asking.

"You have my permission to use force," Paola said.

"Yes, ma'am." He opened a link.

"Wait." Alistair frantically searched records. Where had they stored the Songyan machine? Storeroom 313. How unsurprising. "You didn't corner them at all. They're here to steal the genemod machine." And Paola had just given the order to use deadly force. "Rescind your order, Paola. We need these people alive."

He was too late. The guards had already stormed the door.

16

Nika glanced toward Snow.

"Oh, don't worry about Snowshoe," Wickmore said. "I won't kill him unless he gives me problems. Captain Norris may even give me a full complement of mercs for a little war I'm about to start, he'll be so grateful to have his lost lamb back in the fold."

"We'll be going nowhere if the Justice Department agents get in." Nika looked around the storeroom. This must be where they stored larger items, for there was a loading-bay door at the back. It was flush with the wall; thin lines of pale blue power crisscrossed in front of it.

The noise over at the other door intensified.

There was a fire door in the wall beside the loading bay, but the Songyan wouldn't get out of that.

Plus, there was still Wickmore. She turned back to him. "What now?"

"If you'd arrived quietly, we could have gotten out without any fuss. Could have had time for a little chat even, to see how cooperative you plan on being. We no longer have that luxury. I won't forget this."

"We did arrive quietly," Snow said. "And we didn't ask you to come. Don't take it out on us."

Nika shrugged. She put her hand to her face to turn on the link. She had to let Josune know what was going on.

Wickmore fired.

Thousands of hot needles ripped through Nika's body. It was only seconds, but she dropped to her knees, concentrating so hard on not screaming, and not throwing up, that it took a moment to realize the high keening she could hear was her. When she could, she gulped in air. Wickmore was dead. He was so dead. She was going to kill him.

But first they had to escape.

Otherwise Roystan would die.

Snow knelt down beside her. He put his hand on her face, turned her to look at him. All she could think about was how much it hurt.

"Nika." He used the tone that said she really needed to listen to him.

She forced herself to concentrate.

"Needlers cause pain, but they don't disable you."

"Isn't that touching." Wickmore's voice was a distant sound. "The apprentice telling his master how it works. But it's time to go. Pay attention, Nika."

Nika swallowed her pain and turned to Wickmore. He indicated a large panel to the left of the fire door. "The code to open the loading bay is nine, eight, seven, six, five. So unimaginative, don't you think." He waved the needler in Snow's direction. "You can do the honors."

Snow punched in the numbers quickly. The bay door slid open.

At the same time, the door at the other end of the storeroom disintegrated.

Could they wait for the Justice Department, who at least weren't trying to kill them?

Blaster fire caught the edge of Snow's arm, the one he couldn't use properly yet.

Damn. That order had changed. Now they were trying to kill them.

Wickmore was already out of the loading bay, his needler still aimed at her.

Coward.

Nika hauled herself to her feet using the Songyan to pull herself up. Thank the stars it was still on the trolley it had arrived on. She blinked away the sweat stinging her eyes and swung the genemod machine around. She pushed it between them and the oncoming agents.

She was seconds too late. Snow grunted, spun, as blaster fire raked down his right side. The rest of the fire—from at least three agents, at Nika's guess—raked the Songyan crate, setting it alight.

Snow fell. Nika dropped too. Under the cover of the fire, she rolled Snow through the exit. Next body she'd build for strength.

"Hold your fire," someone roared from the passage outside.

Wickmore turned, snarled. "Laughton! What are you . . . Can't you die like you're supposed to?"

Four Justice Department agents waited outside the loading bay.

"Going somewhere, Brand?" one of them asked. It was the agent they'd met in the foyer coming in. "I will enjoy bringing you in." He straightened, almost to attention, as he recognized Wickmore. "Executive. What is going on?"

The whine of a stunner came over the top of the voice. The four agents, and Wickmore, dropped.

Josune ran over to help with Snow. "I didn't want to take them out earlier because that would bring others."

She'd brought the aircar down to the loading bay. They ran for it. "The Songyan?"

Nika shook her head. "Burning." Even if it was only the crate that burned, they would be captured if they went back for it. "Let's get Snow to a modder."

"Drake's?"

"Perfect." And it was. The Justice Department would go to the hospitals first. They'd eventually try the modding studios, but Nika would have enough time to keep Snow alive.

Josune lifted off as more agents spilled out of the loading-bay door.

Drake's studio was dark. Nika rang the bell. Rang it again. And again. If he was like Snow, he'd live on the premises. She rang a fourth time.

Inside, a light came on, and Drake peered up blearily over the counter.

Nika leaned on the bell.

He finally came over and opened the door. "A modder's got to sleep, you know. How am I to do . . . Oh, it's you again."

"A thousand credits to use your machine again."

"Two."

"Fifteen hundred," Josune said before Nika could agree.

Nika let them negotiate while she helped Snow across to the machine. Snow was bad, because he climbed into the machine without even checking it.

She knew Snow's body almost as well as her own now, set up the machine automatically.

"You might want to slow down," Drake suggested. "You're liable to make a mistake."

She didn't make mistakes. "Where's that leftover mutrient we gave you?"

"That'll cost—"

"Don't charge us for our own products," Josune said.

"But you gave it to me."

"I'll pay him," Nika said, which told Josune how bad Snow was. "But don't try and pass off inferior product, or I might kill you myself."

Drake looked at her, looked at Josune. "That'll be—"

"Get it now, or I will kill you. We'll pay cost price," Josune said. "And remember that Nika knows cost price better than you do, for she bought it to start with."

Nika pulled down the first program she had for Snow. The original, when she'd taken a read of his hair. It wasn't optimal, but she didn't need to code it in. Not only that, it was Snow's design, so it wasn't as if she were overriding his mods.

Afterward she sat back and watched. How many times had she sat by a client, watching the genemod machine? It all seemed so far away from her life of spaceships and blasters and deadly enemies.

She looked at Josune, who looked as exhausted as she was. "Wickmore was waiting."

He was never going to get out of her life. Not unless she killed him. Or ran, like Goberling had. Changed his name, changed his identity, removed his memory. She didn't want to do that.

"We should have killed him." She glanced at Drake, listening avidly. "Laughton's people were waiting for us too. We set off alarms as soon as we arrived, or just after."

"The ID didn't work?"

It should have worked. "Unless they were after Brand and Bouwmeester." They might even have been, for one of the agents had said, "Back to their prison cell."

"Unlikely," Josune said. "Scum like that seem to get away all the time."

"I mucked up badly."

"And the Songyan?"

"On fire, last we saw."

"You trying to steal a Songyan?" Drake's eyes opened wide. "You people have balls, I'll say that. But you should know I don't do illegal here, and I don't want to get caught in your backlash."

As Snow said, how could you steal something that you'd bought and paid for?

"The Songyan is ours," Nika said. "They stole it from us. We're not thieves."

Drake flexed a scaled muscle. Admired it. "And I can fly too. If you really owned a Songyan, no one would steal it from you. It would be snug in a studio, and you wouldn't be here illegally using my machine."

"Excuse me. There is nothing illegal about hiring a genemod machine for a few hours, provided you have certification. I should make you apologize for that."

"How?"

"She'd put you in your own machine and pour orange crystals in until you did so." Josune's hand was close to her stomach. She always reached for the sparker first. Nika would prefer she went for her blaster this close to a genemod machine. But then, Drake didn't realize how close he was to someone pulling a weapon on him.

Drake checked his hairline on the screen. "She wouldn't. She couldn't."

"You'd turn orange."

Idle threats didn't help their predicament. "I have to get a Songyan." Nika needed the extra inlets, and the fineness it provided. In time maybe she and Josune could build something that would approximate what Conrad Songyan had done, using the base of one of the other machines—like the Netanyu—to do it, but that would take months, and Roystan didn't have months.

It was time to share their resources with someone else. "Who do we know has a Songyan?"

SaStudio. Jolie Sand. Esau Ye.

What would she have done if a desperate modder had come into her studio and demanded to use the Songyan? Said no, to start with, but if she knew them, and they persisted, she might eventually agree. But she'd make sure that she controlled the reads. And the mods. And their machines were customized for them.

"How many of them are on Kitimat?" Josune asked.

Exactly none. And Josune had a point. How long could they run to get this machine and keep Roystan alive? Even now, back on ship, he'd be feeling the effects.

"We don't have time to go somewhere else." They'd make the time.

"Think," Josune said. "What about Songyan themselves? Was yours the only machine they had waiting to be sent?"

"They're custom built." Every connection soldered by hand, every fastening hand-fixed, the box hand-molded. "They do them one at a time." All of it customized to the purchaser's requirements.

"What about a demo model? Most showrooms have a demo model, at least, especially if you have to order it."

"Are you kidding?" Drake said. "This is Songyan we're talking about. They don't need demo models. The results speak for themselves."

"A damaged one, in for repair."

"The engineer goes on site." Not that Nika's had ever needed repair. Sinead had serviced it once a year, but she'd never had to repair it. "The only machine they have on the premises is a museum piece. The very first—" Nika's voice trailed away. Giwari's machine, and Dagar had said they serviced it regularly, so it would be in working order. She looked up. "It's too old and doesn't have my add-ons. But I'm desperate, Josune."

"So am I." Josune glanced at the genemod machine, where Snow's mod was half-done. "How long?"

"Another hour."

"I'll make plans."

17

ALISTAIR LAUGHTON

Leonard Wickmore looked as if he was about to have an apoplexy. "What are you doing here? Are all my staff imbeciles?"

Alistair was glad he wasn't in Wickmore's office right then. "Funnily enough, I work here. What's your excuse?"

Alistair had better things to do than question executives. He wanted to follow the aircar. It was being pursued, but he knew it would be gone. Luck? Planning? Or both?

Agents had stopped the fire spreading and finally managed to put out the genemod machine itself—whatever it had been packed in, it generated a lot of heat as it burned.

"What were you doing in the store, Executive?"

"Your people nearly killed Nika Rik Terri. If I hadn't been there to save her, they would have done so."

"You still haven't said what you were doing there."

"And you destroyed the genemod machine. Purpose built to Rik Terri's specifications. I had plans for that machine."

"I'm sure you did. I ask again. What were you doing in the Justice Department store?" He could hear his voice getting louder, consciously quietened it.

Paola caught Alistair's eye. "Upstairs."

Her office, she meant. Alistair took hold of Wickmore's arm as they moved across to the lift.

"Do you mind?"

"Not at all. You had no right to be in there. You're lucky you're not under arrest."

"Yet," Cam murmured quietly from behind.

Alistair saw the heat surge through Wickmore's body, stepped in instinctively to block. Wickmore's blow would have knocked the smaller man off his feet.

"And you're about to be charged with assaulting an officer of the Justice Department."

"You stepped into it. When my lawyer is finished, you will never work in the Justice Department again."

"This is Alistair Laughton you're talking to," Cam said. "Has he ever worried about things like that?"

Paola gave a grim nod.

"You keep out of this," Wickmore said.

"He works with me," Alistair said. "You'll answer him as civilly as you would answer any other Justice Department agent working on a case you're a suspect in."

"How am I a suspect?"

"Executive Wickmore," Paola said as she ushered him into her office, "the Justice Department is a combined-companies initiative and can reasonably expect no interference from individual companies. We have a job to do. We are expected to do it. Especially right now, when we are under such heavy media scrutiny. Twenty agents saw you in the storeroom. You need a good reason for being there, else you will be charged."

"I don't like being threatened."

Paola raised herself to her full height. "Perhaps we should call the Eaglehawk board representative. Have him explain things to you."

He was going to love that at four o'clock in the morning.

"You call Green. I am calling my lawyer. I don't trust Laughton not to frame me."

"Just tell us what in the hell you are doing in the middle of a Justice Department job?" Alistair said.

"Saving Nika Rik Terri's life. Which is more than you people were prepared to do."

Alistair couldn't stop the snarl. "How did you know it was Rik Terri?"

Wickmore calmed suddenly, pulled himself together. It was unnerving to see a man who'd been so apoplectic a moment ago so collected now.

"Agent Laughton, I had information that she would be there. Someone had to save her life. I didn't trust the Justice Department to do so."

"If Eaglehawk cleaned up their act, the galaxy might become a more trustworthy place," Paola said.

Alistair spoke hurriedly, over the top of her: "That doesn't explain why you were in the store. Or how you got in the store, to be in a position to save her life." He didn't want Paola on a defamation suit.

"Agent Laughton. We've been over this."

"One of the intruders was injured. Was it Rik Terri?"

"Why should I tell you?"

"The sooner you help, the sooner you can go."

"And in the meantime, Rik Terri disappears again." Wickmore turned to Paola. "Is this how your thugs apprehend criminals?"

"No." Paola examined the weapon one of the agents had bagged and handed her. "Is this yours?"

"Never seen it before. What is it?"

"Good. Because needlers are illegal, and if it was yours, you would have more than Alistair's questions to answer."

Alistair's link buzzed. Dagar Songyan. Finally. A Justice Department agent stood at her side.

"Dragging me out of bed like this is unacceptable, Agent Laughton."

If she'd been in bed, then the agent had given her time to dress and make up.

"We appreciate your cooperation, Ms. Songyan. Thank you. I do have a question for you. Did Bertram Snowshoe or Nika Rik Terri try to collect the Songyan?"

"The one you confiscated?" She stopped to think about it. "Why yes, Snowshoe came in earlier today."

"And you didn't call me? Even though you knew I was waiting for Snowshoe? Even though the genemod machine had been confiscated? Even though I asked you to?"

Dagar said, "Agent Laughton, we were attacked not long afterward. It slipped my mind."

There was rap on Paola's office door. Lawyer Demetriou—even more immaculately suited than Paola—entered. Alistair had met him before, had been threatened with lawsuits every time. None of the lawsuits had eventuated, but he had no doubt Demetriou could have ruined his career if he wanted to. The fact that he hadn't followed through on his threats was telling. It meant he wasn't sure Wickmore would win.

"About time," Wickmore said.

Alistair turned back to Dagar. "Attacked? How convenient."

Dagar's voice was frosty. "It was most inconvenient, actually. Someone used a sparker. We have to rewire half the building."

Alistair caught the slight movement of Wickmore's lips as he hid a smile.

"Let me get this straight. You didn't have time to notify me, despite my request, or anyone else in the Justice Department, but you took the time to notify Executive Wickmore?" It was a guess, but how else would Wickmore have known?

"I object to that accusation," Wickmore's lawyer said.

It was going to be a long night.

Meantime, Rik Terri was getting farther away.

Alistair sent out requests to the various hospitals to report anyone coming in with blaster burns. So far they'd had three, none of whom was their quarry.

It was, according to the nearest hospital, a quiet night for blaster-related incidents.

"I don't think she'd go to a hospital," Cam said. "She's a body modder, Alistair. I think she'll go to a modding studio."

"To repair someone who's been burned by blaster fire?"

"I bet modders never set foot inside hospitals. I wouldn't have gone to a hospital earlier tonight if you hadn't forced me. I would have gone to a modder. My modder, if I could."

Alistair hadn't told Cam what the doctor had said. But then, Cam knew his body was full of transurides. "You know, Cam, I can't see why anyone would go to a modder when they need to save someone's life."

"You can't," Cam said. "I can." He looked at Alistair. Alistair was the first to look away. "I would go to a modder."

"Fine. I'll get agents to check the modders," Alistair said.

Cam was right.

Gregory "Call me Drake" Eames ran a modding shop down on the docks.

"They left half an hour ago."

Half an hour. So close.

"I didn't do anything illegal. The woman, she had the qualifications. I checked."

"We're sure you did."

Drake held his hands in the air, surrender-style. "Everything was aboveboard. She just wanted to use the genemod machine. People do, sometimes. Pay for the hire, I mean."

"What was her name? What did she look like?"

"Nika James. Qualified seven years ago. From Landers." He paused. Alistair didn't know for what. "That's the preeminent modding school, you know."

Drake seemed to think it was important.

"She didn't look like a modder. No style. But she knew what she was doing, all right. I had no reason to question her."

"How much did she pay you?"

"We bargained." Drake looked coy. "Can I put my arms down now?"

"No one's arresting you."

"That means yes," Cam said.

"Thank you." Drake folded his blue-gray arms. They were scaled. He looked as if he'd been trying for a reptilian effect. Or maybe it had been an accident. Alistair wondered if he should sympathize at the mod gone wrong.

"They came into the store. Three of them."

"Three?"

"Yes. Two women. Nika James and I don't know who the other woman was, but they called the guy Snow."

Bertram Snowshoe. It had to be.

"Was the other woman a modder?"

"She didn't use the machine. She just linked in. Bought things, by the sound of it." Drake scowled. "Drove a hard bargain. Not like Nika James."

Nika James was a new name, but someone named Nika might adopt the name James. "Find out what you can about Nika James," he murmured to Cam.

"What sort of information?"

Sometimes he forgot Cam wasn't, technically, a qualified agent. "Don't worry, I'll do it." He opened a link, pushed the details and the inquiry through.

"Is this going to take long?" Drake asked. "I've been up all night and I have a customer coming this morning." He yawned, showing slightly pointed teeth.

"Can I see your security feed?" Alistair asked.

"My feed." Drake hesitated, looked as if he was considering what might be on the feed. "What would you be doing with it?" he asked cautiously.

"Watch it."

"I didn't do anything illegal. She had certification."

"If you don't give us the feed, I'll arrest you for obstructing justice."

"It's not a crime to overcharge, you know."

"All of last night's feed, and I want it now.

"Where do you think they went after they left your shop?" he asked while Drake reluctantly downloaded the feed.

"I want you to know that I had nothing to do with the idea to steal the Songyan."

Every second they delayed, Rik Terri was getting farther away.

"I only knew about it after they tried it." He pushed the feed through. "It's all there. You'll see I didn't."

"Thank you."

"Why don't I check this quickly?" Cam suggested. "You keep talking."

Cam had a bionic implant in his eye. He could check it without needing a screen. And it meant they weren't wasting time. "Good idea." Alistair turned back to the modder. "Where do you think they went after they left you?"

Drake scratched his head, a sound that set Alistair's teeth on edge. Did he have scales on his head too? "They stopped talking at the end. She paced. The other one linked in. Then the third one came out of the genemod machine. Nice mod, by the way. He had this lovely red-gold hair. Suited him much better than being a woman. Except he was so much older."

So Brand and Bouwmeester had been Rik Terri and Snowshoe, if Wickmore was correct about Rik Terri. "The two who were modded—that was the one called Nika and the one called Snow?"

"That's what I said."

"You didn't say where they were going."

"I don't rightly know. They didn't exactly say, if you know what I mean."

But he knew.

"I can still arrest you for obstructing the Justice Department."

"I didn't have anything to do with this."

"I get that. You were an innocent bystander. Where were they going?"

"They might have been going to find a Songyan." He looked at them. "That's a genemod machine. The best, most expensive. The rarest."

"I know what they are."

"Well, the one they were trying to steal got burned. They mentioned all the big-name studios." He thought about it. "Except Rik Terri. But then, her studio was bombed, so that's probably why."

"Probably." It was getting harder to keep his voice neutral. Coming so close to Nika Rik Terri had stressed him more than he realized. That, or two years away from interviewing had shortened his patience.

"Got it." Cam looked up, right eye glowing. "We need to move, Alistair, if we want to catch them."

Alistair called for two more agents to interview Drake. They left at a run. If Cam said hurry, they had to hurry.

"They're going back to the Songyan factory," Cam said. "They're half an hour in front of us."

"There's nothing for them there."

As soon as they were in the aircar, Cam brought up the security feed at the point where one of the women—Rik Terri, if Wickmore was right—said, "The only machine they have on the premises is a museum piece."

"Why does it have to be a Songyan? They have their pick of any machine they want, but they want this particular brand. Why?"

"It is a famous brand. All the best modders have them."

Maybe it was an image thing, but Rik Terri had claimed she was desperate. So had the woman with her. Why did they need a Songyan so desperately? And if Alistair could help get her one, would that help his chances of getting her to come to Zell?

"Why didn't they just come and talk to us?"

"They might have," Cam said. "We were otherwise occupied, remember."

And Leonard Wickmore had been surprised to see him alive.

Alistair called Paola. "I want to know all Wickmore's calls for the last twenty-four hours."

She pursed her lips. "Going after an executive. Give me a good reason, Alistair, or I can't."

"He was waiting for Rik Terri last night, and something he said made me think he had something to do with tonight's bombing."

"You'd better be right, Alistair, or I'll hang for this."

Was he prepared to risk Paola's job for this? Harassing an executive could bring her down. Especially if Wickmore was clever enough to cover his tracks. Alistair might be wrong, not that he thought he was. "Leave it to me. I'll check it."

But first he had to get Nika Rik Terri.

18

JOSUNE ARRIOLA

The lock on the Songyan Engineering front door was a Verter. Verters took seven minutes to hack with a dedicated lockpick system, let alone in the dark, when you were aware this was only the first stage in your plan. Josune didn't try.

She shorted the power to the door. "Five minutes starting now." She pulled out the laser and cut the mechanical lock that had automatically triggered when the electronic one went down. At least they had a mechanical lock. She'd worked in some places where they relied solely on the electronics.

Thank goodness the walls weren't reinforced. But then, this was a manufacturing plant. Why would they be?

"We'll have to pay for damages when we return the machine."

Nika cut off a giggle. "There'll be more to pay. The glass case." She sounded breathless. No matter what she said, stealing didn't sit well with her.

Josune was a bit breathless herself. Five minutes and counting. "We're in." She pushed the door open and stepped into the dark building.

Snow pushed the trolley in behind them. "They fixed the power, anyway. That was fast."

They paused inside. No sound, but a sliver of light under a door down the passage.

She started to cut the glass around the Giwari.

"Josune."

Nika pointed to the lifts, where a floor light had started to move. The lift was coming down.

Josune handed Nika the laser. "I'll deal with it. Get the Giwari."

She was glad she'd brought a stunner as well as a blaster. She ghosted over to the lift.

The smell of hot glass wafted behind her.

The lift pinged.

The door opened.

Dagar Songyan—for it was her in the lift—was linked in. She'd pushed the call onto the screen on the walls of the lift. Leonard Wickmore.

"Laughton threatened me."

Josune raised the stunner, sprayed the lift. Dagar thumped to the floor. Behind her, the glass of the Giwari's display case crashed to the floor.

On the screen Leonard Wickmore's face stared back at her. He smiled.

Josune left Dagar where she was, pressed a random floor—because Wickmore was still on the screen—then stepped away from the lift. "Wickmore knows we're here. I'll get the aircar. Be ready when I get back."

19

ALISTAIR LAUGHTON

Alistair brought the aircar down right to the door of the Songyan Engineering building.

"They're already here," Cam said.

The door was open. Two people—one of whom looked a lot like Agent Katrin Brand and must have been Rik Terri, the other a redhead who matched the original image they had of Bertram Snowshoe—were pushing a machine onto an antigrav trolley.

Alistair ran for the door, Cam close behind.

"That was quick," Rik Terri said, then her eyes widened as she realized he wasn't who she expected. Her gaze flicked to Cam, widened further. "Cam Santiago, what are you doing here?"

Santiago. No surprises there.

Rik Terri's hand edged toward the blaster at her side.

Alistair grabbed for her arm. "Wait."

She flinched. He stopped. He'd seen that kind of flinch before— on an executive's daughter whose father used to hit her. It was the flinch of someone who expected to be beaten.

Instead he pressed his stunner to her chest. He didn't want to kill her accidentally, and he wanted to stay alive long enough to talk to her. "I need to talk to you. Will you hear me out?"

She tilted her chin, stared at him. "I don't have much choice, do I."

They both froze at the sound of another aircar. It landed on top of the Justice Department car. The night was filled with the crunch of metal.

Nika smiled. "Out of time."

"Cam?"

"Got it." Cam opened the door.

"He's got a weapon," Snowshoe called. "He's holding it on—"

"Isn't that nice." A male voice, and from the shock on Snowshoe's face, not the voice he was expecting. Cam backed into the room, hands held high.

"All conveniently packaged." The speaker stepped forward, a blaster in his hand. "We'll take over now."

Six men, all holding blasters, all in the camouflage uniform of mercenaries, stepped up with him, three on either side. The speaker wore captain's epaulettes.

"Back off," Alistair ordered. "You're interfering in a Justice Department operation."

The captain laughed mockingly. "There are more of us than there are of you."

"I don't know who you are," Alistair said. "I don't know what you are doing here. But leave. Now." He could see heat images of at least another ten mercenaries around the aircar, all of them in a battle-ready stance, arms in a weapon-ready pose.

"Big words," the captain said. "For the record, I don't believe you are from the Justice Department. We've all fallen for that one before, haven't we?" He laughed merrily. "I wonder where you got the idea. Do I let Wickmore know his tip-off was correct, or don't I? Hmm? Thinking, thinking."

Another aircar came down to land, hovered, then lifted off again. The captain listened until he was sure it had gone.

"Move your men away," Alistair ordered. "This is the only warning you get."

Rik Terri started to ease her own weapon out of her holster.

"Agent Brand? Last I heard you were under arrest." The captain looked closer. "Or is it Brand?"

"Of course I'm Brand." Truculent, with a lot more swagger.

"Somehow I doubt that. Mez Arriola, perchance. I've been looking for you." He gestured with his weapon. "Keep your hands away from your body. Above your head would be nice. You, too, Snowshoe."

"Arriola?" It couldn't possibly be.

The woman looked at Alistair briefly, eyes curious, then turned back to the captain. "You're making a mistake, Norris. Let the Justice Department people go." She put her hands above her head.

"Oh, I want you, too, Arriola. You're a nice little bonus for collecting Snowshoe. Pol's told me a lot about you. Including your penchant for sparkers. Keep your hands well above your head."

Snowshoe sighed. "What is it with people thinking other people—"

"Snow," Rik Terri cautioned.

Alistair glanced at her. Did Snow's comment mean she was or she wasn't Arriola?

"Kill those two," the captain ordered, indicating Alistair and Cam.

Four men raised their weapons. Alistair grabbed his firebreather, pressed the controls. Blue lightning spurted in a sheet; molten-red beams flared from the other side.

Cam went down. Four of the men with Norris went down. Norris was already moving, diving out the door, out of the way. The edge of the sheet of fire caught his left side.

Rik Terri and Snowshoe fired seconds after. Six down.

It was a sickening waste of life. "Let's get out of here," but Alistair dropped down to check Cam's inert body. He couldn't be dead.

"Not without this." Rik Terri turned and grabbed the antigrav trolley holding the Songyan.

"Leave it. There's more coming."

They were too late. Ten guards stormed the Songyan foyer and fanned out, the heat signature of a further ten visible behind them. Alistair couldn't have got to them all before someone else got hurt.

Twenty armed mercenaries surrounded them.

"Don't kill anyone," Norris said through gritted teeth. One of them had hit him, at least. "I want that weapon. I want to know where he got it."

One of the newcomers aimed straight for Rik Terri.

Alistair pushed her aside.

A hot, searing pain lanced down his left side. That was all he knew.

20

JOSUNE ARRIOLA

Josune had taken the aircar up as soon as she saw the mercenaries outside the Songyan office. She took it four blocks away, just in case they watched her, then circled back and landed a block over.

She made her way silently to the end of the street, keeping away from any streetlights.

The orange flare of blaster fire, and the crackling blue-white light of something that sounded like a sparker but wasn't, stopped her. A familiar voice—Captain Norris, from the *Boost*—yelled, "Don't kill anyone. I want that weapon. I want to know where he got it." She saw him lurch to his feet. He'd been injured. "And if anyone has killed Arriola, I'll personally find them and kill them too."

Josune stayed frozen. Did they know where she was?

There were mercenaries everywhere.

"Load them into the aircar. Take the big guy too. I have questions for him about this weapon." Norris picked up a tube that was like no weapon Josune had seen before. "Now move, before someone comes to see what the problem is."

There were too many for Josune to take on.

Snow saw her as the mercenaries dragged him past. He'd been watching for her. But he didn't look to her for help. Instead he glanced away, quickly, to a dark object floating on an antigrav trolley. It had been pushed into a recess, wasn't part of the fighting.

She got it. Modders and their Songyans. It was the least she could do. She would have nodded, but the movement would have drawn attention.

At least they didn't plan to kill Nika and Snow just yet. It gave them time. But how did a small group of people take on a mercenary ship? They'd work it out.

They had to.

Josune waited ten minutes after they'd gone before she moved.

The carnage was sickening. Bodies everywhere.

"Please."

It was a whisper of sound. She almost missed it. Dark eyes stared up at her from a body fallen too awkwardly to be anything but damaged.

She couldn't leave them to die.

She called emergency while collecting the antigrav trolley. "There's been a shooting at Songyan Engineering. People are hurt. One man looks as if he's dying."

Without the modders it was the only thing she could do to keep them alive.

"You'll be fine," Josune said. "An ambulance will be here soon."

She heard the clop of the big rotary blades that signified a heavy-duty engine. "Here it comes now," and ran for her own air-car, guiding the Songyan in front of her.

She took off horizontally, the way she'd arrived, and exited four streets over.

Now to get back to *Another Road*, where they could come up with a plan to rescue Nika and Snow.

Back on ship Roystan greeted her with a hug. She could feel the heat of him, felt his bones through her jacket. He'd had more flesh than that before, she was sure of it.

"We're tracking the *Boost*. They're moving, but they've requested a flight path for the moment, so they're not planning to nullspace soon. We'll get them."

Provided they didn't nullspace away. If that happened, they'd have to rely on Nika or Snow to let them know where the *Boost* had gone.

"Good." She leaned back from Roystan to look at him properly. "You look terrible." He'd lost weight. How much weight could a body lose in such a short time?

"That's what I've been telling him," Jacques said. "And he brings his food back up. All the time."

"Too much detail, Jacques. I haven't—"

"You don't have to say. We know." Jacques threw his hands out theatrically. "Years of working with the man, and he still thinks we don't know him. You're starving."

Jacques had made it his mission to keep Roystan healthy.

Looking at Roystan, Josune thought he was right to be worried. "How fast did Nika speed up your metabolism?"

"Nika didn't speed it up, I did."

"We're not laying blame, Roystan," Josune said. "If we did, we'd lay it fair and square at Brand and Norris's feet." She brightened. "It looks like Brand did one dirty job too many, anyway. She's in jail."

"This is a tale I want to hear."

"Let me tell you what happened."

All four settled around the crew table, with some of Jacques's spicy flatbread. It would have been comfortable if Nika and Snow had been there.

"Well, we got to the Songyan factory—"

Roystan's eyes rolled up, and he fell facedown onto the table.

21

NIKA RIK TERRI

Nika came around to find a giant bending over her. She backed away, realized she was on a stretcher when she almost fell off it.

"It's okay," the giant said soothingly. "You've been injured with a blaster. We're prepping you for a fix, but there are others in front of you. You might feel like you're dying, but you're not."

He turned out not to be a giant at all, just a big man in her space. His face had dark planes and flat cheeks. His hair was short, black, and curled tightly around his head. His well-modded body was muscular, with a heavy bone structure. She'd bet, before he modded it, it had been chunky as well, with muscle that easily ran to fat.

Nika sat up, pushed him away, inspected her own injuries. Blaster burn, down one side. It hurt, but pain was starting to feel familiar. Not something she wanted to get used to. "Please don't put me into a Dietel."

"We don't have a Dietel. Only the Netanyu."

She looked around the room. Most of it was bare, with fastenings in the floor to clip stretcher beds into. There were seven stretchers. She hoped some of them were people they'd injured at Songyan Engineering. Still, one genemod machine for a merc ship. What did they do when two people were badly injured?

The man moved over to check the machine readings. A doctor or a modder.

Nika realized who he must be. "You're Gramps."

"Gram Pines, at your service. But most people call me Gramps."

"You are nothing like I imagined."

Gramps glanced at another bed down the ward. "What did you expect me to be like?"

Nika followed his gaze. "Snow." She pushed herself off the bed, painful as it was.

He grabbed her good arm. "Why did you bring him back here? He was safe. He was away."

"We didn't choose to come. Norris chased us. Where is Norris, by the way?"

"In the Netanyu. Where else. When the captain gets injured, he gets priority." Gramps scowled. "Even over my boy."

Based on the scowl, Norris might want to check his mod this time.

Nika pulled herself free and went to check on Snow.

"Excuse me," Gramps said. "This is my hospital. You're a patient."

"This is my apprentice."

"And my boy."

They stared at each other. After a moment Nika inclined her head. "Apologies. But he is my apprentice, and I have a duty of care."

"I never heard of a modder who doctors."

"Snow does." She nearly said, "You do too," but bit it off at the last moment.

"Snow's learned some bad habits over the years. That's why he went to college. To learn how to mod properly."

"You taught him well."

"And if he's your apprentice, what happened to that duty of care you talked about? Why is he back here?"

Yes. Modders were supposed to look after their apprentices. "I failed." For the moment, but they would escape.

The Netanyu pinged then. Job completed. That was Norris in there. Nika didn't need Gramps's gaze toward the genemod machine to know what to do. She lay back on the bed she'd come from and closed her eyes.

Norris didn't comment on being healed. "I want that one next." Nika couldn't see which one he pointed to, but it didn't sound like it was in Snow's direction.

"He'll take a while," Gramps said. "He's got hu-skin all down his back. He's been injured before."

"How long?"

"Twelve hours."

"Do it."

"Not the best use of my time." A pause. "It's your choice."

"I'm glad you understand that. It'll be good for young Snowshoe to spend time in pain."

"As you say." Gramps's voice was wooden.

Norris made toward the door. Stopped. Nika risked a peek through closed lashes.

"Don't forget, Gramps. We have two doctors on board now. You're no longer indispensable." He walked out briskly, smiling.

Nika sat up.

"Lie down," Gramps said. "He'll be back to check."

Nika lay down again. Gramps moved over to another stretcher, this one in the direction of where Norris had seemed to be speaking. He began prepping the body, moved it over to the Netanyu, and started to clean the machine. Two minutes later Norris came back. "By the way, that mutrient you ordered has arrived. I'll have someone send it up."

Gramps just grunted.

After Norris had gone, he said, "You can move now." He shoved the stretcher out of the way, strode down to Snow's. "Nobody tells me who goes first. Not when my boy's hurt."

Nika followed and read the machine as keenly as Gramps did. Snow had burner damage down one side. Gramps harrumphed, moved on. "You got old fast, boy."

He looked accusingly at Nika.

"It was a quick repair. He was injured." She didn't bother going through the why of that fight. "We were in a hurry; it was the best we could do at the time. It's his own design. What he used when he first opened the studio, to make himself look more experienced."

"That's a lot of fighting when he's only running away from Captain Norris."

"It is."

"Why? It seems to me, Nika—" He stopped. "It is Nika, isn't it?"

"Yes, but how—"

"My boy can be one-track sometimes. He wouldn't apprentice to anyone else. If you say he's your apprentice, then that's who you are. Although"—he looked at her consideringly—"I thought you'd look better than that. Different. I mean, my boy worshipped you."

"I was trying to look like someone else. She had a bad mod." It felt strange to be defending her own mod to someone else.

"But a Rik Terri design."

He recognized it.

"She got it secondhand, and certainly not from me. I would never have put her body with that head."

"Glad to hear it. So who attacked you before Norris did? And why?"

Nika glanced around. No one seemed to be listening, but she lowered her voice anyway. Gramps would find out, because even if she didn't tell him, Snow would. "We have a couple of people after us. Norris after Snow, a company man after me." Everyone after Josune and Roystan, maybe.

She moved over to the other stretcher. The one she presumed didn't require hu-skin, even though Gramps had claimed it did.

Snow's fix would take around five hours. This man's another four, maybe six. He'd given himself enough time to do Snow's first.

Gramps joined her. "Alistair Laughton. His ID says he's from the Justice Department."

The infamous Alistair Laughton. Who'd stolen their Songyan from them and then caused it to be burned. Nika planned to have words with Laughton. If he survived his visit to Norris.

"Won't do him any good here," Gramps said. "Captain Norris will kill him once he gets what he wants. Sorry."

For a moment she wondered what he was apologizing for. Of course he thought Laughton was with them. He wasn't wearing a mercenary uniform.

"Right now I'd happily kill him myself."

If he hadn't interfered, they'd be fixing Roystan by now, not imprisoned in Norris's hospital, and Snow would be healthy and helping her. Or maybe not. Norris had been at the Songyan office the first time they'd gone. They would probably still be here, but at least their Songyan would be whole.

"Shouldn't he have come around by now?"

"Some people don't," Gramps said. "Some people fake it."

"He's faking it?" He didn't look the sort.

Gramps shook his head. "Some people take a little help staying asleep. After all, we wouldn't want him coming around, knowing he wasn't done first, accidentally spilling that to certain people, would we? I heard the captain wanted to talk to him, so I knew he'd want him done first."

Nika laughed. "I have no idea how you and Snow turned out so different."

Gramps smiled fondly at the Netanyu. "My boy came fully formed, already with opinions. Even so young, even half-starved like he was. He knew what he knew, and mostly thought he was right."

Nika bumped her arm against the edge of a door. She grabbed the door as dizziness swept over her. The blaster burn. She tried to push it to the back of her mind. "I don't suppose you have any nerve-seal."

"I do, but I'm not giving you any."

"Why not?" It was the first thing hospitals gave patients when they arrived, before they went into a genemod machine.

"Because then I'd have to explain what I'd used it for."

"But you gave him—" Whatever he used to keep Laughton asleep would have been counted too.

"I keep a little up my sleeve. You're not desperate enough, and despite you being in pain, it won't kill you. Or me." Gramps smiled at her. "Easy, see."

"How old was Snow when you met him?" Nika had always thought he was around eight or nine, but he'd never specifically said. Nor had he said why Gramps had taken him in.

"Some stories are not mine to tell." Gramps blew out a long breath. "With luck, he doesn't remember much of it anyway."

Nika reluctantly allowed Gramps to help Snow out of the genemod machine, but her fingers twitched. She was not going to get into an argument over whose job it was to take care of Snow. She wasn't. Josune would have called her on her possessiveness, and she would have been right. Snow was her apprentice, but in a small part of her mind, she allowed that Gramps did have first rights. Gramps would always have first rights.

She busied herself reading the screen to make sure Snow was fully healed, giving Snow and his Gramps time to themselves.

Snow finally turned to her. "Nika, this is Gramps. Gramps, this is Nika."

"We've met," Nika said. "How do you feel, Snow?"

"If you mean do I hurt, then no, I'm okay. If you mean how do I feel, then that is a dumb question considering where we are." He said to Gramps, "She's crazy, you know."

Calling her crazy wouldn't help Nika's relationship with Snow's foster father. She turned toward Alistair. "Do we need to get him in now?"

"We do." Gramps glanced at a clock on the wall. "Captain will check on us again in about two hours. Be prepared, both of you, to get onto those stretchers."

"Why not heal Nika first?" Snow asked.

"Captain's orders. Besides, she needs to be injured. Have you forgotten the rules already, Snow?"

"Sorry, no. It's just . . . You should have put Nika in instead of me. After all, she's my—"

Nika laughed. "I'm not that badly hurt, Snow. Besides, I wouldn't have allowed it." Neither would have Gramps.

Once Alistair was settled in the genemod machine, all three studied the diagnostics. Until Snow, Nika hadn't worked with other modders since Hannah Tan. Sometimes it was good to talk shop and share mods.

The reading for Laughton's eyes was wrong. So badly, blatantly wrong that Nika asked, "Are you sure your Netanyu is working?" She peered closer to make sure she hadn't misread it.

"Sure I'm sure. But I've never seen anything like that before."

Gramps put the diagnostics onto the screen, enlarged the eye area. Nika scanned through the data that accompanied it. "Bioware," as the telltale electronic components came up. Who would be crazy enough to do it? You risked sending your client blind. In all probability he was blind, because they'd destroyed the eyeball to put the electronics in. "I wonder who his modder is."

"Whoever he or she is, they can sort him out." Gramps turned away to get supplies. "I'm doing basic healing only. Enough to get him on his feet. Not touching any eyes. Not touching anything not broken. Just the burns."

Nika had never seen bioware like it, and as to how they'd managed the interface between the electronics and the neurons . . . "I wouldn't mind seeing the nerve links that take it up to the brain." How had his body not rejected it? "And a gene read."

Snow leaned over to Gramps. "When she says she 'wouldn't mind,' that means she wants." He brought it up.

"Lucky I've got you to decode for me, boy. I might ignore her otherwise." He looked at Nika. "Some of us respond to plainer messages."

She nodded, but most of her attention was on Laughton's read, which was as normal as any human's except Roystan's. There was nothing in the read to show that he could code for the proteins that connected the electronics in his eye to his muscles and nerves.

She looked back at the diagnostics again. "This body can't code for those eyes."

They both looked at her.

There was more. "Look at the scarring around his eyes." They'd had to cut to put the bioware in. The scars, faint as they were, were still there. They hadn't used a genemod machine to fix the scarring.

She followed the scar around. Why was it so long?

"They did work on his brain too. Got into his brain and—" It was as abhorrent as some of Giwari's experiments. "I need the brain scan."

Snow pulled it up for her.

"Here. And here." The angular gyrus, Wernicke's area, Broca's area. "Language centers." They'd modified him so he could what? Learn languages faster?

Nika looked at Snow and said softly, "Take a read. That is an astounding mod. We can study it later."

"You think there'll be a later?"

"Roystan will follow us. Of course there will be a later. Don't give up so easily, Snow."

"Don't get his hopes up, lady," Gramps said gruffly. "The *Boost* doesn't like people to escape. My boy won't get a second chance."

22

ALISTAIR LAUGHTON

There was no Cam waiting with a cheerful smile or a sick joke when Alistair came out of the genemod machine. There never would be again.

The doctor, a man as big as he was—there weren't many of them—helped him out.

"Captain is waiting to see you. Best head off." The doctor indicated two armed guards. "You don't keep him waiting. Quite a disciplinarian, our captain."

A red-haired young man cleaning out the machine glanced at him, glanced away again. The shattered and hopeless expression on his face caused Alistair to look again. He looked familiar. Where had he seen him before?

Memory crashed back. Rik Terri. He couldn't save Cam, but he still had another forty-nine colonists to save.

"Bertram Snowshoe, isn't it." He turned toward the redhead. "I need to talk to you about Nika Rik Terri."

Snow glanced toward a stretcher.

The doctor inserted himself between them. "Not now. The captain's waiting." The two guards put their hands on their blasters meaningfully.

"Don't keep him waiting," one of the guards said. "Not if you want to live. Captain Norris doesn't like tardiness."

"Is this a merc ship?" Alistair asked as the guards led him to the captain's quarters.

"What do you think?"

What Alistair thought the ship was didn't matter. What happened if the mercenary captain decided to kill him did.

Guards were everywhere. Not all were armed. Many of them had empty holsters. Could he use that? And how?

He laughed to himself. Who was he to think big when he couldn't even save Cam? Even the memory brought the smell of charred flesh.

"You find something funny," Captain Norris said.

Alistair realized he was still laughing, although it wasn't sane laughter.

"My own stupidity."

He'd interrupted an argument, or the makings of one. A woman stood to one side, mouth still open as if she'd been about to speak.

"We're done here, Pol," Norris said.

"We're not done," the woman said. "I'm telling you. That is not Arriola you have in the hospital. It's the other body modder."

She thought the woman was Rik Terri too. Alistair had wondered if he was wrong.

"I said, we are finished."

"I'm calling Wickmore, telling him you've botched it."

And confirmation Wickmore was involved.

Norris nodded at a tall, female merc behind Pol. The woman stepped forward, took Pol's arm. "Captain Norris is busy."

Pol allowed herself to be dragged away, but she said over her shoulder, "You'll answer to the executive."

Norris, hands clasped behind his back, had already turned to Alistair. He looked him over. "I have downloaded your records, Agent Laughton. It's unimpressive. It appears you got booted from the Justice Department two years ago."

"I didn't get booted, I took extended leave." For the first time, Alistair was glad Paola had kept his position open instead of accepting his resignation. It made things easier.

"Involved in a scandal, no less."

"My wife was involved." He was tired of taking the blame for his ex-wife's transgressions.

"Hard for the husband not to recognize what his wife was doing."

"Not as hard as you think." Not when you were living separate lives, living in different apartments, working on different cases. Alistair had spent his final six months in the Justice Department chasing Tamati Woden. He hadn't caught him. Something that annoyed him even now.

"So you're freelance."

"No. I am back with the Justice Department. You know all this, Captain, if you have looked at my record." He couldn't stop himself adding, "So was the man you killed."

"I didn't kill anyone."

"There is little difference between killing someone yourself and ordering them killed."

Norris pursed his lips. "It's a moot point, anyway. You are a dead man, Agent Laughton. Unless you want to deal for your life."

Alistair nearly laughed again. Deals with men like Norris only went one way. Norris's way. "And what would I have to deal with? Knowledge?" He wouldn't need Alistair to get inside knowledge on the Justice Department. Many agents would be happy to supply insider information for a small consideration.

Norris indicated the fire-breather. "I find this an interesting weapon. I haven't seen the likes before."

He wouldn't have. "The fire-breather." Alistair moved to pick it up.

Norris slapped a blaster over the top of it. "Don't even think of it. A fire-breather, you call it." He flicked a glance at one of his crew. The crew member touched his jaw. Researching fire-breathers, if Alistair had to guess.

"They won't find anything."

"You might be surprised how good our security is."

Alistair wouldn't be surprised at all. "You still won't find anything about the fire-breather." He smiled. Norris didn't. If Cam had been the one smiling, would Norris have matched it? Everyone smiled back when Cam smiled at them. Even Alistair.

Memory of Cam sobered him. Blaster fire wasn't always lethal if you got to the injury in time. But Cam had gone down hard.

"Not smiling now," Norris said.

No. And if he was on a merc ship, how was he going to get to Rik Terri and then get to Zell?

"You'll think of something," Cam would have said. "You always do." But for the last two years Cam had been at his side, dependable, reliable, always there with his ever-ready smile and his willingness to do what needed to be done. All hidden behind a fragile self-confidence.

Alistair wasn't thinking fast enough now.

The day Barry and Angel had made their move, he hadn't been thinking all that fast either.

The trip to the Santiago ship and back, including medical attention for Barry and Talli, had taken all day. They'd returned to find a party in progress.

Yakusha came up to Alistair with a glass. She was wearing one of her Zell-made robes. One with the colors that he saw as bright greens and yellows but that the colonists saw as dirty brown and pink. "Drink, Alistair?"

He took it suspiciously. "This isn't one of your home brews, is it?"

"Genuine japonica rice sake, from back in the days when they used to deliver supplies we asked for. Melda complained how much they charged us for it."

It wasn't the only thing Melda had complained about, and with good reason. The Santiago visitors were making themselves unpopular with their unreasonable demands and their prying. Alistair took a sip. "Why are we celebrating?"

"We made quota. We hit a freak current where the transurides had collected. It was only small, but it was enough. Ten kilograms of transurides in the bag. In the safe, rather. Plus an extra eleven grams, just to make sure. These people can pack up the equipment whenever they like now, although they'll probably insist we mine the pocket out. It doesn't matter. We can all go home." She clicked her glass against his—it wasn't really a glass, just one of the plastic tumblers, which was all they had—and leaned close. "Come to me when you need it topped off. Those"—she inclined her head toward the table—"are for our guests."

Most plants and animals on Zell were poisonous to humans, but no matter what world you were on, Alistair had found the residents could always distill a drinkable alcohol. Zell was no exception.

The drinks on the table had the rainbow sheen typical of alcohol brewed on this world. The Santiagans weren't enjoying it. How long before one of them brought out their own supplies?

As Yakusha disappeared back into the crowd, Barry cornered Angel. Moments later he, Talli, and Angel went out.

Melda came in the door they'd exited. Cam came in from the other end of the room. Melda joined Alistair, followed his gaze. "Barry commandeered my office. They didn't want me at the meeting." She finished her sake and held up her glass high. "If I didn't hate Angel so much right now and not even want to be in the same room as her, I'd be annoyed."

"Hate is a reasonable response under the circumstances," Cam said. "Glad you made it back in one piece, Alistair. Some of us were worried you wouldn't." He gripped Alistair's shoulder hard enough for Alistair to know he was one of the ones who'd been worried. "Can you still see?"

Alistair nodded. "As well as ever."

"Good," and Cam's smile flashed out.

Yakusha swept up in a swirl of yellow and green, poured Melda another drink, and held up the bottle inquiringly in Alistair's direction. "There's not much of the good stuff left."

Alistair shook his head. "Not for me, thanks." In a moment he planned to go to his own office, which was next door to Melda's. Santiago's stingy building materials meant the walls weren't soundproof. Maybe he could hear what they were discussing.

"You heard we made quota," Melda said.

"Yes." Would it matter? Unease curdled Alistair's stomach. He had not gotten anywhere by ignoring his instincts, and the crowded ship in orbit would not fit fifty settlers.

"Melda, what are the terms of the contract? What happens at the end?"

Melda sighed. Looked at her glass. "Why does he have to spoil everything?"

She took a long drink and started toward her office. "I think I need this drink even more than I did before. Let's take it out of here. It will be easier for all of us to see on a big screen, and that way it'll only spoil our night. Let the rest of them celebrate."

Alistair put out a hand again. "Your office is being used." And his was next door. "Maybe Cam's."

"If we can even find the screen in there."

Cam shrugged. He hadn't used his office in months.

Yakusha followed them. "I'll clear it," she said. Most of the items in there were hers. Wool from the bovines, more alcohol.

Some reeds she was trying to make cloth from. She cleared the area in front of the screen.

Melda linked in. "This would be so much easier if I was in my own office. I could use it as an excuse to kick them out. What am I looking for, Alistair?"

"What happens at the end of contract? What do they do with us, how do they transport us home?" His own contract had said he would be paid, then dropped off at the nearest Santiago hub station, Enos Three. From there he could do what he liked. His bonus would allow him to rebuild his life. He'd planned to go back to Kitimat, to his apartment. From there he would take stock and work out what he was going to do next.

"Let me see." Melda scrolled through the details. "Santiago takes back the equipment. Minus a percentage for depreciation. Blah, blah, blah. They take off our final fee. They then pay the contract out. Plus bonuses, if applicable. Drop us off at Enos Three. Is that what you needed to know?"

"Do they say when they'll drop us off? Or how?"

"You're starting to worry me, Alistair. I'm jittery enough with Angel here. I doubt it's familial affection. Her job is usually to close down unsuccessful businesses."

"But we're not unsuccessful," Yakusha said.

Cam twisted a hank of wool through his hands. "It depends how you define *success*, doesn't it."

"Don't mess that up, Cam." Yakusha took the hank from him.

"Successful for us might not be successful for them."

Cam was right, and some of Alistair's unease solidified into full-blown misgiving. "Think about it," he said quietly. "They come here early. They are ready to pack up our equipment before we finish, perhaps to ensure we don't make quota. But we do. Our people are good. Now they have to pay out on a bonus. A massive bonus. A bonus they never expected to pay."

"Where are you going with this?"

"Once we get to Enos Three, we have contracts and the Justice Department on our side."

It wasn't a lot of money for Santiago, but they would still hate to pay it.

"Why do you even think this stuff up, Alistair?"

"Because I was up on that ship today and there is nowhere for us. Their people are already packed in. Not unless they plan on taking us as cargo." Right now he wouldn't put it past them. "I want to know how they plan to do it."

"This is nonsense," Melda said. "They'll have another ship coming."

"Before they take anything of ours, make sure of it. They're not taking anything until we see this other ship."

"And until they've paid us," Yakusha said.

Melda looked at Cam, standing to one side. "Do you agree with him?"

"They don't call Angel the Hatchet for no reason," Cam said. "You're as worried as we are that she's here. You said so before."

"Let's sort this." Melda marched out of Cam's office, down to her own. She lifted a fist to bang on the door.

The door opened before she could knock. "Let's do it while they're inebriated."

"Do what while who's inebriated?" Melda demanded.

Angel swept out. "Have you been listening, Melda?"

"No, but I wish I had if you're worried about what I might hear. What are you planning to do?"

"Not in your need to know."

A scream shattered the standoff. Mayeso. Alistair took the steps four at a time. Mayeso crashed into him at the bottom. "They're here. The Ort. They're here."

He steadied her. "Where?"

"The storeroom. They're here. We're all going to die."

"They haven't killed anyone yet." He passed her to Yakusha's care and ran. Barry, Cam, and Melda were close behind.

There was no one in the storeroom, but the safe was wide open. And empty. The transurides were gone. Two years of hard work, gone. Their bonus. Gone.

Melda choked off a cry.

Alistair swung around, moved into Angel's space. "So this is how you get out of paying our bonuses? Why?"

He knew he was big and could intimidate. Right now it was deliberate.

Barry stepped between them. "I wish we'd thought of it, but it wasn't us."

From the rage on Angel's face, Barry might even be right.

"What were you planning on doing while we were inebriated?"

"Closing down the operation," Barry said.

"We won't mind now. We've met quota. We met contract."

Barry gave a shrug.

"What about us? What about our contract pay, our bonuses? Tell me that you plan to pay our bonus. And while you're at it, tell me how you are going to get us home. No lies. Or do you plan to take the machinery and leave us here?"

Angel said, "You're not obligated to tell them anything, Barry."

Barry spread his hands, shrugged. "We owe them that much." He waited till Alistair stepped back. "Santiago owns the machinery. Much of it can be reused. We're taking it back."

"And us?"

"We planned to notify another ship you were here."

"Notify another ship. What ship might that be, Barry? And when do you plan on notifying it?" There was only one type of ship

Alistair knew who would collect people without being paid to do it. A cattle ship. Santiago planned to leave them here on Zell with nothing and then call a cattle ship to pick them up.

"Strictly business, you understand. It's not personal."

Business. They were talking lives here. Fifty people working hard for two years just to be handed off to a slave ship or left to die once past their use-by.

How many times had Santiago done this before? Barry, at least, had the grace to look uncomfortable. Melda just looked angry.

"I don't know how either of you look at yourselves in the mirror each day," Melda said.

Neither did Alistair.

"Unfortunately for you," Angel said, "there has been a change of plan. This latest plot of yours has saved you from that fate."

Unfortunately. So whatever fate Angel planned for them had to be worse than being collected by a cattle ship. That left only one option. Alistair wasn't sure it was worse.

"You're going to kill us. Why?"

"I believe you call them Ort."

Alistair looked at Melda and Cam. At Yakusha and Mayeso. His friends as well as his workmates.

Angel spread her hands in a let's-be-reasonable gesture. "But before tempers get too heated, tell us what you've done with the transurides."

She had to be kidding.

"You're a bastard, Angel. You know that," Melda said.

Mayeso tugged at Alistair's arm. "The Ort. They took it."

"You can't blame these Ort for everything," Angel said. "Return those transurides. Now. Let me show you how serious we are, what we do with thieves." She turned to Barry, pointed at Mayeso. "Kill the thief."

Alistair snatched for the fire-breather strapped onto his back as he stepped in front of Mayeso. "Don't even think it."

Barry grabbed Melda, held his blaster to her head. "Lower your hands, Laughton. Or this one dies first."

"Let's instead talk about what is happening here. Did you really come all this way just to shoot us?"

Barry shrugged. "It happens."

The matter-of-fact way he said the words made it real. How much time did they have? "You're outnumbered."

"But we're prepared to kill. You're not."

"I wouldn't be so sure about that." Right now he would happily kill them all.

Melda pulled free from Barry.

Angel lifted her own—hitherto concealed—weapon.

Alistair tripped Melda as Angel fired. She went down. So slowly it seemed he could see the spurt of heat from Angel's blaster. Could see the way Melda fell, saw the heat pass by her. Saw her hair catch fire.

Angel raised her weapon again, aimed it at Alistair.

"Don't try it. Lower your weapon or you are dead." He hefted the fire-breather meaningfully. She changed her aim, toward Cam.

There was a spurt of blue-white sheet lightning.

Angel dropped.

Sheet lightning. Alistair looked at the weapon in his hand. He hadn't fired.

Mayeso backed against the wall, eyes wide, staring at the door. Even Barry backed away.

Cam dropped to the floor beside Melda and pulled off his jacket. "You realize this is my last good jacket. After this I'll have to wear one of Yakusha's horrible pink-and-brown things."

Alistair turned to the doorway. Eight Ort stood there, fire-breathers raised. A corner of his mind registered the way they held the weapons. He would have to change his grip. He wasn't sure if the timing of their arrival was good or bad.

A wave of white noise swamped him. A strong feeling of safety and security, and out of the white noise came, "No harm. Miracle."

"The smartest thing you can do right now, Barry, is surrender." Alistair lowered his own weapon.

Barry dropped his blaster. "You lied. You do have an understanding with these creatures."

If only it were true, but Alistair was prepared to pretend it was if it saved their lives.

"They're trying to talk to us." He turned to the Ort, pushed the words across as a thought as he spoke. "We mean you no harm either."

"No harm." One of the creatures pointed to Cam.

"Me? What have I done?"

Outside, voices raised. Someone started yelling.

Alistair snatched up Angel's blaster, and Barry's. He tossed Barry's blaster to Yakusha, Angel's to Cam.

The yelling was punctuated with blaster fire.

The timing sucked.

He ignored Angel. He was pretty sure she was dead. He didn't care. He turned to Barry. "Does this put you in charge?" It didn't matter. The people out there were Barry's. "You come with me. You, too, Cam," for he didn't want to leave Cam without protection. "Mayeso, Yakusha, take care of Melda."

There was more yelling from outside. He couldn't make out the words, but it sounded like Cadel's voice.

"I'm sorry," Alistair said to the Ort. "I have a situation I need to deal with. Please wait." He hoped they understood. He picked up his own fire-breather, gestured to Barry. "Come."

"Your problem, you deal." Barry kept his hands up, his eyes on the Ort. He looked as terrified as Mayeso.

Cam waved his newly acquired blaster. "Go with him, Barry. I'll follow. And be warned. I will happily shoot you, even if you think Alistair won't."

Alistair hid a smile as he bowed hastily to the Ort. "Later."

He ran for the door and raised his fire-breather as he did so. If any of his people were dead, then the Santiagans would die likewise.

In the main room the settlers had taken cover. Talli was ordering her troops to circle behind.

"Drop your weapons," Alistair bellowed. "The next person who fires is dead."

Talli spun toward him, then her jaw dropped, and her weapon went slack in her hand. One of the other guards fired. Aiming behind them. His aim was off.

Alistair shot his arm.

Barry scrambled to one side. "You idiot. Do you want to hit me?"

"Boss," the guard stammered. "Behind—"

"I am well aware."

Alistair detected the tremor in Barry's voice. He didn't think anyone else would pick up on it. He guessed from the reaction, the Ort had followed them out.

"Angel is dead." Alistair hoped she was, anyway. "Barry is in charge and will confirm that the situation has changed. Drop your weapons. I'll shoot anyone who doesn't comply."

Two of them were slower than the rest of the guards. From the corner of his eye, Alistair saw one of the Ort step forward. The guards dropped their blasters.

"Cadel, Sims," Alistair said. "Collect all weapons." Cadel had a blaster burn down his left leg, but he limped toward Talli.

"Anyone else hurt?" He didn't ask if anyone was dead.

"Just me," said Cadel. "My stupid fault, really. They stole the keys to the machinery shed."

Preparatory to moving everything out and onto the spaceship. Why bother if they'd been going to kill them all regardless?

"Lock them in an empty store," Alistair ordered once the weapons were collected. They didn't have a lockup on Zell. He'd never thought they'd need one. He left Sims and Cadel in charge and turned to the Ort. "Thank you for your assistance."

A white noise of confusion enveloped him.

He tried again. "Thank you for your help," and thought it at them as well.

More white noise, but among it he picked out, "Least we can do for our fellow abandoneds."

At least that was what it sounded like.

"Abandoneds?"

"Your uncle's uncle's uncle must grieve for you."

Cam came over to stand beside him.

The white noise crescendoed as the Ort surrounded him.

"They really like you."

"It might not be like."

"It's excitement. They're communicating, but it's not making a lot of sense."

"It's not making any sense to me. I hear nothing."

"So far all I've got is that it's the least they can do to help abandoneds like them, and our uncles are grieving for us."

Cam scratched his head. "I think you might need to work more on your translations." He smiled uncertainly at the Ort. "Hi."

The Ort who seemed to be the lead speaker gave a bob, all four legs down, all four arms up. "Ourselves are honored to be in your company, Savior. Miracle."

The others bobbed too. "Miracle."

"Now they're calling you a miracle."

Cam scratched his head again. "I wouldn't go as far as that. But I'll take it, if it brings them onto our side."

The next hours were an exhaustive blur of struggling to understand each other. All Alistair could go by was the emotions he got through the white noise. If he was interpreting them incorrectly—and he might well be—then this historic meeting of two races was doomed.

It was as exhausting for the Ort as it was for Alistair.

While both sides took a break, Alistair summed it up for Cam, Yakusha, Cadel, and an in-pain Melda. "They're plague carriers. And scientists. I think. Or doctors." Only, their doctors seemed a lot more sophisticated than human doctors. "Their race is beset by a plague. It's spread out along their quadrant of the galaxy—don't ask me where, they did tell me, but I didn't understand. They don't have a cure. It's decimating them." Literally, if he understood the figures. "One in ten survives."

He sniffed at the drink Yakusha handed him. "This smells like coffee." Took a mouthful. "Tastes like coffee too."

"It is coffee," Cam said dreamily.

He'd have to get used to the taste again.

"We raided their shuttles," Yakusha said. "Took all their supplies, given they're eating us out. One of them had the cheek to complain about the size of the dinner we gave them."

Both shuttles were still on-world. They'd have to let their prisoners go soon. They couldn't feed them forever. Couldn't even feed themselves. What would Santiago do then? Give the colony up as lost? No. The ship was still out there, and Barry would have reported the Ort. First contact would be a coup for Santiago Company.

"We'll have to make a deal with Barry."

"Over my dead body," Melda said.

It would be her dead body if they didn't. Alistair didn't argue, though. She'd realize the predicament she was in when she could think through the pain. He continued with what he knew—or thought he knew.

"They've been injecting us with an antidote for their plague. Apparently, we humans can be cured. They say they have wanted to talk with us ever since they first met me." Alistair didn't know what he'd done to make them realize he was sapient, but thank God for aliens who recognized sapience when they saw it, because he wasn't sure humans would have done the same with an individual sample. That was why they'd saved his eyes rather than mercifully killing him.

"It's also why I can talk to them. The Ort opened up some . . . thing . . . a pathway in my brain." He'd thought the white noise in his head had been damage to his hearing—or his mind—from the original operation. Instead he'd been receiving sounds via the opened neural pathways.

"Some of us will volunteer to let them do the same for us," Melda said. "You can't do everything. I hope their machines can cope with human anatomy."

How did he put this without making the Ort seem barbaric? "They don't have machines, Melda. They do it by hand."

"Oh my God."

She'd never sounded so much like his old boss, Paola Teke.

Alistair rested his head against the wall, closed his eyes momentarily. All he wanted to do was sleep. But the important information was still to come.

"They're searching for transurides. In quantity. Their calculations say the Vortex has the perfect conditions for transurides." Which was why the humans were out here too. "They have some method—hit or miss, apparently—where they take in enormous amounts of transurides." He'd thought they said they ate it, but that would be wasteful. "Some of it gets into your bloodstream. You only need a trace amount to stop the plague binding.

"Human blood will build antibodies. Theirs won't, not for this plague. But they test us before they inoculate us, just in case."

He opened his eyes, looked at Cam. "Then they got to you. The plague didn't take. You're naturally immune. They say it's because you have transurides in your body."

"I do." Cam brushed back his hair self-consciously. "Dellarine. It makes my skin glow."

"Are you sure?" Yakusha asked. "That's not normal."

"Of course I'm sure. I paid for it, didn't I."

"Where did you get that sort of money?"

Cam came from money; Alistair was sure of that. He cut across the start of an interrogation Cam didn't want. "How did it get into your body?"

"My modder. She said it would be expensive, but it would look amazing." He smiled, this time his regular, open smile that made everyone smile back. "She was right. It does."

"Here's the deal," Barry had said when Alistair went to see him the next day. "Santiago is sending an armored ship. It will be here in two weeks. If necessary, they will rescue us. You know what will happen to you.

"If you're staying on planet with us, you will need to supply your own food."

They couldn't feed fifteen unnecessary mouths for two weeks. Alistair had rather hoped Barry and his people would return to their own ship, even if it left their own people vulnerable because they had no way off the planet.

"And the Ort?"

"We'll make a treaty with them."

"You don't know how to talk to them. You don't know what they want. They see you as the enemy."

Two groups of outsiders, banding together in isolation. A fragile bond. It was risky to rely on an unknown alien culture, to assume they thought the same way, even if the Ort had helped them, but trusting Santiago led to only one result. Death for all their settlement.

"Understood," Barry said. "Your people also know the world conditions better than we do. We'll work with you."

For the moment. Until they learned to communicate themselves. Then the settlement people would be superfluous. "What about the deal we had with Santiago. Our contract?"

"We'll pay you out," Barry said. "Although, you haven't produced the transurides."

"We've still got a week to deliver." The Ort still had the transurides. Alistair would leave that deal for Melda to bargain, once she could talk to them. She was undergoing the surgery right now to change parts of her brain so she could receive and interpret their words—if they were actually words.

Surgery. He couldn't stop his shudder.

Humans had a lot to learn from Ort. Ort might have things to learn from humans too.

"You won't get the bonus," Barry said.

He'd expected that, counted on it. "Then give us the machinery. Legally."

"The machinery's worth more than you are."

"You tried to get out of a contract by killing us. How do you think the Justice Department will look at that?"

Barry started to laugh, then stopped. "That would be funny, coming from anyone but you. The Justice Department is a toothless tiger."

"There are a couple of canines left, if you know how to use them."

"And you do, don't you?"

"I do." But if those steps came to pass, everyone in the settlement would be dead. Santiago might suffer a minor loss of reputation, and the Ort would come under the jurisdiction of the Justice Department, but the forty-nine people under Alistair's care would be dead.

"We want the machinery," Alistair said. "And we want to be recognized as joint settlers here on Zell." For all the good that would do them. Barry would believe they meant to settle. As soon as he could, Alistair was getting them all off-world. Including the Ort, if they wanted to come. Barry didn't need to know that.

"You drive a hard bargain."

"Please don't be facetious. We both know where this will end." He was trying to delay the inevitable and hoping for a miracle in between. Hope was a funny thing. It kept you alive; it kept you trying.

"Point," conceded Barry. "All conditions agreed, provided there's a proviso that all reverts to Santiago if, say, a plague wipes you all out."

Alistair gave a grim smile. "It's funny you mention plague. Are you aware the Ort are plague carriers?"

From the recoil, no, Barry hadn't been.

Alistair's smile widened. "The Ort inoculated us to protect us from the plague. Your medic cleaned it out of yours and Talli's system, claiming it was a virus. You might want to take that into consideration for future dealings with us."

Not that it mattered. Barry and his team had a doctor and a genemod machine. They didn't have to worry. But even small victories could be savored, no matter how short they lasted.

"One last thing," Alistair said. "We have promised to do something for the Ort."

They'd agreed to find Nika Rik Terri and bring her back to explain how she'd worked the transurides. Provided they could convince her to come. Cam thought she would. But what did a client really know about his or her modder, except what the modder told them in order to sell the mod?

"Two of us have to leave this world in order to do that. We'd like to contract with Santiago for the passage."

Santiago would see it as a way they could divide the team and find out more about the Ort. They'd agree to it. Particularly as they didn't want anyone else coming to Zell right now.

"We will provide transport."

"At cost."

"Negotiated price."

"Negotiated," Alistair agreed, and left him to go and see how Melda's surgery had fared.

Maybe there was something Alistair could bargain with Norris for.

"If you're planning to escape," Norris said, "remember there are four hundred trained mercenaries on this ship. You won't get far."

There were two hundred armed men on the Santiagan ship now orbiting Zell. Santiago would attack any ship they thought might be muscling in on their exclusive, especially a mercenary ship like Norris's, hired for fighting wars. How much damage would each ship do to the other? Enough to give Alistair time to call in the charter ship that Paola had arranged? He was out of time, and so were the people on Zell. Desperate times called for desperate strategies.

He prayed he wasn't about to gamble everyone's life on something he couldn't win.

"Pol is right. The woman with Snowshoe isn't Arriola." He had no idea who Arriola was, and if Norris didn't want Arriola, Alistair was making a bad mistake here. "She's Nika Rik Terri." He hoped.

Norris's eyelid twitched, but there was no other visible reaction.

"You give me Nika Rik Terri, and I will take you to the world where they make those fire-breathers."

"And what will be waiting for me at that world, I wonder?"

"You're in no danger from us," Alistair said. "Ours is a small settlement. Fifty people." Forty-nine now that Cam was dead. He shrugged. "I can't answer for anyone else in the vicinity, although it is an isolated area."

"And if I find you are double-crossing me?"

By then it would be too late. Alistair hoped.

"You have my weapon. It's a good one. Just give me Rik Terri. Our settlement depends on her for survival." He let desperation creep into his voice. "She's a modder, and we need a modder to survive on our world."

Norris opened a link. "Pol, you claim Roystan is following us. Are you certain of that?"

"He'll do anything for his crew."

"You had better be right." Norris glanced at the fire-breather, looked at Alistair. "If the woman turns out to be Rik Terri, and not Arriola, then we have a deal."

Norris turned to one of the guards. "Bring me Snowshoe."

23

JOSUNE ARRIOLA

Twelve hours later Roystan still hadn't come around.

He was deteriorating in front of their eyes.

"He's dying," Carlos said.

Probably, and there was nothing they could do about it with their body modder captive on another ship. No, there was never nothing.

The *Boost* still hadn't jumped. It was almost as if Norris knew they were following and was waiting for them.

"I'm going to call the *Boost*," Josune said. "He wants me. We want Nika. I'll arrange a swap."

"You can't, Josune."

"He won't kill me. He wants me for my knowledge of the *Hassim*. I'll take a tracker. *Another Road* can follow. You'll have to pilot, Carlos, until Roystan comes around."

Carlos muttered something that might have been a prayer.

"When I get to the *Boost*, I'll find Snow."

"How will you get back to our ship?"

She had no idea. "I'll think of something."

"Do we trust Norris to exchange Nika?" Jacques asked. "What if he sends someone else over?"

"I'll kill him." That was a promise. "But we'll get him to use Snow to verify it's Nika he's sending."

She started to open a link, before she thought too much about what could go wrong, then paused. "Norris will probably be less suspicious if you try to bargain, not me. Imply that Nika is crew, and that I'm just a late addition. You'll swap me for Nika."

"We can't do that," Carlos said.

"Not even to save Roystan's life?"

Carlos rubbed his arms and shivered. "It's like . . . I don't know. Wrong."

"I'll do it," Jacques said, although his voice wasn't steady. "We do what we have to do, Carlos. That's what Roystan does."

He took a deep breath. "Perhaps you should remain out of camera sight, Josune."

She nodded and moved to a seat where she wouldn't be picked up by the camera.

Jacques opened a link. "This is Jacques Saloman, second officer on *Another Road*, calling Captain Norris, of the *Boost*."

"You just promoted yourself," Carlos said.

"Men like Norris understand rank," Jacques said. "I have to be the second in charge. Otherwise I cannot deal." He called again, this time sounding more impatient. "This is Jacques Saloman, of *Another Road*, calling Captain Norris, of the *Boost*."

Norris took a few minutes to reply. "This is Norris."

"Captain, you have one of our crew members on board. A woman named Nika Rik Terri. We want her back."

Norris's smile was a baring of teeth. "Second Officer Saloman, you have someone on board your ship I want too. I'd say we're even."

"But we could be even and both be happy," Jacques said. "You give us our crew member, we hand over Arriola."

Norris's left eyelid twitched and twitched again. It was his only expression.

"You're prepared to give up Arriola for—"

"For a permanent crew member, yes. We have a duty of care with permanent crew, you know."

"You are aware she is wanted by the Justice Department."

Jacques gave an expressive shrug. "What crew member doesn't have a few things they'd like to keep quiet?"

The corner of Norris's mouth curved up. "Point," he conceded. "But last time I thought I was collecting Arriola I was mistaken. How do I know I'll be getting the real thing this time?"

"We could ask the same thing. How do we know you are exchanging Nika Rik Terri, and not some random stranger?"

Jacques's hands were starting to shake, but his voice remained steady. Josune gave him a thumbs-up. His hands stilled.

"Point," Norris conceded.

Jacques paused, as if struck by an idea. "Bertram Snowshoe. Would he lie to you? He certainly wouldn't lie to us. He could vouch for both."

"So, you send Arriola over to my ship, I will send Rik Terri back."

"Captain Norris. I was not born yesterday. Why don't you send Rik Terri over here, and we send Arriola back?"

Norris permitted himself a smile.

They bartered for half an hour before finally settling on a shuttle, confirmed by Snow to contain only Nika and one crew member, to come over to *Another Road* and make the exchange. The crew member would be armed and could shoot to kill if they tried to double-cross Norris.

Which meant he'd shoot anyway, once he had what he wanted.

"We have an agreement," Norris said. "I will organize a shuttle." He clicked off.

He hadn't once asked about Roystan, who he knew was captain. Why not?

Jacques fell back onto the seat. "I have aged ten years in ten minutes. I am overcome."

Josune made him a coffee. "You did well, Jacques. Really well."

"That man is like a spoiled sharkbeast carcass. Firm and muscular on the outside, rotten when you cut it open."

"I don't trust him," Carlos said. "I don't like this at all, Josune. If Roystan wasn't—"

"None of us like it, Carlos." Roystan, least of all, once he knew about it. But if they didn't get Nika, then Roystan wouldn't be around to like it, anyway.

They couldn't worry about what they liked or didn't. They had to worry about what was. "The guard Norris sends over with Nika will do as much damage as he can, starting with Nika." They had to find a way to neutralize him as soon as the guard confirmed she was Josune.

Josune had her sparker. Nika had the dart gun—which she wouldn't get time to use. What else did they have that wasn't an obvious weapon? Something to neutralize one person, maybe more.

Gas? She needed Nika or Snow here to mix her up something. Or something Nika and Snow had already used? Hadn't Nika once used diluted antiseptic?

Josune found a nozzle from engineering. Fixed a pressure vac to it, so it would come out fast and easy, and slung it over her shoulder, ready to grab if required.

Lastly, she grabbed three tracking markers from Roystan's small but growing collection that they were all helping to rebuild—you couldn't keep a man and his paranoia down too far.

"I'm putting one under my collar," she told Carlos, and suited action to words. "One on the inside of my boot." If they searched her, they'd find them. "This one . . ." She grimaced, placed it into her mouth, and swallowed.

"Let's hope they don't put you under a genemod machine," Carlos muttered. "And what happens if you, you know, get the trots?"

Josune was more worried about the acids in her stomach destroying circuitry of the marker. She didn't mention that. "We'll be out by then." She hoped. "We'll have to steal a shuttle. Expect one to come our way, but don't open the shuttle-bay doors, not even if one does arrive. No matter what happens. I can unlock it from the inside." It was coded to crew. "But Norris's people can't. If they try to board, pretending it's us, they'll need you to open the door for them."

Carlos nodded, short and fast, and way too long. "This isn't much of a plan, Josune."

No, it wasn't.

"It's all we've got."

"I miss the cargo run," Carlos said. "When all we had to worry about was Pol trying to organize new pickups in our break time, and accidents on Atalante Station because it was old and falling apart." He gave an exaggerated sigh. "Still," he said. "Better company nowadays, I suppose. Even if you are all crazy. Airy-fairy body modders, maniacs with guns."

"Even me?" Josune was honored. "Thank you, Carlos."

"You're a good engineer," he said gruffly.

"Thank you."

The silence that followed was filled by Jacques, behind them, sweet-talking his ovens. He must have heard them, but he kept talking to the equipment in the kitchen, pretending to ignore them.

Norris called then, which broke the awkward silence that had fallen.

Jacques answered. Josune stayed out of the way. Let Norris think she—and maybe even her captain—were not in on this.

"I have Nika Rik Terri with me."

"Hello, Nika," Jacques said.

From where Josune sat, Nika looked whole and healthy, at least. They'd given her time in a genemod machine, so she wouldn't have to waste time on repairs before she could work on Roystan. She still looked like Brand—which must have irritated her to no end—but she was whole.

"Hi," Nika returned. "You're exchanging me for Josune?"

Jacques nodded. He wouldn't need to explain why the exchange, rather than a straight rescue, was necessary. Nika knew, probably better than anyone else on board.

"We have made an agreement with Captain Norris. Snow will confirm that you, and one—only one—of Norris's crew get onto the shuttle and come over to *Another Road* in order to facilitate the exchange. Where is Bertram Snowshoe, Captain?"

"Snowshoe is here," Norris said. "He will also confirm that the woman entering the shuttle at the other end is Josune Arriola." He gave a slow smile. "He knows his life depends on providing the correct answer."

Jacques drew himself up to full height. "I am not a cheat, Captain."

"No one is accusing you of cheating, Second Officer. It is simply to ensure Mez Arriola does actually arrive on my ship."

Message received and clearly understood. If Snow lied, and it wasn't Josune who returned in the shuttle, he'd be killed. If Josune chose not to come, he'd be killed.

"Understood." Jacques's face was wooden. "Let me talk to Snow."

Josune wished they'd hurry up and get the talking done. Roystan was still unconscious. Every minute could mean a minute less to save him. She tried to contain her impatience.

Snow's face was as wooden as Jacques's. "We are at the shuttle. Captain Norris, myself, Nika, and one crew member are here. I have checked the shuttle." He enunciated carefully, as if it was the only way he could get the words out. "There are no extra crew stowed away." He moved his gaze sideways, to the crew member.

No, to behind the crew member.

"And there you have it," Norris said. "A careful boy, young Snowshoe. It's one of the things that makes him a good doctor."

Snow gave him a look that had Josune covering her mouth with her hand to stop laughing.

He put his hand behind his back, brought it out, fist clasped as if he had something grasped in it.

What was he trying to say?

"He is a modder," Nika said coldly.

"On this ship, Mez Rik Terri, all he'll ever be is a doctor. If he survives until the end of the week, that is. I'm still considering which doctor I will keep." He gave another thin smile. "Will I go for the doctor who has been with me for years? Or should I choose someone young, more malleable, and recently trained and more up-to-date? Such a dilemma."

Nika visibly bit off what she had been going to say, changed it to, "Can we get on with this? I'm finding the company rather unpleasant. Not yours, of course, Snow."

"Thank you," Snow said.

Norris's eyes narrowed.

Score one for the malleable young modder. *Don't worry, Snow. We'll have you out of there as soon as I can arrange it.*

Snow stepped back, let Nika and the crew member enter the shuttle.

The crew member moved, lifted his arm, and for a moment, under the jacket, she could see a long, straight rod outlined between his spine and the left shoulder blade. Too large to be a sparker. A stun stick? No, too small. It was a weapon, and he'd use it as soon as Snow confirmed that Josune was who she said she was. *Thanks for the warning, Snow.*

How did they counter that?

With speed. It was the only way.

"Thirty minutes until the shuttle reaches *Another Road*," Norris said.

"We'll be waiting." Jacques clicked off. "That man. He leaves a rotten taste in the mouth."

Half an hour. Josune armed herself. Blaster, antiseptic spray, and the sparker. She used an old sparker, one she could afford to lose if they searched her and took it off her. Which they would. But if she didn't go armed, they'd search harder.

"What do you want us to do?" Carlos asked as the shuttle drew closer. He was a better fighter than he had been two months ago, but that didn't mean much. "What if he shoots our ship once we exchange?"

"We'll have time to nullspace before he gets close enough to do major damage. Be ready, just in case. And move the ship back once the shuttle leaves our ship."

"This is a very bad idea," Carlos said.

They didn't have any other option.

"Stay ready with the blaster," Josune said. "Don't shoot unless he tries to come aboard." He shouldn't. Her biggest worry was that the crew member would kill Nika once he had Josune in his sights. It seemed like the kind of parting gift Norris would enjoy. "Otherwise stay out of it. Keep Nika safe." And pray that Josune had collected everything she needed with Giwari's Songyan.

It went pretty much as she imagined it. The shuttle docked; Josune and Carlos went into the shuttle bay. Josune ID'd herself. The *Boost* crew member then beckoned to Nika and directed Josune to board the shuttle. As they passed, Josune caught Nika's gaze and gestured downward. "When I say."

A single nod.

As soon as Nika's back was to the crew member, he reached his right hand down his back.

Josune had been waiting for it. "Now." She sprayed antiseptic into the crew member's eyes.

Nika dropped to the floor.

A stick thudded into the wall, hard enough to put a fist-sized dent into it. That was reinforced metal, which with regular bumps didn't even scratch. The blow would have killed. He dropped the stick to claw at his eyes. A Canning stick. Used by muscle-boys.

Josune picked it up and used it. The crew member went down.

"Pity he didn't try this in the shuttle," Josune said as she dropped the stick. "Now I have to get him back into it. Are you okay, Nika?"

"Fine," Nika said. "Roystan?"

"In your studio. With the Giwari."

"Thank you." And Nika was gone.

Carlos helped drag the unconscious man into the shuttle. "Now we send him home alone."

"No. Norris will kill Snow if I don't go."

Carlos grunted, but didn't say anything else until he dropped the other man's torso onto the shuttle floor. "I'll take his blaster."

"And the stick." It was on the floor of the shuttle bay, anyway. Josune checked him over, removed two knives, a blaster, and a pair of knuckle-dusters. This was a man who liked his fight physical. His well-honed physique told her he'd be good at it too. She'd only get that one chance of surprise. She called up Nika. "Have you started on Roystan?"

"Just prepping the machine."

Good, for if she'd started on Roystan, she probably wouldn't even have answered the link. "Have you got something to knock this guard out for the duration of the trip?"

A five-second pause, then, "I'll bring it down."

Two minutes later Nika arrived with an anesthetic. "How long do you want him out for?"

"At least an hour."

Nika administered the dose. "Will you be okay?" she asked when she was done.

Josune nodded. "Just fix him." She didn't have to say who "him" was.

"I will," Nika promised. "Now I have the right equipment. Look after yourself. Come back alive. With Snow. And Gramps." She patted Josune's arm. "I'll get back to Roystan," which she knew was Josune's main worry.

"Thanks, Nika."

Josune and Carlos watched her go. "That sounds positive," Josune said. "Tell Roystan—"

Carlos backed away. "I'm not passing on secondhand love letters by word of mouth."

Josune grinned. "I was going to say, tell him to be ready. We might need to come aboard quickly. And Carlos, don't lose my marker." She patted her stomach.

"I won't." Carlos paused awkwardly. The words came out in a rush. "You come back." He raised a hand. "You have to come back, anyway. You've a half-dismantled engine down in engineering. I don't want to have to put it together, since I didn't pull it apart."

Josune opened her mouth to remind him to grease the smaller valve before he finished putting it back together, closed it again. "I'll be back."

It was a promise.

Josune called Norris when she was halfway to the *Boost*. "This is the *Boost* shuttle, requesting permission to approach."

"And you are?" Norris said.

"Josune." Snow must have still been with Norris.

"She can speak for herself."

"I am Josune Arriola." She sent through her ID.

"And my crew member?"

"Unconscious."

She could see Snow now, in Norris's screen. Standing behind him, arms crossed, looking grimly satisfied, as if he'd expected nothing less from Josune.

Norris raised an eyebrow.

"You know why he's unconscious," Josune said.

"And yet you still came?"

"You still have Snow."

"Ah yes," and Norris turned to smile in Snow's direction. "So I do."

"Permission to dock shuttle," Josune said.

"Without my crew member, how do I know you are not—"

"Oh come, Norris. I'm not that stupid. Not to mention, *Another Road* doesn't have the crew to waste fighting a four-hundred-crew merc ship."

Nor, having gone to so much trouble to save Snow's life, would she waste it by giving him an excuse to kill Snow at the first opportunity.

"Then by all means, you have permission to dock. I think I'll like working with you, Mez Arriola."

She certainly didn't like working with him.

———

Norris and four guards waited with Snow, his arms still crossed, although this time it looked more defensive than it had earlier. A woman waited with them. Pol Bager, former crew member of *The Road* turned mutineer. She was like a bad smell in life support, always turning up when you least expected it, and so much trouble to get rid of.

She also had a habit of making stupid pacts with their enemies. Thank the stars she wanted Josune dead. Otherwise she might have argued the swap, told Norris that Josune was a permanent crew member, permanent before Nika was.

Josune ID'd herself again into Norris's personal scanner. She had to clench her fists to stop them shaking. So far things were working to plan. Would they continue to?

"And because IDs can be faked," Norris said, "would you two be good enough to confirm this woman's identity?"

"You are kidding me," Josune said. "You want Pol to confirm who I am?"

Snow hid a snigger. "Last time she didn't recognize her. Offered to make a deal with her so they could both go off and find Josune."

Pol gave him a glare that said he was dead when she got him alone. "I don't recall you being there."

"He wasn't," Josune said. "But we laughed about it later." She had no compassion for Pol. She had looked different at the time, so the mistake was reasonable, but Pol had been ready to break Josune out of jail to help with her scheme and leave the rest of the crew behind, to be killed.

"I am going to kill you."

Norris's eyes narrowed.

Snow's snigger was louder. "I heard you tried to kill her a couple of times already. Didn't succeed."

Pol turned to Norris, ignoring Snow. "She carries a sparker, and she's not afraid to use it on a ship."

Norris had already nodded to one of the guards, who was stepping forward even as Pol spoke.

"Full body check," Norris said.

"My pleasure."

"Make it fast. Make it thorough. I don't care about your pleasure."

They took her blaster, her sparker, and the knife in her boot. They found the marker under her collar. They took the tools in her pocket.

A tall, bulky man in a business suit burst out of the lift and into the shuttle area. "You promised me Nika Rik Terri."

"I didn't promise you anything, Agent Laughton."

So this was the infamous Alistair Laughton. Josune studied him while Norris's crew member finished his search. He was a big man, formidable.

"You did, you know. We came to an agreement."

"So have the Justice Department sue me for breach of contract. Agent Laughton. You've heard the saying 'One meeskarr in a cage is worth two in the wild'? Rik Terri may be valuable to you. She is not to me. I want only one thing from the Justice Department right now."

"Which is?"

"The whereabouts of the weapons factory that made that firebreather you carried."

"You won't get that now."

"I believe I will, Agent, once a little judicious pressure is applied. Every man has his limit, even you." He snapped his fingers at the guards. "Take them both down to the cells."

They hadn't found the marker inside her boot. That was something to be grateful for. Personally, Josune would have made her prisoner strip and then destroyed all their clothes. But then, she was paranoid.

Norris looked at another guard. "Take Snowshoe back to the hospital."

"Yes, sir."

"And Snowshoe?"

Snow looked at him.

"You know what will happen if you try to visit your friend. Or if Gramps does."

Snow nodded, expressionless.

"I'm glad we all understand each other." Norris turned. "Come, Pol. You and I have things to discuss."

Pol's glance over her shoulder at Josune had daggers in it. One day soon Pol would come to kill her. She was sure of it. Let it happen. While Josune was weaponless, Pol was her best chance of arming herself.

24

JOSUNE ARRIOLA

The prison cell was one of ten in a row along one wall. Bars made up the other three sides. The door had an electronic lock that required two sets of ID to open. A suction privy was built into one corner, with a showerhead above it. The shower controls were red. Locked, Josune noted, and presumed that it would only work at certain times.

The bars were poly-treated carbon. Stronger than steel, but not hard. Josune had only ever seen them on the vids before. They were used, as far as she knew, for high-security prisoners who were likely to harm themselves. This ship would have a lot of that, if it was as bad as Snow said it was. Most of the people in these cells would have been captured by a cattle ship, their contracts sold to the merc ship.

The cell was three meters by three meters. Generous, compared to some, but when you were sharing one with an almost giant, it felt cramped.

"I would have preferred you were smaller," she told Alistair Laughton.

"Me too, right now."

"And you can't pace. You're too big."

"Sorry." He sat down with his back to the wall.

That suited Josune. She liked to be close to the bars, where there might be an opportunity to arm herself. A guard standing too close, or Pol, making good on her threat to come and kill her. Josune would be ready.

"What deal did you make with Norris?"

"None of your business."

"Why did you want Nika, then?"

"None of your business either."

Josune sighed. "Nika is my friend and my crewmate. If you won't tell me why you want her, why would she even think to help you?"

Laughton closed his eyes and didn't answer.

Josune studied the lock more closely. A Verter Prime. What was it with all these Verters suddenly popping up out of nowhere? *No, be reasonable about it.* Verters were good locks and all the best people used them. And the worst.

If she blasted it, the lock would fuse, and a secondary magnetic lock would come into play. The only way she would get this door open—short of someone opening it for her—was to cut the power to it, which was how the lock worked. One of these bars must have an electrical conduit behind it. Going up into the ceiling? She tested each bar. Sometimes you could tell from the warmth of the bar.

This time she couldn't.

Two guards stopped outside the cell. "Agent Laughton. Captain Norris wants to chat with you." They emphasized the "chat" and laughed at the same time.

"I don't want to chat with him."

"That's too bad." These two guards had a swagger that was completely at odds with other guards Josune had seen on the ship. They were also well built. Both were close to Laughton's height, and they had extra stripes on their epaulettes. "He certainly wants to chat with you."

Josune watched them go, cocky, sure, and in control. Laughton didn't look cowed. Did he realize how bad a predicament he was in? She thought not.

She sat down with her back to the bars. Norris would try to talk to her—about the *Hassim*, presumably, since Pol was here. She could wait.

They brought another prisoner in and put her into the cell next to Josune. The woman screamed and struggled. Josune moved so her back was against the other set of bars.

The guards watched the new prisoner scream.

"Don't worry, Effie," one of them said. "You'll be first down on the next mission. I'll personally see to it."

They left, laughing.

When Effie started battering herself against the bars, Josune stood up and stepped over. "Effie." She timed her grab and got Effie after she'd hit the bars—going, not coming—so she was easier to grab.

Effie started sobbing. "I wish I was dead." She clutched at the bars. "I should have let them kill me rather than sign that stupid contract."

Josune held her arms while she cried herself out.

"I hate it here."

They couldn't save everyone they met, and taking on someone like Norris and his trained thugs—the guards had held their weapons with ease—and an armored merc ship was crazy, but if Josune killed Norris and a couple of his people while rescuing Snow, she'd consider it time well spent.

"There's no way out." Effie's voice died away to a whisper. "They even caught Snow. Norris will come after you. It might take years, but he'll come."

"Effie." Josune gripped her arms hard. "Snow will escape again. I promise you that."

"He won't. You can't escape."

"Snow can. Snow will. You all can. Norris is just another bully with powerful tools."

"That's an interesting way of hearing myself described," Captain Norris said from the other side of the bars.

Effie froze.

Josune turned. Norris gestured to the guards who were with him. One of them opened the cell door. They pushed Laughton back inside. He had trouble standing.

"Did you get what you wanted out of him?" Based on the time they'd spent with him, she guessed not. "Some days are more difficult than others, Captain Norris."

Effie backed to the far side of her cell, tried to go still farther.

Norris gave a tight smile. "I did plan on chatting with you, Mez Arriola. Maybe I'll leave you to contemplate Agent Laughton here, before I do. You might realize the value of talking honestly and truthfully."

"I might," she agreed.

"Provided we all learn something from today." Norris looked over to Effie cowering against the wall. "Including you, Effie. Nobody escapes from the *Boost* and lives to boast about it."

He turned and marched out.

Josune waited until she was sure he was gone before she turned to Laughton. "Anything I can do for you?"

He shook his head.

"You're a fool. No one withstands torture forever. You'll tell him what he wants to know eventually."

Laughton winced as he sat down. It hurt to watch. "I do want to tell him. You can't believe how much." There was a hidden message in that. One she didn't understand. "But I can't. He'll kill me as soon as he knows it."

"He'll kill you anyway, eventually."

"I know that." Laughton finally made it all the way down. He rested his head in his hands. "I've unfinished business. I can't afford to die yet."

Maybe he and Josune had more in common than she realized.

Norris didn't feed them. When Josune saw the dance the two guards made Effie do for her dinner, she was glad he hadn't. If either of those guards got in her way when she was escaping, she'd happily annihilate them.

There was one night guard. She could call him to her and try to take his weapon, but Norris would expect that. Besides, arming herself was only half of what she needed to do. She had to get out of the cell, and if no one let her out, she had to stop the power.

She needed tools.

She had nothing. They'd stripped her of everything.

"Laughton. What's in your pockets?"

"Huh?"

He was only half-conscious.

"I need to check your pockets. I'll be as careful as I can."

He moaned once, cut it off quickly. In the night-light of the cells, she could see the perspiration on his face. His pockets were empty.

"Anything?"

"No."

Laughton grunted.

Josune leaned back to the bars and dozed. There was nothing she could do but wait for an opportunity and conserve energy.

Sometime during the night Laughton toppled down from where he'd been sitting, back against the wall, to lie flat on the floor. The cell floor vibrated with the crash.

She dozed on and off all night.

Pol finally made an appearance at 06:00. She kept away from the bars. "Just so you know. I am going to kill you."

"Why don't you try, Pol?"

Pol stepped back.

Josune would have laughed if she hadn't needed her to come closer. "You'll have to come nearer if you want to be sure to hit me. That far away I can dodge."

Pol turned on her heel and walked out.

Scratch that for a way to get a weapon. She'd have to rely on attacking guards on her way to, or from, her visit to Norris. Whenever that would be.

25

ALISTAIR LAUGHTON

They dragged Alistair away again later that morning for another session with Norris's persuaders. Alistair had no doubts about how this would go. They would kill him in the end. You didn't beat information out of a Justice Department agent and leave him alive.

How long could he hold out?

How long would Norris bother with this charade? Alistair was sure the only reason he was doing it was to be contrary because Alistair was holding out on him. But a new weapon, no matter how good, wasn't enough to keep his attention for long. He'd cut his losses soon, kill Alistair, and go on his own way.

Nika Rik Terri was out of his reach.

So, half the plan, then. This ship was twice the size of the Santiago warship. It should win. Norris wouldn't go straight down and find out about the Ort immediately. If Alistair could somehow get word to Paola to send the ship she had organized, then he could get the settlers off Zell—including the Ort. If he was condemning the people on Zell to a dictator worse than Santiago, then so be it. It was the best he could do, and his best was better than the certain death that would come.

Decision made, he straightened and walked unaided into the small room that served as Norris's interrogation room.

Norris looked him over. "Maybe we weren't persuasive enough yesterday."

Don't come across as too eager. That would arouse suspicions. Time it. If he could. He ached all over, and right now just wanted it done. "I'm not playing your games."

"That's what they all say, Agent Laughton, but they come around in the end. You're—"

He stopped as a message signal sounded. "This had better be important."

The woman at the other end didn't look cowed. Probably his second, or a third. "Executive Wickmore is on the channel."

Norris took the link without any further comment.

"You're holding out on me," Executive Wickmore said. "You have Arriola, but you haven't told me."

"So your tame little spy told you she's on board." A tic pulsed on Norris's right cheek.

"We have an agreement, Captain. I gave you Arriola in return for half of the profits."

The tic stopped. Norris's smile didn't reach his eyes. "Let's not lie to each other about what we want, Executive. I wanted Snowshoe."

"And I delivered."

"We both know Arriola won't give us anything. If she even knows something. All that disappeared with the death of Captain Feyodor, who was notoriously closemouthed. She probably refused to even let her crew record where they went. No." Norris's smile grew wider. A real smile this time. "Let's be honest. You're in this for revenge. You want revenge on *Another Road*."

Wickmore opened his mouth as if he was going to deny it, closed his mouth again. "Then why haven't you delivered?"

Norris's voice was mild. "Why, Executive, as you so rightly noted, I have Arriola, but I don't have *Another Road*."

"Fool." Alistair was sure he saw spittle spray from Wickmore's mouth. "They'll follow you. They're waiting. They'll plan to rescue Arriola and Snowshoe." He laughed mockingly. "If you think

Snowshoe is packed up tight back in your hospital, you've another think coming."

Norris's lips tightened. "I fail to see how a ship of how many—eight, ten crew at most—can take on a merc ship with four hundred trained soldiers. And if that's the case, then I see why you want revenge. Never fear. I won't underestimate them the way you have."

If Wickmore was right—and Pol—and Arriola's ship was following them, waiting to rescue her and Snowshoe, then Alistair hadn't lost Nika Rik Terri. The Ort would still work with Alistair's people over the Santiagans.

Alistair had to survive today and somehow give Norris the information he needed to go to Zell as well.

"By the way," Wickmore said, "the Justice Department wants their agent back."

"I have no idea what you are talking about."

Another figure leaned into the call. Slender, dark haired, arresting looks, well spoken. "Don't lie to us, Captain. I know what you did. I was there."

Alistair staggered back. Now he didn't know what was real or what was imagined. Given his injuries, Cam couldn't possibly have survived. Could he?

He was dead. Alistair had seen him die.

"We collected Snowshoe and Arriola," Norris lied. "I don't know what happened to anyone else."

"You realize that kidnapping citizens is a designated offense," Cam said.

"Snowshoe is contracted to the *Boost*. He has a contract to complete."

"Arriola isn't contracted, and even if you forced her to sign something, she's one of the few individuals who could buy her way out of the contract. Josune Arriola is a wealthy woman, Captain Norris."

Norris cut him off with a wave of his hand. "You sound like a lawyer."

"I am a lawyer." Cam smiled, and even Norris's lips twitched in return. "I'm Laughton's lawyer."

Norris closed the link.

Alistair laughed. He couldn't help it. He couldn't stop laughing either.

Norris turned to look at him. "Take him back to the cell," as if Alistair's laughter left a sour taste in his mouth.

"That was fast," Arriola said when they shoved him back into the cell. "I thought he'd kill you once he got what information he wanted."

"Didn't give it to him." Now that he didn't have to speak clearly, all he could manage was a mumble. He lay down on the floor and closed his eyes. "Am I drugged?" He ached all over.

"No idea."

"Me either. I'm hallucinating. I saw someone who is dead." He rolled onto his back. "He looked—" Alive and as well as Cam had ever been.

He tried to sit up, gave up. "I think they drugged me, even though I didn't notice."

"Maybe he didn't die."

"You didn't see how bad he was. I couldn't even stay around to help him. What sort of friend am I?"

Arriola considered. "It depends on the circumstances. And on how you justify it to yourself."

"You're very blunt."

Arriola's voice softened. "You think I'm blunt. You should have met Nika." He heard genuine warmth in her voice. "When she's honest, she can be blistering." She settled back against the bars. "Why did you want Nika, anyway?"

This might be his chance. Norris would have someone listening, surely. Here, in the cell, there might even be a chance to survive.

"Apparently she's one of the few body modders who can work with transurides properly."

He felt, rather than saw, Arriola stiffen. "Why is that important?" Her voice was cold.

He looked at her, sitting preternaturally still over at the bars. "It's true. My friend, the one who's dead." Or not. "She modded him."

"What's that got to do with anything? Lots of people have been modded by Nika."

He was losing her, and he hadn't given Norris what he wanted. "Everything and nothing. On Zell—" He stopped, looked at her. "That's where the weapons come from. The ones Norris was torturing me to get information about."

"Walls have ears."

He sincerely hoped they did. "It's a little world out near the Vortex."

She shook her head. "I know Zell. I've passed there once or twice. It's a dead-end world with nothing but a failed settlement."

"We have a settlement there. Fifty of us."

Arriola glanced at the bars, at the walls outside, to where Alistair could see a heat line—a wire—leading to a darker heat block, which might have been a camera. "I hope you know what you are doing." She shrugged and muttered under her breath, "Or maybe you really are drugged."

She understood his words were deliberate. Or maybe not understood, but she was playing along. He didn't know why, but it was important she didn't think he was stupid.

"Not a choice I'd make, living that close to the Vortex. Just getting supplies in would be dangerous."

"We survived. We're still surviving. All fifty of us." He emphasized the fifty, realized he shouldn't have. Norris might suspect he was being played.

If he was listening.

Please, God, let him be listening. Even better, let him act on it.

"Fifty?" Arriola was still playing along.

"Two years. Fifty people. On a world like that, you usually lose half the people before the end of the contract. We only lost one person. I'm proud of that." Lennie, the doctor who'd thought he was invincible, with his genemod machine that could cure anything. Except a two-hundred-meter fall onto rocks.

"That is impressive," Josune said. "I still wouldn't be insane enough to—"

Alistair opened his eyes and tried to sit up, to see what had silenced her. Norris, and their ever-friendly two guards.

"Search her," Norris said. "Do it properly this time."

"Rather than have those thugs paw at me," Arriola said, "tell me what you're looking for. I can save you time."

"Apparently, your friends are following us."

Arriola reached down to her boot, prized something off the inside flap. "You're looking for trackers. Why didn't you say?" She handed it over.

"She'll have two," one of the guards said. "They always do."

"We have one already. If you'd done your job properly the first time, we would have had this one too. We have what we want." Norris inclined his head Josune's way. "We'll talk soon. I need to placate a certain executive, and that requires your friends. I want to be sure they're following us, and I'd prefer to meet them somewhere quieter. Like Zell," and he smiled at Alistair.

He had been listening. Alistair covered his face to hide the relief, found he was shaking.

Norris left.

Alistair put his head down to his knees, still shaking. He hadn't really believed it would work. Still didn't believe it would, until the nullspace warning sounded.

26

NIKA RIK TERRI

The Songyan genemod machine hadn't changed much in the years since Giwari had purchased the first model so cheaply from Conrad Songyan. Sure, this was a single box—Nika had to call Jacques to help her lift Roystan in—squarer in shape and not as sleek, but the controls worked the same way.

Best of all, there were still fourteen inlets.

It was strange to realize that what was deemed the state-of-the-art modding machine had been designed over a hundred and fifty years prior. But then, the machines hadn't changed that much. New versions came out, of course, all the time. But the real changes to modding were in the add-ons. Like the add-on that allowed her to change Tamati's hair so it turned green when his hair got wet, like the mods Nika had designed for Alejandro but given to Tamati Woden to make him stand out. There hadn't been any real innovation in body modding itself for a long time.

Not since Gino Giwari.

It was not something she had time to think about. Keeping Roystan alive was more important.

Nika checked the readings, opened one of the inlet valves to add more mutrient to the mix, marveled at the complete control. Milligrams at a time.

She laughed. She felt like she had when she'd bought her first Songyan.

She wished Snow was here to share it.

"Will he be okay?" Jacques asked.

"Josune will have a plan." Even if she didn't, she'd make one. All they had to do was stay close and do what they could when Josune called.

Jacques gave a look that said she was clearly out of her mind. "A plan for Roystan?"

Roystan was the least of her worries. She had the Songyan. "I'm stabilizing him."

He'd be fine. She could feed his body the nutrients it required, in the order and the amounts he required them. They could perform miracles.

Not, she admitted to herself hours later, that it was going to be easy. She could have done with her apprentice right now. Someone else to watch the feeds with her. Someone she could trust to manage for a few minutes while she got herself a coffee, at least. She sat back wearily, saw someone had left a coffee and a plate of something that had congealed into a cream-colored mess. A stew of some kind.

The coffee was cold. She drank it anyway. Adjusted the feeds. Ate the stew. It was delicious, even cold, even as bad as it looked. Adjusted the feeds again. "See how such minute changes make differences to the body," she said, then realized she was talking to herself.

How long had it taken her to get used to having someone to share knowledge with? Two, three months. She put her head down. No. She couldn't do that. She'd sleep, and then they'd have to start this all over again.

She adjusted the feeds again.

"Any word from Josune or Snow?" The link was always open. They'd hear her.

"Not yet," Carlos said. "We're still tracking them. How's Roystan?"

"Stable for the moment." It was all she could promise them.

She adjusted the feeds again.

An hour later Jacques brought down a welcome hot coffee and a plateful of something that smelled so heavenly her stomach rumbled. He stood watching the genemod machine while she fell on the plate as if she hadn't eaten in days.

"The *Boost* has nullspaced," Carlos said.

Everything stopped, and they waited, long, slow, heartbreaking minutes while he fussed at the boards, until finally, "Tracker signal coming through."

Nika finished lifting the fork to her mouth.

Jacques blinked. "I cannot take all this stress. I must cook," and turned on his heel to go.

Carlos swore. "He can't possibly."

Jacques paused.

Nika pushed her empty plate away. She adjusted the feeds. "Can't what, Carlos?"

"I think this is a trap. He's taking us to the most dangerous part of the galaxy."

Was it? Could they afford to follow?

Could they afford not to? When they escaped, Josune and Snow would be depending on them being there to collect them.

"I'll need you on the calibrator, Nika," Carlos said. "I'm not a pilot like Roystan. If I make a mistake, we're done for. The more accurate the calibrator, the safer we'll be."

She looked at Roystan, adjusted the feed again. "Give me a minute." She reprogrammed the flows quickly. This one wasn't a cure; it was a holding pattern. He'd be fine provided she didn't take more than half an hour.

"Watch him, Jacques. Let me know when something goes red."

Then she ran for the common room—their new bridge—while Jacques muttered, "When, she says. Not if." He raised his voice.

"You'd better nullspace fast, Carlos. We have a life-and-death situation here."

"It's not that bad," Nika said as she slid into the calibrator seat. "It will just delay him coming out."

"I wish he was here now. Look." Carlos gestured at the star chart up on the screen.

It looked like a normal star chart to her. Not many stars. Maybe an unknown sector of space, for half the screen was black. Unknown space was dangerous. Below the black was a small, red star, and close to that was a pulsing signal she thought might be Josune's marker.

"I don't know what I'm supposed to be looking at."

"That big hole there."

The black area.

"That's the Vortex. It sucks you in. Kills you."

"Oh."

Josune had mentioned the Vortex once, when talking about Feyodor. Even Roystan had said it was dangerous.

Carlos jabbed at the black area on-screen. "Keep away from the Vortex, okay? As far away as you possibly can. You can't fight it. Every ship. Poof. No more."

Why would Norris take the *Boost* to the Vortex? According to Josune and Roystan, it was dangerous. An experienced pilot like Norris would know that.

"He's trying to kill us," Carlos said. "This is how he does it."

"Isn't he putting himself in danger too?"

"Bigger ship. Stronger engines. He can escape it. We can't." Carlos tapped the console. "I do not like having to make decisions on where to take the ship. Understand." He glared at her. "Roystan had better get out of that box soon and start doing his job."

"We can always wait until he does come out," Nika said. What about Josune and Snow? But Carlos and Jacques were nearly at breaking point, and the only person who could fix that was Roystan himself.

Carlos sighed. "We know what Roystan would do, Nika. He is more of an idiot than you or me. Or me, anyway," he corrected himself. "And Josune and Snow expect us to be there for them." He took a deep breath. "I'm just scared."

"Me too," Nika said, although she wasn't necessarily scared of the same things. She was scared that Roystan might still die. She was scared they may not rescue Snow and Josune in time. She was scared of what would happen when Leonard Wickmore caught up with her.

She wasn't scared of a big, black hole, even if, from Carlos's reaction to it, she should be. "Let's be scared and do it, anyway."

"Let's," and with an unholy scream that could have curdled blood, Carlos entered nullspace.

27

JOSUNE ARRIOLA

Laughton looked at his hands, said wonderingly, "I didn't think it would—" He glanced toward the camera. "We have to get out of here."

Yes, they did. "How?"

"I don't know." He rattled the bars. "We'll be stuck here if we don't."

"Calm down." He looked as if he was about to have a full-blown panic attack. At least he'd forgotten his injuries for the moment. Unfortunately, given those injuries, that meant that whatever he was worried about was bad.

He pulled himself together. "Sorry. Forgot myself there."

On the whole, she preferred him panicking.

He looked down, lowered his voice. "I was so busy trying to—" He waved a hand. "You know. I didn't think about the consequences. For us, I mean."

He'd manipulated Norris into coming to Zell, of all places.

"A trap?" She kept her voice low, even though Norris wouldn't be listening right now. No captain would, for Zell was close to the Vortex, and the only way in was through the Funnel.

Josune had been through the Funnel twice now in Captain Feyodor's ceaseless, useless search for Roy Goberling. She hated it more each time. You came down the Funnel directly into the Zell system. Most people stopped at Zell, the system's only human-habitable world. Humans tried to settle there every generation. None had survived.

A few prospectors went farther in, mostly with disastrous results. They ended up being caught by the Vortex.

So far as Josune knew, the *Hassim* had been the only ship to successfully go farther into the Vortex and come out again. They'd crept around the edge, every single one of them convinced they would die. Farther around past the Funnel there was enough room to nullspace again. They'd made tiny hops onward.

Five jumps in they'd discovered a yellow, Earth-type star with an Earth-type planet that would support humans. They'd called it Sassia. They'd returned to known space when an asteroid had hit the ship, taking out their aeroponics section.

They'd restocked and tried to nullspace back, found they couldn't. There was something about the Vortex that stopped them. So they'd done the whole horrible trip back through the Funnel and crept around the edge of the Vortex until they knew it was safe to nullspace again.

They'd probably still have been there, moving inward and on, looking for Goberling, if Feyodor hadn't had her epiphany and sent Josune to infiltrate Roystan's ship while she headed to Pisces III.

Where the crew of the *Hassim* had been murdered by Wickmore's people.

The *Boost* juddered, kept juddering.

They had entered the Funnel.

Laughton put a hand to his mouth, covering it. "I told you there were fifty people on-world."

At least that's what Josune thought he said. She had to strain to hear him. This part wasn't meant for Norris's ears, obviously.

"There's a company warship above it. Two hundred armed soldiers, ready to repel anyone who goes near Zell."

What was on such an obscure world that a company sent a warship to protect it? And she really hoped Norris wasn't listening to this, couldn't hear the words if he was.

"They'll fire on this ship as soon as it gets close."

It was a brazen idea, and it might just work. The *Boost* was a larger ship, but they wouldn't expect an attack. Not out here on the edge of the legal zone. Especially not when they were exiting the Funnel.

A small ship could do a lot of damage before a larger one realized it was under attack. A larger one, though, even partially disabled, could then do a lot of damage once it retaliated. It was quite ingenious, really. Both ships would come out of the fight badly.

"We have to get out of here," Alistair said. "I have a ship ready to rescue the settlement, but I have to call them."

He shook the bars again.

Josune really hoped Norris was too busy with the Funnel to listen.

"Calm down," she said. "We've hours before anything happens. We're in the Funnel. No one will do anything until we come out of it."

"Funnel?" He looked at her as if he didn't know what she was talking about.

"I thought you lived here."

"I do, but—" He stopped. "I don't know what you mean."

"How often have you done this trip?"

"It was a two-year contract."

Twice. Once in, and once out. You had to use the Funnel. Two years, and if it was a contract, the company probably hadn't explained it to him anyway. "What were you doing down there?" So far as she knew, there was nothing on Zell.

"Mining transurides."

"Any success?" There must have been if a company warship was perched above them.

He winced. "Enough to make our bonus, which didn't make the company happy."

There had to be more to it than that. "Surely they would have just killed you, then." That was how most companies would deal with it on a way-out world like this. The Justice Department wouldn't interfere. Although, he was with the Justice Department.

"They tried."

But something had happened, something that had brought a warship to protect the world, to hold fifty settlers there as prisoners—if that's what this was about. Something Laughton wasn't telling.

"I'd like to hear the story one day," she said. "But right now let's keep calm. Nothing will happen until the *Boost* comes out of the Funnel." That would take four hours. Josune had never been sure which was worst: the jarring, shuddering of the forces of the Funnel that made you feel as if the ship was being pulled apart, or, once you were through, creeping around the Vortex, praying you didn't get close enough for those same forces to grab your ship and drag you in.

She checked the time. If Laughton was right, then the *Boost* would be attacked as soon as it came out. Four hours to plan. "I don't suppose you collected any tools in your trips to and from the torture room?"

"Sorry."

A pity. Josune looked around the jail. Nothing, and no inspiration. "We need a guard." It was their only hope. They'd have to take the guard's blaster.

The shudder would ease as the ship exited the Funnel. "When we're nearly out, we need to call a guard."

"How?"

"Not sure." Her gaze fell on Effie, cowering in the corner of the next cell. Could she get Effie to help? The guards would be more likely to come for her. She was easy to taunt, and by the sound of it, Norris was less likely to worry if they played with her. Or would they kill her?

She moved over to that side of the cell. "Effie."

Effie had her hands over her ears and didn't hear her.

Over the next three and a half hours she tried to call Effie several times, but the other prisoner either didn't hear her or didn't want to hear her.

"This isn't going to work."

Alistair shrugged.

"We need to get the guards. Start shouting."

"Shouting?"

"Yes." Josune wasn't a screamer, so she yelled insults and sang. After a few minutes, Laughton joined in. Effie screamed at them to shut up—they'd bring the guards.

Josune was fine with that. It was what they wanted.

The guards, when they came, went to Effie's cell first.

Of course.

Effie cowered at the back of her cage.

"Stupid guards. Don't even know when someone is in trouble," Josune yelled. She came close to the bars. "What's wrong with you? Buckets for brains?" Rattled the bars, which made no sound. "No brains at all." She made an obscene gesture.

What sort of insults would rile a soldier? She couldn't think today.

"Gutless," Laughton yelled beside her. "You're scared of us." He jeered, started yelping, and got down on all fours. "Less brain than a dog."

That annoyed one of them, at least. He took out his blaster.

"Big boy," Laughton jeered. "Go on, fire. Then explain to Captain Norris what you did. Go on."

He tried to stick his head through the bars.

The guard came over, stuck his blaster in Alistair's face. "You think I won't?"

It was enough.

Josune grabbed his arm, turned his wrist, took the blaster off him as he screamed. Shot the other guard in one smooth movement.

"Thanks," she said to Laughton.

"Can't say it was fun." He wiped sweat off his face. "I thought he would fire there for a moment."

"You two are crazy." Effie was as far from them as she could possibly get.

"Don't move or I'll shoot," Josune told the guard whose weapon she'd taken.

"You can't get out. It takes two people. You've just killed the other one."

"I know," she said. "Turn out your pockets."

The ship rocked. Josune was familiar with the exit from the Funnel.

Two seconds later a klaxon warning sounded.

"Under attack," blared from the speakers in the outer room. "All staff on duty report to positions."

Laughton's plan was underway.

"Not you," Josune said as the guard edged toward the door.

"But I'm on duty."

She fired at the door. He jumped back as if she'd burned him.

"Empty your pockets onto the floor. Here. In front of me."

He did so.

The ship rocked again, and again in quick succession.

The loudspeaker blared instructions. Patient voices counting down.

Another plasma bolt rocked the ship. This time a grinding shriek flared through the ship. Four alarms went off. Then two more. The portside engine went dead.

They'd been hit.

Josune looked at the paltry collection in front of the guard. A knife. A consumer card, and two metal buttons.

"Give Laughton the knife. Don't try anything funny, or I'll kill you." She'd risk electrocuting herself trying to open the lock, but it was all they had.

The door opened. Pol ran in, a weapon in her hand. Josune's sparker. She tripped and almost fell as the ship rocked again. A waft of hot metal and burnt plastic came in with her.

Pol raised the weapon. Josune fired. Pol went down.

The sparker rolled across the floor, came to rest against the bars of Effie's cell.

"Grab that tube for me," Josune ordered Effie. Would she recognize it for what it was? Most people didn't.

Effie stared at her wide-eyed.

"Do it, or I'll kill you." She turned her blaster on Effie.

Effie snatched it up.

"Hand it over."

The guard seized his chance, ran out the door. Josune let him go. It didn't matter.

"Now."

Effie dropped it into their cell.

The ship tilted. Rolled. Josune dived for the sparker, snatched it as it was about to roll away. Properly armed once more, and it felt good.

"We haven't got anyone to open the door now," Laughton said.

But she had something that would short it out.

Josune looked at the door. "Where do you think the circuits are?" She tested each bar, as she had the day earlier. No, none of them felt warmer.

"What are you doing?" Laughton asked.

"Trying to find where the electricity runs to this door."

"Two bars down. It comes around and goes into the wall back here." He touched something near his shoulder. "There's a junction here."

She looked at him. Was he serious? Or was he making it up? "That's interesting knowledge?" She made it a question.

"Wires are hotter," Laughton said.

She didn't have anywhere else to start. "You'd better be right." If he wasn't, she'd probably electrocute them all. "Stand back, both of you."

Laughton stood back. Effie didn't move.

"You, too, Effie," Josune said. "As far back as you can go."

Effie backed away.

Josune aimed the sparker for the bars Laughton had indicated. Voltage arced out. The current surged along the bars, heating so red even Josune could see it.

Bull's-eye.

Thank goodness Nika hadn't put another bio-connection into her eye, even though they'd talked about it. Nika hadn't felt it was safe. Josune was sure, if they had, she'd be experiencing headaches right about now.

She pushed against the door. The electronics were dead. The handle was too hot to touch. "Where's that knife the guard gave you?"

Laughton handed it over. "You're quite something."

She took it as a compliment, even if he hadn't meant it that way. She used the knife to push the handle down to open the door.

"Stand back," she ordered Effie. No one would think of a prisoner in a cell in a battle situation. If anything happened, no one would come for Effie.

"You're crazy," but Effie got as far away from Josune and her sparker as she could.

"Where's the current?" Shooting the door mechanism would

just damage the door. She had to stop the current getting to the door.

Laughton showed her the bars.

She raised the sparker, fired. Voltage arced again, and the bars ran red-hot. "You really do know—"

The jail door burst open. Josune swung around.

"Don't shoot, Josune." Snow. And a deeper, older voice. "Medical." A stretcher came through first.

"No one's shooting," said the deeper voice. "Don't know what you were worried about, Snow."

The speaker entered. He was an older man, as big as Laughton, with dark hair and a modder's body. Snow followed.

"That's what I was worried about," Snow said, looking at the sparker. "We couldn't get any weapons." He handed Josune a tool bag. "But we got some tools."

Josune clipped the bag around her waist. "For a modder, Snow, you are a great fighter." Dressed, finally. She felt as if she could take on the ship. "Let's get out of here."

"We heard one of you had been tortured," the older man said. Gramps, she presumed.

"I can run," Laughton said. "Provided it's not too long or too far."

"Take this." Gramps handed Laughton a pill. "It's what we give our mercs when they are too injured to fight. Numbs everything. Nerveseal for the innards."

"Let's take the stretcher anyway," Josune said. "It's a good disguise." Escape pods or shuttle? They'd need permission to use the shuttle. Pods, she decided. Anyone could use them. They were designed for emergency exits from the ship. "Where are the nearest escape pods? And does anyone have a working link?"

"I do," Gramps said. "But Norris will hear everything you say."

Maybe later, then. "Can you use it once you're in an emergency pod?"

"I presume so. I've never had to try before."

Gramps's link beeped. He answered it. "Hospital."

"Two dead on port engine. Four injured."

"Send them down." He looked at the stretcher. "I should—"

"Norris will kill you," Snow said. "He said he would."

If Snow escaped and Gramps stayed, Norris might not kill Gramps, but he'd certainly make him pay. "You'll only ever have one chance to escape," Josune said.

"Please," Snow begged. "Please, Gramps."

"I would like to see my boy fulfill his potential."

"Where are the nearest escape pods?"

"Portside."

Josune turned back to the cells, to Effie's door. The lock was still hot. She kicked the door open. "Come on, Effie."

Effie shook her head, backed as far away from them as possible. "Nobody escapes the *Boost*. Ever."

"But we're about to." If they could get the stubborn woman to move.

Effie seemed to be trying to shake her head off. "He'll kill me slowly and make an example of me. Everyone will come to hear me scream."

"Isn't it better—"

Gramps touched Josune's shoulder. "She's right. If Norris does catch her, he will make an example of her. And every second we delay here makes it more likely we'll be caught. Come on."

"But—"

"Zef will tell his boss about the escape. Norris will come and check soon. If we don't go now, we'll never escape."

Josune looked back at Effie one more time, then turned away.

"Come on." Snow gestured impatiently from the end of the corridor.

Josune started to run.

The emergency pods on the *Boost* were actual lifeboats, able to hold twenty people for a maximum of three days. Josune would have preferred individual pods that could carry their cargo of one person for a hundred days. She set the controls to head back toward the Funnel and prayed the crew of *Another Road* would find them in time.

"Belt up." She glanced back toward the cells once more. Maybe Effie had changed her mind.

She hadn't.

Josune closed the airlock and set for auto-exit.

The pod fell away from the ship. Just them, and space.

And one rather noisy life-support system. Whoever had done maintenance on these lifeboats should be forced to scrub the decks by hand. Or take each pod's life support apart and put it back together again until they could do it in their sleep. She hoped it was spaceworthy.

28

NIKA RIK TERRI

Roystan had stabilized. Finally. All Nika wanted to do was fall onto a bed and sleep. But not until she was sure the stabilization was permanent and he wouldn't regress again.

Jacques handed her a glass of water. "You need to drink more. You need to eat. If you collapse, we won't be able to fix Roystan."

She drank the water in two gulps and moved over to get more. "I don't have many clients who take so much effort that I forget."

"Yes, Roystan. He is a handful." Jacques sounded fond and despairing at the same time.

Nika smiled down at the Giwari. The Songyan—combined with their whole supply of dellarine—had done its job. "An amazing machine, this. It's so sensitive. The mods it can do."

What must it be like to have been Gino Giwari, who'd taken a chance and bought the first model. No wonder he'd delved so deeply into the DNA. Because he could. Because only the Songyan could do it and make it work.

To do it in the era of Roy Goberling as well, and to believe that transurides would soon be plentiful and relatively inexpensive. He'd dared to dream, dared to experiment, which was why his work with transurides was so groundbreaking.

"I'm so hungry, I could even eat garfungi stew."

"Garfungi is not for you. I am not wasting it."

"Don't worry, Jacques. I'm not that desperate. Yet. How's Carlos?"

Jacques spread his arms wide. "We're all going to die, he says."

She'd left Carlos some time ago, swearing at the Vortex, creeping down the Funnel at minimum speed. If Josune and Snow needed rescuing, it wasn't going to be instant, for the *Boost* was nowhere in range.

Carlos believed the Vortex would suck them all in.

She could still hear him, only he wasn't swearing anymore. He was praying aloud, to any and every god who would listen.

Jacques stared down at the Giwari. "I would hate for him to die without coming out of that box."

"Me too, Jacques. Me too." If this was true stabilization, he would be out soon, but she didn't tell Jacques that. In case she was wrong.

"He's so still."

"We want him still. If he's moving around, I'd be worried."

Roystan's hand twitched.

Jacques jumped.

"That's normal." At least he hadn't been here earlier, when Roystan's whole body had struggled against the repairs. The twitches were involuntary reactions, but if you weren't used to them, they could be scary. It was a common joke that lecturers played on new modding students when they entered university. Watch the body twitch, see which students tried to rescue the person inside the machine. Nika had known about the twitch long before she'd gone to university. Snow probably had, too, since he'd spent most of his life in a mercenary-ship hospital.

They stayed in silence for a while. Nika watched the settings.

"He'll be hungry when he comes out." It was true: a good mod nurtured the body, but it left the stomach empty. Everyone was hungry when they came out of the genemod machine. But Nika really wanted Jacques out of the studio. Roystan needed to be alone when he came out, not surrounded by anyone except modders, and maybe Josune.

"Spicy flatbread," Jacques pronounced. "It will be like old times." His face fell. "Or maybe not. Not without Josune and Snow."

The ship rocked. Five alarms went off. Even Roystan, unconscious in the Songyan, twitched at that. So much that she thought he might drag himself into consciousness. The Songyan prevailed, and Roystan's body dropped back into a more relaxed state.

Carlos's voice rose. "Nika. Jacques. Somebody. Get here. We've been hit."

"I thought you said nobody used weapons in the Funnel. That it was too dangerous."

"It is, and they're not. Someone's firing toward the Funnel, and the plasma is being sucked up. We're caught in the flux. We'll get dragged in." His voice rose even more. "We are all going to die."

He started praying again. Extra loud and extra fast.

Jacques left at a run.

They needed Roystan.

Nika checked his vitals. Not finished, but stable enough.

"I am not planning on making this a habit," she told the unconscious figure. But there was no way she, Carlos, and Jacques could manage the attack on their own. She was glad Snow wasn't here to witness. Although if Snow were here, he'd be helping Carlos and she wouldn't need to do what she was about to do.

Roystan had, at least, stabilized, so his body wasn't producing more chemicals than it could use. He wouldn't get any worse, and he'd live.

Everything else would have to wait. Again. What repairs could she put off for another day?

"I am so tired of this," but there was no one to hear. She set the machine for finish. She hated leaving jobs half-done.

The ship rocked again.

"Nika," Carlos wailed. "I need you. I need someone on the cannon. And Snow's not here."

"I'll be up as soon as I can."

All the lights on the Songyan went green at the same time.

Nika checked Roystan's DNA. As tight as it had been when she'd first cured him. Would it stay that way?

The lights stayed green. She set the wake-up process.

The cover of the Songyan rose, and she turned to help Roystan out of the machine. Normally she gave him a robe so he could shower.

Today she gave him a shirt and pants.

"That bad?" Roystan said as he pulled on the pants. "I dreamed we were being attacked. I don't usually dream."

The ship rocked again.

Roystan paused. "We're in the Funnel?"

"Yes. Getting the effects of an attack from outside, and Carlos says plasma is being sucked in.

"Also according to Carlos, we're all going to die." She said this last to his back. Roystan was already out the door, running. "I want you to know," as she followed, "that I normally finish my mods."

If Roystan had heard her, he gave no sign of it as he slid into the pilot seat Carlos vacated for him. "What's the status?"

"There is a god," Carlos said. "Everything is shit and I don't know what to do."

Roystan looked around. "Where's Josune? And Snow?"

"Still on the *Boost*," Nika said. "Waiting for us to save them."

Knowing Josune, she was probably saving herself.

"We followed the *Boost* down the Funnel," Carlos said. "There's another ship. I think it's firing on the *Boost*, and we're caught in the plasma flow. We've damage to four external sensors, and we've lost all the starboard cameras. I can't see anything. That section is a blind spot."

Roystan nodded. He opened every screen in the crew room and tuned it to view the outside space. One set of screens was black.

Nika presumed that was the starboard side. Although, she wasn't sure the port screens were any better, for they showed a small area of black just outside the ship, and the rest was predominantly gray. She'd never seen space like that before.

"Jacques is on the laser cannon, for all the good that will do us." Roystan wasn't listening. He stared at the view outside.

"I know this place," he whispered at last. "We're near the Vortex."

"We are," Nika confirmed. He'd recognized earlier that they were in the Funnel. Didn't that automatically mean they were close to the Vortex? He hadn't necessarily associated the two before. That initial recognition must have been subconscious.

"Why do I remember the Vortex? We've never been here before?" He turned to Carlos, energized. "We're still in the Funnel."

Carlos looked at him as if wondering if Roystan was okay. "We are."

Roystan's words had been a statement of fact, not a question. Reconfirming to himself something that he already knew.

Something he remembered, but he hadn't remembered before.

The screens that showed the portside flared bright again. "Cannon ready," Jacques said. "Do I fire back?"

"Don't fire in the Funnel," Roystan said. "It's too dangerous. We'll just have to sit out the damage. Stay on the cannon, though, Jacques, for we'll come right out into a firefight."

The ship rocked again. More heavily this time.

"Starboard again," Carlos said, for they didn't register any damage. "That means the fight will be on our blind side when we exit."

"Not necessarily," Roystan said. "The plasma swirls. You can't tell where it originates." He checked the ship stats. "You came in nice and slow, Carlos. Well done. Most people come in too fast."

"If it hadn't been for Josune and Snow, I wouldn't have gone in at all," Carlos said. "Now you're here, I'll see if I can repair those cameras."

"Don't go outside the ship."

"Believe me, I am not going out there, not even if the last camera goes out."

"What about you, Jacques?" Roystan asked once Carlos had gone. "How are you doing?"

"I'll tell you when I'm back in the kitchen, cooking that flatbread Nika ordered for you."

Roystan laughed. He touched the panels again. Lightly, with a deftness that said he knew what he was doing. Even Nika relaxed.

She wanted to sleep.

She stood up, went into the kitchen, to the area they'd designated the coffee area, which was the only place Jacques allowed them to go. She turned on the coffee machine.

Carlos came back as the coffee finished brewing. He looked pleased with himself. "Josune builds redundancy into everything." He did something on one of the control boards. The starboard cameras changed—three of the screens that had hitherto been black went the same gray as the portside screens, with the patch of black close to the ship. Now they really looked as if they were in a funnel. "There's nothing I can do for that last camera. I need to replace it on the outside."

"We'll be out soon," Roystan said. "Ah," and suddenly the image on-screen changed so the port cameras showed all black, and the starboard ones retained most of the gray, but it was farther away.

Roystan tapped that gray. "That's the Vortex." He tweaked the controls, zooming in to a specific spot on-screen in front of them. "Two ships."

One of them recognizably the *Boost*.

"The *Boost* and a Lotus fighter. That's a company warship. What is it doing in this part of space? Maybe they've found—" Roystan hesitated. "That would explain why they are firing on the *Boost*. I assume the *Boost* didn't fire first?"

Carlos shrugged. "I don't know. I was too busy trying to keep us alive."

"Understandable. All right. They don't appear to have noticed us. Let's keep it that way. Jacques, you haven't fired that cannon yet?"

"No," Jacques said promptly. "And I don't plan to now either."

Did Jacques even know how to fire the cannon? Nika felt better, now Roystan was in the pilot seat. All they needed now was Josune and Snow, and they'd be fine.

After they escaped from the *Boost*, of course, but even that didn't seem so hard right now.

The light that signified the *Boost* split into two. Roystan leaned forward, magnified the image. "Escape pod exiting from the *Boost*. No. A lifeboat."

Nika didn't know how a lifeboat differed from an escape pod, but obviously it did.

Carlos shouted, loud and unexpected into Nika's ear. "The marker. It's moving. That's Josune."

"There's still a marker on the ship," Nika said.

"Three markers she took. One was destroyed an hour after she arrived on ship. One she ate. There were always two. I bet that's Josune in that first lifeboat."

"Josune knows how to escape," Jacques said.

That had all of them smiling.

"Of course she does." Roystan's voice was soft.

"Don't get soppy on us now, Roystan. We have to pick up the pod. And make sure we're not killed in the process."

"I'll save the soppy until she and Snow are safely on board. Will that do?"

"The sooner you pick them up, the sooner I can get back into the kitchen and things can get back to normal."

Even so, it was a relief when Josune finally contacted them.

"This is the lifeboat from the *Boost*, calling *Another Road*. Requesting pickup."

"Josune." Carlos and Jacques capered around the crew room. Nika might have, too, but she could only see Josune on the screen.

"How many of you?" Roystan asked over the noise.

"Roystan." Josune's own voice was a controlled shout. It was all she said, but there was a whole world of messages in it. Her voice turned professional, although she couldn't stop smiling. "Four. Myself, Snow, Gramps, and Laughton."

"Alistair Laughton," Nika said. "Did you have to bring him?"

"It's a long story."

Roystan couldn't stop smiling either. "Which we'll have time to hear, I'm sure. We'll have to use the grapple."

"It's a pity Jacques is a better cook than he is a cargo master. We'll be ready."

"Chef, please," Jacques said.

Roystan looked at Nika. "Can you help Jacques? I need to be on controls."

She nodded.

"Pulling you in soon, Josune."

"We'll be ready," she said again.

Roystan clicked the link off. "Take a blaster, Nika. I'm not expecting trouble, but you never know."

Nika was. Alistair Laughton. Why did he have to keep turning up? She took a blaster, the dart gun, and the same bottle of antiseptic Josune had carried earlier. Sometimes the simplest solutions were the best. An unexpected spray in the face often gave you the seconds you required.

Jacques took her down to the cargo bay.

"Not the shuttle bay?" Nika asked.

"We need the grapple to collect them." Jacques swung himself into place. "If Roystan can bring us close enough alongside."

Carlos came partway with them. He was doing a more thorough check on the starboard side, while they had the time.

It wasn't long before Roystan's voice came through the speaker. "Coming alongside lifeboat now. You might feel a bump."

They didn't feel anything.

"Roystan does line them up nicely," Jacques said as he, in turn, lined up the grapple. "He makes it easy."

"I heard that, Jacques. I'm going to play that back to you every time you remind me of the time I landed twenty-five degrees off at Atalante."

"You be nice to me," Jacques said. "Or you won't get any of that spicy flatbread that's coming out of the oven in fifteen minutes."

"I'll be nice."

"We can hear your stomach rumble from here," Nika said, although it was more likely hers.

"Can you? Really?"

Nika didn't answer.

"Lifeboat caught," Jacques said. "Bringing it in now." He eased the controller dial counterclockwise five degrees. Half the lights went green. The red lights showed there was no air.

Roystan pushed the cameras up to the screen nearest Nika and Jacques. "I'll keep the door locked as they come out. Be ready."

Nika watched as the oxygen light switched to green.

"Cleared to exit," Roystan told the occupants of the lifeboat.

The first one out was Josune. She made for the nearest link, not the door. "It's us," she said. "Snow and me, along with Snow's Gramps, and Laughton."

That was Josune, direct and honest, and covering immediately what they were worried about.

Snow stumbled out after her, looked around the cargo hold as if he wasn't sure where he was. He turned to the older man who exited next, the man Nika had met in the hospital on the *Boost*, said something quiet.

Gramps patted his shoulder. Snow smiled and looked around again, his smile getting wider. He was happy to be home.

The last person out looked larger standing than he had on a stretcher. He looked around, then looked directly to where Nika and Jacques waited outside. Alistair Laughton. Was it coincidence that he looked their way, or could he see them?

The ship rocked as Jacques opened the door for them. This felt like a real hit, albeit not a hard one.

Roystan's voice came out of every speaker. "Need someone on the cannons. For when one of those ships turns on us."

"On it," and Snow took off running.

Josune looked to Nika and Jacques. Nika laughed.

"Go, Josune. We've got this." She turned to her companions as Josune gave a hasty thanks and took off running.

"Why is my boy answering the cannon call?" Gramps asked. "He's a body modder."

"It's a small ship. We multitask."

"Nika calibrates," Jacques said. "I am the cargo master." Which wouldn't have meant anything to these two, but Nika knew what he was saying.

"Speaking of which, Jacques. What I said about food earlier is still valid. Roystan will be hungry. And you said that flatbread was in the oven."

"On it," Jacques said, and he, too, quickened his pace and left them.

Nika gestured for the other two to go in front of her, and they followed at a more leisurely pace. She trusted Gramps. Although he was armed, she thought he would put Snow first. But Laughton— she didn't know about him and wanted to watch him.

Laughton looked around the crew room as if he was memorizing it, stopped when he saw the kitchen where Jacques was pulling the spicy flatbread out of the oven.

"You put your galley next to the bridge?"

"Do you have a problem with that?" Nika asked. Let him think it was the bridge.

"No. But I don't think I've ever seen it done before."

"This is not a galley." Jacques struck a dramatic pose. "This is a kitchen."

"Full commercial range, by the looks," Alistair said.

"You know cooking?"

He'd made a friend for life.

Laughton shook his head. "I remember a case, a few years back, where someone was murdered in a kitchen like this. It was a restaurant."

"Which restaurant?"

Laughton hesitated, shrugged. "A place called the Highest Kite."

"Mia Gonzales's restaurant? She has a Mengar Range? Are you sure? She prefers the Live 8900 series. Did it have a yellow trim or stainless steel?"

Laughton shrugged again.

"Jacques," Carlos said through the link, "do you know how much you sound like Nika when you say that?" He did something that ended on a clang, said cheerfully, "Starboard side as secure as she can be. I'm coming back."

"A bit more to the left," Roystan said to Josune.

Josune adjusted a setting. "Ready, Snow?"

"I am not talking about silly machines," Jacques said. "I am talking about life-support systems." He patted the stove reassuringly. "Machinery that does good in the world."

Roystan fired one of the jets. Jacques, halfway to the table with a plate of flatbread, watched the flatbread go one way as he went the other. Josune caught the pieces before the forces could separate them.

"Nice catch," Nika said.

Carlos, somewhere on his way back, yelped. "Warn us next time."

"Sorry," Roystan said. "But better than being hit. You should all strap in."

Josune handed him a piece of flatbread and dumped the rest back onto the plate. Laughton looked at the plate as if he didn't want to eat any of it.

"If you're worried about germs," Josune said, "Nika can put you into one of the genemod machines afterward. She'll clean anything bad out of your gut."

Laughton looked around at them as if he thought they were all crazy. Which they probably were, but right now they were together. They just had to stay safe.

Nika took flatbread for herself, and some for Snow. "This is for Snow," she told Gramps, who nodded and took his own piece as he got up to follow her.

"He's been tortured," he told Nika as they walked down the passage. "He'll drop soon, even if he doesn't realize it."

"Snow?"

"No, the big guy."

"Some people can go longer than you think." She'd seen both Josune and Roystan do it.

"Not after a session or two with Norris's bullies."

Nika shivered. "I don't know how you and Snow put up with it."

"He couldn't really touch us. He needed us."

Gramps had found ways around Norris's demands, based on how he'd still managed to get Snow into the genemod machine before he'd gotten Alistair in.

"Snow must have contacted you in the time he was at Landers. Why didn't you join him?"

Snow had once told her they'd arranged a code and a place to meet. Gramps had never turned up.

"Norris was watching me. He would have followed, found my boy."

They reached the cannon station. They'd come a long way from the early days of *Another Road*, where the controls had been the simple wired controls direct from the camera. Josune had wired up a seat and cameras from all around the ship. When she had time, she was going to link all three cannons into the crew room. And add a fourth.

What would Laughton make of that?

Gramps smiled at his protégé. "You fell in with good people, Snow."

"I was taught well."

They weren't related at all. Nika couldn't see a single feature that tied them together, except their mannerisms. How had Gramps ended up taking on Snow? One day Snow might tell her. Or he might not. How much of his silence about Gramps had been due to worrying about Norris? A lot, she suspected.

Now they had two enemies to worry about. Wickmore and the *Boost*.

"You okay here, Snow?"

"Never better," Snow said.

Nika left Gramps talking to Snow and went back to the crew room.

She took her blaster out of its holster and put it on the table in front of her before she took another piece of spicy flatbread. Holstered weapons took longer to draw.

Roystan and Josune were talking tactics.

"We come in down the side here." Roystan tapped the star chart. "Slow, steady. Let those two ships fight it out."

"That's too dangerous," Josune said. "You're going closer to the Vortex. You'll kill us all."

"It's safe if you do it right."

"No way. I've been here before. You're going to kill us. We need to get as far from the Vortex as we can, before we're sucked into it. We're out of the Funnel. Nullspace out. While we can. While we're still alive."

"I know this place," Roystan said. "I've been here before too. Four times."

Nika stopped, flatbread halfway to her mouth, forgotten. Four times. The memory of an earlier conversation slipped into her mind. Josune, saying Feyodor had spent a lot of time around the Vortex, because she thought that Goberling had been there.

Nika moved over to the calibrator console, which was next to the pilot seat. "You got your memory back." She made it a murmur but knew Roystan was listening to it. "How much?"

"All of it." His murmur was equally low.

She hadn't touched his memory. Not since he'd started avoiding her because he didn't feel well, two weeks before the arrival of Brand and Bouwmeester. Was that all it took? The ability to fine-tune the feeds to achieve real balance in the body? Or had his recent problems tipped some chemical balance and cleared some pathways in the brain?

How was she going to find out?

Nika looked at the calibrator, glad she didn't have to manage it right now. Hadn't had to manage it for a while, in fact. Roy Stanley Goberling remembered.

Feyodor had been right all along.

She was sweating suddenly. "I hope the *Boost* doesn't kill us. Or that other ship."

"Me too," Roystan said. "And we need to get out of this space while both ships are distracted. We'll come back another time."

"I can't believe—"

"What about Zell?" Laughton demanded. "Why don't you just go to Zell?"

"Zell is the first place the *Boost* will look for us."

"We have to go to Zell," Laughton said.

Roystan looked at him with some pity. "It is the only place around here. It's the logical place we'll head for. Doing what they expect us to do is foolish."

Laughton snatched up the blaster Nika had left on the table. Pointed it at Roystan. "You're going to Zell, and you're going there now."

"Hey," Nika said, partly to distract him from noticing Josune, who was reaching into a drawer for a weapon.

"We have two warships between us and our destination," Roystan said. "They're still too busy to do anything about us, but you can be sure that by now they've noticed us. One of them is the *Boost*. Norris will come after us."

Jacques came up behind Laughton from the kitchen. "You're not our captain." Smashed a pan down on his head. "You don't get to tell us what to do."

29

ALISTAIR LAUGHTON

When Alistair came around, he was in another genemod machine. He surged upright and looked around. He could still see. He couldn't tell what was normal anymore, so he didn't know if the colors he was seeing were the colors he was used to. He couldn't tell here, in this room, which didn't look like any ship room he'd been in in his life.

"We didn't touch your eyes," Rik Terri said. "Although, we would like to know how they happened."

All three modders were there. Rik Terri, her apprentice, and the doctor from the *Boost*.

Alistair looked at the walls.

"What do you see?" Rik Terri asked.

Snowshoe cleared his throat. "We don't have time, Nika. You can ask about it later."

Alistair felt better than he had in a long time.

"Nor did we change whatever it was you had in your blood. Or the tiny changes in your brain. You had those before, and it didn't seem to bother you. Besides, we didn't know how important it was for your eyes. Or your mods. You have a few."

"Thank you." The Santiagan doctor had called it a virus.

"We fixed the physical damage Norris did." Snowshoe frowned repressively at Alistair. "And the hit from the fry pan. I wouldn't have bothered, given what you did, but we thought you might have brain damage. Don't forget we rescued you. It's not the best way to thank us."

He would have been embarrassed, but they had to get to Zell. "I'm sorry, I've been chasing Rik Terri for weeks. My goal was to get her to Zell. Urgently. And Zell is right in front of us." Assuming they hadn't jumped. "I'd do it again if I had to."

Rik Terri looked at Snowshoe. He shook his head back.

"Josune told us," Rik Terri said. "Or she gave us some story you told her about your people being captive on Zell, and you manipulating the *Boost* to come here so it could shoot up the ship that's holding your people hostage."

"Which is pretty stupid," Snowshoe said. "For then you have the *Boost* instead. Which would be worse."

"It was the best idea I could come up with. I didn't have time to plan." He'd been hoping the Santiago warship and the *Boost* would wipe each other out. Or at least damage each other so badly they weren't a threat. Just long enough for the settlers to escape from Zell. "I needed time. And now that they've had their battle, I also need to call my boss to arrange the rescue ship."

Rik Terri waited.

"We need to get the people off Zell."

She crossed her arms. "You told Josune you had promised to take me to Zell. Now you're telling me you want to call a rescue ship."

"Whatever that is," Snowshoe said.

"Yes, I did, and yes, I do."

"Explain."

How could an unarmed woman look so forbidding?

"And don't muck around. Tell it straight and tell it fast. Because of you, we're about to be attacked. Roystan's waited longer than he should to hear your story."

"Then let's go talk to him." He'd feel more comfortable on the bridge.

"I can hear from here," Roystan said.

Alistair looked around. "What?"

"He's stupider than the other Justice Department agents we've met." Carlos's mutter came through the link clearly. "And that's saying a lot."

Alistair took a deep, steadying breath and looked around the studio while he collected his scattered thoughts. This crew was . . . unusual. Even down to the fact that the studio contained three genemod machines, which was bizarre for a spaceship this size. One of them a Songyan.

"Is that the machine you stole from Songyan Engineering?"

"Well, it's certainly not the machine we ordered. That was destroyed while it was under your care." Biting and more than a little angry. "The Justice Department will pay for it."

He nodded. It was only fair.

"We don't have time for small talk," Roystan said. "Either tell your story or shut up and let us escape. We are here only because you arranged it, so do us the courtesy of being honest. And make it fast."

"Harsh words from your captain." Gramps frowned at Snow. "Not what you led me to believe."

"He's normally mild," Snow said.

"Except when his crew is endangered," Josune said through the link. "When he'll do anything to protect them."

Was everyone listening in?

"I am trying to save our settlement." It was Alistair's home. "We took a contract with Santiago. Two years, plus bonuses if we delivered on time." He took a deep breath. "We made the bonus, but the company never intended to pay it out. They came to kill us instead." It was harder to tell than he thought it would be. Especially now Cam was gone.

If he was gone. He still wasn't sure if he'd hallucinated Cam on Wickmore's ship.

"Except they didn't know about the Ort." He paused, ostensibly to give them time to ask the obvious, but really to breathe again.

His audience of three didn't ask. Nor did the four other crew members on board, who might or might not have still been listening. Josune and Roystan kept a quiet murmur of stats going.

"The Ort are sapient, but nonhuman. At first we thought they were local to Zell, but they turned out to be just as foreign as us."

"Aliens?" Nika asked.

"Yes. They'd been watching us. They saw Santiago attacking us and came to our assistance. They wanted—" What did they want? They'd wanted Cam, and, "You. You modded Cam with transurides."

"Why is that important?"

This would be where he lost her. He continued regardless. "Their race is dying of a plague. They've been inoculating us." *Gloss over how the inoculations happened.* "They have a vaccine that's effective on humans, even if not on themselves. When they tried to inoculate Cam . . . whatever it was you did with the transurides in his body blocked the plague virus. They think that if you could show them how you did . . . whatever you did with the transurides, they might be able to use it to save more of their own people."

He didn't understand her quick glance toward the screen. Snowshoe did, for he looked concerned.

"What happened with Santiago?" Roystan's voice, coming out of the speakers, made him jump. "No company will give up on aliens, especially if they're advanced enough to travel to other worlds."

"Santiago sent in an armed warship. We knew we were safe as long as the Ort dealt with us, not Santiago." Alistair closed his eyes. He wasn't proud of the next bit. "I said I'd find Rik Terri, because we all knew that if Santiago found her . . . you . . . first, then the Ort would work with Santiago." They'd work with anyone who could help them save millions of lives by doing it. Alistair would have done the same.

"Nika," Snow began warningly.

She waved him quiet.

"My promise to collect you is the only thing keeping us alive," Alistair said. "Santiago can't talk to them, or they couldn't before I left, and I haven't told Santiago what the Ort need from us."

They must know by now that he was after Rik Terri. They just didn't know what value Rik Terri was.

"What happens when the *Boost* and Santiago finish fighting?"

"The victor will still be weakened. Santiago hasn't told anyone more than necessary. Not even their board. I have a ship on standby—if you'll let me call them. They'll come and get our people." His agreement with Paola wouldn't last forever.

"Your people. What about the Ort?"

"They're our people too." He supposed he'd better be honest. "They're plague carriers. They can't go home."

"It's a stupid plan."

"Desperate times," Josune said through the link, making Alistair jump again. "It might even have worked, Nika."

Nika sniffed.

"We've done stupider things."

"I never said we hadn't. You just don't go against companies like this and win."

30

NIKA RIK TERRI

"The Santiago ship has been destroyed," Roystan said. "They're deploying lifeboats. The *Boost* will come for us next."

Nika looked at Snow, then at Alistair.

"There are lifeboats everywhere right now," Roystan said. "If you're going down world, it will provide some cover, but you've less than five minutes to decide."

She'd already decided.

"I'll take the Netanyu. Snow, help me prepare. I need—" She didn't know what she needed. "Do the Ort use genemod machines?"

Alistair shook his head. "Not that I've seen."

"How did they do your eyes?" They had to be the ones who'd done his eyes.

"Surgery. I think."

She forced herself not to shudder. Hundreds of years ago, that was the way of medicine, and they'd been good at it too. But still, his eye operation must have been awful.

Snow packed a basic workroom for her. "Mutrient. Naolic acid. Arrat crystals. Sodium salts. Aluminum salts. Nerveseal. Plasmas. We should take the Songyan."

"No. That stays with Roystan." Snow was going to stay with Roystan, too, although he didn't know it yet.

Or maybe he did, given the way he took time out from packing to glare at her.

She finished the packing for him. "Let's go."

They hurried down to the smaller shuttle, where Josune waited. "I've programmed it to land on Zell. It will land automatically, but if it doesn't—"

Nika didn't know how to pilot a shuttle.

"I've piloted shuttles," Laughton said. "Not well, but enough."

"Good." Josune gave him the codes.

Snow pushed past them both to get onto the shuttle first. Nika grabbed him.

"You're staying, Snow."

"I'm your apprentice. I go where you go."

"Not this time. One of us must look after Roystan. He needs more time in the machine. I took him out early."

"You have to stop taking people out early, Nika. You know it's bad."

"Sometimes you have to do what you have to."

"I'm still coming with you."

"What about Gramps?"

Gramps tried to push his way into the shuttle. "I'll come too."

Nika grabbed for him. He shrugged her off easily.

Laughton reached over, pulled him out. "The lady has spoken," he said.

"Thank you." Nika had thought he'd want as many modders on planet as he could get.

"Snow," Josune said, "Nika's likely to get into trouble. She'll need rescuing. And someone will need to put her in the machine when she comes back. Let's not put all our modders, and our gene-mod machines, into one little shuttle." The ship lurched. Not a hit. Flux. "Thirty seconds before the shuttle auto-launches," Josune said.

"Nika, don't break our shuttle." This was from Carlos in the crew room.

"Why should I be any different to the rest of you?" Nika tried for upbeat.

"I didn't break our other one. Besides, it's repaired. I checked the engine myself."

The door closed. The shuttle exited.

Inside the shuttle it was quiet. Nika linked in to *Another Road*. "All clear here."

"Good." It was Roystan who replied. "With luck, no one will notice you've detached. Your trajectory will take you into the center of the lifeboats."

"How are you doing?"

"Not too bad." Roystan sounded as if he was talking through gritted teeth. "The *Boost*, at least, is cautious enough to get away from the Funnel before they take a shot."

Another Road would soon be too busy to talk. Nika clicked off.

Laughton flicked open the controls to display the outside scene. It seemed all too soon before they slid into the middle of a group of other pods and shuttles their own size or smaller. Spatially speaking, they weren't even close, but they felt it, and Nika had to force herself not to hold her breath.

Josune had planned it well, for their shuttle stayed in the middle of the fleeing crowd.

"How do you talk to the Ort?" Nika asked. "Do you speak Standard?"

"It's a combination of hearing and thinking and—" Laughton shrugged. "The Ort operated on us to make it work." He shrugged again. "You'll see when you go through it."

Not to her, they wouldn't. Not if she could get a genemod machine to do it for her instead.

"They've operated on all of you?"

"Some of us. I was the first. Then some of the others. Probably most of them by now." He took a breath. "They never operated on Cam. They weren't sure—"

Cam Santiago, whose body she had modded with transurides. The only person whose body had more transurides than Cam's was Hammond Roystan.

"How big are the Ort?" Would they fit into a genemod machine? Machines were set up for human, not alien, anatomy. Could they even use it? Would such a machine kill them? Maybe they could diagnose with it still? Veterinarians used modified genemod machines on animals. Would she have to reconfigure the Netanyu to alien specifications?

"Tall." Alistair turned to the screen. "I have to call Paola to arrange the pickup."

"Go ahead."

The woman who appeared on the screen was dressed in white nen-silk. Nika was surprised she even recognized nen-silk after all this time. Her old life seemed so long ago.

"About time you called, Alistair. Where the hell are you?"

"Time to make good on your promise to supply a ship, Paola. A hundred people."

"Probably more." Nika indicated the lifeboats that had been moved to the smaller screen so Alistair could make his call.

One of the lifeboats on the screen blew apart.

Laughton covered his eyes briefly. "Or a bigger one. Get it to Zell as soon as you can. Within a day."

"Have you heard of this thing called the Funnel?"

"You were aware of that before, Paola."

"Where are you, Alistair?"

"I'll meet you at Zell." He clicked off. "Did that ship just—"

Another lifeboat exploded into smaller pieces.

Laughton scrambled for the controls. "Norris is shooting at anyone trying to escape."

"How long before we get to Zell?" Maybe they'd arrive before their shuttle was destroyed.

"An hour."

They wouldn't make it. The *Boost* would destroy them all long before that. Nika checked the screens again.

She zoomed in, searching for *Another Road*. Had Norris taken it out before he started on the pods?

"Finally," Laughton said as he managed to wrest control off auto. He increased the power. "Who'd have thought it so hard to take over a shuttle on auto."

Debris spun toward them, slammed into the side of their shuttle. The shuttle spun. Their screens went out.

31

JOSUNE ARRIOLA

Josune checked on Snow, back at the smaller cannon. Gramps sat on the floor, relaxed against the wall, watching him with a promise etched into his eyes, a promise that said, "Now I've found you, I'm not losing you again."

Once they stopped running, she was going to rig the smaller cannon to controls in the crew room, where it would be battle ready.

"We should have sent Gramps with Nika," Snow said. "Along with the Songyan. He'd be safer."

She wasn't sure she agreed with him.

"I should have gone too. I'm her apprentice. It's my job. But she didn't want me. She left me behind on the ship."

What a time for the normally confident kid to have a crisis.

"She needed you here, Snow. Roystan isn't finished." Josune couldn't think of anything else to say.

"She never finishes. She always takes people out early." Snow put his head in his hands. "She should have trusted me."

Gramps spoke before Josune could think of anything to say. "Sometimes, boy, you do things because you think it's best for the other person."

Snow opened his mouth to speak. Gramps put a hand on his arm. "I did stupid things too. I ignored all your messages, thinking it best. Thinking it safer. Even if I didn't want to. Even if I was wrong."

Gramps must have carried his own guilt with him.

Josune left them to it. On the way to the crew room, she turned on the big cannon. It would take fifteen minutes to warm up. She wasn't sure they had that time.

Back in the crew room, Roystan's fingers danced across the panels. Jacques and Carlos both watched mesmerized.

"How do you feel?" Josune asked.

He took time out of the finger dance to look up at her and smile. Roystan had a crooked smile. She loved it. "I feel the same way I always feel after Nika has worked on me. A thousand times better."

His smile turned down as he waved a hand at the *Boost*. "But right now I am no better than Captain Norris."

That was unexpected.

"Have I lived too long, Josune? To do what I am about to do. Do I have the right to make this sort of judgement?" It was a whisper, nothing more.

She put a hand over his. His fingers were cold. "I don't understand."

"You will, soon enough." He looked away, as if he couldn't bear to meet her eyes.

"Ahem," Jacques said, making them both jump. "You're scaring us." He placed a plate of flatbread between them. "If we're all going to die, we may as well do it like old times. Eat. If we're going to die, we'll do it on a full stomach."

He was scaring Josune too. Nika hadn't thought they would die. She had left Snow and the Songyan with them.

"We should run," Josune said. "The *Boost* has more firepower than us. It has longer-range cannons." And a captain who couldn't afford to let them get away.

Roystan stared at the screens. "We can't. Not this time. Or it will never be over. None of us will be safe. Ever. So I do this." He inhaled deeply. "The waiting. The waiting is the worst."

Josune's nerves were getting the better of her. She wished he'd stop talking and start acting. If he didn't, she'd fire on the *Boost* herself. "Waiting for what? If you have a plan, tell us about it."

Roystan leaned back. "Some of your prayers wouldn't go astray, Carlos."

Everything seemed too slow. "You know," Josune said. "You are behaving very oddly."

"Am I?" He turned his head to look at her. "This won't be my proudest moment." The *Boost* started to move. "At last. Here we go."

But the *Boost* didn't come for them. It went for the lifeboats, taking them out, one by one. Norris started with the lifepods from the Santiagan ship, which were closest.

The comms sounded.

Life snapped back to normal speed.

Roystan opened a link. Captain Norris was on the other end. "Captain Roystan."

Roystan didn't answer.

"I hope you're watching your screens, Roystan."

"You are shooting at defenseless people."

"A minor matter, I know, but they're in the way. See that shuttle there in the middle. That's the one I'm aiming for."

Nika's shuttle.

"I worked that out myself. You didn't need to call me up to tell me." Roystan gave an elaborate shrug. "I would have said this proves you're a man without an ounce of compassion, but we didn't need to prove that. At least one got away. Again." He opened another link. "Snow, what's the most vulnerable part of the *Boost*?"

"There isn't any," Snow said. "It's a warship."

"Oh, come."

Roystan left the link open to the *Boost*, so Norris was hearing this. Josune thought it might have been to prove that Snow was here, on ship, and not on the shuttle. Norris didn't react. She played along too. "What about engine number four? Number two is already damaged. We could take out both engines on the starboard side."

Not that she'd get a clear shot. Especially now she'd voiced her intentions.

Another lifepod exploded.

"Direct hit, sir," from Norris's bridge.

"One more to go, Roystan. Then the shuttle. Your shuttle. The shuttle that will make a nice, big explosion."

"You're right, Josune," Roystan said. "That starboard engine is a good idea."

It was a stupid idea, for it would draw all the firepower to them. But it might save Nika.

"I'll do it with the big cannon, Snow. Leave it to me."

Roystan cut both links, gave her a thumbs-up. She wasn't sure why. "Beautiful," he said, and opened an internal link. "All crew suit up and strap in. We're in for a bumpy ride. That includes you, Carlos," because Carlos was still sitting at the table. "And you, Jacques," who was making coffee in the kitchen.

"Snow?" Josune went for her own suit. Slid into it. She kept the gloves and her helmet open.

"Kitting up," Snow said. "Both of us."

She brought a suit back for Roystan.

"Thanks. How long till the big cannon is ready?"

She glanced at the panel. "One minute." Did some quick calculations. "You'll need to be closer or I won't do any damage." Or maybe that was the point.

"How much closer?" He was setting the nullspace controls. A bead of perspiration dropped to his collar. "I'd really like Nika here right now on the calibrator."

He was going to nullspace out. "This is a bad idea," Josune said. "It's dangerous to jump here, Roystan."

And it would leave Norris to chase Nika.

"Cannon, Josune." Roystan's face took on a sickly sheen.

Would he collapse on them again?

"Be ready. You'll need to reposition it once I jump."

He planned to nullspace closer. He was insane.

"We're right near the Vortex."

"That's right."

"You do know what the Vortex does. You know it grabs you. You know it sucks you in." He'd told her himself how dangerous it was.

"Yes. Be ready."

"Roystan." Josune bit off the rest of her words. "You're the captain." He obviously had a plan. Could he carry it off? "Get as close as you can."

"Thanks, Josune."

She barely heard him over the yammering of her terror. Calm. It's just another battle. The *Hassim* was forever fighting for survival. Was that so different on *Another Road*? Did it matter that *Another Road* didn't have the firepower, or a fighting crew?

"Snow, do you think you could throw insults at Captain Norris?" Roystan's fingers were dancing over the controls again.

"Are you sure?"

"He is more likely to react to insults from you than from anyone else."

Carlos was praying aloud in the background. He seemed to have lost whatever calm he'd found earlier.

"Ahh." Snow took a deep, shuddering breath. "I'll do my best."

Roystan opened the link again. "Go."

"Captain Norris. You appear to be having trouble keeping your mercenaries." Snow's voice squeaked to start but got stronger as he continued. "How long . . . how long did you manage to keep me this time? A few days? You're losing your touch."

"Snow," Norris purred. "You are next on my list. You can't save yourself this time. But Gramps will be the first to go. You can watch him die."

"Another hit, sir," someone said from near Norris, and on-screen another lifepod exploded.

Gramps's deep voice chimed in. "Got to get me first. I'm with my boy now."

How much courage had that taken?

"Gramps. Me. How many others? You must be hemorrhaging crew." Snow laughed. Josune thought she detected a slightly hysterical timbre to it. She didn't blame him. "All those lifeboats leaving your ship."

They didn't know why the lifeboats were leaving. Maybe the ship was damaged. Although, Josune couldn't imagine Norris allowing his crew to exit in the middle of a battle like that.

Maybe they were the ground crew and Norris was sending them down to take over Zell. Although surely he'd use a shuttle for that.

"You of all people should understand that I always get my man." *Another Road*'s nullspace warning sounded. Norris laughed. "Running away? That won't work. I'll find you. You can run, you can hide, but—"

They nullspaced.

Proximity alarms blared as they came out of nullspace. Out behind the *Boost*. A force grabbed *Another Road*, dragged them sideways.

"The Vortex." Josune clutched at air. She'd had nightmares about this. Being caught by the Vortex, and no way to escape. "Sorry." She tried to get her voice under control.

She realigned the cannon. Fired. Carlos's prayers got louder.

The *Boost* spun from the hit. A shot—fired at the same time from the *Boost* and aimed for the shuttle Nika and Alistair were in—clipped the edge of the shuttle rather than the center.

Another Road's power failed.

Roystan used the emergency backup power to reopen the link. Proximity alarms blared on both ships. Someone shouted at them. Not Norris, one of his crew.

"We're not running away," Snow said over the hubbub. It took Josune a moment to grasp that he was continuing the earlier conversation. Didn't he realize they were doomed? No. He trusted Roystan. She glanced at Carlos. He was white.

"Josune," Carlos whispered.

She understood what she should have known immediately, if she hadn't been so busy getting ready to fire. The emergency lighting and air had kicked in. Her subconscious had known, though, for she'd snapped her helmet on, then released it. It hadn't been a catastrophic ship failure at all. Roystan had turned everything off. They were on backup battery.

"Fire," Norris said.

Another Road rocked. A direct hit, although Josune couldn't tell where. Not without full instrumentation. Breach doors clicked into place—they had their own emergency power systems, because Josune was paranoid about breaches.

"You're wrong, Roystan," Norris said. "Even though you can no longer hear me. The most vulnerable part of any ship is the bridge. And you just turned it face on to us. How amateur."

They didn't need the bridge. Not on *Another Road*.

The ships were getting closer.

Déjà vu. Josune watched the two ships come together. It must have looked like this on the *Hassim*, back when it had nullspaced into *The Road*'s path. She calculated the time to impact. Fifty seconds. Forty-five. Forty.

And they couldn't do a thing, not with the forces dragging at them. Thirty-five. Their space suits wouldn't save them.

"Sir." Norris's crew were calm. Battle ready.

Carlos whimpered.

Josune was glad they weren't on the original *Road to the Gober-lings*, where she could have taken over the controls with a single grab. She sat on her hands so she wouldn't do anything stupid. Roystan knew what he was doing.

Didn't he?

"It's been a pleasure killing you and your crew, Captain. A pity about Snow and Gramps. A demonstration of my ire would have been most effective." Norris's voice faded a little, as if he'd looked away. "Fire engines for evasive action."

The *Boost*'s port engines burst into sudden power, pushed away from *Another Road*.

The alarms coming through Norris's feed increased in signal and urgency. Proximity alarms. Engine alarms. An inhuman, high-pitched squeal that went on, and on, and on.

They sat and listened.

"Get us out of here," Norris hissed.

"Working on it, sir," a strained voice said. The same voice that had been so calm in the face of imminent collision. "We're caught in the Vortex."

"What happens if they slam into us?" Josune asked.

"Then we're dead," Roystan said.

She absorbed that in silence.

"Mayday. Mayday." The voice, calm again. Josune would like to have met him. "This is the mercenary ship the *Boost*, requesting assistance. We have been caught by the Vortex. We require assistance."

"Do everything necessary to get us out of here." Norris's voice was as calm as that of his pilot. Josune imagined he'd have been a successful mercenary.

"There is no escaping the Vortex. Sir."

"Try harder. Try—" Norris's words were cut off by screams around the ship, and the sound of shredding, tearing metal as the *Boost* was torn apart by the forces.

Light flared around them. Then heat.

And finally, silence.

Josune whispered a quiet, "May your Afterlife be happier than this life," for Effie, who'd refused to leave.

Roystan gripped Josune's hand. His own hand was still icy. "It's done," he whispered.

They waited.

Josune turned to the boards to see what the damage to their own ship was.

"Don't," Roystan said. "No power. None at all. You'll kill us."

"Internal emergency comms?"

"We can use that." He flicked it on. "Snow, Gramps? Are you okay?"

"That was awful."

That was Snow, as blunt and honest as ever. Nika would take that to mean he was all right. Josune took it that way too.

"Come back to the crew room. And Snow, power's out. Don't try and use it; it being down is all that's keeping us alive."

"All?" Josune asked.

Roystan shrugged. "I don't really know, but it pays not to test it. I have found that if we stick to emergency power, we're fine."

"You've done this before?" No one survived the Vortex. "You knew what would happen to Norris."

How were they still alive? And for how long, for the Vortex still had them trapped.

"I guessed." His voice was barely audible. "I hoped. I've seen it happen before."

He started to pull away. She closed her hands tight around his. Norris wasn't anyone she'd mourn.

"Four hundred people, Josune. I killed them all. I knew I was going to do it."

"Not four hundred. Some got away. Besides, we're all monsters in our own way." Josune spoke as much to herself as she did to him. "None of us want to die. It's only human to do what we can to stay alive. Snow is safe. Nika is safe." Maybe, because Norris had hit the shuttle, even if he hadn't hit it head-on. "The colonists are safe-ish."

How cold must he be if she could feel it?

Was his body starting to regress already? She said a prayer of thanks that Nika had left Snow here. And the Songyan. Except they couldn't use the machine while the power was down.

An eerie howl started to build inside the cabin.

Snow and Gramps arrived with a dash. Snow closed the door carefully behind him, pulling it manually. He locked it.

They all looked at one another.

"We're in space," Carlos said.

Space was a vacuum. Sound waves didn't travel through it. They required molecules, a medium, to vibrate through. Which meant what? That there was atmosphere outside?

It was better than the alternative, that something was on the outside of the ship.

"I don't know what it is," Roystan said. "But I remember it." He shuddered and tried to laugh. "I don't remember it being so bad."

"You've done this before?"

The howling increased.

"Four times before." Roystan let go of Josune's hand to reach over and give Carlos's shoulder a reassuring pat. "It gets worse before it gets better, but it does get better."

Four times!

"You remembered?"

Roystan looked at her. Nodded. They didn't need to speak.

A consortium of three companies, each supplying ten people, had followed Roy Goberling on his last trip. They'd had a ship called the *Undertaker*. The captain—who'd been somewhat deranged, by all accounts—had a macabre sense of humor. The weapons list for the *Undertaker* had included five plasma cannons, seventeen blasters, and enough ammunition to fill a cargo hold. No one had ever found the ship. Some people thought they'd found Goberling's lode, killed Goberling, and then fought to death over the proceeds.

"The *Undertaker*," Josune said. "Is that how you knew what would happen to the *Boost*?"

He nodded.

For a young Roy Goberling, that had probably been the decider. The reason he'd chosen to forget it all. The first people he'd killed, or been responsible for the death of, anyway.

"You must have been so lonely."

The expression on his face was so raw Josune had to look away. Here he was, remembering it all again now, without even a hundred years to dull the pain of it.

"No wonder no one had ever found Goberling's lode before. The *Hassim* would have hunted forever and never found it. How did you find it?"

Who would think to jump into the middle of the most dangerous natural object in the galaxy, something that spanned twenty light-years across, just to find transurides?

But then, it made sense in a weird kind of way.

The metals were high in the periodic table. There were metals lower than them that could still only be made to exist for fractions of a second inside a laboratory. It had long been speculated that transurides had to be made under intense stress. How else would the atoms ever be pulled together in the higher formations that allowed them to become stable?

The Vortex was the most dangerous known natural pressure cooker in the galaxy.

"We are all so stupid," Josune said.

How did their ship survive pressures strong enough to smash atoms together or pull them apart? It didn't. Which meant that eons in the past the Vortex must have been much stronger than it was now.

"Let me tell you a story," Roystan said, raising his voice above the increasing noise of the Vortex. "About a young explorer. Let's call him Roy."

No prizes for guessing who Roy was.

"This Roy was determined to find new worlds. And he was fascinated by the Vortex, had been ever since it had been discovered. For there were transurides around the Vortex, you see. Not in any great quantity, but more than in other places."

The external creaking and groaning didn't seem anywhere near as bad, with Roystan's voice holding back the cold of space.

"Roy learned the hard way about forces in the Funnel. He sped up to get out and nearly wrecked his ship doing so. Then, to compound the problem, he nullspaced as soon as he exited, and learned the hard way that you don't do that while your engine has any force at all."

Roystan smacked his closed right fist against his left palm. "Straight into the nearest gravitational force. Which, luckily for him, turned out to be an asteroid. He lost his engine."

"Literally lost it?" Carlos asked.

"Not literally, no. But smashed it up so badly it wasn't even worth the scrap that was falling off the back of his ship."

Josune glanced at the others, all sitting around, all of them close. At Carlos, curled into a ball; Jacques, staring at the wall as if it would rip away at any moment; Snow, flinching at every new sound; and Gramps, staring at the blank screen as if he could still see the *Boost* there.

None of them seemed to realize what Roystan was telling them.

"But young Roy didn't despair," Roystan said. "Not yet, anyway. Because he was like Josune. He liked to be prepared. He had a spare engine in the cargo hold. All he had to do was put it together. But then—"

Roystan paused as a particularly loud squeal came from outside.

"Sound doesn't travel in space," Snow said.

Josune wasn't sure they were still in space.

"If you look at the controls," Roystan said, "you'll see nothing is out there."

"You call that nothing?"

"I call it a force, or a wind, or a tunnel, or something, but it doesn't seem to harm the ship. And it spits us out eventually, without harming us."

"That's assuming we're not providing opposing forces," Josune said. Like an electromagnetic engine.

"That's what I think, yes," Roystan said. "I think that it's some sort of medium, which allows it to come through as sound waves when it hits our ship. I don't know what it is. I only know it's not dangerous to us, provided we don't exert any force on it."

"Scientists are going to have a field day," Snow muttered.

That they were.

"So back to the story," Josune said.

"Yes. Back to the story. Where was I?"

"Engines died," Carlos said. "You had spares."

"One spare, anyway. But while I . . . while Roy was congratulating himself on his forethought, the Vortex caught him. Dragged him in."

"Like we are now?"

"Yes. Now, young Roy may have panicked a bit, even tried to restart his engines, but they were as dead as Earth-cats. Not even a sputter. As you can imagine, that saved his life, for anyone who's caught in the Vortex gets ripped apart as soon as they try to fight the force."

Roystan attempted another smile, this one not so successful. "Young Roy didn't appreciate, at the time, just how lucky he was. He spent a harrowing sixty hours convinced he was going deaf, or going mad, or he'd be pulled apart by the Vortex."

"Sixty hours," Josune said. Less than one hour had passed.

"Sixty hours."

Carlos moaned.

The emergency battery should be good for a week. Suits for a week after that. They had enough suits to go around. Josune would check supplies later. After Roystan finished his story.

"Until finally, Roy was so tired he went to sleep. He woke to silence. Nothing but the hum of circulating air."

"I meant to ask about that," Josune said. "Isn't the emergency system another force?"

"I think it's because the emergency system runs on a chemical battery," Roystan said. "I've only ever tried the battery." He shrugged. "If it works."

Which was why power was the first thing he'd turned off when they'd gotten caught by the Vortex. Josune shuddered. What if you couldn't get out? What if you ran out of battery before you got anywhere?

"After a bit, Roy suits up and goes out to look at the damage to his ship. It's a mess. Unsalvageable. And there is nowhere on the ship he can attach his new engine without it pushing right through the bridge the first time he fires it. All that's left between him and space is a thin metal wall and some insulation."

Josune shivered.

"Oh, and the cargo truss underneath, which Roy had bought to carry back all the treasures he was going to find on the worlds he was sure he'd discover. Along with the nets to carry that cargo in.

"His ship is losing power. Slowing down. It's going to stop soon. There's a big asteroid in front of it. It's three kilometers long."

Josune tensed. She knew all about that three-kilometer-long asteroid.

"Roy uses the rockets on his suit to nudge his ship toward the asteroid."

"That's impossible," Jacques interjected. "A ship's heavy. How can a man push it?"

"Force, mass," Carlos said. "You could do it, Jacques. The heaviest part of your ship is your engine."

"What about the cargo?"

"He doesn't have any cargo. And any action will cause a reaction. Give a good blast with the suit rockets. It doesn't have to be much. It's not as if you have gravity to fight against."

"It's kind of like finessing the angle on an airlock with the smaller rockets," Roystan said. "The ship was still moving, you see. It was more a matter of stopping it before it overshot the end of the asteroid. That was hairy, I tell you. And when it was done, the ship was three meters above the rock. I had to winch it down."

This was living history. The story Josune had dreamed about all her life. Being told to them by the man who had lived it.

"But why?" Carlos asked. "Shouldn't you have been trying to escape?"

"I had no engine, Carlos, and nowhere to put my spare. Nothing but a broken shell, which at least was keeping me alive."

Roystan laughed suddenly. "The funny thing was, I wasn't scared. Not that first time. Not once the noise stopped. I was too busy trying to stay alive. I'm in space, and I figure that if I can get my little ship started, I can still nullspace out and get rescued. The ship doesn't care where the rockets are; all it cares is that it can use them, and nullspace will bend around whatever is moving at the speed."

Within reason. Nullspace had limits, but some of the big ore carriers were as long as ten kilometers.

"What about the Vortex?" Josune asked.

"Not there. You come out the other end into I don't know where and space is as calm as anything."

"You can nullspace out. Can you nullspace back in again?"

"I tried that. You have to go down the Funnel and let the Vortex take you."

Snow shuddered. "Sixty hours every time. You have to be joking."

"Unfortunately not."

"How horrible."

It was horrible.

"And that," Roystan said, looking at Josune, "is the story of how young Roy jumped out into space near Kitimat with a three-kilometer chunk of rock. He wasn't looking for transurides. He had no idea what he had."

Josune's eyes misted over. She had to swallow before she could speak. "I think it's the most romantic thing I've ever heard."

"Romantic," Snow said. "How?"

"Ingenuity. Inventiveness. Perseverance. Snow, this is about a man who didn't give up, even when the odds were stacked against him."

"I suppose." Snow thought about it a minute. "Like Nika doesn't give up when a mod's not working."

"Exactly like that." Josune was proud of him, that young Roy she'd never known, who—stranded and alone—had worked out a solution and saved himself.

"It's not how most people imagine it," Roystan said.

Was he embarrassed? She couldn't tell under the dimness of the emergency lights. He sounded it.

"They want something amazing, swashbuckling. It's just . . . ordinary."

"Ordinary for you, maybe," Josune said. "To the rest of us it's rather inspiring."

"But I didn't know—"

"What you had. That makes it even more amazing."

"People like you," Roystan said. "You've been chasing a dream all your life. You have done so much more than me. Roy Goberling was a stupid kid who wrecked his ship, got lucky getting out of it, and then he spent the rest of his life running from that luck."

Carlos leaned over and awkwardly patted Roystan's shoulder. "None of us are perfect."

"This is what happens when you fall in love," Jacques said in an apparent aside to Snow that Josune thought he made deliberately loud enough for them all to hear. "You try to impress the other person. A hundred and twenty-five years old and he's worried about something he did in his twenties."

"If he's like this now," Snow said, "imagine what Nika's going to be like when she's a hundred and twenty-five."

It made them all—except Gramps—laugh, even though it wasn't in the least bit funny.

Josune pushed her way over to sit on the arm of Roystan's seat. "For that, Jacques, I'm going to cuddle, and there's nothing you can do about it." Roystan was cool to her touch. "Snow?" His cool was their regular temperature.

"Unless he's dying, I can't do anything for sixty hours." He sounded so much like Nika it made her smile.

Josune draped an arm across Roystan's shoulder, leaned into him. "I was young and foolish once, too, Roystan. Chasing a dream that was mostly in my mind. Hounding a man and I didn't even know it. But do you know what? Sometimes reality is better than the dream."

32

NIKA RIK TERRI

At first the damage to the shuttle seemed—relatively—minor.

"We've lost communication and sight," Laughton said. "But auto-pilot seems fine." He switched auto back on. "We're still moving, anyway."

"Deaf and blind," Nika murmured.

Laughton flinched.

"Sorry," although she wasn't sure what she was apologizing about.

He shrugged. "Sensitive subject. Going blind. My biggest worry when I came out of that machine of yours, and the one on the *Boost*, was that you'd have tried to fix my eyes."

"Surely you know that's impossible." She'd seen the mods, seen the way the electronics had been connected. "You don't have human eyes, Agent Laughton. Why do you think I agreed to come?"

"Call me Alistair."

"Likewise, Nika." Her reply was automatic. "You do know you have to be careful which modders you go to." What if he went to someone who didn't understand his eyes? Or even to a hospital?

Laughton—Alistair—nodded. "I know."

Good.

Nika busied herself inspecting the contents of the shuttle. "There are space suits," she said. "Can we use them to communicate?"

"Maybe." Laughton—Alistair, she'd have to think of him as Alistair—came over to look.

They pulled one of the suits out.

Suits had a range. Nika remembered Roystan saying that, after Josune had been lost in space when they had escaped from Atalante. She couldn't remember how far the range was, but in space it was tiny.

They both suited up so they could use the suit communicators.

Nika tried to contact *Another Road*.

She'd known how unlikely it was to get an answer, but she had to swallow hard when she couldn't.

"Nothing from Zell either." Alistair sounded as depressed as she felt.

"What about the other shuttles? There were some out there."

They found six lifepods nearby, but the occupants weren't answering. Nika remembered Josune saying some lifepods put you into suspended animation. Maybe the occupants of these were unconscious.

Or maybe no one was talking to them.

"I hope they all brought food," Alistair said. "There isn't much on Zell."

One of the lifepod signals dropped out.

Then two more.

"I think we're off course." Nika didn't want to think of the other option. Surely Norris wouldn't destroy potential mercenaries, especially if he didn't have to pay a fee for them. "One of us needs to go outside this shuttle and see what's happening."

She'd been in space twice. Both times attached by rope to Josune, who'd given some basic instructions on what to do if you found yourself out there. Not panic, breathe evenly, and use the suit link to call.

None of which looked to be of much use right now.

"How will that help?"

She had no idea, but it was better than sitting in the dark, knowing you were off course.

She checked her suit to be sure it was airtight and found two ropes with latch hooks on either end.

It had been a lot simpler when Josune was there to help.

"Talk to me while I'm outside. It can be scary out there."

"I presume you know what you're doing."

She didn't, but she didn't think he knew any better than she.

"Something other than that, please." She closed the inner airlock door. "Can you still hear me?"

"Yes." Suit sound was clear. But then, it would be, wouldn't it? This was *Another Road*'s shuttle. Josune and Carlos maintained it. She cycled the air out of the airlock. Opened the outer door. "Talk to me."

She didn't want to step out. Not into that vast blackness of space. Although, it wasn't exactly black. Half the sky was a dirty, pulsing gray. The rest—there was light. A dim red star, nothing else. She hoped the suit was strong enough to cut the radiation she'd be exposed to.

Weren't they supposed to be heading for a planet? Shouldn't she see it if they were only an hour away?

"Talking," Alistair said. "What do you want me to talk about?"

Anything. Didn't he understand she needed conversation, something to concentrate on rather than what she was doing? "Tell me how you met the Ort. Zell. How you see. Anything." She moved cautiously away from the airlock.

"The Ort. They're like cylinders with four legs and four arms. They're almost as tall as I am, and they don't turn, they just change direction."

That would be an interesting mod. How would you manage the joints?

Nika turned around again. There had to be a world out here somewhere. The only explanation was that the shuttle was blocking it.

Josune had shown her the holding loops built into the outside of the ship, and the markers on the ship itself that showed where each loophold was in relation to the ship. It was a way, Josune had said, to move around the ship without using power. "Always, always, always, be sure one latch is securely attached to the ship loopholds, the other attached to you. You can drag yourself around the ship by attaching and releasing the ropes. Always hook and unhook the right-hand side so you never accidentally break the loop."

No knowledge was ever wasted. Unfortunately. "I'm going to the other side of the shuttle."

"Do you have to?"

"Trust me, I wouldn't be doing it if I didn't have to." Nika found the next loophold to latch on to. "Keep talking."

"The Ort are green, except I see them as white. You'll meet them soon." He paused.

"Keep talking."

"It's amazingly difficult to talk to order, you know."

"If you were out here, you'd understand why I need you to."

"Let me think. I have a different range of vision. When I look at walls, I can see the wires because of the heat passing through. I can see the heat of a person from the other side of a thin wall or of plastiglass."

"Like infrared?"

"I suppose so, yes. Ultraviolet too."

"Doesn't that make it awkward?"

"At times. But I wouldn't want to lose it."

"I would love to see how you see." Nika clung to the side of the ship while she looked around. It was worse than waking up early in the Dekker.

"Are you still out there? Are you all right? You're breathing heavily."

"So would you be if you were walking around the outside of a spaceship."

Snow's vitals hadn't increased when he'd gone out to help Josune or Roystan do repairs. How many times had he been outside a ship? When would a modder, or a doctor, ever have had the need?

"Do you want—"

"Just shut up and keep talking about something else."

Nika kept moving. Attach loop. Unattach. Attach. Unattach. Until finally she was at the top. Off to one side, no longer hidden by the bulk of the shuttle, was a planet.

"I can see Zell."

"Are we heading toward it?"

She had no idea. She looked around. There were several specks reflecting red from the sun, heading toward the planet. "We're not going the same way as the other lifeboats." She hoped they were lifeboats. "Can you see what I'm seeing?" She'd been pushing her camera feed through all the time.

"Yes, and I don't think I like it."

Neither did she.

"I can't steer this thing blind."

How did you steer a shuttle? By firing the rockets. Nika didn't plan on staying outside while Alistair fired rockets around her, trying to get them back on course, but maybe that was what it took.

"I'd also like you to know that while I have landed a shuttle on manual, I've only done it the once, and that was twenty years ago. Back when I did the training."

He was really inspiring confidence.

"We can only pray the autopilot's still fine and will land us, once we get back on course."

Nika looked around again. "How many suits do we have?"

Josune liked a lot of suits. One for everyone, even on the small shuttle.

"Six, counting yours."

There were four engine jets. Two on one end of the shuttle, two on the other. Coming in to land you fired the jets to slow you down, which said to Nika that you'd enter the atmosphere with one set of the jets facing forward, the other facing back. "I'm going to take two of the suits. Fix them to the ends of the shuttle. I'll set the camera to transmit, then we'll have a view from outside."

There was silence from inside. Eventually, "That might work."

If her logic was wrong, they wouldn't be alive for her to regret it.

She'd have to do it fast. They'd only been an hour from Zell when they'd started. "Prep two suits. I'm coming back in. Keep talking while I do."

He had the suits, sans oxygen, prepped and ready. "Thanks." She clipped both suits to her own and went back into the airlock.

It was worse going out the second time.

"How did you start working for the Justice Department?" People who took contracts on places like Zell weren't generally Justice Department material.

"I was a career agent. I—" He checked himself. "You mean after Zell?"

"Yes." Although, she wouldn't mind hearing the rest of the story one day.

"We—Cam and I—went back looking for you. That's what we'd promised the Ort. Initially I thought it would be easy. I thought I could do with any modder."

Of course he'd think that. Alistair Laughton had no appreciation of the body as art.

"Cam knew where to find you, but there'd been the explosion at your studio and you'd disappeared. We were still looking for you when Paola, my old boss, sought me out. She was looking for you too."

Everyone seemed to be looking for her at one time or another. "Why?"

"You killed an executive."

"I what? Me?" She missed a loop, had to scrabble for the rope. Yes, she'd killed people, from Alejandro and Wickmore's hench-mates on, but this? "When?"

"Six months ago. You did it publicly, and you leered at the cam-era while you did it."

She knew where this was going.

"Paola ran the stats. In every way, except for it being public, the killing matched the modus of a known assassin."

"Tamati Woden."

"Yes."

She'd kill him if he wasn't already dead. "So he plastered my image all over the vids, and used my new body to do it."

"Yes."

Nika shivered.

"Paola knew I was looking for you, and I had worked on the Woden case before I was suspended."

"You were looking for Tamati Woden, and you never caught him. In all that time."

Alistair ignored that. "She was worried Woden had found a way to steal bodies. I thought he'd taken on an apprentice. It turned out she was right."

At least he'd come to that conclusion.

Nika reached the first two jets. She pushed the feed from the other suit to her own camera so she could check it was positioned correctly, then lashed the suit to the outside of the shuttle and ad-justed it until the camera faced forward.

One done.

"I took the job," Alistair said. "Two people looking for a woman who'd gone to a lot of effort to disappear were never going to find her. But with the Justice Department behind us—"

"So we have you to thank for putting Wickmore back on our trail." Eaglehawk had used the Justice Department before. It made sense.

Nika started across to the other end of the shuttle. This was easier somehow, as if she was getting the hang of it. Or maybe she was starting to panic, for Zell was looming so large in her visor—and off to one side—that it didn't matter where she was on the shuttle, she could see it.

"We didn't know Wickmore was involved," Laughton said. "Although, I must say, I certainly suspected him in the past. How did you manage to get both him and the *Boost* on your trail? And is it true that Arriola came from the *Hassim*?"

She didn't answer that. They didn't need another treasure hunter on their heels.

He continued after a few moments of silence. His voice sounded strained. "After I agreed to work temporarily for the Justice Department again—to find you—I looked up the report Cam and I had made about Zell."

She didn't need him to tell her what had happened. "Case closed?"

"There was no record of it."

Nika had been like that once. Naïve, believing that justice was justice and people were basically decent. Some people were, she supposed, just not the ones who were supposed to uphold decency.

She couldn't help Laughton with his demons.

There. Last camera in place. "How does that look?"

"Terrible," Laughton said. "We're way off course."

"I'm coming back in."

As soon as she was inside, Laughton fired the jets to correct their course. It took two tries, but eventually there was the bulk of a planet in front of them.

"We did it," she told Alistair as he set the autopilot.

Just in time, for an alarm sounded. "We're coming into atmosphere."

A moment later it seemed every alarm on the shuttle went off. Lights flashed amber, warnings screeched, and numbers scrolled across the screen in an energetic stream. The jets fired, front first, then back. The shuttle slowed.

"Are you doing that?"

Alistair shook his head.

At least something was going to plan. Nika hoped it was, anyway.

The flashing lights turned to red.

Maybe not fully to plan. The cabin was getting hot. "Is it just me, or is it stifling in here?" Shuttles could take a reasonable amount of heat. They had to, on entry into the atmosphere.

"It is stifling," Alistair said. "We're not slowing down fast enough. If this is a cheap shuttle, we're done for."

Josune bought quality, but sometimes, like Nika, she had to buy what was available. They'd find out, Nika supposed. She went through the shuttle cupboards, found some fire blankets. "Help me wrap these around the Netanyu."

"Shouldn't we use them for ourselves?"

"We have the suits." The suits would protect them better than a fire blanket. Besides, what did they have to offer the Ort if they didn't have a genemod machine?

She hoped Snow and Giwari's Songyan were safe.

"You're crazy. You know that."

"That's not exactly a new insult. Wrap this."

The jets fired again. From the front, this time. The pressure knocked them both to the floor.

"At least it's slowing us down," Alistair said. "Provided it's not too late."

"Are you always such a pessimist?"

"Under the circumstances—" He struggled to his feet again, helped her pull the blanket over the Netanyu. Even lifted it so she could wrap it around. She used all four blankets. "Are you sure these wouldn't be better around us?"

"Yes."

Nika snatched up the fire extinguisher, waved it at him when he looked as if he would take the blankets off. "Our suits will protect us."

He picked up his own extinguisher.

The alarms increased in frequency and volume.

"Time to strap in," Nika said. If they could, with their suits.

They managed, although she wasn't sure how. It was suffocating in the cabin. She sealed the helmet and hoped the oxygen tanks on the suit were safe.

A speaker blared. "Crash positions."

The shuttle hit the ground, kept going.

The cabin grew hotter.

Nika blacked out.

33

ALISTAIR LAUGHTON

For one awful minute when he came around, Alistair thought he was back with the Ort. Strapped to a bench. He couldn't see, couldn't move. He tore at the restraints, the thunder of his blood pounding through his body, deafening coherent thought.

A blinking red light he hadn't seen changed to green.

He could see. He wasn't blind.

He fumbled at the release, his hands shaking so hard he could hardly feel them. The catch was jammed.

Broken.

Breathe.

Finally he heard a click, and his body was released from the restraint. He pushed at the exit latch, forced it open, and fell out. Daylight. Blessed, blessed daylight under the cold Zell sun.

He forced himself to calm and pushed himself upright. No one was near to witness his panic.

Where was Nika?

The shuttle had broken apart on crashing. One crumpled side settled farther into mud and water. Nika's side. The mud on Zell was greedy. Once something got stuck, it was almost impossible to drag out. He ran—slid—toward it, careful to avoid the slick. He'd be no help if he got stuck.

Wreckage bobbed on the water, including a rectangular box shape. That damned genemod machine.

In the muddy water, barely visible, was a space-suit-shaped tinge. Heat signature. The suit was cooling, but it was still slightly warmer than the surrounding water.

Alistair plunged in. No time to think about how stupid he was being, no time to think about what would happen if he got stuck.

The suit was already three-quarters immersed in the mud. *Don't think about how heavy it is.* He shoved his hands under one end. Heaved. Heaved again. And again.

It was like trying to lift an aircar.

He kept heaving. His muscles bulged. He thought he would burst.

Slowly, slowly, the end of the suit came out of the mud, then, with a final sucking, the suit broke free.

Alistair fell back into the water.

He was up again immediately, turning the suit over, pushing at the emergency latches.

The oxygen indicator was red.

He tried to open the helmet. It stuck, glued by the mud. He grabbed a floating shard and prized the helmet apart from the suit.

Nika lay lifeless and still.

Not breathing.

He was too late.

She was still warm, and there was a faint gold glow under her skin. He couldn't be too late. To have found her, to have come all this way, and now, this.

Then Nika gasped, breathed in hard, and choked.

He carried her across to dry ground, held her while she finished coughing.

Their entry would have lit up the sky. The only question was, had it been anywhere near the settlement, and would anyone come to find them?

He sighed at the sharp bladed grass around him. The northern marshes, not far from the lake. The worst place they could have landed except for the lake itself.

They called it a lake, but it was really an inland sea. A sea that covered a thousand square kilometers. Their landfall could be worse, but not by much. If they went the wrong way, they would have a long, long walk, with the only food on them what they could scrounge from the shuttle.

The marsh had softened their landing, probably saved them.

"Get the Netanyu," Nika croaked.

She had to be kidding. But she wasn't. When he didn't move, she struggled to her feet and staggered toward it.

"Wait." She didn't know the area like he did. Couldn't see it like he could either.

The marsh was treacherous, but the deeper, more dangerous areas were colder. Easy to see the warmer parts from the less warm when you could see into the infrared, so he knew where to step.

And while the wildlife nearby would have run when the shuttle landed, the salynxes, with their double rows of sharp teeth, and the bovines, large two-headed cattle that had few natural enemies, would be back quickly.

Alistair checked his blaster and looked at Nika's empty holster. One blaster between two. It would have to do.

"Stay there. If you hear anything, yell." He waded out to get the Netanyu.

Of course, she didn't stay, but at least she followed exactly in his footsteps. She grabbed one end of the machine and backed away, retracing her footsteps.

"This way." Alistair spotted a drier piece of land.

As soon as they were on dry land, Nika examined it. "It doesn't look damaged."

Modders and their crazy priorities.

She scanned the sky. If she was looking for a ship, Alistair could have told her there were none. He'd already checked.

"I hope you're not planning on us carrying this all the way to the settlement."

"Will it be safe here until we get transport?"

"That depends." They could come back to a swarm of salynxes making it their new home, or to it having been flattened, crushed by a bovine.

"Then we should take it with us."

"You're kidding." He hoped.

She wasn't. But she did scrabble around inside the broken shuttle shell and come out with an antigrav trolley.

"Seriously?"

"Seriously." She smiled sweetly at him. "What's a modder without her tools?"

They pushed the Netanyu onto the trolley, then Alistair piled all the supplies they could find—not many—into the machine.

"Limiting," Nika muttered.

"Let's go." They couldn't waste any more time. The settlement was south. They had a full day's walk ahead of them. And they'd have to stop for night. "We can't eat much food from this world. Or drink the water without putting it through a purifier."

"It strikes me as that kind of place," Nika said.

"We'll take the suits," Alistair decided. His, anyway, and another one from the shuttle for Nika. "They'll provide some protection at night." They were too heavy to wear and walk, but it did solve some of the problem of being out at night on Zell, which was dangerous.

They settled the suits on top of the genemod machine and set off. Nika guided the trolley while Alistair acted as guard.

"I'd offer to swap," Nika said as he blasted another salynx. "But half the time I don't see what you're firing at until it's dead."

Alistair hoped the blaster would last. He wanted his fire-breather. "They're certainly plentiful around here." It made him nostalgic for the settlement, where the salynxes were controlled and it was safe to walk outside.

It was getting on for twilight. They'd been walking for hours. Nika hadn't complained, but he could see she was flagging. He wasn't any better. He was about to suggest they stop for the night and put on their suits—the salynxes were more numerous just before dark—when they heard the *wap-wap* of an aircar. They both stopped and waved. Danced.

The aircar passed over, heading toward the crash site.

Nika snatched up a suit, put the helmet over her head, linked it. "Hello, aircar that's passing overhead. Hello. Hello."

The aircar circled, came back.

"They heard us." Nika sounded as if she hadn't believed they would. Alistair certainly hadn't.

They waited while the aircar landed. It scared the salynxes away, but not for long, and not far. Alistair could see the boldest of them already bellying back.

The door opened. A man jumped out. Same engaging smile as ever. "Alistair."

He was alive. Really, truly alive.

Alistair went forward to hug him. "Cam."

"Alistair." Nika yelled and shoved the genemod machine at them, knocking him to one side and Cam off his feet.

Cam spun away. Dropped.

"What the hell?" Then the stench of burned human and cloth assaulted his nose. Blaster fire.

Alistair looked at the aircar. A man stood in the doorway, a smoking blaster in his hands. Leonard Wickmore.

Wickmore smiled. "Hello, Nika."

34

NIKA RIK TERRI

Alistair Laughton was paranoid about salynxes, so when he started forward to greet Cam, Nika kept watch for the flickering shapes that were all she could see of the creatures. A movement out of the corner of her eye made her look up, to the aircar door.

Leonard Wickmore. Raising his blaster. Aiming toward . . . Cam. Or Alistair.

"Alistair!" She shoved the antigrav trolley forward as hard as she could, pushing both of them out of the way.

Cam went down in a sickly smell of burnt flesh and burnt cloth. Too slow. She'd failed, and Alistair had the only blaster.

Cam rolled over.

He was alive. Wickmore had missed getting him square on, but by then Wickmore had turned his blaster toward her.

"Hello, Nika."

She stood behind the Netanyu, seeking what flimsy protection it offered. It wasn't much. Alistair swung around, hand reaching for his blaster. Josune would have fired by now. But then, Wickmore would have aimed for her first, knowing her to be the dangerous one.

"Leonard Wickmore. Like a bad smell you can't get rid of." She looked down at the injured body in front of her.

Josune would have told her to never take her eye off her enemy.

"Drop your weapon, Agent Laughton," Wickmore said. "My blaster is aimed. I'll fire before you can."

Think.

All she could think about were salynxes. Her brain didn't want to think about the rest. They'd never be rid of Wickmore, not unless they killed him. "Should we pick Cam up before the salynxes get him?"

"What?"

It was a stupid question, she knew. But Cam was still breathing. For how much longer, she couldn't tell.

Alistair Laughton wasn't a stupid man, but she'd bet in all his years in the Justice Department, he'd probably never been directly threatened by a company executive. Or maybe he had. He was starting to pull himself together.

"Talking of salynxes," Alistair said, "they will be back soon," and his eyes flickered in a specific direction.

"Your weapon, Laughton."

Alistair dropped it to the ground.

"Kick it away."

He kicked it—toward where he'd indicated the salynxes were. Nika didn't know if it was deliberate or not.

"Now, Nika," Wickmore said, "let's be sensible about this. Come inside, or I'll kill the two agents."

Nika edged in the direction of the blaster, keeping the Netanyu between her and anything that might attack them. "Please, Leonard. We know each other better than that. You'll kill them anyway. You've never been a man of your word."

Alistair had better understand the message in that. Wickmore wouldn't save them, no matter what he promised, no matter what deals Alistair tried to make.

"I kept Alejandro away from you for two years."

"Because it suited you."

She edged farther away.

"Of course." Wickmore came out of the aircar, blaster high, ready to fire. "Stop creeping away, Nika. There's no escaping me. I said get inside."

He sounded so much like Alejandro she flinched.

"Down, Nika," Alistair yelled, and she dropped, felt the wind of something small as it jumped her. Another landed on Wickmore's arm, clung, teeth shredding the flesh.

Wickmore fired the blaster. It went wide. Two more salynxes charged for his legs. He attempted to shake them off. Couldn't. He dropped the blaster and dragged out a knife. Three salynxes down. How many were there?

Nika rolled toward the blaster.

A salynx tore into her back, ripping skin off. She screamed.

She didn't see Laughton snatch up his blaster, but a wide sweep of blaster fire swept around her.

Salynxes ran.

Alistair thumped her back, hard, with the barrel of the blaster and dragged a salynx off. She was sure half her back went with it.

Nika snatched Wickmore's blaster and scanned for more. Nothing that she could see. Wickmore was bleeding, but he would live. Unfortunately. She tightened her grip on the blaster and bent to examine Cam, one eye on the executive. Excruciating pain sent her to the dirt.

"Aircar is secure." Alistair's voice cut through the haze. He bent to pick up the younger man.

"Don't move him," Nika said. "His injuries are bad. Have the salynxes gone?" Her back was on fire, but she could move. She pushed the pain to the back of her mind to deal with later, after she'd seen to Cam.

"For the moment."

"Good. Watch him." She indicated Wickmore. "Get me power from the shuttle." She emptied the contents of the Netanyu onto the floor of the aircar. And yes, there was some nerveseal. There was a god. "Strip him."

"Wickmore?"

"Cam."

Wickmore moved a hand toward his knife, which he'd dropped close to his body. "And get his knife."

"Do you have a priority list?" But at least Alistair was thinking, for he got the knife first.

She finished emptying the Netanyu. "Put Cam in here."

"We can't fit the Netanyu in the aircar."

"We don't have time to take him to a hospital."

"We don't have a hospital on Zell."

Why was he arguing, then? "Just put him in."

Nika tucked her blaster into her waistband. "And cut off his clothes."

She connected the feeds with fast, experienced hands. "Get me some power to connect to the Netanyu. When you've done that, I need you to spray some of that nerveseal on my back."

Wickmore moved. Nika grabbed her blaster and swung around.

Alistair pushed her arm down. "Don't kill him."

Rage tore through her. For a moment she couldn't see. If Alistair hadn't been stronger than her, she might have used the blaster on him instead. Leonard Wickmore and his people had chased her and her friends across the galaxy; they'd framed them; they'd tried to kill them. And while Wickmore was still alive, none of them would be safe. She wanted him dead.

"He's going to stand trial," Alistair said. "Let's do it legally, Nika. You don't want murder on your hands." He unwrapped her white and clenched fingers from around the blaster—carefully—and took it from her.

Nika shook his hand off her arm. "Do something about him, then," she said coldly. "Since he's planning to escape. I don't want to watch my back all the time."

Wickmore smiled.

They weren't finished, she and Wickmore, and as soon as Nika got him somewhere private, and she had a blaster in her hands again, they would finish what Wickmore had started, so long ago.

Alistair must have seen by her face that she meant it, for he raised the blaster and clubbed the side of Wickmore's head.

"Make sure he stays that way." She jumped into the aircar to connect the power, yelped at the pain in her back. No point waiting for Alistair. He was dragging Wickmore into the aircar.

At least he thought to tie the executive's wrists to one of the support bars. It would have been easier, and safer, to kill him. Unfortunately, it went against even her morals to shoot an unconscious, tied captive. Although, with Wickmore, she might have made an exception.

The Netanyu ran smoothly, despite its crash, despite its use as a barrier. Something to be grateful for. She snapped in the most important feed—mutrient. Turned to Cam, whose eyelids were flickering. "Relax, Cam. It's Nika. We're putting you into a genemod machine. I know you're in pain, but it'll be gone soon. Just relax." She made it as reassuring and as confident as Cam needed.

Alistair hadn't removed the clothes.

"Where's that knife?"

"What are you going to do?" but Alistair let her take it.

"Sorry about your clothes, Cam. I know that's nen-silk, but it'll get in the way of your healing." Two quick slices through the front of the jacket and everything he wore underneath it, another two on each sleeve. She pulled the cloth out and away from underneath him. It must have hurt, but he didn't utter a sound.

She wadded the cloth into a ball. Cam could go through his own pockets later.

"Nen-silk, huh. It always looked so muddy, and—" Alistair shrugged.

Nika sat back with the semiprotection of the aircar at her back, the Netanyu in front of the doorway, and watched the figures as the machine started its diagnostics. What was Alistair seeing right now? "Can you see his body?"

"I can see a shape. It's warm." Alistair fired over the top of the Netanyu. "Are we staying here till he's fixed?"

"I can't fix him fully. Not out here. Not with what we brought." Snow would say this was typical Nika, bringing him out before he was cured, but Cam needed a Songyan for proper healing. He was like Roystan.

She hoped there was still a Songyan to work with.

She looked out over the bleak marshes. "We have to stay awake and fight salynxes?" Half a statement, half a question.

"Not sure. They're attracted by heat and by scent." Alistair checked the marshes too.

Nika looked back at Wickmore, lying still against his restraints. Or maybe not so still, for she saw his eyes blink. Once. Twice. Thrice. Four times. Five. The right lid glowed.

He was in communication with someone.

She grabbed the knife, scrambled over to him. "Wickmore, close down." She held the knife at his throat.

He opened his eyes. Smiled. "You can't stop me, Nika."

Oh, she could. She could kill him. Alistair was watching her too closely to let her do that. But she had removed an eye-link once before. She prized his eye open.

"What are you doing?" Laughton demanded. He reached over to grab her arm.

"You think he doesn't have friends on-world? Either I kill him or I do this. And if you fight me, I'll cut his eye out by accident."

"You're insane."

"Watch Cam. And for salynxes. I promise I won't kill him. This time." She studied the back of the eyelid. There. That was the wire that transferred the link to his synapses. And all she had was a knife big enough to stab someone in the ribs and kill them.

Wickmore stopped smiling.

Alistair looked at the Netanyu, looked at the knife she held to Wickmore. She could see he wanted to grab it.

She put the blade to Wickmore's eye. "This will hurt. Don't move, or you'll lose your whole eye. That will be a lot harder to fix." She nodded at his eye, said to Alistair, "See that light? He's still in contact." She sliced up and across. A clean cut that severed the wire and any links he'd had open.

Wickmore screamed.

"Don't be a baby. I've seen you do worse to your own staff." She sliced off a sleeve of his jacket and made a pad to sop up the blood. He backed as far away as he could.

"Stay still. Unless you want to bleed out."

The silence was strained, only broken by Wickmore's heavy, agitated breathing. Or was it Alistair's?

She took the pad away. Looked critically at the eye. The bleeding was easing. "You know, that's the same angle as Tamati Woden's scar was. All we need to do is take the scar up higher and bring it all the way down across your mouth."

"You are disgusting," Wickmore said.

"No more disgusting than you, who had a team of assassins do your dirty work for you. No more disgusting than you, who threw acid into an employee's face because he made a mistake. No more disgusting than your friend, Captain Norris, who tortured a man to get information out of him." She noted the widening of Alistair's eyes. Yes, let him think about that.

She shrugged and tossed the sleeve at Wickmore. "Hold it to your eye. You can manage that. And remember. It's thanks to him it's only your eye, because you and I both know that if I had my way, you'd be dead." He'd be dead as soon as Alistair left her alone with him, but she kept that to herself.

She turned back to the Netanyu. Cam was stable, repairing nicely.

"I'm going to call the settlement," Alistair said.

"Do you trust them? Cam came with Wickmore. Presumably they came from the settlement."

At least she didn't have to convince him Wickmore was the enemy. He'd shot Cam in cold blood. If Alistair had been through as much as the crew of *Another Road* had, he would have killed Wickmore too. He thought he was experienced, with Santiago trying to kill the people of the settlement, but he was still naïve.

So was Cam.

Alistair blasted at something behind the genemod machine. Another salynx, she presumed. "I don't know who to trust."

Right now he sounded as if he didn't trust her either. That was mutual. She glanced at the scorched ground around them. "If they come, ask them to bring something large enough to fit a genemod machine, will you."

They came, in an aircar large enough to take heavy machinery—which, based on the mud tracks on the floor, was the last thing it had carried—and ten workers. Four of the seats were occupied.

Alistair knew them all. He hugged one of the women, whom he introduced as Melda.

He looked around the aircar. "This is new."

"Not ours," Melda said. "Theirs," and gestured a thumb at the man who'd been introduced as Barry.

Alistair frowned at the mud. "They're getting into mining?"

"Not mining. Building. You won't recognize the place, Alistair. It's tripled in size since you left, and it's still growing."

The look that flashed across Alistair's face made her wonder what he was thinking.

"When did Cam arrive?"

"About that," Barry said. "The Justice Department here, Alistair? Tell me it's not your doing."

"I can't tell you that."

Barry looked at him. "You took a risk."

Alistair stared back. "You must know that the first thing I did was report what had happened here."

"And you know that report disappeared." He gestured at Wickmore. "What's Eaglehawk doing here? How did they come prepared? Armed."

Alistair started to laugh. They all looked at him as if he'd taken leave of his senses. He kept laughing.

Nika finally leaned over, patted his cheek gently. "Alistair. They slap your face for hysterics." She made it quiet.

Alistair tried to sober up. It took him two tries. He finally took a deep, hiccupping breath. "Sorry."

"Are you okay, Alistair?" Melda asked.

"I am. I'm fine. It's just been . . . are the Ort—?"

"They're still here. They got excited when he"—she nodded at Wickmore—"and Cam went out to collect you. They wanted to come too."

A pity they hadn't. Wickmore might not have tried to kill them all, then.

"They think you have Cam's body modder."

"I do. I didn't introduce her properly before. Nika Rik Terri, who modded Cam. And who, by the sound of it, created a machine that Leonard Wickmore was desperate to get hold of." He looked at Nika, to see if he was right.

She nodded warily. Was there going to be more demand for her to create a monster machine? Somehow she was going to have to remove all trace of the notion that there had ever been an exchanger.

"So desperate he sent a merc ship after her. What happened to the mercenary, by the way?"

"Caught in the Vortex," Melda said flatly. "That and the ship it was chasing." She shuddered. "A terrible way to die."

A shuttle-sized rock inside Nika hit the bottom of her stomach. "Both ships?" Melda didn't mean it. Couldn't mean it.

Leonard Wickmore sneered. "Didn't you know your precious captain and his ship had been destroyed?"

"I don't believe it." It couldn't be. Not Josune and Roystan and Snow and Carlos and Jacques. Not her friends. "I had an apprentice. I'm supposed to look after him."

She turned numbly back to the Netanyu. It wasn't supposed to happen that way. They were supposed to be saved. Roystan had agreed with her, told her they'd be all right on board the ship.

Wickmore laughed and kept laughing all the way to the settlement.

The whole settlement, it seemed, had turned out to welcome Alistair back. There was also the well-dressed, well-modded woman in cream nen-silk, the woman Alistair had called from the shuttle. She stood apart with her own group, all of them suited, although none as immaculate as the woman at the front.

"What's going on, Alistair?" the woman demanded. "And why

did I have to hear about the attempted massacre of this settlement from the Honesty League, not from you?" She indicated the four sober-suited people behind her.

"Hello to you, too, Paola." Alistair looked pleased to see her. "You got here fast. Thank you for coming."

Paola looked momentarily nonplussed. "Did you think I wouldn't deliver?"

"I no longer knew. As for this"—he waved a hand to indicate the settlement—"I reported all of this to the Justice Department. That was for them to take up."

"There's no record of your report."

"Why am I not surprised?" Alistair shrugged. "I did report it. To Agents Wick and Santos. Cam and I recorded the interview. Would you like a copy?"

"Very funny, Alistair."

Nika looked past Paola to the two figures hovering behind. Cylindrical, Alistair had said. Four legs, four arms. Eyes at the top, in line with the legs and the arms. Alistair had said he saw them as white, but to Nika they were a bright green.

How did one greet a member of another species? She made a final check of the Netanyu—everything was fine—and stepped toward them. Hadn't realized she'd done so until Alistair moved with her.

"And somehow you managed to leave that particular bit out," Paola said. "Don't you think something like that should have been mentioned?"

"Excuse me," Barry said. "This is company business. Santiago only."

"This is not something to keep to one company."

Alistair glanced at Nika. "Ready?"

"Always."

"Greetings. Your uncle's uncle's uncle must grieve for you."

Alistair raised his arms and bobbed his knees at the same time. "Ourselves are pleased to be here to assist. I am honored to present . . . miracle . . . Nika Rik Terri."

Nika was a good modder, but "miracle" took it a bit far.

"Hello." She imitated his movements.

That started a flood of conversation she couldn't hear, couldn't understand. Melda came over and joined in.

Paola stood to one side, hands on her hips, watching.

Nika finally held up her hands. "Please," she said. "How do I learn to communicate?"

A tall, dark woman standing nearby said, "They do an operation. You'll also need to be inoculated."

Maybe. Nika wanted to check it in a genemod machine first. "Have you had it done?"

She nodded. "We all have, all of the settlers." She glanced across at Barry, who was in a scowling standoff with Paola. "Not them. I'm Yakusha, by the way."

35

JOSUNE ARRIOLA

They went to sleep, eventually. Despite the noise. All six of them on the floor of the crew room. No one wanted to go to their cabins. Josune shared a corner with Roystan and fell asleep to the rhythm of his breaths, in and out, against her cheek.

When she woke, Roystan's breaths were deeper, longer. He was truly asleep now, relaxed, even smiling in his sleep. The ship was quiet. Something had woken her. There. A faint bump. And another one.

Josune lifted her head.

Roystan tensed beneath her. Awake, without her needing to wake him. "Hit?" he asked quietly.

"I think so."

It was only a small bump. When the power was on, part of that power was an electrostatic force that repelled foreign objects. The same force that had repelled the *Hassim* that fateful day when the *Hassim* had nullspaced in front of their ship.

"Some of us are trying to sleep," Jacques grumbled. "Now that it's quiet, we can."

They were out of the Vortex.

Roystan scrambled to his feet and followed her across to the controls.

"This'll be loud, after the silence." Roystan turned the power on.

It woke everyone.

"Let's see what's outside." Roystan turned on the cameras.

"Oh, my—" She wanted to close her eyes, cover her ears. Everything was so close. She couldn't tear her gaze away. There were asteroids everywhere. Even as she watched, another asteroid bumped against the outside of the ship. They were lucky they were almost stationary, ship and asteroids, and nothing was hitting with any force.

It was like being in a dark star field. Or a minefield.

"All this is transurides?"

Roystan shrugged, held his arms out, palms up. "How do you tell?"

She looked at him, started to laugh. "You're telling me you came out here four times and you never tested it."

"I never said I was smart in my twenties. Or my thirties. In fact, I was a bit of a fool."

"Snow." Josune turned to the body modder. "Would you recognize transurides by sight?" He'd spent the last few months talking transurides with Nika.

"I'm not sure. Dellarine looks kind of oily. I don't know about the other metals." Snow glanced at the lights on the panel. "If we have power back, should Roystan go back into the Giwari?"

"Let's wait until we're out of here."

He nodded.

"Body modders with sense. An oxymoron." Jacques moved into the kitchen. "I missed you beauties."

Josune presumed he was talking to the stoves.

"How soon can we get back to Nika?" Snow asked.

They all looked at Roystan.

"We can nullspace out of here, but we have to go back through the Funnel to get to Zell. I'll get as close as I can, but it'll still take a full day."

"Are you sure?" But of course he was sure. He'd done the trip four times. Josune looked at the minefield outside. "How safe?"

Roystan knew what she was asking. "She's either dead already or she's working with the Ort. A few hours won't make a difference."

If they were wrong, neither would ever forgive themselves. *Please let this not be a bad decision.* Josune turned back to study the field outside.

"How did you avoid being hit by all those asteroids?" It was a miner's dream.

"It's not as bad as it looks. They're farther apart than you think, and everything—including us—is moving slowly. After the first trip, as soon as I turned on the engine, it was fine." Roystan moved over to check the cargo hold. "What did we bring to collect transurides with?"

They'd brought a lot. Collecting lumps of rock was part of exploring new worlds, and Josune had known what was required for that. They had drones packed away in cargo that could harvest some of the bigger rocks.

They could have let the drones do all the work, but they were in a hurry. Roystan, Josune, Carlos, and Snow took suits and two cargo nets and went out. Roystan and Josune went one way, Carlos and Snow the other, holding the nets between them, gathering any rocks as they went. When their net had captured enough rocks, they tightened into a loose pack and brought it back to the ship.

"Oof," said Roystan as they entered the higher gravity of the ship and found they couldn't even pull the bag. "Hold a moment."

He moved to the bridge, cut the gravity down to ten percent, then came back.

They emptied the net onto the shuttle-bay floor and went out again.

They brought back load, after load, after load. Tiny asteroids, bigger asteroids, some as big as a human, some as small as their hand. Gramps and Jacques packed them into the cargo space, pulling them down with the nets when they had enough to fill an area.

"Thank goodness we're not doing this in full gravity," Jacques said. "I'd be dropping by now."

Roystan called a break after six hours. "Is there anything on this ship to eat, Jacques? I'm starved."

"I thought you'd never ask. Five minutes to wash up."

They stopped to survey the half-packed cargo store. It was only a small room, but there was a fortune in transurides there. If it was transurides.

"Too easy," Carlos said. "Like taking candy from a baby."

Yes, it was, and maybe Roy Goberling'd had the right idea not telling anyone where the transurides came from. Josune could imagine the chaos and greed that would come when the information became public. "We'll have to work out how we're going to do this. License it, or—" She didn't know what. If someone like Leonard Wickmore got control of this, there'd be little hope for the Nikas of this world. Or even the Roystans. Especially not the Roystans.

Roystan nodded, then yawned. "That's enough, I think. Let's nullspace out of here. We've dinner to eat, a modder to collect."

Repairs to do too. The *Boost* had damaged their bridge. The wonder was over, and it was time to get back to work.

Carlos snorted suddenly. "We did all this, and it might just be worthless rocks, you know."

Roystan fell behind to walk with Josune as they made their way to the crew room. "It's always so ordinary, isn't it?"

"Anticlimactic," Josune said. "Too many things happening at once." She put her arm around his waist. "The important things are still special, Roystan. You." He raised her spirits just by being around.

Roystan made a face. "Not me, so much. I've got old memories overlaying my new ones. I don't like young Roy Goberling much. He was a . . . an overconfident young man."

Josune laughed. "Not sure I liked young Josune much either. She was outright arrogant." She gave him a quick hug. "We'll give you time to get back into yourself, Roystan. Or if you truly hate yourself, we'll get Nika to take your memories away again."

Provided Nika was still alive.

36

NIKA RIK TERRI

Nika tried not to think of *Another Road*. If Roystan had believed he would die in the Vortex, he'd have sent Snow and everyone else with Nika in the shuttle. He'd been sure he could save them. Maybe he'd nullspaced out.

Despite what Alistair—and her research—said about how impossible that was.

Roystan had said he'd been here four times before. He remembered the Vortex. There had to be some way they'd escaped. No matter what Paola or Wickmore or Barry told her. She hadn't finished training Snow.

Was this how Josune had felt when the crew of the *Hassim* had died? She'd been with them for ten years. Nika had been with Roystan's crew a little more than six months.

She coped, right now, by concentrating on the one thing she could do here. Communicate with the Ort.

Using Melda and Yakusha as translators was exceedingly slow, and if the Ort were getting the same garbled messages as I was, they must think she was crazy.

"Let's try again later," she finally said. "I need to look at Cam."

She had the feeling that she left them disappointed. They'd been hoping for a miracle, and she wasn't it.

After Cam came out of the Netanyu, Nika put Yakusha and

Melda through for a read. She found an antibody she didn't recognize, and the same changes to the angular gyrus, Wernicke's area, and Broca's area of the brain that had been made to Alistair.

She double-checked, just to be sure, and sought out Alistair, who was talking to Cam. "I need to read your mods," she told him. "I won't change anything."

Cam came with them. "I haven't seen Alistair go willingly into a modding machine since he came back from Zell. In fact, he avoids them."

"I didn't say it was willingly." Alistair pulled off his shirt. "Although, I am getting used to going naked in front of strangers."

"Nika's hardly a stranger. And I was naked too. Someone cut my suit off."

"Speaking of which." Nika thrust the damaged nen-silk at him. "You might want to empty your pockets."

Alistair crawled into the machine. "You were telling me how you didn't die, Cam. Even though I saw you get killed."

"Blaster damage doesn't always kill," Nika said.

"You didn't see his wounds."

"I'm going to close the lid now," and Nika did.

Cam emptied the pockets of his damaged suit. "Thanks for saving this for me to do."

There wasn't much in them, from what she could see.

"Respect of property." He looked up. "Most people wouldn't. Or not people I know."

"I'm surprised," and Nika was. "Not even him?"

"Alistair." Cam laughed. A bright, bubbly laugh that suited his looks and his new personality. He had changed so much since he'd arrived in her studio two and a half years ago. "He's a practical man. If he thought to empty the pockets—which he probably wouldn't—he'd dump everything into a bag, just so he could throw the suit away as rubbish. Easier to carry."

Yes. Some mods were good mods.

Paola came in. "Where's Alistair?"

Nika indicated the genemod machine.

"Are you sure? He showed a distinct aversion to them last time I suggested it."

"With good reason." She'd have to train people like Paola. "He's got specialist mods. You need to be picky about which modders he goes to." Her or Snow only.

"I didn't want him to go to just any modder. I offered him mine. She said she'd fit him in."

"Ronda Knapp?" He'd have come out with toned muscles, which he'd never be able to see. Ronda wouldn't have looked at his eyes before she put him in.

Paola bristled. "How do you know who my modder is?"

Nika sighed. "I'm a modder, Paola. Most modders leave a personal signature. Toned muscles are Ronda's." And they all came out with the same ivory-colored skin.

"And your signature?"

She didn't want to think she had one, although she had no doubt other modders would recognize her work.

"Me," Cam said. "I'm her signature, Paola."

Paola sniffed and looked Nika over. "She looks a lot like an agent I arrested not so long ago."

Agent Brand had gone to a modder who'd ripped off one of Nika's designs.

Nika shrugged.

Paola looked at the closed lid of the Netanyu—for a moment Nika thought she was going to try and open it—then at Cam. "Tell Alistair that a ship is coming to take Executive Wickmore back to Kitimat to await trial. I'll let him know when it has arrived."

If she waited five minutes, she could tell him herself, for they were only doing a read.

It was a relief to know Wickmore was going. The sooner the better.

Paola turned and left.

Cam scratched his head. "She's a . . . I think Alistair likes her." He took a breath. "She certainly . . . protects him. And I think she wants him to work for her again."

"Does he want to?"

"I don't know. You'd have to ask him."

The Netanyu blinked green for the completed read. "I'm opening the lid."

She studied the reading while Alistair dressed. Cam continued the conversation he'd started with Alistair before he'd gone into the Netanyu, as if there had been no break.

"Her friend." Cam gestured at Nika. "The one who stayed behind afterward and collected the genemod machine."

Josune.

"She called emergency. They took us back to the hospital. I got the same doctor who treated me last time. He said I was lucky to be alive and shouldn't have been. He said he thought the transurides might have slowed down the damage."

Nika looked up. "Of course it did."

"He said he wanted to meet you, Nika. To talk about it."

Nika wanted to meet a doctor who could talk intelligently about the fact that transurides might prolong someone's life. She went back to the read. Yes, Alistair had the same unusual antibodies Yakusha and Melda had, plus the same alteration to the brain areas.

She reprogrammed the machine for her own body while Cam turned back to Alistair.

"When I got out of the hospital, I went to see Paola. Paola was stressed because someone had sent the Honesty League the report about Zell, and they wanted to know why nothing had been done about it. Paola couldn't find any record of it in the files, and so she had to go back to them, to see what it was all about. By now she was really, really angry at you—and me—because it had to be one of us who sent it to them.

"The only connection I had was Wickmore, because we saw him when Nika came to collect the Songyan at the Justice Department. So I went to see him. He told me he had to come along, as he knew who'd taken you, but that they wouldn't listen to the Justice Department."

"You are aware he tried to kill us? That he blew up my apartment."

Cam half shrugged, looked embarrassed. "He tried to kill Nika too. But he was the only lead we had, and so I figured Wickmore was my only chance of rescuing you."

Sometimes you had to take your chances with the enemy because it was the only way you could win.

"Continue this discussion elsewhere," Nika said. "I want the room to myself for a while." She shooed them out, locked the door. If you did take chances, you also did what you had to do to protect yourself while you took those chances.

She checked the program again. Couldn't see any problems.

She set the machine to start in one minute, disrobed, and climbed in.

37

JOSUNE ARRIOLA

Zell space was crowded.

"I count eight ships," Roystan said. "One of them is armed."

It was a big, wallowing Class Three. The Justice Department was the only group who armed Class Threes. Josune would bet this ship belonged to them.

"We should turn around and go away."

They couldn't. They had Nika to collect.

Besides, they were already being hailed. If they ran now, they'd be fired on.

Roystan took a deep breath. "I don't know why, but this scares me more than the Vortex. Maybe even more than the Funnel." He opened the link.

The man at the other end wore a suit. His expression was severe. "This is the Justice Department. You are entering a restricted area. Only ships with prior approval can enter the area."

"We have approval," Roystan said. "We are expected."

"Identify yourself. Identify your ship."

Josune and Roystan looked at each other. She could see he was going to laugh. She wanted to laugh too.

"My name is Captain Hammond Roystan. Our ship is *Another Road*. We are expected on Zell. Please confirm with them."

If Santiago or the *Boost* were in charge, this was where they'd get shot. Josune itched to warm up the cannons.

The Justice Department man glanced to one side, perused something quickly. "You are not on my list of approved ships. Please remove yourself from the vicinity, or we will be forced to fire on you."

"This wasn't a restricted area last time we came through," Roystan said. "Why is it now?" He knew as well as Josune did what the trigger must have been.

"Don't play ignorant. We all know what you're here for. The same thing as everyone else. I notice you haven't tried to bribe me yet."

If he was trying to intimidate them, it wasn't working. All Josune wanted to do was laugh.

"I want to talk to Nika Rik Terri, please."

"Never heard of her."

"Alistair Laughton," Josune said. If this really was the Justice Department, maybe his name would carry weight.

The Justice Department agent paused, said something quiet to someone off-screen that Josune didn't catch. He sniffed, then said, "Putting you through to the agent in charge. If she says you can go through, you can, but none of this backdoor stuff."

A minute later an immaculately coiffed woman came on-screen.

"This had better be important."

"These people claim they are expected, Agent Teke."

"You have a list."

"They're not on the list."

"Then don't—"

Roystan cut in smoothly. "Agent Laughton is expecting us. As is Nika Rik Terri."

She left them hanging while she switched over to another link—calling Agent Laughton, Josune presumed—then came back in under half a minute. "Who did you say you were?"

"Hammond Roystan and the crew of *Another Road*."

She left the link open while she spent longer on the other link.

"Must be some conversation," Josune said.

"Apparently you're dead," Agent Teke said when she came back. "All right, Alistair, don't be impatient. Switching you through." She turned to the original agent. "If Laughton says let them in, then let them through."

And finally, Alistair was on-screen. "Roystan." His smile was broad. "Everyone swears they saw your ship destroyed by the Vortex."

"That was the *Boost*," Roystan said. "But you know when you nullspace out, it can take a while to get back."

"Personally, I'd never have nullspaced that close to the Vortex." It was amazing what people assumed. "Nika will be delighted. She's working with the Ort. Come on down."

"That's classified information, Alistair." Agent Teke may have closed the link to *Another Road*, but she hadn't closed it to Laughton.

Alistair laughed. "They know, Paola. That's why Nika's here. Come on down."

"You go, Josune," Roystan said. "We can't leave this—" He glanced in the direction of the cargo.

"I'll call you as soon as I get down there."

"Take care."

"I will."

Snow, Gramps, and Josune went down. No one argued with Snow's right to go, and where Snow went, Gramps went.

38

NIKA RIK TERRI

Communicating with the Ort was much simpler after her mod, and even simpler still once they'd established a scientific basis for their discussions. Eight of the outcasts—the leaders of their colony—were Earth's equivalent of microbiologists crossed with body modders. Except they modded the body surgically rather than via machine.

They were as skeptical of the modding machine as Nika was of their knives and scalpels, but they did concede that she had modded herself to communicate with them.

The communication got easier. They'd all been working in different labs, across different worlds, and had become plague carriers trying to find a cure. That could happen if you caught the plague and survived. Plague carriers were normally killed because the plague was so virulent, but because of their knowledge they had been banished so they could work on finding a cure. Forty plague carriers working other branches of science and medicine had been sent with them, all of them trying to find a solution.

"How do you get supplies?" Nika asked. "Or do you live off the planet?"

From what Yakusha and Alistair had said, there wasn't much on Zell that humans could eat. Could the Ort eat anything local?

Those sorts of questions caused more confusion than the scientific ones. When they finally understood what she was asking: "Not. Food here poisonous. We bring . . . supplies . . . enough for thirty lunar cycles."

Which Nika ultimately took to understand as being they'd brought thirty months of supplies, and when they ran out, they'd starve.

"We have to find this cure fast, or you'll starve."

"Abandoned . . . cannot go home, even if we find a cure . . . none would trust—"

A suicide trip.

Alistair entered. Did the weird leg-and-arms bow that was better suited to four legs and four arms than it was to two, went through the daily "uncles grieve for you" ritual that seemed so important to the Ort. "Please excuse . . . I must talk to Nika."

He drew her out. "Do you want the good news or the bad news first?"

"Bad news." It was always better to get the worst out of the way first.

"A shuttle has arrived to collect Leonard Wickmore."

"That's the bad news?" Maybe it was. She didn't want him where she didn't know where he was.

Alistair hesitated. "His lawyers claim there is no proof he did what we claim he did. Chances are he'll be out on bail by the time he reaches Kitimat."

It was hard to get past a company lawyer. "Not even the word of two Justice Department agents and a body modder?" She should have killed him.

"I'm a disgraced agent, no matter that I was reinstated. You killed Shanna Brown—on vid."

"That wasn't me."

"And then tried to kill Leonard Wickmore by bombing your studio."

"I wish I'd been successful. What about Cam?"

Alistair shook his head.

The Santiago family had known who Cam was when they'd planned to kill everyone at the settlement. They wouldn't support Cam's claim. Nika had sat down and talked with him about his mod, late last night after everyone else had slept.

As Cam had said, "I've been chipped since birth. The whole family is. They knew I was here, but I'm no use to them because I'm not executive material."

"And that's a bad thing?" Nika would have thought a company with multiple heirs would be happy one of them didn't want to take over. From what she'd heard, the infighting among the executives in most companies was more vicious than anything they did outside it.

"I'm a terrible lawyer."

"I'd make a terrible lawyer too. Does that make me worthless?"

"But you're a body modder."

"So. You're part of Zell's security team."

"Alistair is. Not me."

"Cam. You've been working with Alistair for the last two years. I don't care what your official title is, I only care what you've been doing."

She'd talk to Melda later, to ensure the position became official, but right now neither member of the Zell security team could protect her against Leonard Wickmore.

"You should have let me kill him," she told Alistair.

"I uphold the law. We don't take justice into our own hands."

Nika crossed her arms. "I don't know if you're truly naïve, Alistair, or just plain stupid."

They were talking about a man who'd tried to kill them both, who'd killed other people, who would never let either of them go free. "Now he knows about the Ort, he'll want part of Zell too."

Alistair rubbed his eyes tiredly. "Now that the Honesty League has spread word about the Ort, every company wants a part of it. They know Wickmore's reputation. They're unlikely to let him in."

Wickmore would go where Wickmore wanted to go.

Nika had never heard of the Honesty League before she came to Zell. They'd turned out to have some big names behind them, along with pirate media that proliferated both inside and outside the legal zone. The four grim-faced representatives who were still here, waiting to ensure that the Ort were treated fairly by the Justice Department, had sent images of the Ort to the pirate media. According to Paola, half the galaxy was headed to Zell. So much so that she'd called in armed Justice Department ships to protect them. She was thinking of hiring merc ships as well.

Which was funny, in its own way.

She said to Alistair, "If I see Wickmore again, I will kill him." Even if he wasn't doing anything to harm her. "Don't get in my way."

"Then you'll end up on a murder charge."

"Even if it's self-defense?" It would be worth it if it stopped Wickmore chasing her crewmates.

"You'd have to prove it."

You could never argue with someone like that. Nika changed the subject. "Alistair. Yesterday I saw a Dietel gathering dust in one of your storerooms. Can I have it?"

"The genemod machine? I'll check with Melda," who was official head of the settlement, but if Alistair asked, Nika knew he would get it. "I don't see why not. It's no use to us. We don't have a doctor who can use it."

If they stayed on Zell, they'd get a doctor and need the machine themselves, but she didn't point that out or he might change his mind about allowing her to have it.

"What are you going to do with it?"

"Extend it." Build a new container and transfer the electronics to it.

He looked blank.

"The Ort won't fit into a standard genemod machine. They're too tall, and they don't lie down."

"Don't they?"

"No."

"Oh. Well," and he brightened. "There's even some old supplies with it. You can have those as well."

Please tell her they hadn't kept the mutrient. It went off. "Alistair, I hope you didn't just offer me two-year-old mutrient." Still, they might have other supplies that remained usable. "Show me."

The building where she worked with the Ort was one of the new prefabricated ones that Cam said had been brought in by Santiago. If Alistair was right, and the Justice Department did try to control Zell, what would Santiago do? Call in the lawyers?

Alistair led the way past all the new buildings and into the huge, weathered machinery shed behind it. Cheap building materials, a cynical part of her noted. It was already falling apart. It must have come in with the settlers, two-plus years ago. He took her down to the darkest, dustiest area of the shed, she was sure.

It didn't matter what world you were on, there was dust. Even in space, where there was no world and no atmosphere to speak of, tiny particles of dust eventually settled.

"Any chance of some light?" Alistair may have been able to see everything clearly. She couldn't.

There was a light above the shelf. The illuminated circle made the rest of the shed look darker.

Nika covered her nose with her arm to stop a sneeze. There was little here worth collecting. The standard crystals and solutions of a basic hospital kit—some of which she had, some she wouldn't bother to use, and some she might have used if they hadn't been two years old.

"When was the last time you used these things?"

Alistair picked up one of the plastic jars. "Two years, four months, and three days."

"It's not like you have the date memorized."

He laughed. "He thought himself pretty good, our doctor. No doubt he would probably have improved on acquaintance, but we never got to find out. He loved rock climbing, you see."

"He fell?"

"Mmh. There's not much you can do when someone falls head-first down a two-hundred-meter rock."

"No."

"We think it was quick. The body was cold when Cam and I found him."

Which reminded her of Cam, and the conversation she planned to have with Melda. Maybe she should have it with Alistair, instead.

"You said you had good—"

Alistair looked away, over to the doorway.

"What's wrong?"

He shook his head. "I thought I saw . . . No. Nothing."

Nika looked to where he'd been looking. Alistair didn't imagine things. If something caught his eye, and she couldn't see it, then she wanted to know what it was.

She couldn't see anything.

"The good news?"

Alistair turned his head again, not quite in the same direction he'd been looking a moment ago, but slightly farther to the left, and sighed heavily. "Come on out, Barry. No need to skulk around."

"Barry?" Alistair had introduced him when they'd first arrived. "Why would he be sneaking around?"

"He's done it before. He sends people to spy on us."

Call her paranoid, but if someone was sneaking around, it was more likely to be one of Wickmore's people. Or Wickmore himself.

If his lawyer was any good, he'd be out on bail a lot sooner than Alistair believed.

"Where is he?"

Alistair pointed. "Coming up the side there."

The skulker might have been Barry, but until Nika was sure, she wasn't taking chances. She looked around for something to use as a weapon. The out-of-date mutrient was nearby, but there was no acid of any type. It was probably locked away. Normally she'd approve of that.

They were targets with the light on.

Alistair didn't need the light. She flipped the switch and tugged him behind the Dietel. It wasn't much cover, but it was better than nothing, and it placed the genemod machine between them and the still-unseen person.

In the sudden darkness the figure between them and the daylight from the open door cast a long shadow that stretched up the Dietel and onto the back wall. The chunky barrel of a blaster elongated the shadow of the right hand; a longer, slimmer weapon elongated the left.

The right hand was raised.

"Back. Back," but Alistair was slow, and the blaster caught the edge of his foot.

He grunted, and she grabbed him before he could step back into the line of fire. The shadow had aimed downward. Whoever it was knew that neither of them was armed, or they wouldn't have chanced the shot.

It also meant they were playing with them.

A Dietel was no protection against a maniac with weapons, especially when two of them were crowded behind it. Nika glanced around to see where they could retreat to. Nowhere.

"You live a charmed life, Nika."

Leonard Wickmore. And it seemed that even though he'd just

been released from his makeshift prison, he had his hand on a ready supply of weapons.

Wickmore moved out of the light from the doorway. Nika lost sight of him in the gloom of the shed, had to rely on the direction Alistair turned to watch.

"How are you out of lockup?" Alistair pushed them around the machine, presumably to keep them out of the line of fire. He put his weight on his injured foot, gripped Nika's shoulder for sudden support. She thought her shoulder would break.

Wickmore laughed. "You had to ask? We control the Justice Department, Laughton. Not you."

Alistair shoved Nika aside a second before Wickmore fired with his left hand. The Dietel wasn't nearly enough protection. Hot, molten needles burned her legs. Alistair jerked and dropped.

A needler. Snow said they didn't kill, but for a moment, she wished they did. Then she'd be dead and the pain would be gone.

Focus. The jar of solution Alistair had been holding rolled toward Nika. She grabbed it, concentrated all her efforts on holding it. Her legs. Next time—if there was a next time—she was going to build a mod that would turn off the pain sensors in her brain if they were overloaded.

Wickmore's voice came closer. "It hurts, doesn't it. But don't worry, Nika. Needlers don't do lasting damage."

She aimed for the voice. Alistair wasn't looking Wickmore's way any longer, so she couldn't use that as a guide. Raised her arm, threw the jar as hard as she could.

It hit him in the face. She hadn't realized he was so close.

Both weapons jerked up, and back, loosing a blast. Nika's arm was still up. It saved her eyes, but the blaster raked along her side.

Alistair charged Wickmore, who casually turned the blaster to him. Alistair collapsed.

Nika grabbed another jar from the shelf. Threw it. And another. If she could make him drop a weapon, they might have a chance.

Wickmore, close enough now to see—or maybe her eyes were adjusting to the darkness—hunched his shoulder against the missiles and fired at Alistair again.

"I can keep doing this all day, Nika. It won't change the end result. You, me, exchanger. I take over the galaxy."

Figures blocked the sunlight from the doorway.

"Ah. My friends. I suggest you surrender now."

She couldn't escape, not right now. But there'd be other opportunities, and Alistair was still alive for the moment. If she surrendered, Wickmore might take her and leave Alistair.

No. He wouldn't leave Alistair alive.

Her own body would shut down soon from the pain.

She was out of ideas.

Wickmore stepped forward to stand over Alistair's prone body. He raised the needler this time. Fired down. "I owe you this, Laughton. If you had died at your apartment as you were supposed to, I wouldn't have had to travel to this dead end of space. I wouldn't have had to spend time placating my own company. I wouldn't have had to dip into the chairman's fund to be here now."

Alistair's body jerked with the pulses.

"But still, I got to hear about the Ort. Which I can use."

He turned to Nika. "Did you really think the Justice Department would keep me prisoner, send me to trial? No. You and I both know that won't happen in your lifetime."

"You won't get to trial, Wickmore. I am going to finish you once and for all."

He fired the needler at Alistair again. "Justice Department. Never there when you need them, are they."

Nika came out into the open, her hands up. "Stop torturing him."

"That's better. You and I have unfinished business, Nika. Deliver my exchanger, or Alejandro will be an angel compared to what I will do to you."

She couldn't stop her shudder.

"I'm glad we understand each other. And with your friends now space debris, there's no one to rescue you this time." Wickmore holstered the needler, aimed the blaster downward. "I must say, I'll be happy to see the last of Agent Laughton."

It was futile, but she jumped him anyway. Landed short.

Blue light silhouetted Wickmore. Lightning sparked out from his body. He danced inside it. Kept dancing. On and on, while his skin shriveled and his screams grew less and less, until they finally stopped.

"We're not space debris yet, Executive." Josune stepped over the charred body. "I'm glad your jump was short, Nika."

Nika lay back, her smile wide, despite the pain. "I know what the good news is, anyway." Laughton must have been about to tell her *Another Road* was here. He should have told her that first. "Roystan?"

"He's good."

Snow pushed past Josune. He dropped to his knees beside Nika. She knew the shape of him, even in the dark shed. "Snow. Don't put me in the Dietel. Please."

"I want to see Roystan," Nika said as soon as she came out of the genemod machine.

"He's still on board *Another Road*," Josune said.

Snow crossed his arms. "I ran the mod you had programmed." She'd left it coded, ready to go. "Pulling him out early doesn't seem to have done major harm, but you can't keep doing it, Nika."

Nika laughed. "I missed you, Snow." She had. She'd missed them all. Not just because she'd thought they were dead—she'd tried not to think about that—but she'd missed not having them around. "I need to see Roystan," then belatedly remembered she wasn't the only one who'd been injured. "How's Alistair?"

He'd gone into the genemod machine before she had because he'd been more badly injured. "You didn't touch his eyes."

"Gramps told me."

She'd forgotten Gramps was here.

"You told me too. Five times before the anesthetic took."

She'd been in too much pain to think straight. At least she'd remembered the important things.

"We nearly put him in the Dietel, but it hasn't been used for two years. We gave him nerveseal."

"You should have brought Roystan and the Songyan down," Nika told Snow as they went looking for Alistair. "We could have finished his mod, made sure he really was okay."

Snow hesitated. "Nika, there's something we haven't—" He looked at Josune, shrugged helplessly.

Nika stopped. "You said they were all okay." She'd never thought to ask about the others, just assumed they were all right. Neither Snow nor Josune looked upset. "Tell me."

Snow stepped back and raised his arms helplessly.

"Everyone's fine," Josune said. "It's not that. As soon as we're done here, we'll take you up, Nika."

Nika looked at Josune. "It's not bad," Josune said. "Just something we need to tell you."

They found Alistair talking to Paola.

"What am I going to tell Eaglehawk?" Paola asked.

"Tell them that they'd better not have had anything to do with trying to kill us or they'll end up spending the rest of their life in jail." He looked up. "That was fast."

"It was a repair only," Snow said. "I wouldn't dream of doing anything else."

Alistair looked as if he had no idea what Snow was talking about.

"How are your eyes?" Nika came over to check anyway.

"Good, thank you. I can still see."

They reacted properly to light, at least. How did she know what was normal for Alistair? One day she would. "I'm going back to *Another Road* to check on Roystan."

"But—"

"We'll still help with the Ort," Nika said. "And we'll have expert engineers on hand to help, as well as two extra modders. We'll make good progress converting the Dietel. But we'll do that after I've checked Roystan."

Nika, Gramps, Snow, and Josune went back to *Another Road*.

Carlos waited for them just outside the airlock. "Have you told her?"

"No one tell her until she checks Roystan." Snow steered her toward the studio. "She won't listen till then, anyway."

"I'll get Roystan," Josune said.

"No need. I'm already here. And Jacques wants to know how long you'll be, because he's a celebration dinner planned."

Nika looked around at the expectant faces. Carlos was openly beaming. Even Gramps had a smile.

Snow moved over to disinfect the Songyan—even though Nika could see it was sparkling.

"Let's get you in there," she told Roystan. "Before someone bursts."

Roystan was fine.

"Nice job, Snow."

"It was really hard." Snow rolled his eyes. "Preprogrammed and all. My first chance at using a Songyan too. I may as well have been a doctor."

"You'll get other opportunities."

Snow stood, his hands on his hips. "And I don't even see why you needed the Songyan to start with. We could have done it in the Netanyu."

That last stabilization, yes. "Later I'll go through the repair with you. You can tell me what you'd have done. I'll show you what I did."

She rechecked Roystan's vitals. Everything worked perfectly—albeit for a man whose natural body temperature was 40.2 degrees Celsius.

"Ready to come out," she told Jacques. "Five minutes at most, then he'll want a shower. Body modders only. The rest of you—" She shooed them out.

Gramps went, too, which surprised her.

Snow watched him go. "Melda offered to let Gramps stay on Zell. He's thinking it over."

"How do you feel about that?" Snow's envisaged future had always had Gramps with him, Nika was sure.

He chewed his bottom lip. "He says he has to let me fly."

"He's welcome to come with us." Wherever they went. Zell—with less than a hundred humans—wasn't a place to train an apprentice. She looked around the ship. Neither was *Another Road*, not now they weren't running.

Roystan came out, damp hair slicked down. Nika studied him critically. He hadn't changed much from the day she'd first met him. More relaxed, and she was sure she'd find out why very soon, but otherwise the same. No longer starving, but certainly thinner than he'd been two weeks ago. She walked around him, studying him.

"I think . . . this will be you forever, unless we mod you." Or unless the transuride bonds broke down.

Roystan shuddered. "I'm never going into one of those machines again."

"Roystan," Josune said through the link, "don't fight it. You may as well give up. This is Nika you're talking to. You'll be going in every month, at least. Probably more. Now take her down and show her, because we're all waiting for dinner."

They weren't waiting for dinner. They were waiting at the entry to the cargo hold. Even Jacques.

Roystan opened the cargo door. "We collected this on the way through."

Rocks. They'd collected rocks.

Nika picked out one small enough to fit into her palm. Studied it, saw the oily sheen. She looked closer, picked up another. The rocks she held had a heavy seam of the most precious transuride of all. Dellarine.

"So, do we have worthless rocks? Or do we have something else?" Roystan asked.

"You don't know?"

Roystan's neck heated slightly, and he gave his crooked smile. "No."

"You are kidding me. You have all this, and you don't know." Nika shook her head. "Let's go and have this celebratory dinner, and I will teach you all how to recognize dellarine."

"What happens now?" Nika sat back and pushed away her empty plate.

"We have to decide how we're going to sell this stuff," Josune said. "We don't want to mine it ourselves, and we certainly don't want to let a single company have control of it. They'll be ruling the galaxy in ten years."

"A consortium," Roystan suggested. "Although, I can imagine the power battles that will go on."

Jacques laughed. "We know what happened to the last consortium the companies built. It's as corrupt as anything."

"Which consortium is this?"

"The Justice Department."

They didn't want to build another entity to rival that. The Justice Department was bad enough.

"So what do we do, then?" Josune asked. She put up her hands to cover her face. "In all this time I never thought about what we'd do when we found the treasure."

Roy Goberling had known, though. Nika saw the realization in Roystan's face. It was one of the reasons he'd run, tried to forget. If he'd remembered that six months ago, when he'd first met Nika, would he have been so willing to get his memory back, even for Josune?

Maybe. Maybe not. Eighty years was time enough to forget how bad it had been.

Josune dropped her hands. "Should we walk away?"

"No," Roystan said. "Running doesn't work. It just makes a different kind of pressure."

He was right. They had to control it, or otherwise one of the companies would. Someone would find the transurides one day, especially with so many ships coming through the Funnel to see the Ort.

They couldn't let that someone else be a single company.

They couldn't do it themselves, because they'd be annihilated. Wickmore and the *Boost* would be minor problems compared, and they wouldn't survive it.

Jacques was right. The Justice Department, monster that it was, represented all the companies, plus the non-company worlds like Lesser Sirius. It was the logical organization for a cross-company outfit. Not only that, Zell, and thus this part of the Vortex, was in the legal zone. The Justice Department would muscle in, whether they wanted them to or not.

The best they could do is control who did the muscling, and how.

"Who can we trust?" Nika asked.

"With something like this? No one."

There were only two people she would even consider trusting in the Justice Department. Alistair Laughton, who was more naïve than they were, and Cam Santiago Le-Nguyen, whose company had been prepared to kill him because he was no use to them.

Alistair had a boss, Paola Teke, whom she thought he respected—or who respected him—who had brought the Honesty League with her.

"Hear me out," Nika said slowly. Thinking aloud. "Let's make a consortium. Ourselves. The citizens of Zell," which included the Ort. "The companies. All overseen by the Justice Department, who in turn will be overseen by the Honesty League."

"They've finally gone mad." Jacques looked at Carlos and Snow and lowered his voice to a whisper. "Do they remember how many times the Justice Department has screwed us around?"

Even Roystan shook his head.

But Josune was nodding. "You want Laughton as the Justice Department representative."

"Not just Laughton. His boss too." Paola Teke was one step below the board; she wielded a lot of power, and Cam had said she listened to Alistair.

Teke was far more politically savvy than Laughton was. From what Nika had seen of Laughton, he wouldn't follow a corrupt woman. Not knowingly. So Teke may not have been "good," but she likely wasn't on the make the way Brand and her team had been.

Roystan said, "It sounds great in theory, but if they're any good, the Justice Department will kick them out and put someone else in their place. Someone more aligned with company goals."

"Not if they were appointed permanently to those positions." And not if the consortium had the power to appoint replacements, and those replacements didn't have to come from the Justice Department.

"And that's about as likely as—"

"It will happen if the Ort push for it."

"And if they don't?"

Josune said, "Laughton was already worried Santiago would—"

"No," Snow breathed. "Don't you see. We've got the genemod machines. We're going to cure their plague for them."

That little gem stretched into silence. It was broken by the gurgle of the coffeepot.

"Might work," Roystan conceded, and even Josune nodded.

It would work, Nika knew it, and Alistair would even push for it, because he wanted to save his people on Zell. He might not appreciate it when he realized what he was in for, but that was his problem. He could deal with it. Nika thought he would cope with it too.

Jacques brought out freshly brewed coffee for them all. "Santiago will want part of it. Didn't they start the settlement?"

And then decide to abandon them. "We'll have a permanent Santiagan representative."

"Barry?"

"Cam." And she'd make sure whatever lawyer they got—and it wouldn't be Cam—built in a clause to say that if Cam died, a representative from another company would sit in his place. "Maybe Jerome Brown as well." Brown Combine was one of the most respected companies, reputed to be the most honest. He was a smart man. He'd cope with intercompany politics. "Once we explain, he won't turn us down."

Jerome Brown was also a long-term Goberlingophile. He'd bought the *Hassim* from them when Roystan and his crew had claimed it as salvage. He'd even been decent enough to try to save their life once, when Wickmore's people were after them.

Roystan rubbed his hands together. "People might even think it was him who found the transurides, not us."

"We could call in Feyodor's lawyer," Josune said. "We used him on the *Hassim*. He's a good negotiator and for a percentage he'll look after us."

"Sounds like a plan," Roystan said. He hesitated, then asked the question Nika had been dreading. "What are we going to do afterward?"

"We're rich," Carlos said. "We can do whatever we want."

Nika knew what Carlos and Jacques would do. They'd follow Roystan. Roystan and Josune would most likely go exploring.

"I have an obligation to Snow, to my apprentice. I have to train him." She didn't want to leave, but they couldn't continue to mod four people, three of whom didn't like being modded.

Carlos waved it away. "You can do that on the ship."

She couldn't, not if she wanted to teach Snow properly. Although, they might learn a lot about transurides and longevity.

"There's the Ort too. We can't go anywhere until we've sorted out their plague." She glanced over at Snow. Gramps wanted to remain on Zell. Could she train an apprentice properly there? There'd be a lot of people on Zell soon. All come to look at the Ort.

Snow might almost have been reading her thoughts. "I don't think I'm going to be a normal modder. I'll probably specialize in human-Ort relations, or how to work with transurides." He looked toward his foster father, bit his bottom lip.

Nika wanted to go with *Another Road*. "We'll stay on Zell awhile," and tried not to brighten at the way Snow winced.

Once, all she had wanted was to be a good modder. She hadn't realized she was lonely, or that she'd had no friends. And she was going to lose them, just after she'd found them.

"Face it," Carlos said. "Zell is a horrible place."

"Does it have to be Zell?" Josune asked.

Nika shivered. "Where else have they got?" Ort and settlers alike. Zell would never be anything but hostile to either race.

"We . . . the *Hassim* . . . found another world further in," Josune said. "We called it Sassia. Earth-type, and no one has claimed it. Or not that I know of. Someone will discover it soon, so we may as well get the benefit from it. We could claim it, and combine it with the transuride agreement, Sassia-Zell rather than just Zell. It wouldn't be company run, then."

It was a generous offer.

From what Nika understood of what the *Hassim* had done, that was how they had made their money. They discovered worlds, but they didn't work them. They sold the license and the location to the highest bidder, then took a percentage of everything.

Only this time it wouldn't be the highest bidder. It would be their consortium. And this time a company wouldn't rule the world—it would be governed independently. She hoped Laughton and his team would be up to it.

She'd be there, too, helping to make decisions. While her friends were off exploring the universe.

Josune touched her hand lightly. "No one has to decide immediately. We'll be around awhile. There's a lot to do to set this thing up."

Nika tried to smile. She looked around at the faces. They should have been happy, but Carlos and Jacques were scowling. Snow was still biting his bottom lip. Even Roystan was frowning. "So it's a plan?"

Gramps put a hand on Snow's shoulder. "My boy doesn't need to be tied to my lifeline. He needs to get out, explore the galaxy."

Coming from a merc ship, Snow had probably seen a lot of the galaxy already. More than Nika had, anyway.

"Besides, what happens if Roystan gets sick again and you're not around to fix him with our stolen Songyan?" Carlos asked.

"Borrowed Songyan, Carlos. Borrowed. We'll return it once the

Justice Department replaces ours that they had in their care." Alistair could make that happen. They didn't need to be involved.

The words came out shakier than she meant them to. This was stupid. She'd been on her own before. And she had an apprentice to train now.

She blinked, looked up to see Josune put her hand over Roystan's, smile, and nod. Roystan smiled back.

"We'll be around awhile," Josune said. "After all, we've found the ultimate treasure. We plan to enjoy it for a time."

"We don't have to go exploring immediately," Roystan said. "And you and Snow will want to visit Ort worlds. That's new territory. We should be the ones to take you."

They were explorers, both of them. "Don't give up your dream just for us."

"We're not. But when you've lived as long as I have—and we all will, because we'll have you and Snow around to make that happen—an apprenticeship isn't all that long. And I can see a cargo route ripe for taking. Between Zell, Sassia, and Kitimat. We'll make a fortune if we are the first ones in."

They didn't need the money anymore. Or the work. Even so, around the table, the frowns turned into smiles. Even Josune's.

"We'll make sure you get quality supplies, Nika," Carlos said.

Nika would have thanked them if she thought she could get the words out. Instead she nodded.

Roystan sat back, rubbed his hands together. "Good. I think we have a plan."

ACKNOWLEDGMENTS

Books are collaborations. With your writing partner, if you have one, but also with your agent and your editor.

This isn't the first story we wrote as *Stars Beyond*. Our agent, Caitlin Blasdell, was honest enough to say the first versions weren't good enough. Then she and our editor, Anne Sowards, helped us work through the new story, after which Anne gave us the time to make the changes.

So a huge thank-you to Caitlin and Anne. It's a better story now.

Thanks also to our beta readers, Jenny and Arthur. For your patience, your feedback, and your willingness to read multiple versions of the same adventure.

Thanks to the Ace/Berkley team at Penguin Random House for all their work on the book. A special mention to Fred Gambino, the artist, and Judith Lagerman, for cover design. We love the cover of *Stars Beyond*.

As always, thanks to our family and friends for their support and encouragement. You are always there for us when we need you.

And finally, but definitely not least, thank you, our readers. For reading our stories and for the encouragement you give us.

S. K. Dunstall is the pseudonym for a writing team of two sisters. Together, they are the national bestselling authors of *Stars Uncharted*, *Confluence*, *Alliance*, and *Linesman*. They live in Melbourne, Australia.

CONNECT ONLINE

SKDunstall.com